FRACTURED

ANACONDA TALES - BOOK ONE

FUTURE

J ROSE

For those who survive by being the strong one. By wearing a
brave face and swallowing their feelings. Forging their protective
armour by fighting the entire world and everyone in it.

For the warriors.
The sarcastic. The bruised. The bloodied.
The quietly vulnerable. The *strong*.

It's okay to let yourself break too.

1
NOT CROSS

"We know so perfectly how to give birth to the monsters inside us, but for reasons I will never figure out, we have not the slightest clue what to do with all the love."

- Christopher Poindexter

1
CROSS

Fractured Future (Anaconda Tales #1) is a slow burn, why choose romance, so the main character will have multiple love interests she will not have to choose between.

This book is dark and contains scenes that may be triggering for some readers. These include strong mental health themes, human trafficking, allusions to sexual assault, psychological/physical torture, undiagnosed chronic illness and graphic violence.

If you are easily offended or triggered by any of this content, please do not read this book. This is dark romance, and therefore, not for the faint of heart.

CONFIDENTIAL

Suspect?

DO NOT CROSS

POLICE

Suspect?

NOT CROSS POLICE

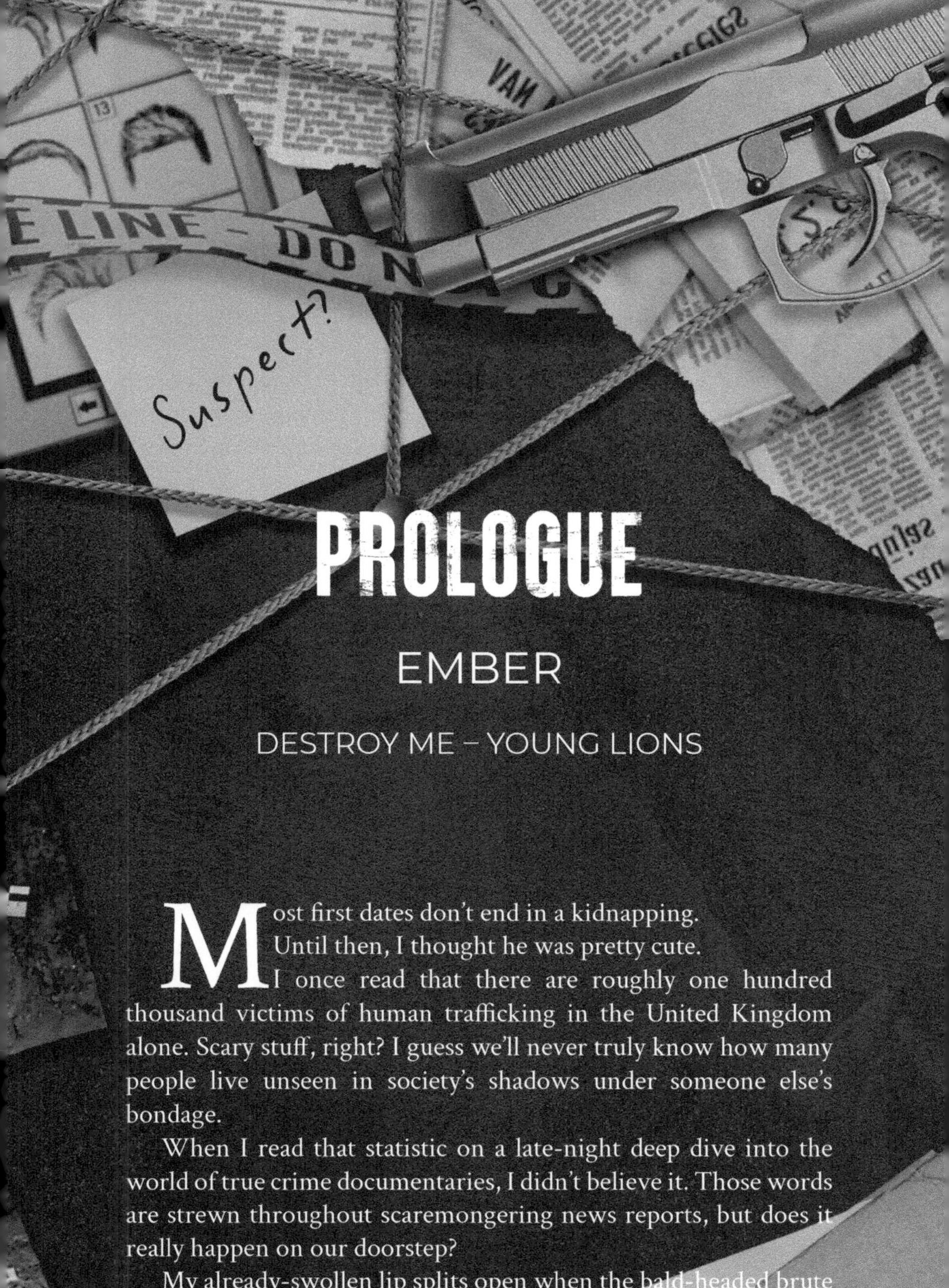

PROLOGUE

EMBER

DESTROY ME – YOUNG LIONS

Most first dates don't end in a kidnapping.

Until then, I thought he was pretty cute.

I once read that there are roughly one hundred thousand victims of human trafficking in the United Kingdom alone. Scary stuff, right? I guess we'll never truly know how many people live unseen in society's shadows under someone else's bondage.

When I read that statistic on a late-night deep dive into the world of true crime documentaries, I didn't believe it. Those words are strewn throughout scaremongering news reports, but does it really happen on our doorstep?

My already-swollen lip splits open when the bald-headed brute looming above me throws a punishing backhand. *Yep. It fucking happens, Ember.* I'm living proof of my own ignorance.

FRACTURED FUTURE

White-hot pain burns a path through my veins, spreading a poisonous lava that fills every last sense. But at least when they're hurting me, I can feel my extremities. My fingertips. My toes. Each cold, naked limb, caked in dirt and blood.

I have proof that I'm still alive.

They haven't taken my life from me yet.

It's far worse when they move us, whether from the subzero shipping container filled with the scent of human waste or the convoy of tinted vehicles we've been transported in since then. We're all loaded with sedatives on those days.

"Put it on!" Diego barks, tossing a hot-pink bra and panties set at me. "You're coming with me."

"Fuck. You."

Peering through my throbbing black eye at the asshole trying to intimidate me, I gather moisture in my mouth to spit directly in his ugly face. My saliva is red-stained, hitting his cheek.

"What was that?" he yells in my face.

Licking the coppery dribble spilling from my mouth, I refuse to look away. We've been down this road several times. He threatens, I taunt, something breaks. I still haven't learned how to shut up.

Taunting this motherfucker won't get me out of here, but after laying in the damp darkness listening to other women sob all around me, I've lost all sense.

Now I'm fucking angry.

And I want them to know it.

"Are you deaf?" My mouth stretches in a semi-sane smile. "I said fuck you."

"You really are the dumbest bitch."

"I've been called worse."

Diego's wrinkled face flushes purple. "How many times do I have to tell you to shut your mouth?"

Rage is a welcome heat curling around my bones. One that keeps my blood circulating and heart pumping. Without a single possession, scrap of clothing or clue where I am, all I have is a blanket of anger to wrap myself up in.

"Try it once more?" I blink innocently.

"If that's what you desire."

"Come on! You piece of shit!"

Excitement shines in his cruel black eyes. I hate the way my fresh blood coats his gnarly knuckles, but I'll never admit that to him. He'd enjoy that knowledge far too much.

Despite feeling dizzy and weaker than a newborn baby from being half starved, I manage to duck his first swing. I'm thankful we're no longer tied up like we were before being tossed in the metal cages.

At least in these makeshift prisons, lined up in what seems to be a subterranean warehouse, I have a fighting chance. The swaying shipping container and constant screams we endured before almost broke me.

Almost.

"Stupid slut!" He viciously catches a handful of my greasy, dyed blonde hair. "You need to learn when to admit defeat."

"I wasn't taught to give up," I garble.

"Then allow me to teach you!"

Misjudging his next move, I don't avoid the thick fist sailing straight towards my face. The impact hits hard—my teeth snapping together, vision blurring and more warm, tangy blood filling my mouth.

Quakes ricochet through me as something in my cheek audibly cracks. The explosive aftershock reverberates, my bones grinding together with an awful crunch.

There aren't words to sufficiently describe the white-hot, liquid fire stabbing into my tissue, igniting nerve fibres into a vision-blackening pain that rivals any punch I've received before it.

"Not such a smart mouth now. Are you?"

I choke on a strangled sob. "F-F-Fuck!"

"That's it." He wipes his knuckles off on his filthy black jeans. "Show me those tears."

"Leave her alone!" someone else screeches.

"Shut it, bitch," he fires back.

I don't know all of my fellow captives. There are too many tearstained faces, contorted with terror, for me to memorise. At least thirty women of varying ages, builds and ethnicities. A veritable smorgasbord of unwilling victims.

"That's what I thought." Diego's gaze refocuses on me, boiling with hatred. "Your mouth is giving these sluts the bravery to speak to me."

All I can muster is a broken whimper.

"Do I have to beat your ass in front of them?"

I won't give him the satisfaction of an answer.

"I'll happily do it," he adds, lips curling in a grin. "With pleasure."

My life back home feels like a million miles from this soul-crushing low. I don't know how long I've been missing. Hours. Days. Weeks. Perhaps even months. A lifetime could have passed.

Time is only marked by the fading and inflicting of more injuries. For each new bruise, cut or scrape, another strike is etched onto the walls of my mental cage.

I count my survival in each beating that I outlive. For every drop of blood slicked across their fists, I buy myself another hour. Another day. Another breath. Perhaps if I buy enough time, I will find my way out of this nightmare.

"Got nothing to say to me now?" Diego jeers.

"N-No," I sniffle.

"Time to get dressed then. We have somewhere to be. Perhaps you'll learn to keep your stupid mouth shut in the future."

Diego is one of the few men who doesn't wear a mask. He's overweight, his rounded belly testing the boundaries of his jeans. While he screams at us in English, his voice has a slight exotic twang.

Our captors are all the same. Violent. Sadistic. Merciless. Well-tanned with accented voices, wearing the same nondescript uniform: basic and dark enough to hide the bloodstains.

He picks up the skimpy bra and thong that started this fight then waves them in my face. "Dress."

"Fuck you!"

"Once you meet the customers out there looking for a piece of your ass, you'll wish it was me fucking you."

Pushing my shoulder, he roughly shoves me to the hard cage floor. I have to bite down on my tongue to hold a cry inside, the sudden movement jolting my new injuries.

"You have two minutes, or I won't hesitate to break your leg next."

The lingerie lands on the floor before the cage door slams shut. The sound of the lock clicking rattles throughout the gloom, causing a chorus of whimpers and cries from the others held captive all around me.

"Two minutes," Diego repeats over his retreating shoulder. "Pull yourself together, bitch."

Can't wait.

Letting my limbs go loose, I go limp on the floor. Frigid cold leaches into my bones, freezing my naked body. The pain in my face is so fierce, I have to pant for air through clenched teeth.

When I was studying for my license to qualify as a personal trainer, I took a self-defence class with an overzealous instructor. He was a misogynistic asshole who should've been sacked.

The pain of the broken nose I gained in an accident there didn't hurt half as badly as this does. Nor did the hours-long screaming match that followed with my stupidly overprotective older brother, Tom.

Still, I'd take his worried ranting giving me a migraine over this hell any day. In fact, I'd give just about anything to see him one last time and accept one of his big hugs.

"You shouldn't taunt them," Gracie whispers to me. "You're only making it worse."

"I'll taunt them until they cut my fucking tongue out," I wheeze, testing how much I can move my mouth. "I'm not going to lay here and take their abuse."

At sixteen years old, she's blue-eyed, dark-haired and full of heartbreaking innocence. We were taken from the same vicinity. Gracie was tied up in the moving van when I woke up after being drugged.

Our shared horror when our tear-logged eyes met formed a deep trauma bond. I even held her close in the echoing metal prison we were thrown in, keeping her warm with my own body heat.

She follows their barked commands without a hint of hesitation. I understand why. Gracie can't handle the daily terror or their leering stares. Her mind is shattering, and I don't blame her.

Fighting back is the only thing keeping my sanity intact. The moment I give up, I know the widening fissures in my mind will grow into deep crevasses that will swallow me whole.

"They stole us from our lives," I say through calming breaths. "Like we're nothing more than cattle to be shipped from place to place. I refuse to make their jobs easier for them."

I hear movement from inside her cage, the iron bars revealed by light emanating from ancient bulbs high above us.

"What about when you get killed? When they hit you too hard one day?" Her little voice trembles with terror. "Who will I have then?"

"That isn't going to happen."

"You can't promise that. We were taken for a reason, Ember. They won't keep us in these cages forever."

She's right.

I knew it the moment I woke up gagged and bound.

The man who arranged my kidnapping, Charles, was smart. We were far from the prying eyes of Liverpool's city centre where we met for drinks. I never should've agreed to go back to his apartment.

But he had seemed so normal. Plain. Workaday. Perfect for a quick fuck followed by an easy goodbye—the only kind of relationship I have time or energy for. I knocked back my vodka martini and pretended to laugh at his jokes until he invited me back to his place.

The concrete-paved streets turned blurry before we reached his apartment. If that's even where he was taking me. I can only assume that boring 'Charles' isn't even his name.

He played a role. Providing a false construct while truly being a middleman with a dangerous secret. The kind who adorns his dates in handcuffs and gags before driving them to the coastline to be shipped off.

One spiked martini and the promise of an easy lay. That's all it took to land me in the pages of a news story that you read over the safety of fresh coffee in the morning.

"Ember." Debbie's older voice emanates from behind me. "Just put it on."

"You first," I scoff.

"I'm not the one they're prepping to ship off." She coughs wetly, the sound rough and guttural. "You've caused them too much trouble."

God, if there weren't metal bars keeping us apart, I'd slam my fist into her face. From the glimpses I've gotten, she's one of the oldest women here, and she has no shortage of unhelpful opinions.

"She's right." Layla sounds weaker than ever from her cage several metres away. "Don't f-fight them."

Nausea swirls in my belly. Three masked men used a baseball bat on her not long after we arrived then laughed as they forced themselves into her, making us all watch.

Humans have a way of getting used to suffering. We adapt. Become complacent. Stronger. Our survival instincts kick in. Every single one of us has endured this long by tuning out each other's torture.

"Ember," Debbie hisses. "Look at me."

Biting back a groan, I twist my pulsing head to see her dimly-lit cage. She's tucked into the farthest corner, her bony knees pulled up to her chest to hide her bareness.

"Wear the panties, and go with them." She drops her voice lower. "You're not getting out of here if you're locked in this cage."

"What?"

"You heard me. This is your chance to do something."

Prickly surprise washes over me. "I thought you wanted me to be all quiet and shit?"

"I never said that." She sucks in a breath. "Go with them, find an opening, and give them hell."

"They'll kill me!"

"You're going to die anyway if you sit here."

Not a single one of the guards has slipped up when I aggravate them. Not long enough for me to make an escape. If I'm going to get out of here, it won't happen behind these bars.

"You're the only one strong enough to do it," Debbie adds, keeping her words hushed. "Just don't forget about us."

"What do you expect me to do?"

"Something. Anything."

The risk is an unspoken weight in her voice.

Or die trying.

But I can't die here. Not like this. I have to get back to Tom. To my business. To the life I've worked so hard to build for myself. This can't be how my story ends.

"If I don't come back…" My throat dries up. "Look out for Gracie?"

She ducks her chin, staring at the blood streaked over her legs. "I can't even protect myself."

"None of us can, but you have to try. Promise me."

After a long beat of hesitation, Debbie reluctantly nods. I nod back, the movement causing my injuries to flare. But I don't have time to sit and wallow. He's coming for me.

Gingerly lifting myself, I lightly poke my face again. My cheekbone definitely feels broken. It takes all my willpower to hold a cry inside as I reach for the discarded bra and panties.

The thin lace is so cheap and plasticky, it will offer little coverage. My black and blue frame trembles as I slide the lingerie on, stopping several times to blink aside the dizzy fog that's descending.

"I'm going to go with them and find a way out of here," I announce loudly, trying to keep my voice steady. "Someone has to."

Exhausted voices whisper through the din, murmurs of terror and anxiety. Not everyone is lucid enough to respond. Several cages remain silent, their occupants lost to a catatonic state.

A shuffle comes from the adjacent cage.

"No!" Gracie cries. "Please don't leave me here."

"It's going to be okay. You're not alone."

"B-But… Please, Ember. I need you to stay."

"I have to do something. Diego is coming for me."

"But I'm scared." Her voice sounds thick with tears. "What if you don't come back?"

"Take a deep breath for me."

Snapping the bra into place, I shuffle across the floor to reach the side closest to Gracie's cage. Even though I can't reach her, I have a better view into her shadowy cell.

Similar to Debbie, she's curled up in a ball, only slumped on the concrete instead. If I couldn't see her shivering, I'd think she was already dead. I can just barely make out her sweet, tear-streaked face.

"Listen to me. I need you to be strong."

"I'm so tired." She shakes hard, more tears slipping over her hollow cheeks. "So hungry."

"Think about home, Gracie."

Her rocking pauses for a brief second. "Home?"

"Yeah. Home."

"I… I c-can't remember what it looks like."

"You told me all about your two little sisters, remember? Annie and Gabby. And your mum's homemade baking? Think about those oatmeal cookies. You made me hungry just by describing them."

"Annie," she mumbles through her folded arms. "I think I remember her. Those cookies… They're the best."

"You're going to eat them again soon with your little sisters." My broken heart twists, filling me with anguish. "We didn't go through hell just to die now, did we?"

The silence from the other women being held with us is deafening. It's like they can taste the lies I'm feeding the terrified teen to keep her from shutting down. Maybe it would be kinder to let her soul die.

Just as her breathing starts to even out, the sound of a door clanging open marks my doom. Diego is back to see if I've complied with his demand.

"Keep breathing for me," I say in a rush, dragging myself into position. "I'll be back."

"No!" She suddenly jerks upright, her face red from sobbing. "Don't go with them!"

The wide shoulders and bulging belly of my tormenter return. Only he's packing this time and has company with him. Two other men, both wearing woven balaclavas, follow close behind him.

They too carry weapons strapped to their hips. I've only seen guns once. It was when we were marched through the windswept night over to a shipping container already full of gagged women.

One girl made a run for it before our kidnappers could load me and Gracie inside. She almost made it to the end of the rain-soaked dock before a masked man shot her in the kneecap.

I can still remember the bloodcurdling scream she unleashed. The high-pitched shriek nearly burst my eardrums when the men proceeded to beat her. Silence came when her carcass was tossed into the sea.

"Learned your lesson?" Diego bellows at me.

I lean against the cage bars to hold myself still. "Hardly."

"Your face begs to differ. Looks awful sore."

Teeth gritted, I don't take the bait. He'll only break another bone.

"Are you going to come quietly this time?"

Silent, I nod in response.

"Well, isn't this a turn of events. Wrists up then, whore."

Hold it in. Hold it in.

If I play the game, I'll get my opening.

The inflamed circles that mark my wrists become clear when I hold them up. He unlocks my cage, skulking inside to bind me in a pair of black handcuffs. The cold metal bites deep into my wounds.

"Keep that mouth of yours shut too," he growls in warning. "The boss ain't as forgiving as I am."

"Is this forgiving?" I can't help but snark. "You broke my fucking cheekbone."

Grinning, he trails a fingertip over my face. "Could've been worse."

Hauling me by the chain that connects my cuffs, I'm pulled from the cage. Each tug adds to the furious bonfire turning my innards into a furnace, but I wrestle with the red haze to keep a level head.

I'll bide my time. Allow them to think I've given in to their taunts. When I'm above ground, I can make a plan.

Before I'm escorted from the dank expanse, a shout freezes my blood.

"And her. She's been requested for this auction."

"No," I gasp in horror.

Diego's staring right at Gracie. Her puffy blue eyes fill with burgeoning horror when she realises he's talking about her.

"Our customers enjoy unspoiled products." His disgusting breath tickles my earlobe. "She'll be snapped right up."

"No! Don't you dare touch her!"

"Oh, I won't. That's what the auction is for, *cariño*."

Despite kicking and thrashing with every ounce of strength I possess, I'm still pinned tight by the handcuffs. The other men prowl towards Gracie's cage, unlocking the bars to enter.

"Stop! Leave her alone!"

"Now, now." Diego laughs, still lording himself over me. "I'll make sure she goes to a good home. They'll break her in nicely."

"No! Gracie!"

Attempting to wrench myself free, the twinge in my shoulder transforms into an intense burn when the muscles strain. Still I buck and thrash, searching for any escape.

They can't take her. Not a chance. I'll rip myself in half and carry my severed limbs with me if that's what it takes to reach her cage and protect the poor girl.

Frantic shouts and cries form a sick harmony all around me as the other women watch the unfolding scene. The two men have picked up Gracie's arms and legs, but she's jerking between them to shake herself free.

"We've got a wriggler, boss."

"Then teach her to behave!"

The second man momentarily drops her feet so he can snap out his curled fist. She's unprepared, the impact landing with a hollow crack that causes blood to explode from her nose.

Just the sound of Gracie screaming is enough to tear at those widening fissures in my mind until I'm barely hanging onto my sanity.

"Gracie," I screech, now overflowing with panic. "Stop. Don't fight."

I can see how weak she is from being starved. Another punch like that and she may crumble into dust.

"No!" she howls through pouring blood. "I want to go home!"

"Just do as they say!"

Her small, bird-like limbs finally go limp between them. They adjust their grip as they carry her ahead of us, leaving Diego to drag me behind. His chuckling feels like needles stabbing into my brain tissue.

"She looks up to you," he hums. "Perhaps I'll make you watch when she's packaged up and shipped off. Make you understand who's in charge around here."

The red haze intensifies.

"I'm going to kill you."

He guffaws loudly. "Sure."

"You can watch while I cut your dick off for hurting her."

Yanking me into his side, the stench of his sweat and cheap aftershave creates a noxious cloud.

"As entertaining as this is, we have somewhere to be. Shut up and smile, or else I'll fuck that tight asshole of yours until you can't walk straight."

I seal my lips shut while we ascend, leaving the greyscale gloom behind. Small details enter my awareness as we enter a cluttered space above ground.

Two wooden desks, overloaded with scattered paperwork. A half-full bottle of tequila. Overflowing ashtray. Next to a gun holster, there's an outdated mobile phone.

These pigs are living like slobs. The air is so stiflingly hot, it causes sweat to dribble down my exposed spine.

We're dragged across the office then through various rooms, all mirror images of the last. Cigarettes, booze, weapons. Bright lights blind me in the confusion after so long spent in half light.

Ascending another flight of stairs, I'm leaning heavily on the asshole yanking me along by the time we emerge into a room with tall ceilings, blacked-out windows and an array of widely spaced chairs.

At the front, a raised platform made from glossy, black wood boasts several floor-to-ceiling steel poles. We're handcuffed to our individual poles when the situation becomes clear.

This is a viewing stage.

A place where cattle are paraded.

Each chair sits empty but will soon house an occupant with cash to burn and a desire to acquire new property. The living, breathing kind.

Head lolling forwards, Gracie spits blood on the floor. "Oh, God."

"It's okay. Breathe for me."

"We're going to be sold! That's what this is!"

Dismissing his two men, Diego observes us from below, hands braced on his hips.

"You're right, *chica*." He chortles in amusement. "Now smile and behave. You're going to make us a pretty penny."

"Or what?" I challenge.

Hand moving to grip the weapon at his hip, he lifts a silvery brow. "Customers will still purchase you with a bullet between your eyes. Just think about the things they'll do to your corpse."

With a wink, he turns to leave the room. It won't be long before their precious customers are escorted in. Frenetic energy clouds my thinking, throwing too many obstacles at me.

My head spins with dizziness as I flash between hot and cold. Pinned against a pole, I sag in defeat. Powerless to help Gracie. Powerless to do anything. I can't run. Can't hide. Can't escape. And we're out of time.

What was my fucking plan here?

Footsteps echo above us. Each thump feels like a knife being pushed into my gut, finding new organs to pierce and rupture. If we don't die here, we'll die soon enough once we're sold.

The steps grow louder as company arrives with Diego. Several men are all dressed in varying degrees of finesse. Tailored suits. Pressed shirts. Gelled hair. Clearly wealthy.

Strolling ahead of them, the leader of the pack stands apart. He isn't dressed to impress. His suit trousers have a dark-blue shirt tucked into them that's rolled up to his elbows, showing a flashy gold watch.

"These are Assets 768 and 777?" His voice is cold and firm.

"Yes, Luis," Diego answers him.

Unfriendly brown eyes sear beneath his black locks, the strands curling and hanging over his forehead. Tall and lanky, he's slimmer than the men surrounding him but walks with obvious authority.

Luis.

He's the boss.

"Gentlemen." Luis halts in front of the stage. "These assets are a sample of our newer products. And 777 is unspoiled and available at an enhanced rate."

Memories of the assessment we endured, one by one, to gain the information he's rolling out in a marketing pitch push to the surface. I've refused to acknowledge them since enduring that traumatic experience.

"This one..." A heavy-set, older man wearing charcoal-grey looks at me. "She is a natural blonde?"

"No. We don't believe so."

Nodding thoughtfully, his beady eyes search over me. "Good. I deplore blondes."

His focus causes my skin to crawl in visceral revulsion. He's good looking for an older guy. Self-assured. Commanding. But that isn't what provokes my unease.

Something incredibly sinister glistens in his gaze. The devil soul shines through his handsome looks. The way his lip curls in pleasure at seeing me, beaten and bloodied, is a screaming alarm bell.

"I will take a closer look."

Luis gestures, causing the gold signet ring wrapped around his pinkie to twinkle. "By all means."

The walking predator stalks towards me, leaving the other men to continue looking and quietly discussing. My muscles lock up as he climbs onto the platform to approach.

Evil drips from his gait, an invisible smog clinging to each silk-covered muscle. He must be in his late fifties, but his light, honeydew eyes are razor-sharp and full of calculating threat.

"Buenos días, señorita."

Striding around me in a circle, he examines every inch of skin on display in the skimpy lingerie. Revulsion bubbles in my throat until it feels like I'm going to choke.

"They could've cleaned you up a little, hm?" he croons from behind me. "Sloppy."

Moving in front of me, the sick fuck stares at me like I'm a shiny new piece of jewellery he wants to purchase and display.

"Luis." He snaps his fingers. "Here."

The boss purses his lips but doesn't refuse the summoning. This yellow-eyed man holds even more power than I thought.

Luis climbs the stage to join us, gesturing for Diego and his two men to stay with the other customers. They've all moved over to the other side of the stage to take a closer look at Gracie.

"Yes, Mr Gael?"

"You know I do not purchase without a trial run. Especially at these prices."

"Your last... ahem, *trial run* didn't end so well for our product. We had to scrap the asset."

I think my eyeballs might bulge out of their sockets.

"Nevertheless," Mr Gael smoothly replies.

"But—"

"Do I need to call your father to inform him that his son denied my request? It's no trouble."

Jaw flexing, Luis flicks his eyes to me. "Very well. We have a room available. Diego, move Asset 768!"

Leaving the other sleazebags lingering, Diego hops up onto the platform while pulling my handcuff keys from his pocket. I grit my teeth in a tight clench when he approaches.

"Apologies for the state of this one." He chuckles. "She's caused us some trouble."

Mr Gael musters a thin smile. "You could've avoided her face. But I do not mind a bit of spirit."

"She has plenty of that."

"Good."

Diego stops behind me to unlatch my cuffs. Once unlocked, he leans in to whisper into my ear.

"Fuck around with this guy, and he'll have a pistol rammed inside your tight snatch before I can find something else to break. Behave."

As soon as my sore wrists are released, I slump forwards. All of my focus is on the sharks now circling Gracie with lascivious hunger behind their grins. I've got to do something. *Anything.*

Before Diego can re-fasten my cuffs to escort me to the room, I burst into action. No matter how suicidally reckless it may be. He howls when I snap a fist backwards to hit him in the face. The idiot must've thought he'd scared me into submission.

Without hesitating, I spin around to slam my fist into his

temple, offering me a few precious seconds. I've snatched the gun from his holster in the time it takes him to refocus, quickly leaping several paces away.

"I'll pass," I snark back.

"Fucking *puta!*"

"You should've left me down there."

"I'm going to ki—"

Finger trembling on the trigger, I don't think before squeezing as hard as I can. I don't know shit about aiming, but the shot fires off in his direction. Those split seconds feel infinite.

"Argh!"

Diego slams a hand down on his left thigh where the bullet vanishes inside him, creating a bloody eruption. He crumples in half, howling through gaping lips.

I've barely swung the weapon around to aim it at Luis's stunned expression when I feel movement, the displaced air warning me that someone has snuck up on me.

Pain flares behind my right knee from a brutal kick, causing my legs to buckle. Clattering to the floor, the gun slips from my hand, landing a small distance away.

I throw myself forward to recapture it, frantically scrabbling. My fingers brush the metal right before they're crunched beneath a shoe sole, making a scream erupt from my mouth.

Wrinkled hands snatch the gun up, taking it out of reach. The foot squashing my hand twists, causing my bones to grind together. I cry out when it lifts, leaving my index finger bent at a crooked angle.

"You're fast, *señorita*. Untrained, but fast."

Hands seize my hips then roughly flip me over. My back smacks into the floor before a heavy weight straddles my waist. Hands move to trap my arms above my head.

I'm made to stare up at the embodiment of evil peering down at me with raised eyebrows. Intrigue has propagated into a look of fascination. And that's far, far more petrifying.

"So much fire," Mr Gael mutters, still looking over me. "What will we do with all that?"

"Get the fuck off me!" I screech maniacally.

"Hush. I'm thinking."

"No! Gracie! I'm here!"

The heart-wrenching sound of her screaming my name through sobs is too much to take. Still, I can't shake Gael off to reach her. For an older male, he's unbelievably strong.

"I don't have room for disobedient products in my business," Mr Gael explains like we're discussing a fucking car purchase. "Thankfully, I have multiple ventures, and I enjoy brave animals."

"I am not an animal!" I spit at him.

His lips twitch in a smile. "You will be with a little training."

"Let me go!"

Barking at his men who are moving to assist a semi-conscious Diego, Luis curses at the madness that's engulfed the room. The other customers have scuttled far back now.

Yet he doesn't seem surprised that Mr Gael is the one imprisoning me. With a head shake, Luis dashes over to us, his eyes now blown wide in concern.

"Antonio, please allow me to apolo—"

"I'll take her," he interrupts.

Luis halts, his mouth falling open. "Excuse me?"

"It's been a while since we had a product with a backbone. I have a use for her."

"Well..."

"And it's Mr Gael, Luis, as you rightly know. Enough bumbling. The others may fight over the weeping virgin. I've made my choice."

Attention landing back on me, Mr Gael flashes white teeth that could be pincers for all the dread the sharp points inspire.

"You will be my new champion, 768."

CONFIDENTIAL
Suspect?
DO NOT CROSS
POLICE
Suspect?
NOT CROSS
POLICE

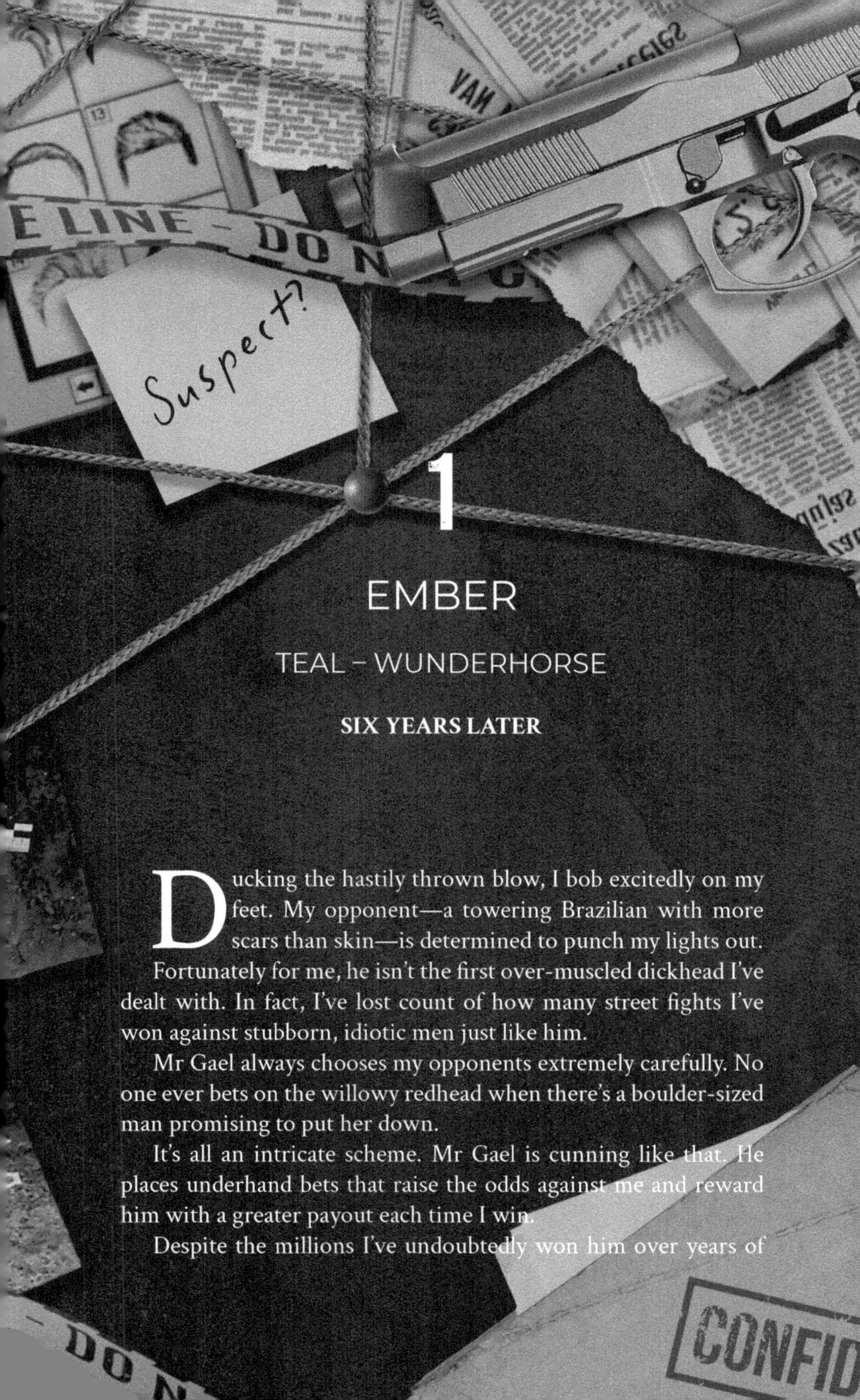

1

EMBER

TEAL – WUNDERHORSE

SIX YEARS LATER

Ducking the hastily thrown blow, I bob excitedly on my feet. My opponent—a towering Brazilian with more scars than skin—is determined to punch my lights out. Fortunately for me, he isn't the first over-muscled dickhead I've dealt with. In fact, I've lost count of how many street fights I've won against stubborn, idiotic men just like him.

Mr Gael always chooses my opponents extremely carefully. No one ever bets on the willowy redhead when there's a boulder-sized man promising to put her down.

It's all an intricate scheme. Mr Gael is cunning like that. He places underhand bets that raise the odds against me and reward him with a greater payout each time I win.

Despite the millions I've undoubtedly won him over years of

fighting, I haven't earned my freedom. Only a few less beatings and whippings. Protection from the assaults that other guards indulge in. And moderately better living conditions than the other women in his possession.

Unlike those women—hollow-eyed and silent when they're summoned to work at one of his parties—I exist solely to fight. Nothing more, nothing less. He stayed true to his word when he proclaimed to have a purpose for me.

It was a long time before he rolled me out for my first bout in a seedy, underground fight club somewhere in southern Mexico. Months of lessons taught with fists and broken bones gave me enough skill to survive. Barely.

Mr Gael's operation is the definition of *do or die.* I had to adapt fast to survive. Learning how to fight dirty and obliterate my opponent became more necessary than breathing.

I drink spilled blood now.

Not oxygen.

The sweat-soaked Brazilian charges towards me. It's a pathetic move. As I suspected, he's allowing rage to cloud his judgement, and that will be his undoing. I'm quick to dodge sideways.

The brute slams straight into the graffiti-tagged concrete wall that encloses the sunken fighting pit. His agonised bellow is like a shot of liquid dopamine straight into my heart muscle.

"Argh!" he roars.

Moving in, I run fast at his wide, scarred back. My bare feet springboard off the ground, sending me flying through the air until I latch onto him like a violent spider monkey.

With my bootie short clad thighs wrapped around his midsection, I scissor his neck with my arms. I'm slimmer than him but strong and muscled enough to choke the bastard out given a chance.

He spins around and slams backwards, crashing me against the concrete he just headbutted. Intense agony sprints along my spine from the impact, forcing the air from my lungs.

"Fuck!" I wheeze.

His response is a garbled tangle of Portuguese I can't comprehend, but he sounds smug. I cling on when he moves again, arms wringing. Muscles straining. Chest heaving. I ride the asshole's back like my life depends on it—because it fucking does.

I've lost enough fights to fear the consequences. The punishments were so severe, I'd rather die in the ring than lose again. After the first loss, Gael whipped me until I couldn't move for a week. But my worst defeat left me out of action for months with a life-changing injury.

Each slam into the solid wall feels like it's going to shatter my skeleton, causing every single part of me to rattle. I can already feel the vivid black clouds that will soon mark my skin.

"Die, fucking bitch!" he bellows.

Now that I understood.

"Never!" I holler back.

His power is reducing. Each backwards hit carries less weight. The more he tires, the louder the baying crowd looking down on the enclosed pit screams their heads off.

All they want is a show. I've built a fearsome reputation for providing exactly that. Some hurl beers while others slam their fists against the chain-links high above.

"768! 768! 768!"

That's who I am now.

Three motherfucking numbers.

The next collision hits a weak spot in my back, the strained muscle still healing from a recent fight. A young, travelling American who I fought wanted to make a quick buck by kicking the shit out of me.

My tight cinch around my opponent's neck falters, causing my bodyweight to lurch dangerously. I fall sideways, tumbling off his back and smashing hard into the ground.

His massive bulk is on top of me before I can suck in a stunned breath. The first punch hits my stomach, opening up a canyon of sizzling agony that rips through my organs.

Spittle and saliva smack me in the face each time he swings his fist, finding a new, unobstructed part of me to pummel. My tight sports bra leaves him a myriad of visible targets.

Smack.

Smack.

FRACTURED FUTURE

Smack.

Desperately searching around me, I spot a chunk of dislodged concrete that's escaped. The piece is slim and jagged, but I bet I can jam it somewhere.

When his fist slams into my jaw, my teeth click together so hard, I worry that my molars will split wide open. Tears involuntarily pour from my eyes.

He smirks, enjoying the sight. *"Tá fodido."*

I spit blood that's pooled on my tongue. "I don't speak asshole."

"You… fucked," he enunciates.

"Not quite."

Using his distraction to my advantage, I strain my arm, hoping my fingers can reach the concrete sliver. He's far too busy laughing at me, revealing gap-filled teeth that are now stained red.

Come on, come on, I mentally chant.

Another punch to the face arrives before I can locate my potential weapon, making my head wrench to the side as I feel my skin split open. Warmth dribbles down to my jaw in a slippery wave.

It hurts like a son of a bitch, landing right on top of the cheekbone that once took two months to heal. Blinking through the haze, I can distantly see the shard I'm searching for.

I've shifted enough from each blow to strain my fingers to a breaking point. The very tips catch on the concrete shard, but I don't have a spare second to rejoice.

Nudging the ridged point, I draw it into my palm. Screaming and hollering echoing all around in a deathly bay soon fades away. The filthy fight club vanishes from sight.

All I can see is the wide, pleasure-filled eyes of the man who thinks he's beaten me. He's not the first. Certainly not the last. But he will be the latest to learn just how wrong his entire species is.

"Smile for the crowd, buddy."

The chunk sails into his head, packing a heavy weight that stupefies him. His bulk wavers on top of me, but he's still conscious. *Good.* I want him to feel this next part.

Repositioning the shard, I ignore every fresh injury wailing at me and aim for his face. The tip is angular enough to push into his eye socket with an audible squelch that would turn a weaker stomach.

His resultant howl could break the sound barrier, it's so inhumanly loud. Blood spatters against my face like spitting oil, mixing with my own.

Pulling my arm back, I take in the sight of his contorted face. Hands slapped over his eye, mouth frozen open on a pathetically high-pitched scream. Beautiful.

It's child's play to shove him aside, allowing me to shakily sit up. Every limb protests against the movement, but I'm a master at locking my pain away. It barely registers as I draw to my feet.

I'm prepared to take out his other eye or perhaps tear his throat out with my teeth when the piece of shit begins to plead. At least I think he does. I can't understand his language, though he's clearly cowering.

"*Tiempo!*"

The announcer's voice and a blare of an air horn marks the end of the fight. Tossing the slick shard aside, I raise my hands as high as my battered body will allow.

"768! 768! 768!"

The cheers are a confusing mixture of English and Spanish. I've learned enough of the latter to communicate with Gael and his men, no matter which lawless city we rock up in to fight.

"768!"

Slowly rotating around the pit, I relish in the jeering onlookers. Their praise isn't what I'm here for, though. It's their exuberance which marks another day of my survival.

Only one person isn't responding to my victory. The figure stands out among the revellers who clink beers and rush to collect their earnings or stand wallowing in their financial losses.

A tall, frozen statue.

Silently watching from afar.

Nimble fingertips tangled in the chain-links, as if he was attempting to rip them open and climb into the pit himself, his undivided attention is locked solely on me.

The feel of his stare drinking me in across bloodied concrete and untold horrors feels weirdly intimate. In a crowd of drunkards, he's just standing there. Unmoving. His patience is seemingly infinite.

"768! Here!"

Carlos's bark pierces the strange moment, tearing me free from the bubble that's formed around me in the mayhem. I look over to my trainer's scowl, waving for me to follow him.

When I glance back at the crowd, the strange onlooker is gone. Not a shred of evidence remains to prove that he wasn't a figment of my likely-concussed imagination.

With Carlos banding an arm around my midsection, I limp away from my now-sobbing opponent to leave the pit. No one is attending to him yet. Whoever he's fighting for—a gouged eye is the least of his problems now that he's lost.

"That was pathetic," Carlos criticises in his usual way. "You were weak."

"I won the fight."

"By the skin of your teeth."

Flinching, I breathe through the lava collecting around my spine and ribs. "I gave them a good show. That's the whole point of these stupid clubs."

Walking me down a dimly-lit, underground corridor, thick with the stomach-turning scent of cooking drugs and spilled liquor, Carlos scoffs. It's a derisive, unpleasant sound.

"Don't pretend like that shit was all part of your plan."

"Perhaps it was."

"*Mierda.* I taught you better than that."

Mr Gael's trusted trainer is a cruel piece of shit with sky-high standards and a penchant for beating skill into you rather than teaching with patience or humility.

Illegal fights are only a small intersection of Antonio Gael's business empire, spanning across borders to reach vast swathes of South America. My knowledge is limited, but he's heavily involved in the skin trade too.

I've seen enough traumatised girls come and go on his grand, rural estate. Most vanish when they outlive their purpose. For years, I've held out hope that I'll see her face.

Gracie.

The poor girl I left behind.

But sometimes, I hope I don't see her. Not here. I hope she's dead already and far from this depravity. The thought of her enduring six years of relentless torture is too much to bear.

"Clean yourself up and be ready to leave in ten minutes." Carlos stops outside the changing rooms. "We're needed in Ciudad Obregón by tomorrow."

"Is he meeting us there?"

"Señor Gael's schedule is none of your concern."

His bushy, black caterpillars drawn together in a deep frown, Carlos waits for me to leave. I want to bite back, demand to know what he's going to tell the man who decides my fate, but I swallow the question.

"Yes, sir."

Limping into the small room, I take in the old cardboard boxes that once held cheap tequila to be poured down the necks of the fight club's regulars.

Rather than avoiding the mirror, I've taught myself to rip the Band-Aid off fast by assessing each fight's damage in the immediate aftermath. No sense in avoiding my own reflection.

Lukewarm water drips into the dirty sink as I study the unfamiliar woman staring back at me through one working eye, the other blackened and nearly swollen shut.

I used to see a leggy, blonde bombshell when I looked in the mirror. Someone I liked. She was attractive. Athletic. Ambitious. But so incredibly naïve and foolish. I just didn't know it at the time.

Now the muscular stranger staring back at me looks nothing like the person I used to be. Flaming-auburn hair has regrown from my roots over the past few years, leaving me with an odd inch of blonde at the very tips of my long locks.

Pulling out my tight bun, I finger brush the obnoxiously bright strands. I have the same vivid auburn hair as my older brother, inherited from our half-Irish mother, and it makes my porcelain skin gleam.

My narrow nose, the centrepiece of my oval-shaped face, now sits eternally crooked after years of fighting. It didn't take long for my curved brows to grow back to their natural red, crowning my forever-changing eyes.

FRACTURED FUTURE

Some days, they're akin to a restless sea, churning in shades of tranquil azure. Other times I see my mother looking back at me in the stormy-grey colour that invades to form a muddied ocean.

Russet streaks pour from my nose, mouth and a shallow cut that's opened in my cheek. The blood obscures most of the bruising, but the purple marks will shine through soon enough.

Violent green and black storm clouds are already forming on my midsection, the relentless throbbing mirroring the beat of a war drum wreaking havoc on my spine. As the adrenaline fades, it's harder to ignore.

Tipping my head down, I splash my face with water then scrub my cheeks as roughly as my bruises will allow. Pink swirls escape down the drain, removing a small fraction of the blood I'm doused in.

"You're a savage creature, sweetheart."

The crisp, formal British accent is a startling shock. It sends me hurtling to a place that I haven't allowed myself to dream of seeing for a very long time.

Rearing back, I wobble on the balls of my feet, spotting a stranger lingering in the doorway through the mirror. My heart lurches against my breastbone.

It's *him.*

Letting the door swing shut behind him, the observer from the crowd stalks into the room. His legs are long, powerful rowing oars that devour the space between us with each assured step.

Midnight-black hair—shaved close to his skull on the sides while the tousled strands are left long on top—perfectly matches his intense onyx eyes.

Up close, I can see a thin, wiggling scar that curves from the end of his right eyebrow to his exaggerated jawline. The puckered skin is pale and faded, evidencing the age of the uneven mark.

He's tall. Lithe. Packing muscles that strain his dark shirt and jeans, the all-black clothing screaming bad boy. While he isn't oversized, anxiety still prickles over me. He doesn't need bulk to look dangerous.

"How did you get in here?" I blurt.

Bottom lip curling inwards, his tongue flicks out to tease a silver ring that pierces the soft swell.

"Your trainer is having a chat with my associates."

"A… chat?" I turn to face him properly.

His sly smile drips with confidence. "Less talking and more bleeding on the floor, last I saw. I expected more from the infamous Carlos Morello."

I'm not sure my mouth could fall open any wider.

"To confirm… You are Ember Lawson?"

Hearing my real name out loud knocks me for six. I have to blink several times to stop a hot wave of dizziness from sending me to my knees.

"What the… Who… Who are you?"

Lifting the edge of his leather jacket to tuck a big, veiny hand into the pocket of his black jeans, he spreads his feet. I've never seen a total stranger act so casual in the middle of an illegal club.

"Is that a yes?"

Awash with numbness, I summon a loose nod.

"Good. I'm Blaine Madden. Pleasure."

A disbelieving laugh spills out of me. "Well, Blaine Madden. I have no idea what you want from me, but I've already gouged one man's eye out tonight. I can make it another."

His chuckle is rough, throaty. Full of raw masculinity and amusement. It rolls down my still-screaming spinal cord, leaving a tingling imprint in its wake.

"I saw. Impressive work."

"He was cocky." I shrug stiffly. "A bit like you."

"You think I'm cocky?" His black gaze twinkles, revealing flecks of navy-blue undulating in his irises. "Seems presumptuous."

"You're an easy read."

"Is that so?"

Smiling to himself, Blaine pushes up his jacket sleeve to unveil a silver Rolex. Though lines mar his forehead when he frowns at the time, he can't be much older than early thirties.

"I'm all for foreplay, Ember, but we're on a tight schedule. Get your shit."

"Excuse me?"

"Our men are on guard shift for the next three minutes. I don't mind a fist fight, but you're in no state to punch your way out of here once that shift changes."

I must've taken a harder hit to the head than I realised. He's making zero fucking sense.

"Back up like… a thousand miles." I grab my threadbare sweatshirt to cover up. "Explain."

Those dangerously intense orbs watch me wincing while trying to pull the sweatshirt on. I can't twist my body in the right way to even lift it over my head without wanting to throw up.

"Need a hand?" He lifts a single brow.

"Not from you, asshole."

"I'm not sure what I expected from Thomas Lawson's missing baby sister. But a foul-mouthed street fighter working for the Mexican cartel didn't cross my mind."

Stilling mid-struggle, I gawp at the smirking stranger. "What did you just say?"

"Come on, Ember." He pulls down his sleeve to cover the expensive watch. "I need you to get up to speed a bit faster. Let's move."

"I have no idea who you are!"

"That's an irrelevant detail."

Taking the final steps into my personal space, he lifts the hem of the sweatshirt. I swear, something soft and gentle flickers in his obsidian gaze, tangled with the sapphire flecks.

"Dress," he demands.

"I… W-Why?"

"If you go out there looking like that, I'll be forced to take a page from your book and blind my men so they can't look at that beautiful body on display."

Yanking the fabric over my head, I shove my head inside rather than respond. Blaine tugs the sweatshirt down over my skin, covering up my sports bra. He spots my nearby shoes then kicks them towards me.

"Better. Ready?"

"For what?" I blink rapidly.

Sighing through his nostrils, his long fingers curl around my forearm. Even through my sweatshirt, I can feel his cold skin sending icy swirls deep into my sore muscles.

"Enough questions. Walk."

After shoving my trainers onto my bare feet, I stumble beside him. I'm propelled by his momentum, the sound of not only my name but also my brother's name, ringing in my ears.

I haven't heard either since I was taken.

Not once.

How does he know who I am?

CONFIDENTIAL
Suspect?
DO NOT CROSS
PO
POLICE
NOT CROSS
Suspect?

2

EMBER

MR. RAGER – KID CUDI

Marched down the corridor, three shifty-looking characters are gathered around an unconscious heap on the ground. One glowering, light-haired man looks up at the sound of us nearing.

"He's still down, boss."

Blaine lengthens his strides to carry us towards his crew. "Good."

"Their security is held up with our friend upstairs, collecting Gael's earnings. We've got one minute until guard change."

Their friend?

"Then let's hurry, hmm?" he responds, his grip on my arm flexing. "Watch our six."

Gesturing for one of the others to follow, the duo take position behind us. We're left following a third, blue-haired figure. It takes a moment for me to register that it's a woman.

"This is stupid," she hisses under her breath. "What are we

doing here, Blaine?"

"I don't want to hear it. You know I have my reasons."

"We should be focusing on your fath—"

"Enough," Blaine interrupts icily. "You have your orders, Raye. Follow them."

Shaking her navy pixie cut head, showing off rows of multicoloured ear piercings, she doesn't bite back. The sounds of the jam-packed club roar in the subsequent silence as we near the rear exit doors.

With a final surveying look behind us, Blaine tows me outside into the blazing heat. Even after years, the raw intensity never fails to steal my breath. It's the kind of heat that crisps bare skin into a dry lake bed within minutes.

"*Gracias.*" Raye stops to shake the hand of the first guard we meet, palming him a roll of Pesos. "You'll want to split quick once we're gone."

Both guards nod in deference, avoiding looking at me. I've seen them here before. This underground club has been on my fight list several times before, and they're regular staff.

"Head down," Blaine murmurs to me. "We don't need attention."

"Why should I trust you?" I snarl at him.

"Believe it or not, sweetheart, I'm not here to hurt you."

"That means nothing to me."

"Fine, try this... If I meant you harm, don't you think I would've done so by now?"

My next sassy remark dies in my throat. He had the opportunity to take me out in the changing room. But that doesn't mean I'm ready to trust these unknown people who sound like home.

Something inside me breaks when I lower my head as told. Instead, a defiant animal, salivating for its next kill, tucks its tail. Even if I wanted to, I couldn't fight off this group.

"Get in." Blaine nods towards an unmarked blue van close by. "Quickly."

Raye throws open the back door, her feet remaining planted on the dusty road. The abandoned warehouse that conceals the fight club seems so unsuspecting in the early evening sunshine.

Teeth gritted, I climb into the van as quickly as my injuries will allow. Not even the return of my surging adrenaline can distract me from the pain wracking my entire frame.

The other two men climb into the front while Raye joins me and Blaine in the back of the vehicle. We take off in a squeal of spinning tyres, causing me to clatter against the thin metal wall.

The impact jolts my spine, aggravating nerves on the verge of splitting apart. The pain from being repeatedly acquainted with a concrete wall is quickly making itself known.

Rubbing a hand over his five o'clock shadow, Blaine looks at me. "You're not gonna like this next part."

"Try me." I hold in a cry while straightening.

"Where did they put it?"

"Huh?"

Crouching on the van floor, Raye unzips a backpack to pull out a small travel case. She clicks it open, exposing two glinting scalpels embedded in foam and a compact suture kit.

"The tracking device," Blaine explains grimly. "Our intel says that all of Gael's assets are implanted with one. He can still track you."

A solid lump gathers in my throat.

"Quickly, Ember. We don't have time for you to deliberate."

"Fine." I sigh. "Forearm."

His nostrils flare, the sapphire in his irises churning with anger. "Lay down. We're getting it out."

"Here?"

"You got a better plan, princess?" Raye quips sarcastically.

"We're in a moving vehicle."

"Fuck, Blaine," she grumbles. "I can't believe we're risking everything for this dumb bitch."

Lips thinning, I narrow my eyes on her while dropping myself to the van floor. Her dyed-blue brows lift as she watches me lay down without another word.

"Just do it," I grit out. "Before I break your fucking nose for calling me a dumb bitch, you miserable cunt."

Bursting into laughter, Blaine moves to kneel beside me. "You are a miserable cunt, Raye. She's got you there."

"She has not." Raye scowls while selecting a scalpel to disinfect.

"Right. We don't have any sedatives." Blaine quickly sobers, returning his gaze to me. "And this ain't gonna tickle."

"I can handle it."

"Of that I have no doubt. Let's take this back off."

He helps me to remove the sweatshirt, exposing my right arm. The tracking device was surgically implanted not long after I was sold to the cartel. It bulges beneath a puckered scar.

Accepting the antibacterial swab that Raye passes to him, Blaine deftly cleans the incision site. An inch or so below it, closer to the crease of my elbow, lies another scar.

The mangled skin is far darker and messier, twisted from a severe burn. But no ordinary burn. It was delivered by what can only be compared to a cattle brand, the warped iron glowing with heat.

"What the fuck is that?" Blaine's voice is low and dangerous.

Memories I've long held back threaten to break free from their prison. The brand. My sobbing. Gael's whip slicing deeply into my back. It takes all my willpower to hold the horrors at bay and stuff them back into their prison cell.

"My name." I stare up at the ceiling. "768."

There's a muttered curse.

"Your *intel* didn't tell you about that?" My laugh is forced.

"No."

A muscle in Blaine's neck convulses, his jaw clenched tight. Even the vein at his temple seems to throb, visibly pulsing beneath his skin.

"You're the first person to use my old name in a very long time," I admit croakily.

An unknown emotion seems to cast a shadow over his features as he contemplates. "Your name is Ember. Not 768."

"I stopped being that person the day they took me." I watch him finish cleaning my arm. "If she survived the kidnapping, she died in the years that followed."

Blaine halts to glance at me. "Someone told me you have 210 undefeated fights under your belt."

"More or less. I have plenty of defeats too."

"Yet you're still alive."

My stomach flips and twists. "I suppose so."

"Well that doesn't sound like dying to me. In fact, I think that makes you a survivor."

He shifts to let Raye slide closer, the blade poised in her hand. Blaine moves to my head, yelling at his men to drive carefully while we work. We're careening along at breakneck speed.

"Hold still," Raye instructs.

She offers no further warning before pushing the scalpel into my forearm, slicing through my skin to access the device. If I wasn't physically spent, I could probably hold my cry inside.

Instead, it rips out of me, ricocheting around the van's hollow interior. The blade feels like a scorching laser point, carving into my flesh. Sweat quickly breaks out on my forehead.

"Shut her up, Blaine. I need to concentrate."

A large, calloused hand moves to cover my mouth, clamping down on my whimpering. The faint scent of spicy peppercorns and citrusy bergamot emanates from Blaine's wrist.

Trust this smooth talker to wear expensive aftershave on some kind of fucked up kidnapping mission. I know a fine cologne when I smell one. My brother's lifestyle used to demand no less.

"Not the way I usually like to make a stunning woman like yourself scream." Blaine's smirk hangs over me. "In an ideal world, I'd buy you a drink first."

"Stop flirting," Raye mutters.

"Ignore her." His night-sky eyes seem to sparkle good-humouredly. "She's just jealous because a chick broke her heart. Now something tells me you're a wine drinker on a date."

Knocking his hand aside, I pant raggedly. "The last m-man I dated had me kidnapped and trafficked."

Lines arch around his mouth when he laughs. "I'm not opposed to kidnapping, though I'd prefer it to be consensual."

Is he for real or just insane?

"I suppose the cliche is for people like me to swirl whiskey in their crystal glasses and smoke a cigar, right?" he continues. "In reality, I'm partial to a fine pinot noir."

"People like you?" I repeat shakily. "Who are you?"

Blaine winks at me. "Spoilers, sweetheart."

With a sudden stab of pain, I feel something in my arm pop. The rapidly spreading heat feels like I've been branded all over again, joining the medley of injuries sapping my strength.

"Gotcha." Raye lifts her head, a metal chip caught between her wet fingers. "Slippery little bugger."

"Undamaged?"

"Do I look like an amateur to you?" she barks.

"Don't bite my fucking head off. Put it somewhere safe, it's coming with us. We need to throw Gael's men off the scent until she's clear."

Nodding at Blaine's command, Raye deposits the tracker into the foam-packed case. "I need to stitch her up."

"I've got this," Blaine intervenes. "Your sutures are shit."

"You've never complained before."

"Look at my damn face. Your fault I look like this."

Rolling her eyes, she clambers out of the way to clean up her supplies. "Whatever, pretty boy."

Blaine swipes the suture kit then shuffles to pull my bloodied arm into his lap. With his head lowered, he preps the suture needle then moves to apply pressure to my forearm.

My hazy vision clears long enough for me to study the scar that bisects the right side of his face and defined bone structure. It's pulled taut as he concentrates on my arm, causing the corner of his eye to crease.

"She stitched your face?"

The faintest shudder rolls over him. "Yes."

"The scar looks old."

"It is."

"You get stitched up by friends often?"

His lips twitch. "On occasion."

Each clipped response tells me to shut the fuck up. I don't know this dangerous man, and I certainly don't want to piss off the person getting me away from that seedy warehouse.

The feel of the needle slipping into my skin delivers a familiar jolt. I've been patched up enough times by Gael's well-paid doctor. Sedatives weren't on offer then either.

My mind clouds, floating in an exhausted fog. Flashes

accompany my semi-conscious daze. A filthy, constrictive cage. Gracie's begging. The doctors who took our measurements. Years of half-assed examinations that followed after a fight.

Locking the memories away and giving myself no option but to remain strong has kept me alive. I survived not through skill but sheer stubbornness. Never once allowing myself to break or feel.

When the sound of low voices rouses me, I jerk back to the present. I must've drifted for a while. Blaine has halted the bleeding, and he's now almost done stitching me up.

"You're back." He lifts his lips to form a small smile. "Thought we'd lost you there."

"I'm back." I blink moisture from my eyes.

"Good."

Taking a few seconds to steady my breathing, I swallow hard to lubricate my throat. My voice still comes out raspy.

"Why are you helping me?"

"Purely selfish reasons." He shrugs casually.

"What does that mean?"

Blaine ties off a suture then snips it. "Curious much?"

Weak laughter balloons in my chest. "I was held captive for six years before you showed up. I think that warrants a few questions."

"It does. I'm not obliged to answer them, though."

"Ow! Careful!"

Pulling the needle back out from where he pushed too hard, Blaine tuts. "Stop distracting me."

"Asshole!"

"And that's the second time you've called me that. I may start taking it personally."

"You should." I shudder at the suture being tied.

"Quiet. Let me finish."

Squeezing my eyes shut, my logical side tries to find a reasonable explanation for his insanity. No one pays attention to me. Not even the other women unwillingly tied to the cartel. They hate me for my position and the protection it brings.

I have no friends. No allies. Not even Carlos can stand the sight of me after the hundreds of hours he's spent beating his lifetime's fighting experience into me. No one would ever help me.

FRACTURED FUTURE

So why him? Why now?

Tying myself in mental knots while Blaine continues working, I can't find a viable explanation. I've never met this man. Not once. He's a total stranger, offering me a chance at salvation.

"What's the plan, boss?" a voice shouts from up front.

"Near Acapulco airport like we discussed," Blaine calls back.

"Coming up."

"Airport?" I jerk in surprise.

"Still," he snaps. "Last one."

"I don't have a passport!"

"I said still! For fuck's sake, Ember."

The use of my real name is equivalent to being sucker-punched all over again. I hate the way he cherishes each syllable, letting them roll off his tongue in a sensual, whiskey-smooth drawl.

"There." Blaine catches the bandage that Raye tosses him then begins to wind it around my arm. "You're clean."

"Fantastic," I hiss out.

Sitting back on his haunches, he trails a critical eye over me. "How badly are you hurt? Those bruises look pretty bad."

"Had worse."

"Don't fucking tell me that."

A raspy chuckle pulls from my lips. "Why do you care?"

Ignoring my challenge, Blaine tips his head towards Raye. "Check to make sure nothing's broken. This doesn't work if she's dead before they arrive."

"I'm no doctor," she argues. "Or at least I'm a severely underpaid one."

"Do you ever shut up?"

Flipping him off, she knee-walks across the cramped space to reach for me. I ball my busted hands into fists at my sides to stop myself from hitting the sour-faced bitch.

"This isn't your first rodeo." She probes my stomach, watching my reaction. "Not even a flinch."

"Look where you found me," I growl at her.

"Hard to tell without an X-ray, but I'd expect more swelling by now if you had a fracture. You are bruising bad, though."

"Then stop poking me, dammit!"

Raising her hands in surrender, Raye pulls back. "Want to show me your back?"

"Not a fucking chance. You'll stick a knife in it."

"Whatever." Her tone is thick with sarcasm. "She'll live, Blaine. Nothing a personality transplant won't fix."

"Then go sit up front," he orders.

Raye clambers to her feet, disappearing between the seats to find an empty space. Blaine shakes his raven head at her retreat then stretches out a hand in offering to me.

I reluctantly accept, allowing him to slowly pull me upright. It causes more tears to spring into my eyes when I twist to rest my back against the wall, but I keep my teeth gritted tight.

"Listen to me," Blaine says urgently. "Gael isn't the kind of man to let his assets run off. He will come for you, no matter where you run or hide."

"You think I don't know that?"

"I don't care what you think you know. This is real life now."

"Get to the point," I demand in frustration.

"We'll buy you a few hours before tossing the chip, but he's going to throw everything he's got into getting you back, if your fighting record is to be believed."

"Then what do you suggest I do?"

"Exactly what I tell you to."

I was wrong earlier when I labelled his swagger as confidence. It's more like blind stupidity if he thinks I'm going to follow his orders. I've listened to enough men telling me what to do.

"What exactly do you want from me? Spoilers or not, it's abundantly clear what *people like you* want in return for their help."

His mouth hooks up in a pleased smile. "I just want you to tell the truth, sweetheart. Nothing more, nothing less."

"What truth?"

He leans closer, causing his black t-shirt to strain over his chest. While muscular, Blaine is svelte and wiry like all good hunters are.

"That Blaine Madden saved your life. Think you can remember that?"

"Well, it's rather bloody complicated."

Snorting, his tongue flicks out to touch his piercing again. "I like your smart mouth."

"I'd like to know who the hell you are."

"Call me… an acquaintance of an acquaintance." He grimaces at his own choice of words. "That's not right. More like an enemy of an acquaintance."

My blossoming headache triples at that head fuck.

"Meaning?" I press.

"Meaning you're gonna sing my praises from that gorgeous, pouty mouth of yours to those bastards at Sabre Security. Capiche?"

My lungs tighten into a vice.

Sabre… Security?

Too many old memories resurfacing at once make my skull throb harder. Acquaintance is definitely not the right word. I can make a good guess at who he's looking to manipulate.

"We're ten miles out, boss," the voice calls again. "Seems as good a place as any."

Reaching into his leather jacket, Blaine plucks out an old flip phone. It looks like a relic from decades ago, all bulky and scratched. He quickly tosses it at me.

"This is yours."

I manage to catch the phone. "What's it for?"

"You have a phone call to make."

"Wait, I don't understand…"

Squealing fills the rear of the van as the brakes are hastily applied. I'm thrown forwards by the momentum, straight into Blaine's awaiting arms. A surprised grunt hums in his chest.

Every hardened inch of his cut frame presses into me. It's a solid, steady weight that elicits feelings I didn't think I was still capable of after years of watching and experiencing unfettered violence.

Aside from beatings, the odd whipping, and Gael's physician, no one has touched me in years. Not a single time when I sobbed, begged or pleaded. Nor when I pondered whether it would be better to die than continue living.

I survived alone.

Until now.

"I swear, I'm usually more of a gentleman." His formal accent rolls over me again. "Maybe next time."

Releasing me, Blaine reaches behind his back. I hear the van door click open, but the sluggish realisation comes too late for me to react. I'm spun around then unceremoniously shoved outside.

"Apologies again!" he shouts.

"Argh!"

Thin air wraps around me, failing to slow my rapid plummet. Bracing myself for a hard collision, the impact feels minimal when I smack into a relatively soft surface.

Breath swooshes out of me, cutting off my ability to yell his name. A split second later, my balled-up sweatshirt lands on top of me.

Sprawled out on what feels like a sandy bank, I have to watch that son of a bitch sweep his devilishly dark gaze over my body.

"See you very soon, sweetheart." His grin reveals a single dimple on his unscarred cheek. "I'll buy you that drink."

"Stop! Wait!"

"Don't forget whose praises you're singing."

His lips pucker up to blow me a kiss. Then the slamming doors swallow him. When the van takes off, it leaves a thick sand cloud behind.

Staring after them, I watch until it vanishes from sight. I'm on what appears to be a deserted road, littered with rocks and surrounded by sun-scorched land and distant farms.

"What the fuck?" I scream into the nothingness.

Part of me wonders if I'll wake up to find myself being driven to my next fight. Or perhaps back at the infamous Gael estate, preparing for another punishment in my constantly monitored room.

No matter how many times I squeeze my eyes shut and reopen them to blazing sunshine, the scene remains unchanged. Those insane people rescued me then... What? Dumped me?

My fingers clench around the flip phone still clutched in my hand. *You have a phone call to make.* Blaine's self-assured drawl fills my mind as I wrestle myself upright and flick the phone open.

It takes me a moment to remember how to use the keypad. I'm hardly green at thirty-one years old so this isn't my first Nokia. After fumbling for a second, I locate the contacts menu.

FRACTURED FUTURE

There's just one.
My stomach churns in shock, loss… and hope.
Warner Mead — Sabre Security.

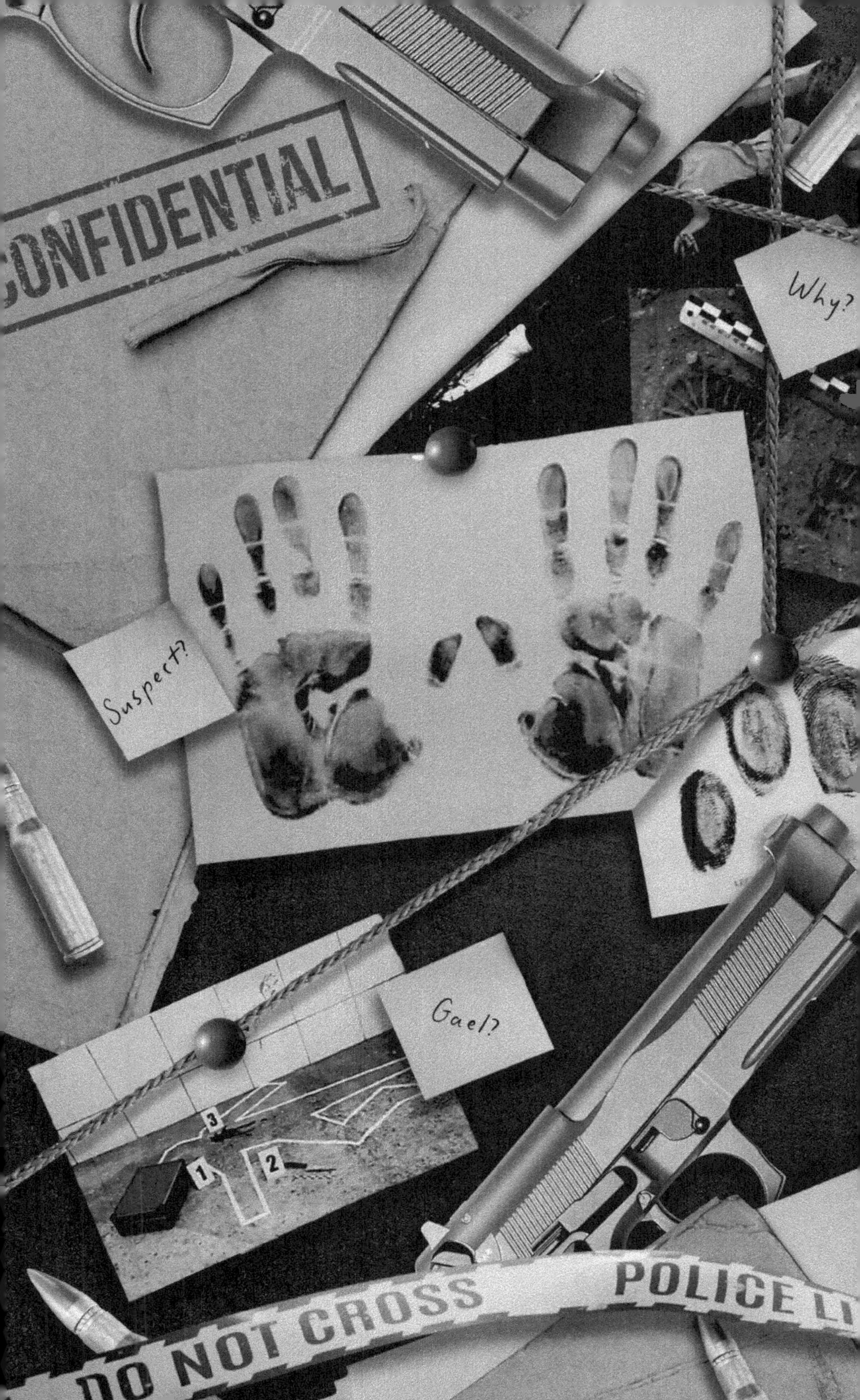
CONFIDENTIAL
Why?
Suspect?
Gael?
DO NOT CROSS
POLICE LI

POLICE LINE – DO NOT CROSS

Gael?

Incoming Call

8:20 AM

Unknown

Victim

DO NOT CROSS

POLICE LI

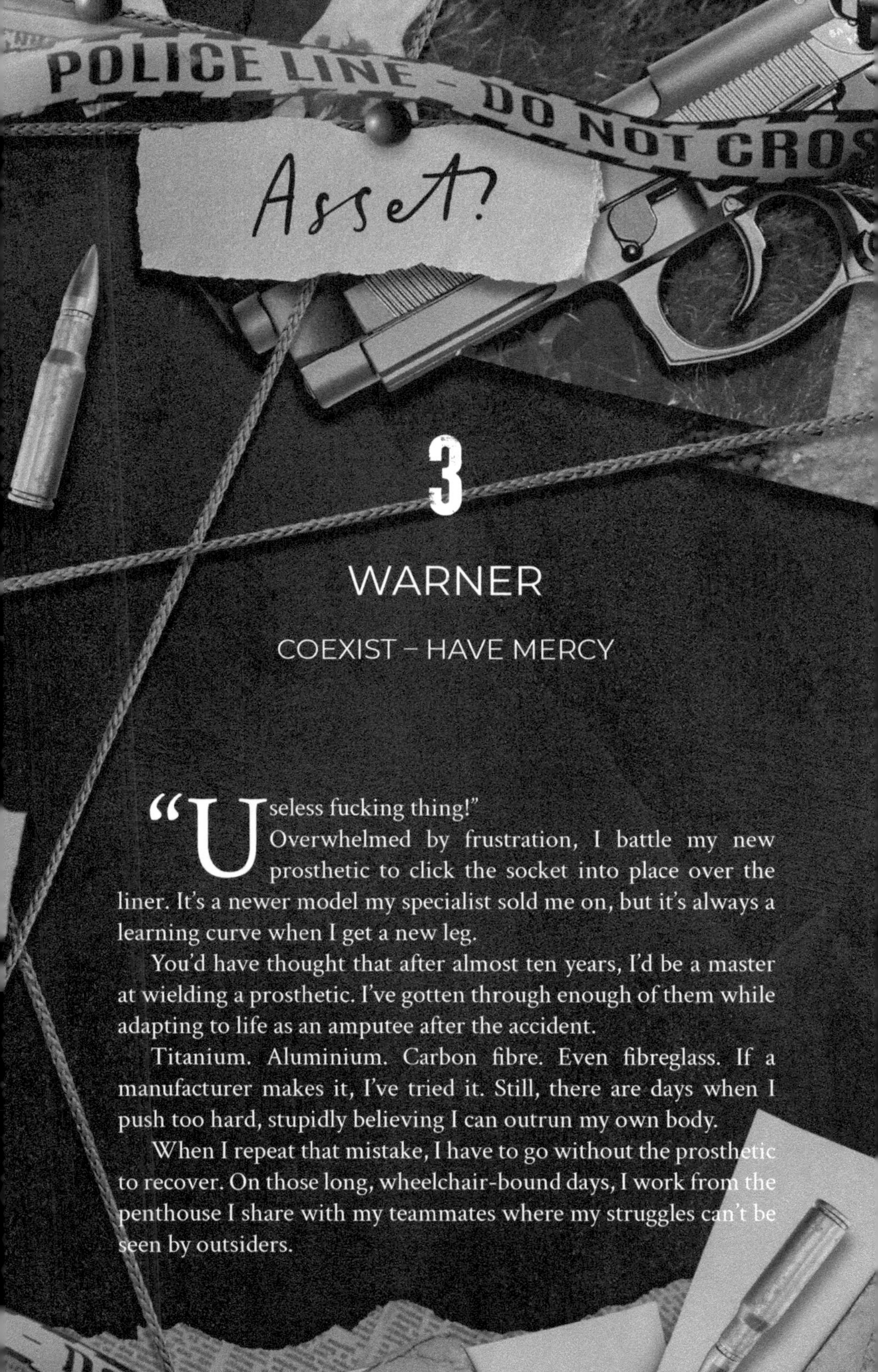

3

WARNER

COEXIST – HAVE MERCY

"Useless fucking thing!"

Overwhelmed by frustration, I battle my new prosthetic to click the socket into place over the liner. It's a newer model my specialist sold me on, but it's always a learning curve when I get a new leg.

You'd have thought that after almost ten years, I'd be a master at wielding a prosthetic. I've gotten through enough of them while adapting to life as an amputee after the accident.

Titanium. Aluminium. Carbon fibre. Even fibreglass. If a manufacturer makes it, I've tried it. Still, there are days when I push too hard, stupidly believing I can outrun my own body.

When I repeat that mistake, I have to go without the prosthetic to recover. On those long, wheelchair-bound days, I work from the penthouse I share with my teammates where my struggles can't be seen by outsiders.

FRACTURED FUTURE

Or I did before our recent long-term work placement in Mexico. The heat aggravates my residual limb further, making it more difficult to be mobile. But I'm not a complainer, and I won't leave until we find her.

Alive or… well, alive.

I won't entertain another possibility.

"You all good in here?" Axel pokes his head around the door, waggling his eyebrows. "You're not supposed to insult the new leg, you know."

"It doesn't have feelings." I sigh loudly.

"I bet John Connor said the same thing before he had a freaking terminator on his ass. Not so fun insulting the machines when they rise up, is it?"

As much as I appreciate our newest and youngest team member's perpetual playfulness, I am in no mood for his teasing today.

"You got something for me, Ax?"

Stepping into the shitty motel room, he bobs his head, though his obnoxiously bright, purple-dyed faux hawk doesn't move. He spends a stupid amount of time styling it each damn morning.

Axel has fully embraced the teen runaway look, despite being a fully grown man. His revolving wardrobe of oversized slogan shirts and ripped jeans match his baby face and bee-stung lips. The head-to-toe tattoos are another thing altogether.

"Picked up some online chatter on the dark web about an incident down south near Chilpancingo, but nothing concrete. Just a few players murmuring about a search party."

"Searching for what?"

He shrugs. "Beats me."

"Fine. Monitor it."

"Already sent a request to the intelligence team in London. Kade told me to suck a dick for waking him up at 2 am."

"Charming," I mutter.

"Isn't he just?" Axel rolls his eyes.

Head shaking, I refocus on fitting my prosthetic. With some gentle manoeuvring, the socket finally clicks into place. I stretch the stiff limb out, testing the weight. It always feels odd at first.

Axel whistles dramatically. "Nice. You had it shipped from the

UK?"

"Sure did. We don't know when we'll go home. I'm not being uncomfortable and in pain until then."

"That's fair."

Climbing to my feet, it takes a moment to adjust to the foreign sensation. This new model is cutting-edge, the best money can buy. It still doesn't replace the right leg I dream about at night.

"I miss my bed." Axel's heavily-inked arms fold across his chest. "And Mary's bagels. Reckon she'd ship some out here for us?"

"All the way across the Atlantic Ocean?"

"Yes!"

Honey-hued eyes curving into a puppy dog look, Axel juts out his bottom lip. It's an insane expression on a thirty-year-old who I've seen break every bone in man's leg in alphabetical order before.

He will play the jokester until the cows come home, but since he joined us, recent investigations have taught me that our new transfer from MI-5 is the most dangerous of us all.

Axel is even more violent than our team enforcer. Not to mention utterly unhinged when the jokes cease. You know what to expect with Hyland, but Axel will skin a man alive while wondering what to eat for dinner.

"Sure." I shrug.

"Hell yeah! Really?"

"If you want a box full of mouldy crumbs to arrive two months later, then yes. Call her."

He deflates, the swirls of black ink that completely cover his throat barely concealing the way his Adam's apple lurches. It feels somewhat akin to kicking an excited toddler who wants candy.

Not like I've done that.

"It's unkind to tease, you know."

"Life is fucking unkind, Ax."

"You don't have to help it!" He throws his arms up in annoyance. "Pay for your own tacos tonight."

"Technically speaking, I am your boss. And that is a business credit card. So I'm paying for my own tacos tonight and every night."

"Bloody smartass," he grumbles.

FRACTURED FUTURE

Watching him stomp off, I pull on a fresh shirt. After staking out a local underground club all night—rife with illegal fights and prostitution—we didn't sleep until midday. A matter of hours later, duty calls once more.

Every time I think we're getting close to a breakthrough, it's snatched from our fingers all over again. I'm getting tired of delivering my weekly phone call to Tom with no updates.

Mexico is a vast country, seven times bigger than our patch of land back in the United Kingdom. Sure, we've dealt with criminal conspiracies, illegal empires that rival the royal family in wealth and even government corruption before.

Nothing this large-scale.

And nothing this personal.

Sabre Security is the finest private investigative firm in the UK. Our fearsome reputation is second to none. Ever since the groundbreaking Blackwood Institute case nearly a decade ago, we've conducted business in the limelight.

We only take the hardest criminal cases, the ones that no one else can crack. The kind that takes years' worth of painstaking work, the best investigators and unlimited resources.

I've headed up our division—the Anaconda Team—alone since my partner moved to live in the middle of nowhere. After all this time and years of military service before joining Sabre, it's safe to say I feel comfortable in enemy territory.

Then I came here.

We've tackled human trafficking cases before. One of my best pieces of work was wrapping up a case a few years back, granting the young mother justice when she fled a depraved individual who forced her into marriage.

We're still unravelling the complex web that huge case exposed. It takes time to identify an intricate ring of traffickers, mobsters and criminal masterminds wreaking havoc.

Our continuing work became personal when my best friend's sister was kidnapped. When she vanished into thin air, several exhaustive investigations pointed towards human trafficking.

Ember.

Just her name fills me with grief and pain.

Weeks of searching turned to months, and months turned to agonising years. From the intel we've gained and tied to a complex ecosystem of cartels and trafficking rings, we've moved our search to Mexico.

"Warner!" Hyland hollers through the door.

"Yeah?"

"Coffee. We're late."

"Alright, I'm coming."

Staring into my vivid-blue eyes, the vibrant gleam dulled by exhaustion, I hate to admit that we're getting nowhere. This web is a living, breathing manifestation of evil. Constantly shifting and changing, throwing us in all directions as we search for evidence.

After six years, the likelihood of finding Ember alive feels remote, let alone finding her at all. We're searching for a needle in a haystack, chasing ghosts in a country that's suited to quick disappearances.

Limbs heavy with fatigue, I head out into the small kitchenette that connects our two rooms. Hyland is crouched over an ancient-looking coffee machine, scowling at the blinking red light.

"Why is it still cold?" he asks the lifeless pot. "You stupid lump of junk."

"Careful. Axel will tell you off for being mean to the machines."

"Go fuck yourself," the man in question hollers from their shared bedroom. "I hope Arnold Schwarzenegger kills you."

"If I get a break from you, I'm game!" I shout back.

Clapping Hyland's massive shoulder as I pass feels like petting the face of a mountain. At well over six foot two, he outweighs us all in size, height and muscle. The man is the walking embodiment of overgrown brawn.

His shoulder-length, dirty-blonde hair is pulled back in a loose ponytail today, leaving his glower front and centre. Not even his olive-green eyes, full lips or wide, flat nose can soften his perpetually furrowed brows.

The toothy smile he occasionally unleashes does counteract his monstrous height and grumpy disposition, but it's reserved for family only. And nine times out of ten, we get gruff Hyland, not gentle Hyland.

"You get some sleep?"

"Some," he grunts.

"We need to see who arrives for the club's night shift. That government official was approving shipments for the cartel for years. If Ember was in one of them, she passed through here."

"Women," Hyland corrects.

"What?"

"I said women." He stabs a thumb into the control pad. "Not shipments."

"You know what I meant."

"We're talking about people here."

"Shit, man. I bloody know!" Tiredness coupled with frustration causes me to erupt. "And she could be one of them!"

Turning my back on him to grab coffee cups, I feel my mobile phone vibrating in my trouser pocket. Probably Kade calling to try his luck moaning to me about the late-night wake up call.

"All it takes is one sighting." I reach for three mugs, setting them on the stained countertop. "This venue funnels victims from across the globe through its doors. She could've come through."

"We need to shut it down."

"And we will. As soon as we've verified whether Ember was there. I don't want to spook the owner—it's a front for the Gael cartel, and we both know it."

"Do we?" he chuffs.

My curled fist slams against the countertop, rattling the empty mugs. I've been awake for ten minutes, and already I'm fighting the urge to batter my teammates.

"What is your problem, Hyland?"

My phone stills in my pocket as I stare up at him. His narrowed, moss-coloured gaze is full of challenge. I know how hard it is for him to be away from home, but I'm not going back to England without answers.

"I want to finish this just as much as you do." He forces a calmer, even tone. "But after all this time… don't you think it's cruel to keep getting Tom's hopes up?"

"He's my best friend." I blow out a tense breath.

"Exactly. You should be helping him move on."

"And if it were someone you loved out there? Lost and alone? Could you move on?"

Eyes lowering, he stares down at his long, tree trunk legs. "No."

"Then don't lecture me."

Taking the coffeepot to pour myself some liquid patience, regardless of whether it's hot or cold, I cast him a final glare then retreat to the window to drink. I know he's exhausted. Fed up. Impatient. We all are.

That doesn't mean we quit.

Not in this business.

Studying the few old cars parked up outside, I focus on slowing my rapid breathing. As team leader, it's my job to keep my cool. I'm the level head guiding two fearsome weapons to their targets.

But fuck if they don't get under my skin sometimes. We're a close-knit team, and like any family of choice, we live in each other's pockets. That makes us strong. Reliable. Dependable.

It also means we drive one another crazy. Especially on long, emotional cases like these. I love them both like family, and I'm proud of our team, but that doesn't make this career even remotely easier.

Vibrating emanates from my pocket again, forcing me to tug my phone out. I'm going to chew Kade out for being so impatient. I don't care if he and his brother pay my salary now.

Two words light up the screen, giving me pause.

Unknown number.

Staring at the phone, I wait for the call to ring out. I'm not looking to get scammed by whoever's purchased my personal number from some dodgy online data broker.

I've barely swallowed my next mouthful of lukewarm coffee when it starts to vibrate again. Still flashing the same words—*Unknown number.* They're persistent.

You know what? Fine. I'll take my frustrations out on whichever unlucky twat chose me to harass. Smashing the accept button, I take another gulp of the gross coffee.

"What?"

A dead silence answers me.

"Is someone there?"

More strange quietness, stretching long enough to send unease down my spine.

"Warner Mead speaking."

I think I hear faint breathing. The featherlight sound tickles the receiver, making me hesitate before disconnecting the call.

"Hello?"

"Langley. It's me."

I'm faintly aware of my fingers releasing the coffee cup, causing it to crash to the floor. Not even the loud smashing sound the impact creates can pierce the intense ringing that fills my ears.

Surely... it can't be.

"Langley," the ghostly whisper repeats. "Are you there?"

Shock nearly bowls me over.

"Em?" I croak.

Even as children, Langley was a silly nickname. The kind invented when kids create make-believe characters, horsing around outside during those endless, hot summers after school finished.

Sometimes, I watched my best friend's little sister while he cared for their sick mum. Even if she was five years younger than us, I liked playing with her. I was always a secret agent—code name *Langley*—while she was an astronaut.

I later adopted my made-up character's name when I needed a cover story for an undercover job. Ember laughed when I told her about the false identity I used once the Harrowdean case was wrapped up and I was back home.

Grabbing the window ledge to hold myself up, I clutch the phone hard enough to crack the plastic case.

"Ember?"

Shock, panic and disbelief battle for supremacy inside my misfiring brain as footsteps behind me abruptly still.

"Fuck. Em? Is that really you?"

"I n-need help." The line crackles, relaying movement on the other end. "He told me to call you."

My heart somersaults, twisting and turning faster than a fucking laundry machine. It takes great effort to unlock my jaw and suck in a breath.

"It is you."

"Yeah," she wheezes. "Surprise."

"I… Shit. Shit!"

Her breathing catches, pushing me to focus up.

"Are you safe?" The words escape me in a rush.

When she doesn't immediately respond, I feel like my mind is on the verge of a cataclysmic implosion. I'm struggling to remain upright as it is.

"Answer me! Fuck!"

"N-No." Ember releases a painful-sounding hiss. "Need h-help. Please."

"Jesus Christ, Em. I can't believe it's you."

Tapping my shoulder, Hyland frantically waves to gain my attention. Axel has set his laptop atop the cramped bar connected to the kitchenette, his fingertips already racing.

"We can track this call. Stay connected. Where are you?"

Placing the phone on speaker, I rush over to Axel so he can plug it into his laptop. We're all linked to Sabre's secure server, giving us access to its vast wealth of shady technical capabilities.

"Something about an airport," she replies faintly. "Acapulco."

"Acapulco?" Hyland repeats.

I offer him a jerky nod.

"That's southern Mexico," he confirms. "Not far from where that trouble they're all talking about online went down."

Axel keeps his attention focused on the laptop screen. "They're searching for her."

Terror razes through my extremities. "Fucking hell. Ember, what happened?"

When she doesn't respond again, I shout her name into the phone. The terror blooming inside me has grown legs and arms. Now it's climbing into my internal cavities to launch a full-scale invasion.

"They're coming for me." Her voice sounds so strained and raw. "I'm not safe here."

"Hold tight, Em. We're going to find you."

"Please hurry," she begs, sounding so unlike herself.

"I've got you. Are you hurt?"

Endless possibilities ping-pong around the inner confines of my skull. I can't begin to think about what might have happened to her. Or what price she paid to escape long enough to call me.

How did she even get this number?

"I'm alive," she croaks.

"That's a start. I can't begin to explain how good the sound of your voice is."

Her barely restrained sob tests my mental restraint. *Goddammit.* I've never heard her make that sound before. Not even when they lowered her only parent into the cold, hard ground.

"Y-Yours too."

"We never stopped searching for you." I push past the brick that's landed in my throat. "Not once. Just took us a long time to trace you this far."

"This far?"

"We're in Mexico."

"Wait, what?" she splutters.

"Farther north than your location, but in the country. We're tracing a ring of trafficking gangs bankrolling illegal clubs, searching for any signs of you."

"Shit." Ember laughs though it sounds more broken than amused. "You were here all along."

"Trying to track your crazy backside down to bring you back home." I smile despite my searing eyes.

"Glad to hear it."

"Listen, can you take cover? We're a few hours away."

"I'm in the middle of nowhere," she replies.

"Then walk a bit. Look for a hiding spot."

Ember sucks in a stuttered breath, riddled with agony. "Walking is tough right now."

"Why?"

"I'm a bit roughed up. Long story."

Cursing colourfully, Hyland fists his long waves. I give him the side-eye, indicating for him to take a breather. The grump isn't as thick-skinned as he'd have us believe. Especially not after recent years.

"What's around you?" I ask urgently.

"Sand. Mountains. A cactus or two."

"Keep looking. Were you followed?"

"Not here," she rasps. "They bought me some time."

Suspicion fills my mind. "Who did?"

"Oh, shit! I think I can see a farm in the distance."

"Nowhere near people!" Hyland reappears, clamping a hand around my bicep. "We don't know who you can trust or who's bought and paid for."

"Thanks, whoever the fuck you are," Ember snarks. "That thought didn't cross my mind."

"Pretty sure you've met Hyland before." I laugh from the acute relief of hearing her sass. "He's a permanent member of the team now."

"Erm... the huge, grumpy asshole with the stupid hairdo?" She puffs between the sound of crunching footsteps. "Yeah, I remember."

"Glad to hear from you too," Hyland scoffs under his breath.

"Got her!" Axel shouts excitedly.

We crowd around him to look over his shoulder at the screen. He's geolocated the call to a remote stretch of countryside not far from the town or its coastal airport.

"Find us a helicopter," I instruct him. "Offer the pilot double if we can get wheels up in under an hour."

"I'm on it," he quips.

"We'll need to find a private airstrip to request the Sabre jet for evac too. Call HQ to update them."

"Way ahead of you. I'll wake the boss up again."

"Good luck." Picking up my phone, I click the speakerphone off. "We're coming for you, Em. You need to sit tight."

"Okay," she replies in a rush of breath. "Um, my brother. Is he... okay?"

"Yeah. Tom's doing fine. He calls me for an update on the search weekly."

"Oh my god... After all this time?"

"None of us ever stopped looking."

It's getting nearly impossible to talk around the boulder of repressed emotion that's growing in my tight chest. I doubt it'll shift until I can lay eyes on her myself and verify she's real. Alive.

Safe.

"He never stopped hoping you'd be found. Not once."

Her sniffles intensify into outright cries that scratch at my battered heart. Hearing her weep is tearing me apart inside. All I want is to hold her in my arms and make it all better.

"We'll be there soon. I promise. Hold on for me?"

"I'll be waiting."

"Good girl," I praise emotionally.

We need to haul ass, but the thought of hanging up on her is literally unbearable. Hyland is already stomping between our two rooms, tossing equipment and suitcases into the living space at random.

"Thank you for not forgetting me," Ember whispers in a tiny voice.

"Forget you?" I repeat in disbelief.

"Well, it's been... Shit, six years."

That's the final straw for the throbbing organ in my chest.

"It could've been sixty years, and I'd still be searching for you."

I'm not sure I'll have a job to return to once my superiors see the bill for our helicopter ride into Acapulco's small airport. We had to bribe the pilot with triple his standard fare to speed up the entire process and bypass official checks.

Even so, it's been almost five hours since we received her call. Five hours since the entire world shifted on its axis. Five hours since I got the first shred of hope that I could bring my best friend's sister home alive.

Sliding behind the wheel of the first rental car we could lay our hands on, Hyland assumes control of driving. I'm too on edge to even think about navigating the dusty roads right now.

We haven't heard from Ember since we landed under the cover of night. Our subsequent phone calls have gone unanswered, the line clicking without connecting. Best case scenario... the phone she's using has died.

Worse case… I'm not considering that.

"Buckle up." Hyland fires up the engine.

Checking the magazine of my semi-automatic pistol, I focus on the solid weight of it clasped in my hand while he drives. I'm not a nervous person, far from it. I've faced enough life and death situations to master my fight-or-flight response.

But having a loved one caught in the line of fire evokes a different feeling. The lack of control, endless *what if* scenarios… It's all too much to hold inside without splitting apart at the seams.

I'd love to unload this round into the motherfucker who did this to Ember in the first place. As soon as she's secured, hunting down the scum who harmed her is going to be my first priority.

"Take the highway," Axel shouts from the backseat. "Head east. I'll holler when you need to turn."

"Hold tight," Hyland warns.

Praying to God that no airport worker is watching us abuse their rental car's engine, we race out of the half-full garage. It's late at night now, and the roads are quiet. Luckily, May is a slow season for tourism.

"Where was her last location?" I ask over my shoulder.

There's tapping on a keyboard.

"She moved about a mile or so to the north," Axel replies distractedly. "Looks like farmland. There are a whole bunch of coffee production sites around there."

"With any luck, she's still there."

"She will be." Hyland bobs his head with certainty.

A sour-faced asshole or not, he knows exactly what to say when push comes to shove. Hyland is a steady, albeit gruff presence in our chaotic lifestyle. And I'm thankful for that.

Though his steadiness is being called into question by his alarming driving right now. We blast past idling vehicles and bright road signs without taking time to consider the consequences.

"Have you called Tom?" Hyland's gaze briefly shifts to me.

"Not yet."

"You need to call him."

"I will once she's secured. He'll want to speak to her."

Mouth tightening, Hyland swerves around what appears to be a loaded cattle truck driving at a snail's pace. My shoulder smashes into the car door while Axel curses from the backseat.

"How far, pup?" Hyland barks.

"Not that nickname. Come on, dude."

"What? It's appropriate."

"We're not having this argument again. Don't think I won't make good on my threats to slit your throat." Axel's fingers click away. "It's about eight miles."

"Shit," I spit. "Keep calling her."

"The line's dead," he points out.

"I don't care! Keep trying!"

Summoning the good sense not to argue with me, Axel resumes dialling Ember's number from his own phone. I drop a hand to my right thigh, tracing the ridge where my residual limb meets the prosthetic socket.

If she's slipped between our fingers now that we're this close to bringing her home, I'll never be able to face myself again. Let alone her brother. Ember's life is in my fucking hands.

Hyland keeps his attention fixed on our surroundings as we speed past. "We will find her."

"How can you be so sure?"

He shrugs a huge shoulder. "Because we won't rest until we do."

"You've changed your tune from earlier."

"We're all allowed moments of doubt." Hyland sighs tiredly. "I haven't seen my son in five months. Can you blame me for being downbeat?"

Swallowing my guilt, I cast him a tight smile. "I guess not. I'm sorry."

"You don't need to apologise. I know it's been hard for you too. We all want Ember found."

Lapsing into tense silence, the screaming of the car's engine fills the time it takes to eat up each mile between us and Ember. The closer we get, the tighter Hyland grips the steering wheel.

"Right here!" Axel shouts, his purple-haired head popping between the seats. "Last location was the outskirts of the farm up ahead."

All around us, the stiflingly hot night causes a haze that muddies our line of sight. We turn off the road then onto an unlit track, the dirt peppered with pebbles and surrounded by sandy plumes.

Each time the car jerks, my heart leaps into my mouth. I swear, infiltrating a hostile encampment in the Sahara desert with no backup was less nerve-racking than this.

"Pull over here." Axel slams his laptop shut.

"Right here?"

"We need to go on foot."

Throwing the car door open, I swing my prosthetic out first, using the frame to haul myself up. All around us, the hum of angry cicadas fills the still air.

We're surrounded by fields of towering, glossy coffee plants, the elongated leaves shining in the moonlight. Axel points towards the field on our right, accessible by a narrow dirt track.

"We'll never find her out here," Hyland mutters, scanning the nearly black landscape. "Why didn't we grab flashlights?"

"It's pretty deserted," Axel muses.

"Yeah, we haven't seen anyone for a while. No residential buildings near the farm fields either."

"Why?" I wonder, suspicion chilling my blood.

Cupping his tattooed hands around his mouth, Axel throws his head back. "EMBER!"

Both Hyland and I physically recoil at the ear-splitting screech. The little shit has the most ridiculous pair of lungs on him.

"For fuck's sake, Ax!" Hyland hisses furiously.

"What? It's efficient."

"It's going to rain down hell on our heads!"

Ignoring him, his hands remain cupped. "It's been a while since I had any fun. EMB—"

Curled fist snapping out, Hyland thumps him in the shoulder. Axel's loud yell is cut off by the blow, causing him to yelp instead, shooting our resident enforcer a dirty look.

"You got a better plan? Like searching the entire farm?"

"Yes!" Hyland booms. "This is a stealth mission."

"You wouldn't know what stealth means if it slapped you around the face!"

"You're such a little bastard."

"Aw. Thanks for the compliment."

"It wasn't a fucking com—"

"Shut up, the pair of you!" I snap at them. "Listen."

In the insect-filled murkiness, a distant shout can be heard. It's hard to tell if it's male or female. The weak sound is far off, carried through the sweltering air.

"Use your phones." Axel pulls his out, lighting up the torch. "Better than nothing."

Hyland follows suit, gesturing for me to follow. "Cover us, Warner."

Unholstering my pistol, we all take off, using the shout as a homing beacon. With the track winding and barely lit by their phones, leafy roughage pulls at our arms and legs as we move through the vegetation.

When the shouting falls silent, I take a leaf out of Axel's playbook and yell at the top of my lungs. We'd know about it by now if any assailants were out here searching with us.

The voice comes again, louder this time.

"That way." Hyland points to the left.

Gun locked in both hands, I follow them through the swaying crops. We move painstakingly slow, dodging roots and thin branches, until the sound of gasping is clearly audible.

Tucking my weapon back into my side holster, I gesture for Axel to hand me his phone. The light beam offers a little visibility into the plants that whisper with quiet cries.

"Wait here."

"You sure?" Hyland frets.

"Yes. I don't want to scare her."

Both nod, allowing me to advance alone. My raging heartbeat roars in my ears, pumping unease and anticipation into my nervous system.

"Em? You out here?"

There's a sniffle in the barely lit din.

"It's Warner. Come out, Em. I'm here."

Swinging the light from side to side, I search for any signs of life in the gloom. The first rustles of movement on my right cause me to whip around, my heart a frantically flapping hummingbird locked in my chest.

"Warner?"

"Yeah, it's me."

"Is it… s-safe?" The voice trembles.

"Yes, Em. We're here now. You're safe."

A long-limbed shape limps through two coffee plants. The phone's light offers me the first glimpse of brilliant, flaming-red hair, a far cry from the expensive bleach-blonde job she used to proudly wear.

Six years of grief, anguish and absolute fucking hopelessness hammers through me at breakneck speed. Every night I've laid awake, wishing I could save the girl I once knew and alleviate my best friend's pain. That I could give him the one person he needed.

Ember.

The inflamed expanse of her oval-shaped face is obscured by violent, dark bruises. Ember's almost unrecognisable beneath the evidence of fists pummelling her to a pulp, she's so swollen.

Even when I illuminate her blood-spattered, scantily clad frame, I'm struggling to recognise her. The girl that I grew up with got into plenty of scraps, but this looks like a life-threatening beating.

With one black eye clamped shut, a single blue-grey orb fixes solely on me. She's wearing a loose sweatshirt and tight spandex shorts that leave her scratch-covered but muscular legs on display.

While working as a personal trainer, Ember was always trim. Yet the muscles that I can see in her thighs and calves now seem bulkier than before. Different. Just like the blonde tips of her outgrown hair.

"Warner," she whimpers.

"Oh, Em."

"You're real."

"Hell yeah, I am." I hold my arms open for her. "Come here, love."

Despite being visibly injured, she runs full speed into me. Our bodies smack together amidst the rustling plants, her hands snaking around my waist while her tearstained face buries in my chest.

"I've got you now," I reassure around tears.

Her shoulders shake up and down, betraying her silent sobs. Every inch of her is trembling like she's wired up to a live car battery. I hate how cripplingly terrified she is.

"W-Warner," she keens.

"Shh. I'm here."

"I w-was so scared…"

"I know, love. I know."

Holding Ember close, I take a deep inhale of her beautiful, tumbling red hair. It smells foul… Dirt, sweat and an aged, coppery fragrance that sets my teeth on edge. She's covered in dried blood.

"You're really here."

"It's me." I stroke my hand up and down her shaking back. "Breathe for me."

"I d-didn't know if you'd come."

"Like I'd ever let my little astronaut down."

Weak sobs rattle over her. "You're still a sweetheart."

"Don't tell my teammates that, Em."

The sound of the other two approaching isn't enough to make me surrender her. We've never been touchy feely—I respect her brother too much for that—but it feels so damn good to hold her at last.

When her trembles subside some, I reluctantly push Ember back for a closer inspection. We're similar in height, giving me a good vantage point to see just how banged up she is.

"How bad are you injured?"

Licking her split lip, she nervously glances at the others. "I'm alive."

"You need a hospital."

"No. I just want to get out of here."

"Em—"

"No! Please let's just go. No hospital."

The high-pitched urgency in her voice is enough to alarm me. For all her bravery, she seems to be mere seconds from losing it. I'm not going to expedite that process while we're exposed.

Reluctantly bobbing my head, I gesture around our small group. "Okay. You know Hyland, and this is our new team member, Axel."

Rocking on his heels, Axel offers her an enthusiastic wave. "It's so good to meet you!"

"Hi," she whispers.

"Okay, first up." Axel claps his hands together. "Is there anyone out here I need to kill? I only need a sec to sharpen my switchblade."

"Get in line, pup," Hyland rumbles.

"Again with the nickname?"

"Ignore them." I keep a firm grip on Ember's elbow. "They're harmless."

"Now that's debatable." Axel puffs out his chest.

"I… I don't think so." Ember sways on her feet. "They took the tracker with them when they dumped me on the roadside with your mobile number."

We all gape at her. Silent. Stunned.

"There isn't a single part of that sentence that doesn't require explaining." Axel crosses his arms, wearing the scowl that usually precludes his violent outbursts.

"Who?" I stare at her intently.

Ember visibly cringes, her throat working up and down, betraying her apparent reluctance to answer me. It makes my gut churn with increasing fury.

"Em?"

"I don't…"

When her whisper trails off, I squeeze her arm in encouragement. "It's okay. Tell me."

"The man… He… He said his name was Blaine Madden."

CONFIDENTIAL
Suspect?
DO NOT CROSS
POLICE
Suspect?
NOT CROSS
POLICE LI

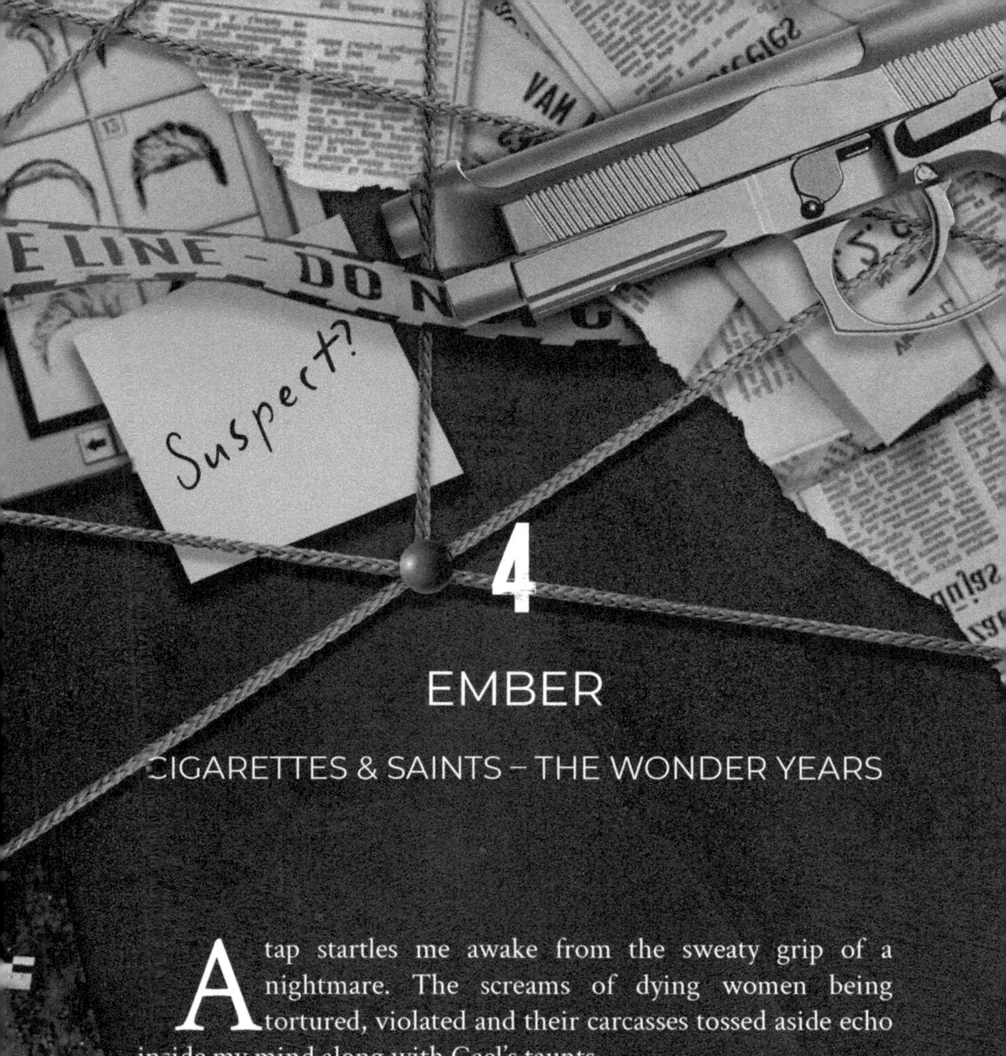

4

EMBER

CIGARETTES & SAINTS – THE WONDER YEARS

A tap startles me awake from the sweaty grip of a nightmare. The screams of dying women being tortured, violated and their carcasses tossed aside echo inside my mind along with Gael's taunts.

You will be my new champion, 768.

Body spasming, I move so fast that I smack my head against what feels like a metal door. Spikes of pain lance through my pounding skull, adding to my confusion.

"Shit." I grip my forehead. "That h-hurt."

"Careful, Ember."

Wrenching my one-functioning eyelid open takes great effort. The other is firmly sealed shut, and the swelling feels a lot worse now that time has allowed my skin to balloon.

So much fire.

What will we do with all that?

FRACTURED FUTURE

For several disorientating seconds, I think I'm curled up on my uncomfortable mattress, pushed into the corner of a room on Gael's estate. The ever-blinking eye of a camera watching me.

At any moment, Carlos will slam the locked and bolted door open. Drag my exhausted body from the bare mattress and toss me into the ring to fight for my life again. Day in and day out. Never once relenting or allowing me to show the slightest shred of weakness.

"No!" I wail in panic.

"Hey, calm down."

"Please, stop… S-Stop!"

"Ember! Come back. You're safe."

The voice repeating reassurances is a far cry from Gael's rich, accented boom. Instead, it emanates from the man beside me in what appears to be a back seat. I'm not in my room.

This is a moving car.

I'm… free.

"That's it," the voice assures. "Look at me."

The soft words come from a blonde-haired mountain sitting next to me. His neck is bent at an odd angle, allowing him to cram his huge height in the car.

Hyland hasn't changed much since we briefly met. Perhaps there are a few more stress-induced lines around his mouth and seemingly endless, olive-toned eyes.

The earthy hue is stark against his tanned skin and flowing, long hair. It's a shame he's known to be a grumpy asshole, despite being blessed with a body and complexion like that.

"Wh-Where am I?"

"Highway," he offers in a deep voice, reminiscent of deafening ocean waves. "Searching for somewhere to stop. Our ride won't be here for a day or so."

Blinking rapidly, it takes time for the greyscale memories of the estate to vanish from my vision. More so than a nightmare, I think my mind was convinced I would wake up back in that prison.

I've startled awake from dreams of home enough times to be confronted by my bleak reality. Each time I endured that horrifying realisation, another piece of my soul splintered.

Only now, the bare walls and twenty-four-hour surveillance of my prison aren't the reality that's taunting me. Freedom is. And somehow, that feels even more terrifying to me.

"Our ride?" I clear my dry throat.

"Sabre's private jet," Axel explains from up front.

Hyland shifts in his seat. "We're waiting for evac."

"And getting the fuck out of here! Whoop!"

Slim body twisted in his seat, the newest addition to Warner's team balances his laptop on his lap as he smiles. Axel was incessantly wisecracking and babbling before I passed out.

With his purple hair, slicked up in unmoving spikes, and symmetrical, boyish features that complement his unusual honey eyes, he seems to radiate an intoxicating kind of energy.

It's a bizarre contrast to the countless inches of visible skin that he's wrapped in black tattoos. Arms. Hands. Throat. Even his fingers are tattooed. The ink fits well with his quirky style.

"This delay is ridiculous." Hyland scratches the light blonde scruff that smothers his jaw and cheeks. "We should just take a commercial flight."

"You know as well as I do that it isn't safe." The back of Warner's salt-and-pepper head shakes in the driver's seat as he speaks.

"Holing up in a shit motel isn't safe either," Hyland groans.

"It's the best option we have, and that's final," Warner deadpans. "We'll rest up in the meantime."

"Fine."

The power dynamic behind their terse exchange reveals a few things. When I was taken, Warner was a part of the Anaconda Team. Now he seems to be the one leading it.

"I hate this." Wincing, Hyland rubs his awkwardly bent neck. "Tell HQ to hurry up."

Axel concentrates on the map that fills his laptop screen. "Stop complaining."

"Fuck off, pup."

"Believe me... If I could, I would."

Flipping the bird over his shoulder, Axel studies the two-lane road we're driving along, searching for stopping points. We must've been travelling for a few hours if dawn broke while I was out of it.

I'll chalk my worn-out state to the hysteria that took over me. In all the years I've involuntarily toured this sun-soaked country, I never allowed myself to break down, let alone sit and sob like a scared kid.

Hearing Warner's reassuring voice on the other end of that phone obliterated the brick wall I'd erected around my fear. It all poured out at the sound of his familiar croon.

Not even that emotional exchange prepared me for the magnitude of seeing him, though. He's a comforting callback to my childhood and my home. For the first time in years, I tasted safety.

"There's a motel up ahead," Axel announces, clicking the laptop shut. "Reckon it'll work."

"How far is the nearest town?" Warner glances to the side.

"Far enough. I'm desperate for a hot shower."

I roll my tense shoulders. "A wash would be good."

"Agreed." Hyland gives me a pointed look.

My glare lands squarely on his face, boasting a strong but flat nose, square jaw, and lips so plush, they resemble beckoning, feathery pillows. The son of a bitch is as grumpy as he is ruggedly good-looking.

I know he's a good guy—Warner insisted as much when they began working together on a few cases. My brother too. Tom has spent enough time getting to know the various investigative teams.

He began offering legal counsel to Sabre Security when he made partner at his London-based law firm. That's what led me to meet Hyland once, when he dropped paperwork off for Tom while I was visiting.

"Are you saying I smell?"

He fixes his stare outside at the passing cacti. "Yes. And not like roses."

"I see you're still a dick." My tone drips with acid. "Nice to know some things never change."

Warner briefly looks over his shoulder. "Nicer than anything he's ever said to us, Em. I'd take it if I were you."

"I'll pass on the insult, thanks."

Tracing a finger over my knuckles, I scratch at a fleck of dried blood. He's right; I am a mess. I'm sure I can't see half of the cuts and abrasions I gained in the fight beneath all this blood and dirt.

The tender skin stretched across my puffy knuckles doesn't hurt. I've developed enough scar tissue to deaden the nerves. When I look back up, I realise Hyland's attention is fixed on my fists.

"Seen some fights?" he asks quietly.

My throat tightens. "Some."

"I'd say so based on those hands."

"What do you know about it, huh?"

"They look like mine," he replies.

Glancing at his oversized paws, similar patterns of calloused tissue warp his knuckles. A twisted part of me feels validated by our matching marks. I've earned my battle scars just like him.

"Just a lot smaller," I joke sadly.

"I guess," Hyland mutters, keeping his baritone low. "Where have you been all this time?"

"That's a long story." My lips pucker and roll together, niggling a scabbed cut. "One I'll need alcohol to tell."

"That can be arranged. You hungry?"

Surprise inches over me at his gently-spoken concern. When I met Hyland, he quickly adopted the scowling, silent persona of a social recluse. This gruff but curious person seems different.

"I haven't eaten since before the..." I trail off before uttering the word *fight*. "Yeah, I could eat."

Hyland leans forward to smack Axel on the shoulder. "Run to the store while we get checked in. Food and booze."

"Sure," Axel volunteers brightly. "I'm fucking starved anyway. Anything specific?"

He looks over his shoulder at me, a brow raised. "Well?"

The simple question stumps me. Once I was purchased by Mr Gael, I was fed regularly. The psychological torture of being starved ended when he needed me strong enough to earn him money.

That doesn't mean I was given a choice. Every aspect of my captivity was still controlled. They didn't use sexual intimidation to control me like the other women. I was quicky designated as off-limits. But my life was still dangled in front of me like a carrot.

When I don't answer, Warner speaks up.

"She has a sweet tooth. Always has. Her mum used to make her sit on the naughty step for an hour when she ate sweets after eight o'clock and couldn't sleep."

Axel chuffs a laugh. "Is that true?"

"She was strict," I offer neutrally.

"Well, I can work to that brief. Leave it to me."

Pulling out a crumpled stack of Pesos, Axel flicks through the creased notes as Warner navigates the car into a corner spot, far from the entrance to the abandoned-looking roadside motel.

"I'll take some of that." He sticks a hand out to Axel. "We need to keep a low profile. No credit cards."

"You think we're being traced?" Axel hands him a thick stack.

"Better safe than sorry." Warner shrugs. "The entire world knows we've been searching for Ember. Now that she's vanished, you can bet they'll be looking at us for answers first."

"Why are you three here?" I blurt out.

All eyes slide over to me.

"Looking for you." Warner's mouth curves down after he answers me. "I told you that."

"No, I mean… You're thousands of miles from home, and for what? I've been gone for six years. Why not give up?"

His disapproving frown deepening, Warner studies me. He's always had an uncanny ability to read people. It goes hand in hand with his caring nature. He's a textbook empath.

But I'm not sure what emotion it is that sears behind Axel's disappearing smile or Hyland's thick brows drawing together. Neither of them know me well. I'm practically a stranger.

"Beyond it being our jobs?" Warner eventually says.

"Well… Yes."

"Em, I swore to Tom that I'd bring you home, one way or another. I'm not in the business of breaking promises."

For someone who doesn't like crying or wallowing, I'm winning awards for holding back tears today. I can barely see them through my rapidly blurring vision.

"I could've been dead for all you knew."

"That changed nothing." Warner shakes his head. "But for the record, none of us doubted for a moment that you would fight like hell to keep on living."

Opening the car door, he battles to heave himself out then slams it shut with a loud rattle. I wince at his departure, swiping a hand over my one good eye.

"He loves Tom like a brother," Hyland adds softly. "Warner never would've let him down by giving up on your case."

"Yeah." I swallow the noxious guilt trying to plug my oesophagus.

"Come on. He'll get us a couple rooms, then you can get cleaned up."

"Hang on!" Axel reaches into the footwell to rifle in a bulging backpack. "Put this on."

He tosses me a scruffy, blue baseball cap. I laugh at the embroidered words scrawled across the front.

"*Less Upsetti, More Spaghetti?* What the fuck is this?"

"My fantastically hilarious cap, obviously." He re-zips his backpack. "Keep that."

Looking over his outfit again—the dark denim tight to his strong legs and full of rips, his shirt displaying some elaborate cartoon of a pizza slice with legs and a cheesy grin—I come up short.

"Do you buy all your clothes in the kid's section?"

Next to me, Hyland fails to smother a laugh.

"Why?" Axel asks in confusion.

"Just sensing a theme." I lift the embroidered baseball cap.

"Wow. That's two for two." Axel's smile fades into a look of supreme disappointment. "Keep it up, and you'll only have this bucket of joy left to talk to."

Casting me a loaded look, he joins Warner in leaving the car with a ceremonious door slam. Fabulous. I've been awake for five minutes and already pissed off two of my rescuers.

"Can you just tell me what I can say to piss you off too?" I remark flatly. "Then I can get three for three."

Hyland's throaty laughter tumbles over me like a rockfall, crashing down a steep mountain face.

"Finding you alive is the best thing to happen to me since I arrived in this bloody country. You'd be hard pressed to piss me off right now."

FRACTURED FUTURE

Giving him the side-eye, I search for any signs of deceit on his golden features. Two honest, mossy pools stare back, a tiny smile playing on his well-shaped lips.

"Huh."

"Problem?" He widens his eyes at me.

"Just re-evaluating my initial opinion of you. For future reference, perhaps you should be nicer upon first meeting someone."

"I'm nice when I have a reason to be." Hyland grabs the door handle. "This fucked up world doesn't deserve any less than my suspicion."

"Sounds lonely."

"Alright, enough analysis. Move it."

Letting him climb out, I take a second to breathe while tugging the borrowed cap on. My door is ripped open before I can attempt to piece my scattered thoughts together.

"You need help or something?"

"No," I snap at him.

"Anytime today, then."

Teeth gnashing, I manage to get my legs out of the car without admitting how badly my whole body is throbbing. But standing up poses a whole other challenge.

"Just ask for help." Hyland watches me struggle to move. "I'm right here."

"I don't need it."

"You're clearly in pain. I can make a good guess that you're hiding all kinds of mess under that sweatshirt."

"Maybe you should keep your guesses to yourself."

Hands braced on his wide hips, he refuses to budge. "Stubborn, aren't you?"

"Infamously so." I yelp at the agony racing up my spine when I try to move. "Shit!"

Hyland taps his thick-soled army boot on the ground. "It's fine. I've got all day to wait for you to pull your head out of your ass."

Ignoring his intensifying glower, I try to heave myself up again yet fail. The first day after a brutal fight is always the worst. I've just never dealt with it around people who notice or care before.

"Dammit!" I curse loudly.

Slumping onto the seat, I'm no closer to lifting myself. My usual routine is to remain horizontal and ignore the world until I can handle my injuries. Not go on the run while barely able to move.

"Just ask, Ember. Fuck's sake."

"I don't want your help!"

"You need it." He allows a thread of sympathy to enter his voice. "Believe it or not, you can trust me."

"I don't trust anybody," I hiss out.

"It's my job to help you. Trust that."

Feeling like a complete fool, I finally crack under the pressure. "Fine."

Hyland stretches out a meaty paw. "That wasn't so hard, huh?"

"Speak for yourself."

"Come on. Nice and slow."

Accepting the hand, I have to bite down on my tongue hard enough to draw blood to keep a whimper in. It's bad enough they saw me having a total breakdown when Warner found me.

Once I'm up, my pounding head spins with nausea. I'm forced to lean into Hyland's muscle-hardened side to stop myself from toppling over. The bottle of water I chugged earlier has done little to steady me.

"Easy," he murmurs.

"Sorry. Dizzy."

"Mind if I touch you?"

"Hold your horses. We hardly know each other."

"Hilarious." Hyland huffs impatiently. "I'm just gonna help you move a bit, alright?"

"Just... be gentle, please."

"I will," he reassures.

Banding an arm around my back, his arm slips beneath my shoulder to lift me. The added strength allows me to put one foot in front of the other, getting blood moving back through my strained muscles.

By the time we reach the deathly silent building up ahead, Warner has emerged from a dim side office with two sets of keys. He gestures towards the farthest two doors.

"Paid in cash, no names. Two rooms."

"They ask any questions?" Hyland grunts.

"Out here? Hell no. The guy was just happy to have customers."

"Sweet. Let's roll."

We shuffle towards our rooms, keeping our heads lowered just in case anyone passes by. Hyland's hand remains clamped under my arm to take the weight off each footstep.

"You're in 302." Warner stops outside the first door, selecting one set of keys. "I need to come in to look you over, Em. You're barely walking straight."

"I'm f-fine," I strangle out.

"Convincing."

"I said I'm fine."

"You're clearly not. Ideally, we'd let Sabre's medics check you out, but I'm not prepared to wait that long."

Extricating myself from Hyland, I try to stand straight. "Look, I've survived worse."

"That's…" Warner pushes out a frustrated breath, "so not the point, Em. You know I was a field medic in the military. Let me check you over."

"Really, I'm okay."

"Still being a stubborn shit, huh?"

Hyland smothers a chuckle. *Dickhead.*

"Yep," I hum.

Reaching for the door handle to escape inside, another rush of pain and dizziness causes me to fall into the painted wood. My body hits it with a thud that can't be played off.

"Ember!"

I slump back against the taut body that moves behind me. "Oh, fuck."

"What is it?" Warner demands.

"H-Hurts. I'll take some painkillers if you have them."

"Get the supply bags from the car," Warner orders, his hands moving to grasp my hips. "Inside, Em. No more arguments."

I'm frogmarched into the dark room, letting Warner pause to flip lights on. It reveals a small, basic space. With a tiled, terracotta floor, simple double bed and rotating ceiling fan, the sparse furnishings fit our needs.

Depositing me on the edge of the bed, Warner surveys me. "Where are you hurt?"

"Ribs," I wheeze. "Spine. Asshole kept slamming me."

"Who?"

"Long story."

"Dammit." He shakes his head in barely contained anger. "What else? Dizziness?"

"Yeah."

"Do you have a head injury?"

Not a recent one.

Saving me having to cook up a lie, Warner moves to let Hyland in when he raps on the door. The pair flash to my side, a backpack ditched next to me on the mattress.

Toeing off my shoes, my bare feet are rubbed raw from being rushed to shove them on. The reminder takes me soaring back to my earlier escape. Or rather, the stranger who orchestrated it.

No one explained when I revealed Blaine's name as he'd instructed. But from the widening of Warner's eyes and Hyland's colourful curse, they have a history. One I'll need to uncover.

"I still need to call Tom to update him." Warner rifles through his supplies, pulling out medical paraphernalia. "You should speak to him."

His words hit me with the ferocity of a destructive hurricane. The thought of talking to my brother in this state threatens to undo all the mental work I've done to lock up my hysteria.

"I can't yet." I squeeze my eyes shut, trying to breathe through the pain shooting down my torso. "Just... Call him and let him know I'm safe. I'll see him when we're home."

"It may help," he attempts again. "Talking to him."

Hit by another wave of vision-blurring vertigo, I drop my head into my hands. I'm fighting a familiar black tide that's threatening to pull me under.

"And tell him what? I don't know how to answer the questions he'll have."

After a beat of silence, Warner sighs. "One problem at a time. Tell me how you got these injuries first."

FRACTURED FUTURE

Looking up at him, I don't immediately respond. The thought of revealing every last horror-filled moment to the sweet boy who once played with me as a kid may just break me.

Back then, he looked at me like I hung the fucking stars and moon just for him. Warner was a sad teen, fleeing his broken home and warring parents mid-divorce. I made it my mission to make him laugh.

But we're not kids anymore.

And no one is laughing now.

Warner finishes spreading out his supplies then moves to kneel in front of me. He stops short of placing a hand on my leg, though he clearly notes my bouncing knee.

"I just want to help." The genuine empathy in his tone pulls at my already aching heart.

"Please…" I bleat. "Don't make me say it."

"Hey. It's okay. I'm just here to get you home in one piece. No judgement, no expectations. You can be honest with me. Tell me as much as you feel able to."

A swarming hornet's nest has gathered in my still-pounding head, applying bone breaking pressure. He wants to help, but he has no idea what kind of monster he's aiding.

"You don't understand what I had to do to survive."

Exhaling, Warner looks down at the tiled floor. "I don't give a shit about that."

"You will."

"No, Em. I won't."

"The things they made me do… It disgusts me."

"You're my friend," he insists. "I would never judge you. The main thing is that you're here. Safe."

My chest rises and falls in a speedy rhythm. Traumatic flashes of every time I've punched, gouged, strangled and beaten a total stranger to buy myself another breath pour into my fracturing mind.

It doesn't matter if the people I hurt deserved it. If they were career criminals or deadbeats looking to make a pretty penny by humiliating me. I survived by embracing violence. *By becoming it.*

"I was sold," I say in a hush. "There was an auction after we were shipped here. I'd caused some trouble, so they put me up for sale first with…"

My voice dissolves into a parched whine. Just saying her name aloud feels insurmountable.

"Get her some water." Warner reaches for a bottle of antiseptic and packaged swabs. "Hands, Em. Keep talking."

Letting him tackle my abused knuckles first, I flinch at the sting of cold liquid. Warner hesitates when he notices the thick layers of battle scars scored across my knuckles.

"Mr Gael purchased me. He said he had a use for me."

"Gael?" Warner repeats thickly.

"Antonio Gael." My hammering heart leaps into my mouth. "You know him?"

Lips pursed, Warner lifts my hands to inspect my wrists. Two thin but jagged bands of silvery skin circle them, evidence of countless handcuffs and restraints. My skin was repeatedly rubbed raw over the years.

"We've spent years researching the Mexican cartels." He lowers my hands. "Our intel gave us Gael's name and a few other high-profile players. You just confirmed what we suspected."

"Great." I laugh icily.

"Tell me about Gael."

"He's… powerful. Richer than God. Ruthlessly violent. I've seen no less than a hundred women come and go in the last six years, all from different countries."

Dabbing at my right hand with a swab, Warner hits a sore spot that makes me suck in a breath. He mutters an apology then resumes with a lighter touch.

"He didn't want me to be his pet. I wasn't ordered to entertain his friends or colleagues. The moment I shot that thug at the auction, Gael spotted an opportunity."

"You shot… Jesus, Em. What the hell?"

"It's a complicated story."

"Evidently," he grits out.

Watching him gently treat my busted knuckles, I try to summon the words to tell him just how much has changed since we last saw each other.

"I don't know what to say," I admit.

"Just start at the beginning. Take your time."

Returning to the bedroom with a glass of water, Hyland hands it over for me to gulp down. The liquid moistens my aching throat, allowing my voice to strengthen.

"It'll be easier to show you."

I hand him back the glass then grab the hem of my sweatshirt. It's no easier to yank it off this time, but I push past the stiffness, needing to get the big reveal over and done with.

With the bloodstained fabric pulled over my head, I hear their audible shock when the room reappears. Beneath the splattered sports bra, my torso has darkened to a miasma of vivid black, sickening green and deep, angry purple.

"Gael wanted to shore up his fight club enterprise with a new champion. Someone he could wheel out and milk dry through underhanded betting schemes. A champion."

Letting them take a good look at my scarred back too, I try not to let the memories of numerous whippings that marked my skin sneak in. The shiny, vertical stripes tell the tale of many punishments.

After the first couple of years, I learned how to play the game. When I didn't follow Gael's commands, the punishments were severe. Once I figured that out, I made it my mission to avoid his wrath.

"This is what I had to do to survive." I sigh in defeat as my secret is revealed. "I had to fight."

Slumping on his haunches, Warner scrunches the red-tinged cotton balled in his fists. His brilliant blue eyes catalogue my bandaged arm and every last discoloured blotch proving my agony.

As the motel door reopens, admitting a beaming Axel with two plastic bags, Warner's voice hits like a thunderclap.

"Who *the fuck* did this to you?"

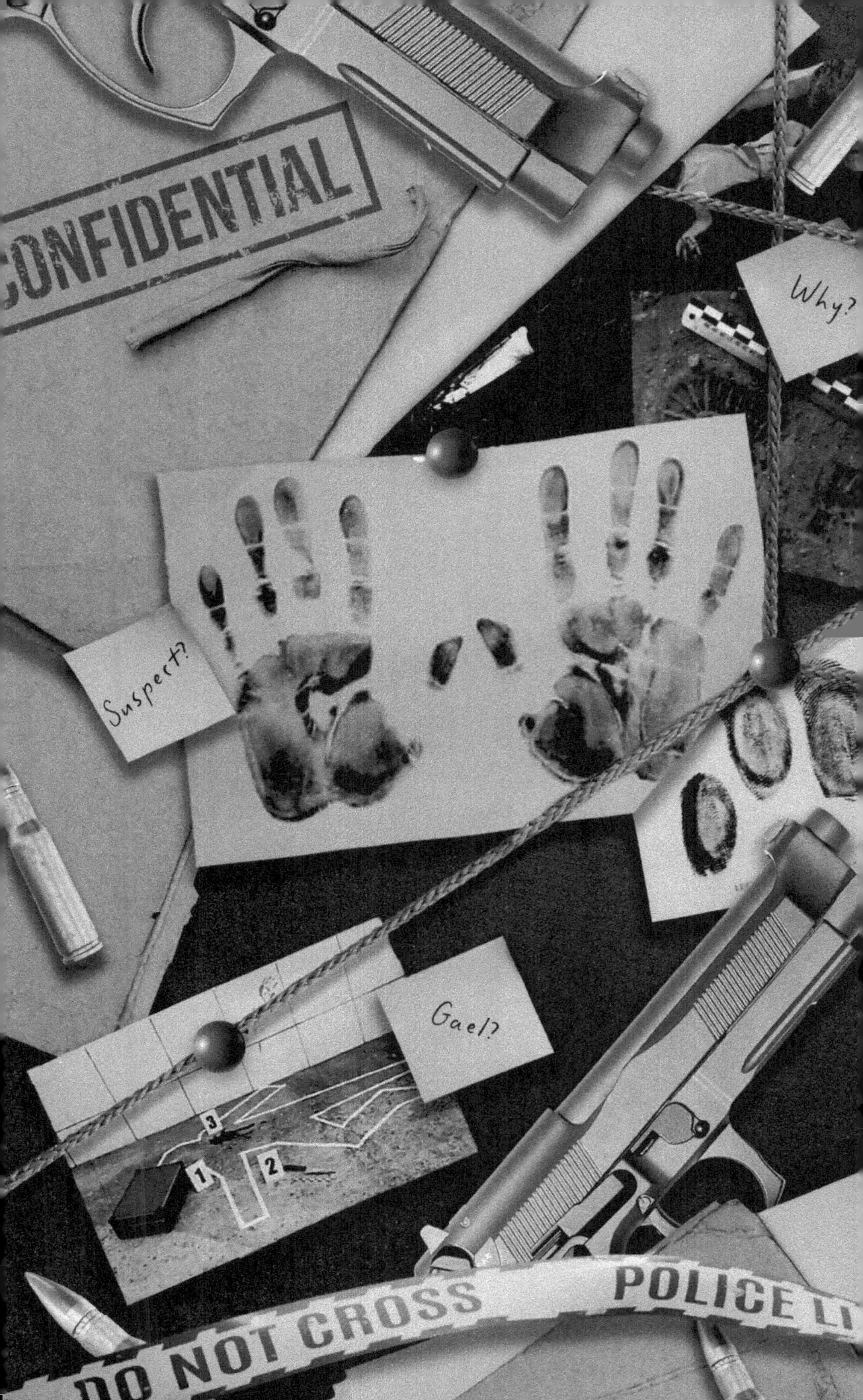

CONFIDENTIAL
Why?
Suspect?
Gael?
DO NOT CROSS
POLICE L

Sec
LINE – DO NOT CROSS
Reasoning?
CONFIDENTIAL
Suspect?
?
DO NOT CROSS
POLICE L
ret

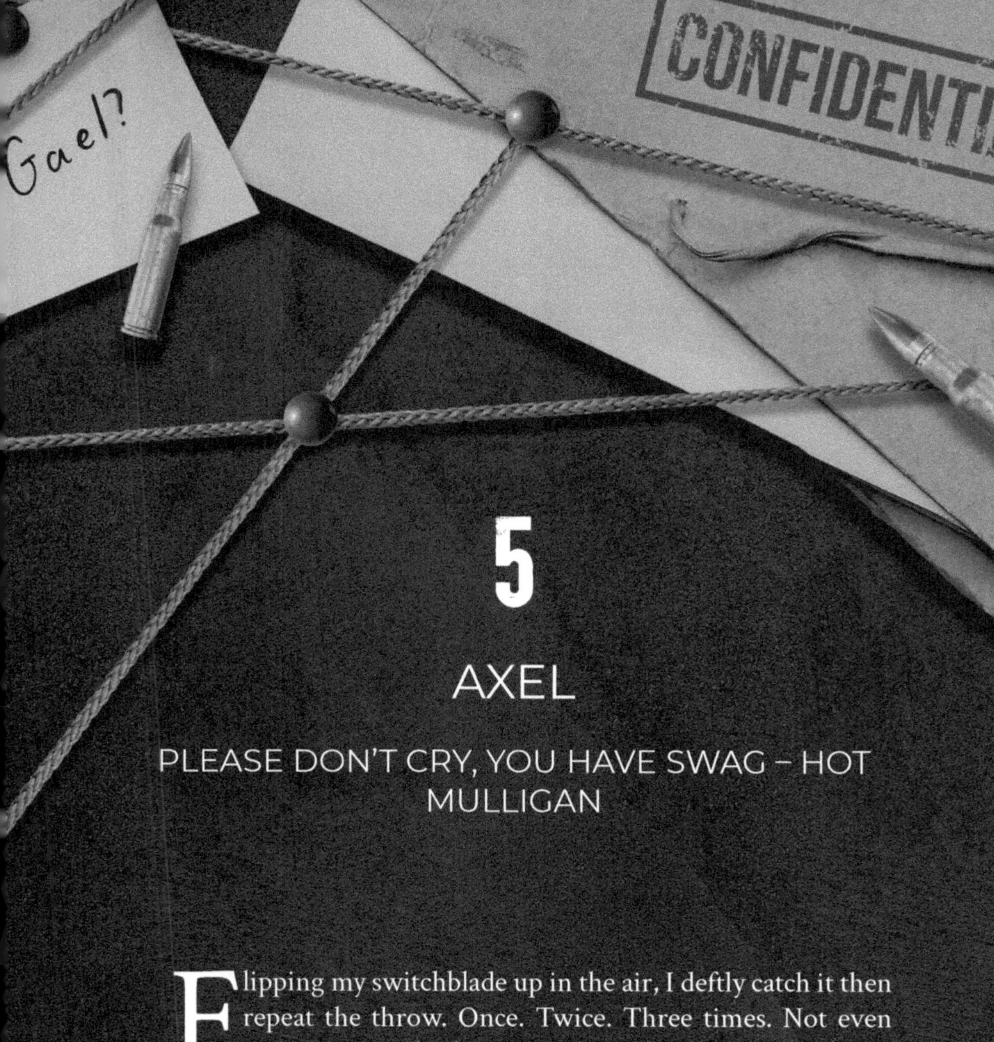

5

AXEL

PLEASE DON'T CRY, YOU HAVE SWAG – HOT MULLIGAN

Flipping my switchblade up in the air, I deftly catch it then repeat the throw. Once. Twice. Three times. Not even staring up at the boring ceiling fan is encouraging my eyes to fall shut.

We've been holed up for fifteen hours, resting and refuelling while keeping a low profile. The jet is scheduled to leave London shortly, bringing our departure from Mexico tantalisingly close.

The snores of my fellow teammates aren't enough to make me feel remotely tired. Not when the foul-mouthed redhead is resting mere metres from where I'm trying hard not to think about her muscular legs and near-bursting sports bra.

Jesus, Axel.

I don't give a rat's ass about what others deem to be right or wrong. People spend their entire lives abiding by meaningless principles, never tasting the sweet release of ending a man's life with your bare hands.

And for what? They're missing out. That rush has no comparison. Not a single drink, drug nor late night fuck can match the sheer power of holding a bloody, still-warm heart in your hands.

I'd say looking at Ember comes pretty close, though.

The things I'd do to those pouty lips. *Fuck.*

It's not hard to imagine the sloping, lickable skin that lies beneath the bruised mess we found her in. The others may not see it, but I do. Or perhaps their morals are holding them back.

But not me.

I don't care whose sister she is.

Setting the blade aside, I stalk to the attached bathroom to take another shower. I'm sick of this godforsaken room. I want to get out of here and hunt the ghosts who marked all that skin currently invading my thoughts.

My timing was shitty when I entered Ember's room with two bags full of snacks and drinks. I saw enough of her scar-striped, purple back to make my awaiting joke dry up.

I too would like to know who the fuck laid their hands on her so I can hack them off. They won't get the benefit of a bone saw. I'll chip away at their bones with a knife and fork if it'll hurt them more.

I'm about to flick on the shower to scrub away my irritating thoughts when an audible *bang* echoes from the adjacent room. Our bathroom connects to Ember's thin bedroom wall.

Straining my ears, there are no further sounds of struggle. Just a quiet shuffling before a soft, muffled sob leaks through the wall. God, she tries so hard to put on a brave face.

It isn't hard to see the shadows writhing in her oddly mixed, blueish-grey gaze. A palpable anguish that haunts the windows to her soul, no matter what sharp retorts roll off her tongue.

How I'd love to dive into that cavernous pit and swim in her inner darkness. Something about the way she holds herself intrigues me. Just hearing what she's spent the last few years doing had me fucking hard.

I wanna see her fight.

Damn, I wanna fight *her*.

When another thud echoes from her room after a few silent minutes, I decide to sneak out. Warner is still sleeping soundly, cuddling a pillow to his chest, while Hyland snores sprawled out on his back.

My first knock on her door goes unanswered. Doubt creeps in, pushing me to turn back. I quickly change my mind and spin back around to knock again before getting very far.

If anyone could see me wavering on her doorstep like some fucking idiot, they'd laugh. I'm not like Warner and Hyland. I don't care for caring's sake. But when someone intrigues me, that's different.

After an eternal pause and several more knocks, I hear footsteps move inside the room. The door creaks open, revealing a bleary-eyed goddess who makes my cock twitch.

"What?" she groans.

My lips fall open, throat contracting tight. "Ah."

She's wearing a massive black t-shirt that can only belong to one person. I'm going to skin Hyland alive for being so damn thoughtful before I could offer her my clothes.

I get a flash of boxers where the t-shirt has ridden up, the cotton disappearing when she lowers her hand from the door. Well, fuck. He lent her some of those too.

"Um." I cough awkwardly. "You alright?"

"Yeah." She stares past me. "Is it time to leave?"

"No… Everyone is asleep. I just thought I heard something."

Ember swipes a hand over her sore-looking face. It's hard to tell with her wounds, but her functioning eye looks red and puffy from crying. She gestures over her shoulder.

"Tripped over the armchair going to the bathroom."

Huh. Something tells me her spatial awareness is far better than that.

"Can't sleep either?" I prod.

Ember shrugs. "I managed a few hours."

"So… want some company?"

"Will you leave me alone if I say no?" she sasses back.

That mouth.

"I'm not a stalker," I argue playfully. "Well, not much anyway. I'll just sit out here and pout."

"Why am I not surprised?" She exhales in a weary manner. "Fine. Come in."

"We don't have to talk."

"Even better."

Passing her, I step into the low-lit room. "If I have to listen to Hyland snore for a moment longer, I'm going to go play in the road."

Ember snickers under her breath. "I can hear it through the wall."

"I'm convinced he swallowed a bloody train before passing out. Try living with that twenty-four-seven for five months."

Her auburn brows raise when I flop onto her unmade bed, stretching my limbs out. She got a double while we're all crammed in on twin mattresses in a single room.

"Nice big bed."

"Make yourself at home, why don't you?"

"Thanks." I jam a pillow beneath my head. "I will."

"Do you have any sense of personal boundaries?"

"What are those?" I watch her move to the armchair.

Snorting, Ember stiffly lowers herself into it. "I'm starting to understand the '*pup*' nickname."

"Watch it. Better to have me as a friend than an enemy."

This time, her laughter sounds genuine. It's a tinkling symphony, far different from the raspiness of her usual sarcasm. I feel a smile spreading my lips wide.

"So… You grew up with Warner? All happy families and shit?"

Ember's expression sobers, a crease forming between her eyebrows. "Something like that."

"How old are you?"

"By now… I guess, thirty-one? I haven't even thought about my birthday since I was taken."

"Five years younger then. I swear, Warner gets greyer by the day. Your brother too."

"You've seen Tom?" She looks over to me.

"Well, yeah. He's always at HQ for meetings and stuff."

"Right. Of course." Ember shakes her head like she's trying to knock the cobwebs out. "It's weird to think that life carried on while I've been trapped here."

"That's a stretch," I quickly argue. "His life did not go on. I'm not gonna speak out of turn, but Tom made it his mission to bring you home."

She smiles to herself. "Sounds like my big brother."

"You're lucky to have someone like that."

After a pause, Ember blinks rapidly to pull herself back. She's a little out of it. I faintly wonder what caused that bang. There's no way I believe she tripped over the damn armchair.

"You don't have any siblings?" she asks.

"Nah."

"Family?"

"Orphan," I volunteer. "Just little ole me."

The pity that usually comes when I reveal a little about my past never arrives. She merely nods in acknowledgement but keeps her thoughts to herself.

I'm thankful. There's nothing I hate more than talking about my screwed-up family or somehow being judged for what happened to them.

"I see. How old are you?"

Crossing my legs at the ankle, I get comfortable on her bed. "We're the same age."

"Huh. I thought you were younger."

"I can find my birth certificate if that helps."

Ember looks down at her bare legs, the cuts and scrapes now thoroughly cleaned. "Hilarious. I can see why you piss Hyland off."

"He makes it too easy. The man can't ever take a joke."

"I noticed. When did you join the team?"

Grabbing a bag of unopened gummies on the nightstand, I rip the crackling plastic open to shove a few in my mouth. I love the way she gawps incredulously. It's cute.

"About eighteen months ago. Got transferred in from MI-5."

"I can see everything in your mouth." Her lip curls in mock-disgust.

"You asked. Want some?"

Shaking her head, Ember watches me stuff another handful of sweets into my mouth. "You seriously worked for MI-5? Like James Bond, top-secret agent shit? That MI-5?"

"It's a lot less glamorous, believe me. And not really a well-kept secret either. You can literally walk past the offices in London."

"Right. So what did you do there?"

"I worked in the counterintelligence division for eight or so years."

"Why leave?" Ember leans forward, appearing to be genuinely interested.

"That's a story for another time. I don't wanna scare you off too soon."

"Come on." She chuckles. "I can handle it."

"Well, put it this way. Government policy didn't necessarily align with my methods. Sabre operates in much more of a legal grey area."

"Christ. You're right; I am scared off."

Swallowing my mouthful, I almost choke on a laugh. "Says the woman who became a vicious street fighter for the cartel. I couldn't scare you even if I tried."

Her fingers lift to cover her wry smile. "Probably not."

Beyond the two men I share my life and home with, there aren't many people who stick around once they get a glimpse of my madness. I wonder if she'll stay when she gets a real look.

"Can I ask you something?"

"Sure," I drawl.

Ember hesitates, her mouth creasing in trepidation. "What do you know about Blaine Madden?"

Munching another two gummies, I attempt to decipher her expression. Her eyes are darting around like she's trying hard not to appear interested.

"That mess was before my time," I answer carefully. "Something to do with a big case a few years back involving an organised crime family."

"In the UK?"

"I believe so."

"Huh." She nods to herself. "Um, he called himself their enemy. Sabre, that is. Warner too."

"I'd imagine he is."

"Do you know why?" she prods.

"I guess the guy was thrown in prison for racketeering and a lifetime's worth of drug charges. Next I hear, he's escaped and vanished off the face of the earth."

"Wait... Seriously?"

"Yup. Never to be seen again. Until now, apparently."

By the time the plastic bag is empty, she's zoned out. That criminal fuck clearly got under her skin. I don't know the bastard, but I want to cave his head in just for stealing her attention from me.

"What are you going to do when you get home?" I attempt to redirect her scattered thoughts.

Ember startles before her gaze returns to me. "What do you mean?"

"The investigation is ongoing. You'll have to cooperate, but you'll be offered protection too."

"Oh." Ember nods slowly. "Shit, I didn't even think about that. I have no idea. I'm not sure what I'm even going home to. I'm sure my apartment is gone by now."

"Would it help if I told you that Warner spoke to Tom?"

She visibly recoils. "How did it go?"

"After he finished screaming at him to put you on the phone?"

"Ah, crap. I should've known he'd react like that."

We've met enough times over the past eighteen months for me to think her brother's a decent bloke. He was heavily involved in my transfer into Sabre and all its legal ramifications.

"It was a tense phone call. Warner didn't reveal much, but Tom will be waiting for us when we land. It took almost an hour of convincing to stop him from flying straight here."

Ember brings her hands up to her face, hiding herself from my sight. "He's overprotective. Always has been."

"Sounds like that's been dialled up to a million now."

"Fantastic. Should we just stay?" Her joke falls flat.

"You'll be alright. Tom just won't let you leave the house ever again. I'll come break you out once in a while for a small fee."

"A small fee?" she chortles.

"London is expensive. I ain't working for free."

"Naturally."

"What? I'm entrepreneurial."

Seeing her smile makes me feel light inside. I want her to keep laughing. To forget how incredibly fucked up this all is, even if just for a moment. Maybe I can do that for her.

"I'm a bit tight on funds right now," Ember adds. "But I make a mean spaghetti bolognaise, if I can bribe you with food."

Propping a hand beneath my head, I peer over at her. "What makes you think that would work?"

"The rate at which you just inhaled the gummy bears I was saving for later."

A full belly laugh rips out of me. "Busted."

Her playful grin is downright intoxicating. The movement lights up her face, offering a taste of what her happiness would look like. Yep. I'm definitely making her smile more.

Cracking a yawn, Ember shifts in the armchair. "When are we leaving?"

"First thing in the morning. Things will be pretty intense once we land. You should get some more sleep while you can."

"I'll be okay."

"You're barely holding your eyes open," I point out.

Her bottom lip releases from between her teeth. "Every time I shut my eyes, I imagine Gael's men breaking down that door and tossing me back in a cage. Only, I'll never be allowed out again."

Watching her wince when she shifts her hips, I roll onto my side then pat the mattress. Warner would kill me if he saw this, but screw it. Ember shouldn't be left alone.

She needs to be looked after. I'm not the person to be doing it, though. The only difference between me and the men who took her are that my crimes were sanctioned by law.

I'm no less diabolical.

But for now, I can pretend. For her.

"Come lay down," I invite.

"Seriously, I'm okay."

"Give it up, Ember. You're safe. No one's gonna throw you in any cages while I'm here. Not if they want to keep their limbs attached."

"How do I know I can trust you?" she asks plainly.

"You don't. But Warner does. Do you think his trust is earned easily after all he's been through?"

"I guess not." Ember eyes the bed with interest. "Promise to keep your hands to yourself?"

"Pinkie swear. I'll be a good little bodyguard."

Drawing in a loud inhale, she raises herself from the armchair to hobble towards me. That damned oversized tee should be illegal. It keeps riding up and flashing her tempting, porcelain thighs.

I hold my breath as she lowers herself onto the bed, leaving a few inches between us. The lemony scent of motel shampoo wafts over me, mingled with something delicately floral and entirely her.

Ember curls her arms underneath her head, careful not to disturb the thick bandage wrapped around her forearm. Her muddied blue eyes lock on me.

Even injured, it's impossible not to notice that she's fucking beautiful. Her flaming hair, delicately structured facial bones and generous pout would make her the object of anyone's desires.

"Sleep. I'll stand guard."

Ember's nose crinkles as she looks over my body. "Maybe you're the one I should be worrying about."

I shift on the bed, wrestling with my urge to pull her close. "Maybe."

CONFIDENTIAL
Suspect?
DO NOT CROSS
POLICE
NOT CROSS
POLICE LI
Suspect?

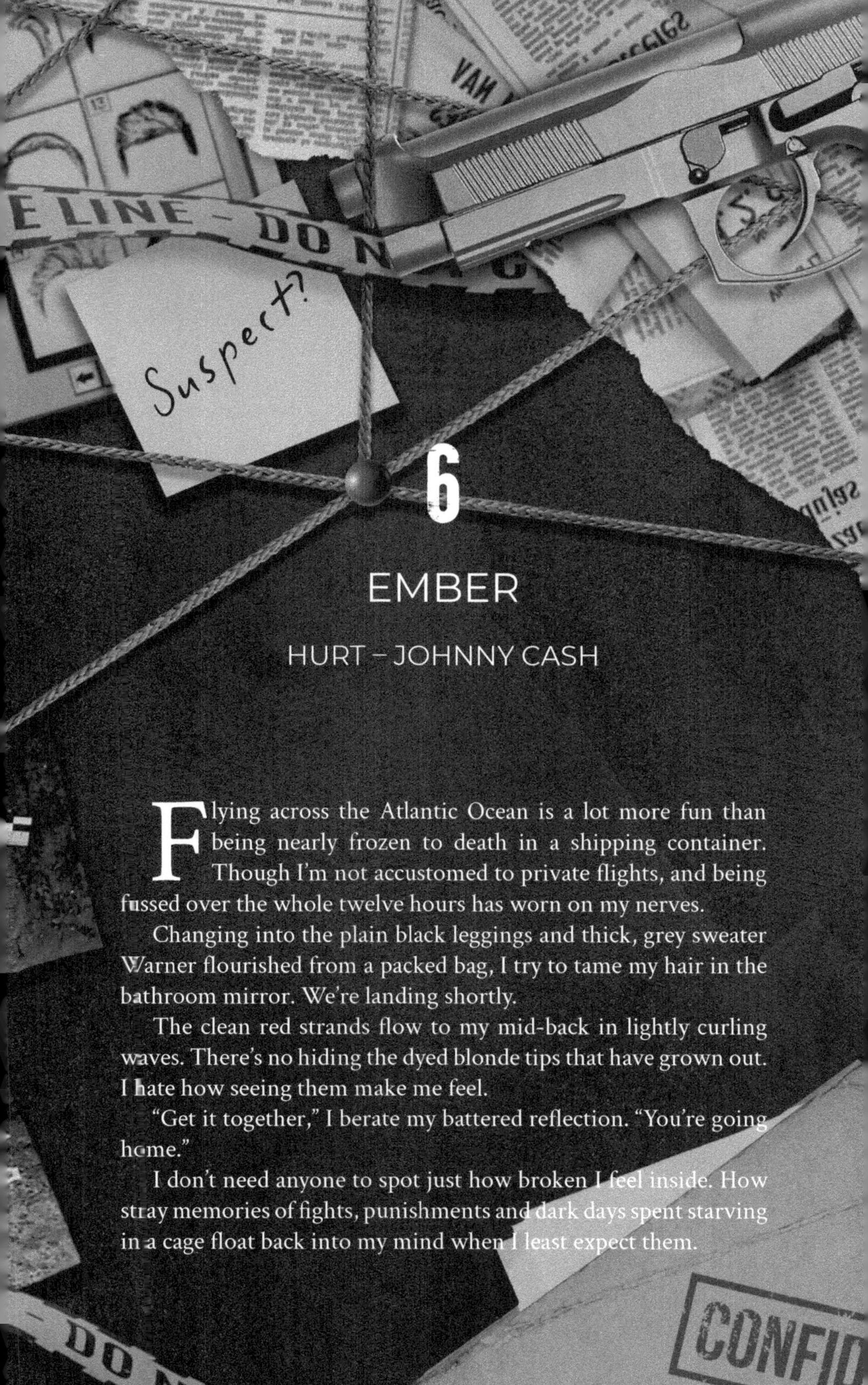

6

EMBER

HURT – JOHNNY CASH

Flying across the Atlantic Ocean is a lot more fun than being nearly frozen to death in a shipping container. Though I'm not accustomed to private flights, and being fussed over the whole twelve hours has worn on my nerves.

Changing into the plain black leggings and thick, grey sweater Warner flourished from a packed bag, I try to tame my hair in the bathroom mirror. We're landing shortly.

The clean red strands flow to my mid-back in lightly curling waves. There's no hiding the dyed blonde tips that have grown out. I hate how seeing them make me feel.

"Get it together," I berate my battered reflection. "You're going home."

I don't need anyone to spot just how broken I feel inside. How stray memories of fights, punishments and dark days spent starving in a cage float back into my mind when I least expect them.

More importantly, I don't want anyone to ever find out the price I paid for surviving the fight clubs. How weak my mind and body have become as a result. I can't handle concern or pity.

Axel came close to discovering my secret last night when he knocked on my door after I came back around. The black out episodes hit infrequently, but each attack is physically exhausting.

I don't know what it is. Sometimes my head splits open, and the world vanishes until I come to, my limbs locked tight. But the thought of admitting to anyone that they happen is abhorrent.

Weakness gets you killed.

They have to remain a secret.

"Em?" There's a tap on the door. "Landing in five. You need to take your seat."

"Gotcha."

Clenching my jaw, I resume rebuilding my mental brick wall. The same wall that kept me alive while other women were violated and sold to the highest bidder. The wall that kept me sane.

I can't let it tumble down now. I've paid in blood, sweat and endless screams to get to this moment. In a matter of minutes, I'll step foot back in England and see my big brother again.

It doesn't matter what I've done.

Now I can forget it all.

Quickly plaiting my long locks to conceal the blonde tips as best as possible, I tie off the braid then take a final glance. The vivid purple bruising is still horrific, but I can tentatively open my eye now.

Warner taps again. "Sorry, Em. The captain is insisting."

"Yeah. Okay."

I'm not sure what he would say if he knew where Axel slept last night. Warner's barely let me out of his sight since I revealed enough of my story to get him off my back.

When I woke up to voices calling my name, Axel's presence in the bed was gone. All that remained was a cold cavern in the mattress to prove it wasn't all some delirious, post black out dream.

"Hi." I step out of the bathroom to find him waiting. "I was just getting cleaned up."

"You look good." Warner smiles. "Did what the Falcon Team

packed for you fit okay? Tom gave them your rough sizes."

Truthfully, the sizing is a little off. My body has changed since I last stepped foot in this country. I've always been fit, but my slight curves now boast hard, visible muscles.

"It'll do. Thanks."

He rubs a hand over the scruff on his chin. "Listen. I can hold our superiors off until you've rested, but we'll need to bring you into HQ for questioning."

"I figured."

"I'm sorry." His mouth quirks. "It's my job, Em."

When he smiles, Warner's entire demeanour transforms. He's a handsome man—slim but muscular with firm shoulders, evenly proportioned features and intense baby blues that radiate warmth.

As a kid, I had the stupidest crush on him. He was the cute, friendly boy from down the street who spent more time at our house than his. Plus, he paid attention to me. Made me feel special.

It didn't take long for those first innocent feelings to bubble up. The older boy with all his burgeoning muscles and thoughtful, caring questions. How could I not fall for him?

As we both grew older, the unwritten rules of our friendship put a stop to those feelings. He's Tom's best friend. For that reason, our relationship has always been strictly platonic.

"Always so dutiful," I joke.

"I'm kinda straddling two horses in this race. I have a job to do, but I'm your friend too, Em. No one is going to rush you while you're settling back in and healing."

"As much as I appreciate your care, there are others out there who need to be helped. I'll tell you everything I know if you can catch the motherfuckers hurting those innocent women."

Warner nods. "I won't stop until I do."

"Promise?"

He sticks out a curved pinkie finger. "You know I always keep my word."

"You do. That's why I'm asking for it."

"Then yes. I promise."

Hooking our fingers together, we seal the deal. Having the reassurance that he'll keep fighting for me and all the others victimised by Gael's enterprise relieves a crushing weight.

"God." A rush of overwhelming anxiety engulfs me. "I can't believe I'm going home."

"Hey." Warner tugs me into a bear hug. "It's going to be okay."

His chin nestles against my head as I snuggle into his broad chest. Despite being smaller than Hyland's towering form, Warner packs the same bulk as Axel and can easily handle himself.

I've never hugged him for long enough to categorise his scent before. It's a fresh, intoxicating blend of patchouli and pine, the combination taking me to a mountainous forest retreat.

"We'll get justice." His hand lightly circles my back, careful not to press on my bruises. "For you and everyone else that son of a bitch has hurt."

Reluctantly extricating myself from his warmth, I plaster on a strained smile. It needs to stay on until I'm alone again and can deal with the trauma clouding my mind.

"Thanks for coming to get me."

Warner fiddles with a loose strand of his salt-and-pepper hair. "You can stop thanking me now. Just doing my—"

"Job," I finish for him. "I know. Still, I'm glad it was you."

"Me too, Em."

His silver-dotted streaks have grown in the past six years. He's one of the few men who looks better with a bit of distinguished grey. Truthfully, he's even more attractive now than before.

Aside from the physical changes of his thirties wearing on, Warner is exactly the same as when he was Langley, the top-secret agent building a pillow fort with me while Tom cared for our ailing mother.

That empathetic boy grew into a caring, loyal man who has given his entire life to helping others. In every case he takes on, Warner finds a lost cause to help. I just never thought I'd be one of them.

"Let's take our seats. A welcoming committee awaits."

"Great." I heave a weary breath.

"Now, now. Everyone's glad to see you home."

"I know. It's just a lot."

"You're not alone, Em. We're going to get through this."

Nodding, I pat his arm. "Thank you."

He flashes me another smile. "I've got you."

Shuffling back to the main cabin of Sabre's jet, I gaze over what is a masterclass in simple elegance. With glossy oak panelling, plush leather seats and a fully-stocked bar, I've never experienced such luxury before.

Setting up my own business was a huge financial investment. I'm far from rich. I used my inheritance and an extortionate bank loan, refusing to take any money from Tom's deep pockets.

I feel eyes on me when I shakily retake my seat. Hyland is back to his silent brooding, a persistent glower fixed in place. Not even his snoring competition last night seems to have cured his foul mood.

"Better?" Axel asks me.

"Yep." I avoid looking at his grin.

"Good. It's home time, baby!"

"I can't quite believe it."

"You better start believing it!" he whoops.

He's been unashamedly staring at me since I emerged from the motel room hours earlier. For a man who didn't stick around for the awkward wake up, he seems determined to let me know he's constantly watching.

Buckled in, my grip on the leather arms is white-knuckled. The farther we descend, the more my gut twists into a wringing knot. This is the closest I've gotten to returning home since I was taken.

It still doesn't feel real.

London's expansive, urban skyline is a familiar sight out of the small window. I visited Tom regularly when he moved to the capital to pursue his career. Though our lives went in different directions, we remained very close.

Towering steel skyscrapers that look like they were hand carved by the gods themselves dominate the landscape. This is an impressive city. England's crowning jewel in all its glittering glory.

It's also an anarchistic cesspit. London's shadowy streets operate under their own laws. While politicians debate legislation in Whitehall, gangs and organised crime families run rife.

"Home sweet home." Axel's nose is pressed against his window.

"Never thought I'd be so happy to see this fucking place."

"Honestly? Same," Warner replies.

"Of course, it's raining, though."

"It's England," Hyland retorts.

"But in May? Seriously? I want some sunshine."

"Be glad it's not snowing or something equally crazy." Warner distractedly rubs his right thigh. "I need to get this damn leg off."

I can just about see the shiny metal ankle joint of his leg sticking out of his trousers. He's dressed smartly for the big reunion, but the Warner I know is far more at home in sweats or shorts.

"Still overwearing the prosthetic?" I watch him cringe.

"No."

Hyland catches my eye across the jet and mouths the word *lie*. I smirk back at him.

"Saw that," Warner mutters.

"Don't lie then, boss."

"I'll do as I damn well please."

When the jet touches down, a seismic judder of nerves rattle through me. This private section of the airport appears quiet, blocked off by huge, slate-grey hangars and ground staff wearing hi-vis jackets.

After the jet finishes taxiing, the guys begin gathering their bags, waving off the attendants who rush to assist them. None of them seem comfortable with the private jet lifestyle. It feels like more of a necessity than a choice.

With nothing to carry, I check that the laces on the brand-new trainers I'm wearing are tight then work on stiffly lifting myself up again. My aching muscles and bruised body are humming with pain.

Familiar dizziness and a dull throbbing in my head accompany me as I slowly follow them to the front. Axel is vibrating with excitement while he waits for steps to be attached.

"First thing's first, I'm gonna eat twelve of Mary's bagels," he announces. "Then take a fifty-hour nap before going back for another twelve bagels."

"Fifty hours?" Hyland snorts.

"Dude, I was serious about missing my bed. I'm never leaving it again."

"You have work to do." Warner lingers behind them so I'm not alone. "I'll allow you one bagel and a change of clothes."

"One? That's a human rights violation!"

"I'll give you a human rights violation." Hyland wraps a massive paw around Axel's neck then squeezes. "Just keep whining like a little bitch."

"Get off! I'm still on duty. If my knife slips into your ribcage, it's a workplace accident."

"Not when the boss overhears you plotting my death it isn't, pup."

"For the last time, choose a new fucking nickname!"

"Nah. You like it too much."

The clank of steps being attached to the jet precedes the hostess opening the door. Hyland pushes past Axel to step out first, carrying two backpacks on his shoulders and a duffel in his hands.

Still grumbling, Axel follows with his laptop tucked under his arm and an equipment bag in hand. When it's time for me to follow, I can't seem to get my feet to respond.

Anxiety is worsening my ever-present headache, making me feel weak and unsteady. I don't know if I'm ready for this. I'm struggling to hold it together.

"Em?"

"What if... He doesn't recognise me?" I fret.

Warner spares me an assessing look. "You haven't changed that much. The old hair's kinda strange, but I'm used to it now."

"I'm not talking about my appearance."

"Then what?" Warner urges.

"It's just... I'm not the same person I used to be. I've changed."

"I still see little Em Lawson beneath those scars."

"You're not my brother."

Warner pauses, his eyes darting around like he's searching for the right words. "Tom will see that too. Give him a chance before letting your fear win."

"Shit. Did you gain another fifty IQ points while I was gone?"

He laughs at my crappy joke. "I know my best friend. He loves the bones of you, and nothing will ever change that."

"Okay." I heave in a final breath for courage. "Let's do this."

"After you."

Lips pressed together, I step out into the drizzly London air. The fresh, chilled breeze feels like heaven pouring into my nostrils after dealing with nonstop heat and humidity for so long.

Hyland and Axel are already heading towards three blacked-out SUVs parked next to the runway, still trading barbs. A tall, pale man running past them quickly captures my attention.

His long strides seem to be fuelled by sheer urgency, an invisible voice screaming at him to close the physical distance between us. My chest is unbearably heavy with the same frantic desire.

"Ember!"

Tom's voice cuts through my startled daze.

"Em!"

His yells cause the searing sensation in the back of my eyes to surge forward, forcing moisture to spill onto my cheeks in dribbling rivulets.

"Em!" he repeats in a rush.

Time freezes.

My heart pounds.

Head spins.

Limbs twitch and tense.

At the feel of Warner nudging my lower back, I break free long enough to launch myself down the metal steps. My breaths come in short pants, making my heart throb harder.

"Tom!" I shout back.

The agonising moments between half-running, half-limping towards my brother and being wrapped up in his arms stretch infinitely. Each second is elongated by grief-tinged catharsis.

Then I'm trapped against his tall frame. Wrapped up in peppermint-scented warmth that's so familiar, it intensifies my cries. I'm convinced I'll startle awake, and he won't even be real.

"Oh my God." He crushes me to his body, nose pushing into my hair. "You're here."

"T-Tom," I wheeze.

"Yeah, trouble. It's me."

Wrestling the back of his polo, I twist the expensive cotton. Too many words to count flash over my tongue without materialising. All I can think about are the nights I spent begging the silent darkness for this moment right here.

Through every last match and the endless beatings, the times I wanted a killer blow to end it all so I could finally be free... I thought of him. My big brother. My family. Home. He kept me alive.

"Oh, Em. It's okay."

The sob building in my chest feels like it's going to rip me in half. "You're here."

"I am." He inhales me deeply. "I'm here."

After all that time spent piecing my brick wall together, it comes crashing down at the strong pressure of my brother holding me close. The avalanche sweeps me off my feet in an instant.

"I d-didn't think I'd s-see you again."

"I know, Em. I know."

"I-I tried to be hopeful, to hold on... I tried so h-hard..."

He presses a hard kiss against my head. "I'm so thankful you kept going. I knew you'd come home."

Letting his shirt bear the brunt of my pouring eyes, I don't let go of him until the hysterics subside. I'm not allowing myself more than a brief meltdown. Not now that I've gotten what I wanted all along.

Releasing his shirt, I take a long look up at my brother's face. His stubbled cheeks are soaked with tears, spilling from his glistening emerald eyes. Tom is always slick, freshly shaven and dressed to the nines.

Today, his artfully cut, auburn hair is sticking up haphazardly, matching his unshaven face and painfully enlarged eye bags. Hell, I haven't seen him in a polo and not a dress shirt since we were kids.

"You look rough," I croak wetly.

He swipes his arm across his ghostly face. "I could say the same about you. Jesus Christ, Em."

"It looks worse than it is."

"Heard that one before." His mouth crinkles into a worried line. "We're going straight to the hospital."

"No! Warner checked me over. I'm alright."

"I don't care."

Looking over at the sound of approaching footsteps, Tom breaks out in a smile for his approaching best friend. I stand alone while they exchange a long, back-slapping hug.

"Good to see you back in the country."

"Good to be back," Warner replies brightly. "Just delivering one baby sister, as promised."

Tom clasps his forearm, using his other hand to swipe beneath his eyes again. He's always been the more emotional of us. Though I feel like I'm catching up to him now.

"I don't know how I'll ever repay you for finding her."

Releasing him, Warner's smile falters. "Wish I could take the credit."

"What?" Tom glances between us.

"It's a long story, but we should get out of here first." He pats my brother's hand to reassure him. "We've got a lot to catch up on."

Stepping away, Tom returns to my side so he can steady me. "She needs to go to the hospital first."

"I said I'm good," I grouse.

Both eye me sceptically.

"Cut it out! All I need is a hot shower, a banana milkshake and three double cheeseburgers."

Warner splutters a short, amused chuckle. "You didn't eat on the jet. Now you want three cheeseburgers?"

"Three doubles, actually. I was saving room for what I'm craving."

Doors slam behind us as the guys finish loading up their gear. I can feel eyes on me from across the tarmac where Hyland and Axel now wait, both leaning against their SUV.

"Well, looks like the lady has spoken." Warner surprises me with a good-humoured wink. "Come on, Tom. Let's feed the beast before she has a full meltdown."

"But—"

"Cheeseburgers," I insist. "No hospital."

He wearily shakes his head. "I was hoping your stubbornness had mellowed."

"Keep dreaming, bro."

All laughing, I snuggle into Tom when he bands his arm around my middle. His smell is a pure slice of home—old, legal textbooks and fresh peppermint toothpaste.

I'm really here.

I'm safe.

I'm free.

Not even the bloodthirsty whispers growing louder in the back of my mind can convince me otherwise. I survived the cartel. I don't need violence to protect me anymore.

Now... I just want it.

CONFIDENTIAL
Suspect?
DO NOT CROSS
POLICE
Suspect?
NOT CROSS
POLICE

7

EMBER

STAY WITH ME – THRICE

"That was shockingly bad, 768. You're getting lazy."
Panting from exertion, I let my sweat-soaked forehead crash against the training mat. We've been in the ring for almost ten hours. I feel like I'm going to throw up if I don't take a break soon.

Looming above me, Carlos makes no secret of how my failing muscles disgust him.

"So weak! Pathetic!"

The powerful kick he delivers to my tender midsection causes me to scream out.

"P-Please…"

"What did I tell you about begging?"

Pleading with him only intensifies his rage. I should know better than to beg for anything after the blows he dealt before I knew what asking to rest would incite.

FRACTURED FUTURE

I roll onto my back, jelly-like arms wrapped around my stomach to protect it from another kick. The motherfucker loves to flex his authority when the boss is watching.

"Get up, puta!"

Sitting silently in the corner of the warehouse with a hand-rolled cigarette clasped between his fingers, Mr Gael hasn't reacted at all. Not even when I landed a punch to Carlos's sneering face.

After weeks of these gruelling sessions, I thought he'd be pleased. Or at least forgiving. I don't want his satisfaction; I just want his mercy. My body can't take another punishment.

"Get up," Carlos spits again. "Now."

"Just... A little water..."

"When you earn it, you'll be given water and rest. Now get up."

Bracing a blood-caked hand against the floor, I use the leverage to heave myself upright. The world twists and spins, threatening to pull me under, but I blink the dizzy fog aside.

Carlos grants me a moment to gather my wits before he comes for me again. With my feet spread, I duck the blow he attempts to land, stumbling beneath his swinging arm.

Fortunately, his lessons are starting to stick since he's unwilling to tolerate failure. If I don't fight, I'll die. Or worse—I'll be like the other women, sent out to satisfy the whims of depraved monsters.

Taking a kick to the side, I land sprawled across the boxing ring. The mat isn't the high-tech, sponge kind that I paid a small fortune to have fitted in my studio. This one is rock-hard and inflexible.

The impact jolts my bones, causing me to cry out. Carlos growls a curse in furious Spanish then stalks off so he doesn't have to watch me writhe around in front of him.

Staring up at the steel rafters high above me, I can almost picture my safe, bright studio back in Liverpool. The polished, floor-to-ceiling mirrors. Workout equipment. Well-stocked smoothie bar. Bustling atmosphere.

I used to think that I was successful. Strong. Independent. Capable of tackling anything the world dared to throw at me after Mum passed. That nothing and nobody could ever hurt me again.

Now I'm cowering here, getting beaten within an inch of my life on a daily basis. Despite all the PT sessions I've taught and workout routines I completed, I still can't defeat this son of a bitch.

If I can't defend myself against Carlos, what hope do I have against anyone else?

I have to get stronger.

Fists curled tight, I push myself up again. My spindly legs are shaking, the muscles shrieking in protest. But still, I launch myself towards where Carlos is glugging water against the ring's ropes.

He hears my thudding steps too late. I strike him in the back of the head, causing him to grunt then topple. The asshole lands so hard, I wonder if I've caused some serious damage.

Spread out in the same position he left me in, I'm free to boot him in the face. Blood erupts from his mouth and nose from several firm kicks, giving me a burst of satisfaction.

"You told me to get up." I stare down at him, his eyes muddled with confusion from the head blow. "Now let me have my rest and water."

A slow, rolling clap echoes through the room. Cigarette now flicked aside, Mr Gael has moved to the edge of the boxing ring. For the first time since I arrived here, a smile graces his lips.

"Finish the job, 768." His savage yellow eyes brim with intensity. "We're not teaching you to show mercy."

Distant sensations pour into my numb state, dragging me from the depths of the traumatic memory. For a few seconds, I float in the unknown, that evil smile at the forefront of my mind.

We're not teaching you to show mercy.

It takes time for awareness to inch back in, eventually feeling the hot water still beating over me. I lay still as the world settles back into place, slick tiles pressing into my screaming muscles.

Pain.

Nausea.

Dizziness.

Numb detachment.

The warring sensations battle for centre stage when my brain catches up to what's just happened. Each time I black out, the result is the same. I wake up in agony, confused and dazed by the force of the latest attack.

Every episode I've had in the past few years is different. Truthfully, I don't know what physically happens in the seconds or minutes when I'm plunged into total blackness.

I've dealt with the anxiety of wondering when the next will hit ever since my worst fight. The one that almost ended my life. Mr Gael was forced to cancel my fights for months while I healed from a fractured skull.

Knocking forces me to peel my eyes open. It takes a few seconds for my sight to settle beyond my swimming vision. I feel like I'm on a swaying ship.

Tom's spotless marble bathroom appears in blurry lines through the shower door. This is… his apartment. His bathroom. His life I've invaded.

I'm free now.

"Ember? The car just arrived."

Lips flopping uselessly, it takes great effort to make my tongue obey, though my voice is strained.

"C-Coming."

His kind response floats through the door. "I'll tell them to wait. Don't rush."

Tom took me back to his apartment when I landed a couple of days ago. True to his word, Warner has held back the questioning until now. But I can't hide from it any longer.

When I try to find the strength to stand, my numb limbs fail to respond. I quickly give up on moving. My body needs time to recover from the total paralysis that each terrifying episode always brings.

Finish the job, 768.

"Leave me alone," I whimper in a tiny, broken voice. "Please… I'm free. I'm safe. Leave me alone!"

I'm not sure how long I continue laying in the shower, curled up into a tight, protective ball while the memory refuses to budge. It's long enough for my muscles to grow stiff and cold.

With great effort, I manage to turn off the shower then stumble out to locate a towel. My jittery limbs feel weak and useless. These episodes drain me physically and mentally. I'm weaker than a baby right now.

They don't usually happen in such quick succession. I woke up in a similarly disorientated state in the motel. The frequency of the attacks is undoubtedly a testament to the stress of the past few days.

I have no doubt that seeing a doctor would give me answers to the constant worry of when my brain will attack me next. It's the warped, terror-fuelled memories of the doctor who assessed us when we were kidnapped that are holding me back.

After arriving at the warehouse, we were individually dragged from our cages and shoved into a makeshift clinical room to have our measurements taken. That's how they confirmed that Gracie was a virgin.

I can't contemplate even seeing a doctor without sweat breaking out on my skin. My body tightens and prickles with panic just skirting the edges of those dark memories.

While they didn't have to do that horrific test on me, being stripped bare and weighed like a prime steak was harrowing. I never want to experience that again. Free or not.

By the time I've shakily dried off, pulled on jeans and braided my wet hair, my extremities feel more stable. My head still feels like it's stuffed full of cotton wool, but I can play that off.

Another knock on the door rings out, interrupting my spiralling thoughts. I clear my throat to call back.

"I'm coming now."

And another knock.

Huffing, I throw the door open. "I said I'm com…"

Shoulders wider than a sprawling mountain range steal my words. Rather than Tom's worried face and signature pressed shirt, I'm staring between the carved pectorals of a glaring giant.

"Oh."

"I've been waiting downstairs for an hour." Hyland's barrel chest vibrates with his low rumble. "What is taking so long?"

Neck craning so I can look into his olive-green orbs, my snarky retort dies in my throat. He's sporting a brilliant shiner, his face and left eye socket blackened by a huge bruise.

"What the hell happened to you?"

"I could say the same about you." He folds his arms over his barrel-like chest. "Who takes that long to shower and dress?"

Mentally burying the truth, I shrug it off. "I asked first."

"Axel," he replies shortly.

"He… punched you?"

Hand braced on the doorframe, Hyland scales his gaze over me from head to toe. "You look pale."

"No, I don't."

"What's wrong?"

"Stop deflecting," I retort.

"Hah." He snorts in amusement. "Pot, meet kettle."

Narrowing my eyes, I glower at him. "Fuck you."

It doesn't take long for the grump to crack.

"I ate one of Axel's bagels. The pup said it's lucky I'm still breathing."

Honestly, I'm starting to wonder if the ball of golden retriever energy isn't the most insane of them all.

"You guys are fucking crazy."

Hyland's mouth crinkles in a reluctant half-smile. "Don't worry. He looks worse."

"What happened to turning the other cheek?"

"I never really bought into that shit as a kid." He chuckles deeply. "Not gonna start now."

"That's really mature of you," I say sarcastically.

"I know, I'm a fucking hero. Look, are you ready? Or should I wait for another hour?"

"Settle down. I'm ready."

Ducking underneath his braced arm, I flick the hallway light on to locate my shoes. A modern crystal chandelier hanging from the high ceiling creates a beautiful pattern on the hardwood floors.

The opulent, two-bedroom apartment in the affluent borough of Marylebone is a testament to Tom's passion for law. He's always been career-driven, working hard for his status and money.

The man in question appears as I'm toeing on my knee-high, leather boots. At least I have my own clothes and belongings here. They've provided some comfort, however shallow.

Tom told me he packed up all my stuff when the landlord

insisted my apartment be cleared as I hadn't been found after a whole year. The life I fought so hard to get back to is gone. Erased. All I have left are a stack of cardboard boxes.

When he revealed that information, I quickly offered an excuse to get a closed door between us so I could fall apart in private. The grief is all-consuming. For so long, I dreamed of home.

And now it's lost to me too.

That really fucking hurts.

"Sorry, Em." Tom fiddles with his glinting cufflinks. "I held him off for as long as I could."

"I doubt anyone is capable of holding him off indefinitely." I cast Hyland's bulked-out mass a side glance. "Thanks for trying, though."

With his dirty-blonde hair pulled back in a messy bun, Hyland's hair-smattered square jaw and perpetual frown are front and centre. At least he looks a bit more rested today.

Much like before, he wears an all-black ensemble that prioritises practicality over comfort. Black cargos hug his bulging thighs and round ass, while his black t-shirt accentuates every last defined muscle.

"Is that supposed to be an insult or a compliment?" Hyland questions with a cocked head. "Because I'm going to take it as the latter."

"You shouldn't."

His nostrils flare, sparkling green eyes betraying his amusement. "Can't take it back now."

"What are you still doing here?"

"Whatever. I'll be in the car."

Once Hyland has stomped off, I'm left to face Tom. We haven't spoken much since we were dropped off by the Anaconda Team. Even at mealtimes, I've silently eaten before crawling back into bed to avoid his questioning.

The distance between us hurts like a bitch after growing up so close, but every time I look at him, all I feel is anger. Pure, out of control rage for all the precious years and memories that were stolen from us.

If I give in to that righteous anger, I'm terrified of what I'll do.

And if I'll be able to ever switch it off again.

"Listen, Em." He gifts me a reassuring smile. "I'll be there today as your legal counsel, and we're going to take this at your pace. Their questions can still wait."

"I want to get it over and done with."

"Of course, I understand that. I'm just saying that if it's too much or you need to rest some more, I have no problem telling them to bugger off."

More fury licks at my insides, turning my blood to molten ash. All I want is to set him at ease. To tell him that no one hurt me like he's imagining. Why can't I do that?

Because it's not true. It doesn't matter how they hurt me or how any of us were forced into subjugation. The injustice is that I'm here—safe and breathing—while others are not.

Others like Gracie.

While those bastards still run free.

"Ember?"

Teeth grinding together, I try to speak past the enraged storm crawling up my throat. "I need to do this."

"You've barely said a word since we got home." His emerald gaze brims with concern. "I know you've been through a lot. I'm trying to protect you from more pain."

"Avoiding the investigation isn't going to help."

"Perhaps not." He gently squeezes my bicep. "But if you can't even talk to me, how will you be able to tell them what happened?"

Typical Tom.

He's never been one to beat around the bush.

"I want to talk to you," I make myself admit. "I'm just trying to make sense of everything first. I lived in survival mode for so long, I didn't stop to process it all."

He sighs, sliding on his charcoal-grey suit jacket. "Which is precisely why we should postpone."

"Time won't make this any easier."

"Then what will?" He stiffens, his posture carved from nervous tension. "Please tell me what I can do. Let me in."

"I don't think you can help."

"Try me, Em."

Unable to look at him, I stare down at the shiny, polished floor. His weekly cleaner came yesterday while Tom took work calls in the living room. I heard them trading polite conversation from the spare room.

I wanted to get up, try to socialise or even show my face. Yet something held me back from taking that first step into the world again. A paralysing fear that came out of nowhere and stole my breath.

I thought I'd feel safe here. Warner even assured us that he would post around-the-clock security outside the building. But in truth, I don't think an entire army outside would make me feel any better.

I'm not scared of Gael and his men.

Rather, I'm petrified of the person he made me into.

After losing the studio I worked so hard to build—shut down years ago without me there to make rent—I have no purpose. No direction. Nowhere to go.

All I have left are my cardboard boxes of clothes and knickknacks belonging to a different woman. My vivid nightmares, jolting me awake in a cold sweat. And the constant threat of another attack forever looming.

How do I tell Tom that although I'm here, it feels like I left a part of myself in the ring? Perhaps the scraps I've brought home are the worst parts of me. The parts I don't want him to see. Parts far too jagged and ugly to create a whole person.

"I just need time. That's all." My voice wavers. "Coming home… hearing how everything has changed… it's been a lot."

"I'm trying to give you time, Em."

"I know."

"I really am. But when you barely eat, won't speak and seem unable to even look at me… it kills me inside."

"I'm sorry," I offer half-heartedly.

"Don't even." Tom jerks his head in dismissal. "None of this is your fault. I just want to help, that's all."

The anguish in my chest detonates, reforming into a new shape each time I try to wrestle it into subjugation. Choking grief is preventing me from saying a single thing to comfort him.

"I hate what they've done to you." He runs a hand over his hair, slicked back in its typical perfection. "And I don't know how to help."

Shit.

Sighing tiredly, I wrap my shaking arms around his midsection. The scent of peppermint and rich, ink-stained paper filters into my senses, soothing the torrent trying to rip me apart.

I want to scream at myself... *This is Tom.* The overprotective perfectionist with a brain bigger than most family homes and a heart that rivals it in size. I can trust him. He deserves the truth.

"You help just by being you," I whisper into his shirt. "Be patient with me."

"Always."

"I'll try to open up more."

He hugs me back, pushing warmth into my bones. "I need you to tell me if it gets too much today, and we'll end the interview. No questions asked."

"I will."

Clasping my arms, his neck tilts so he can look into my eyes. "Promise me."

Weakly, I smile at him. "What are we, five-years-old?"

Tom doesn't crack a smile, his green gaze gleaming. My brother, the formidable legal ninja who breaks multimillion-pound cases wide open before he's had his morning brew, looks afraid.

"Promise me, Em."

That harrowing look is enough to shatter every last defence I've been hiding behind. I never want to be the reason he wears that expression. I'll just have to find a way to pretend. And pretend *well.*

"Promise." I nod once.

"Good." A breath whistles from his nose. "Let's get this done. Then we're coming home and ordering the biggest pile of Italian food you've seen in your life."

"Thought you were on a bachelor's diet?"

He picks up his laptop bag then checks his pockets to make sure he has his wallet and phone. "That ended the moment I got Jamie to commit. I was sick of intermittent fasting."

"Wait... You and Jamie?" My eyes widen in surprise.

Tom shoots me a smile. "He still lives at his place for now, but yeah. We've been exclusive for about three years now."

"Holy shit!"

My brother's on-again, off-again boyfriend—or rather his convenient hook-up, if you'd prefer the truth—has been on the scene ever since Tom moved to London. But they hadn't done labels before.

"Alright, calm down." A flush stains his pale skin. "It's not like we're getting married or anything."

"I'm just surprised. I never thought I'd see the day either of you settle down."

"Thanks for the slut shaming. It's perfectly fine to spend your life having endless threesomes with hot, single men without taking on their baggage, you know?"

Grabbing his keys, we step out into the thickly carpeted hallway. He lives in a beautiful, luxury apartment building, set in a renovated mansion block with all original, Victorian features.

"I agree, but you have taken on someone's baggage now," I point out as we head for the stairs. "So that kinda refutes your argument."

"Bloody know-it-all," Tom grumbles.

"So what's it like? You know, being off the market?"

"It feels really, really great." He grins to himself. "Jamie makes me happy. He got me through the past few years, all the police investigations, everything."

"I'm glad you had someone here to look after you."

"He wanted to come see you, but I thought it may be too much right now."

Guilt crackles through my grief-tightened chest. "I hate that I'm a burden to you."

Halting at the top of the staircase, Tom captures my hand. "No. Don't do that to yourself. You're not a burden, and I would never think that."

"I've interrupted your life. If I had anywhere else to go—"

"You think getting my little sister back after all this time is an interruption?" he asks incredulously.

His fingers cinch around mine, anchoring me in the present moment. Far from the wails and cracking whips that still bounce around my mind.

"Maybe?"

"Jesus, Em."

I bite my tongue to hold another pointless apology in.

"You're my priority," he declares without hesitation. "That will never change. This is your home now. Jamie doesn't even come close to you in importance."

Appreciation warms my skin, pushing out some of the disorientating fog still lingering in my mind. I latch onto the feeling with both hands and drag it to the forefront of my inner darkness.

"You don't have to look after me. I'm a big girl. I'll figure it out."

"Less than forty-eight hours, and you're already done being coddled." He snickers to himself. "Why am I not surprised?"

"At least I'm consistent."

"Consistently annoying. I agree."

"Love you too, bro."

"Yeah, whatever," he groans humouredly.

Tackling the marble staircase side by side, I focus on the pressure of Tom's hand wrapped around mine. Even though I'm a grown-ass woman who shouldn't have to hold her brother's hand. I want to.

For all those times I wished I wasn't alone, I now have what I wanted. Perhaps I can forget the evil I've seen. Forget the way my mind has broken into a thousand pieces. Maybe I can forget the monster Gael's street fights made me into.

I can forget it all.

Can't I?

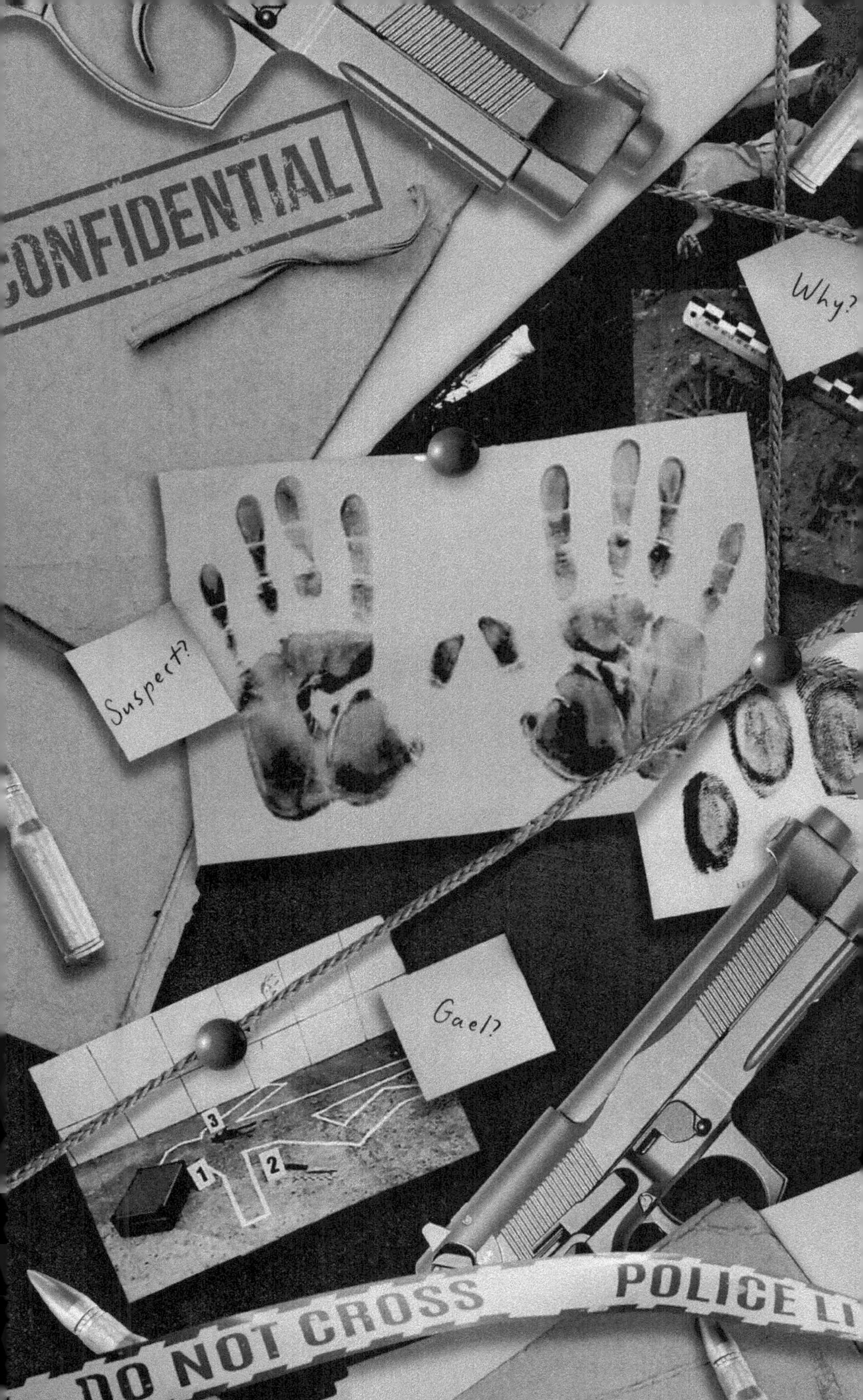

CONFIDENTIAL
Why?
Suspect?
Gael?
DO NOT CROSS
POLICE L

POLICE LINE
POLICE LINE - DO NOT CROSS
E LINE - DO NOT CROSS
CONFIDENTIAL
Weapon?
2
3

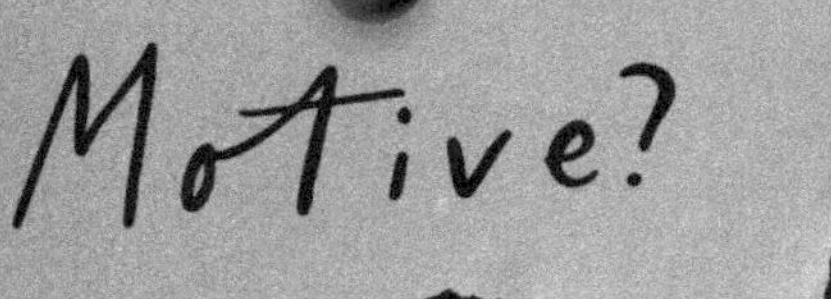

8

HYLAND

MATCHES – JONAH KAGEN

"What's the hold up?" Warner snaps down the line. *Give me strength.* I'm in no mood to deal with his demands today.

"We're two minutes out," I drone.

"You're over an hour late."

"I'm aware."

Between Ember taking an eternity to get ready and London's incessant traffic, I'm perfectly aware of just how late we are. Warner is a stickler for punctuality.

"If you'd like to send a helicopter to pick us up from the fucking road, be my guest. I can't use magic to make the cars go any faster."

"I've got the terrible twosome here breathing down my neck for a progress update," he explains wearily. "Just hurry."

For two individuals who once held the title of clients long before they ever worked for Sabre Security, let alone ran the damn company, Kade and Hudson Knight can be incredibly impatient.

We've been home for less than forty-eight hours, and already, the demands for information are flying. This isn't the kind of case that gets resolved the moment we find our victim after years of investigating.

Gael is still out there, not to mention the vast network of traffickers he's connected to who pluck victims from across the globe. This snake has many heads. Realistically, our job has only just begun.

"Tell them to wait their turn. Ember's our priority."

"Believe me, they got an earful." He huffs into the receiver. "Drive safe."

"See you shortly."

Ending the phone call, I wait for the heavy traffic to shift, leading us into the bustling mayhem of Central London. For a Friday morning it's typically busy, the roads heaving with flashy cars and delivery vans.

After all the years I've spent working at Sabre Security, bouncing between cases and departments until I permanently joined the Anaconda Team, the towering skyscraper up ahead never fails to impress.

It's an intimidating sight, challenging the height of every last FTSE 100 corporation housed around it. Our building is an impressive statue of steel and black glass, stretching high above the ants wandering on the streets below.

Growing up in a working-class suburb in the east of England, the eye-watering sums of money that pass through a place like this seemed staggering to me at first. Far more money than I'd ever even thought about.

I could hardly believe the opportunity in front of me when I was recruited from a decently paid job in private security. Uprooting my family was a tough call, but all I wanted was to provide them with a better life.

As luck would have it, that was the worst decision I could've made. Years down the line, I'm now divorced with a six-year-old son I barely have a relationship with. Not for lack of trying.

My ageing parents tried to convince me to return to my

hometown and start fresh, but I wasn't willing to abandon Sabre. No matter what price working for this firm has extracted from me.

"We're keeping this brief." Tom doesn't look up from texting on his phone beside me. "Ember isn't up to being interrogated so soon."

"Do you really think we'd do that to her?" I clear my throat.

"You tell me."

"No one is interrogating her. Christ."

He shrugs in the passenger seat. "I've seen the way your team operates up close. You can't blame me for wanting to shield her from that."

"For God's sake. We're not animals."

"Tell that to Axel. I had to negotiate with the head of prosecutions to clear his criminal record after leaving MI-5. If he wasn't working for the government, he'd be in a prison cell."

Honestly, I'm not surprised. Eighteen months isn't long enough for me to get accustomed to Axel and his craziness.

"Well... yeah. But that's Axel."

"Just keep him the hell away from my sister," Tom says curtly.

Glancing in the rearview mirror, I check to see if Ember is still asleep. She quickly passed out when we set off, her head propped against the car window. Something about her seems off today.

"With pleasure. How's she doing?"

Pocketing his phone, Tom blankly stares at the traffic. "Honestly? I have no idea. She's barely talking to me. Still refusing to see a doctor too."

"Well, shit. Any idea why?"

"She won't say. Just outright refuses."

Sickly tendrils of suspicion creep through me. I'm a pretty good judge of character. Not Warner-level perceptive, but enough to do my job.

What did they do to Ember?

"You can't push her?" I suggest.

"Believe me, I've tried. She claims to be feeling fine. Short of pinning her down... I'm out of options. She seems healthy."

"Appearances can be deceiving."

"I asked if they..." He grips the back of his neck, swallowing loudly. "You know? But she claims no one touched her like that. She was protected by her position."

"That's something, right?"

"I guess so. She still needs a full medical, I just don't know how to make it happen."

My stomach flip-flops at the possibilities. "She hasn't told you anything else?"

"Not a word." His hands form fists in his lap. "I already knew about the street fights, but she won't tell me anything else. You seen her fists?"

"Yeah. I have."

He wordlessly shakes his head.

"From the little information Ember gave us in Mexico, she was found in some illegal fight club before contacting us. We heard reports of a disturbance in the area via online traffic."

"Jesus Christ." Tom rubs his eyes with his fingers, already appearing exhausted. "An illegal fight club?"

"Yeah," I confirm grimly.

"Those motherfuckers… No wonder she's traumatised. How the hell did she survive?"

"She's strong."

Tom glances up at Sabre's overwhelming height as we head for the parking garage. "She always has been. Even when our mum was dying, Ember held us all together."

"That's how she survived then."

From working a previous human trafficking case, I never held out much hope that we'd find Ember, let alone in one piece. Meanwhile, Warner never doubted for a moment that she'd be alive and kicking.

But I've seen enough from the red-haired spitfire in the past few days to understand the sheer breadth of her strength. No one survives six years of brutal fights and captivity without having nerves of steel.

Her courage and strength… it's fucking formidable. Just like her. I never paid much attention when we briefly met before, but she sure holds my whole attention now.

"And now?" Concern bleeds from Tom's words.

"If she did it once, she'll do it again. And she has the entire weight of Sabre behind her now. We'll make sure she's safe."

Looking at his phone again, he spits a curse. "Why is Warner emailing to ask for all my case files on Blaine Madden?"

I brake to pull up to the gate for a fingerprint and retinal scan. "We were going to debrief you today."

"If that animal is involved in my sister's case, I should've been told. How on earth is Madden wrapped up in this?"

"Seems our criminal friend has made a reappearance," I reply acerbically. "He was the one who got Ember out of there."

"Madden was in Mexico?" Tom clarifies.

"According to Ember."

"What the… Explain. Now."

"That's all I know. Madden left her clear instructions to give his name when he deposited her on the side of a road with Warner's mobile number."

"How on earth did he locate her? Why?"

"Honestly, it beats me."

Frankly, the whole tale is ludicrous.

Blaine Madden's conviction was one of Sabre's best success stories—the son of a prolific mobster, from a powerful dynasty of British criminals. He took the fall for his family's crimes.

Most notably, they supplied half of London's drug trade at one point. The entire enterprise was in Sabre's crosshairs for years before we nailed the sneaky bastard. Only for him to escape and vanish.

"We've been trying to track him down since he escaped." Tom shakes his head. "I always thought he had inside help. No one disappears that quickly and effectively."

"Who cares how he escaped?" I reverse into my assigned spot. "Madden is sending us a message. And using Ember as the fucking envelope."

Cursing again, Tom unclips his seatbelt. "I'll make some calls. We can get all the court files from the firm's archive."

"Good."

I grab my handgun from the car's lockbox then climb out to fit it into my holster. Tom attempting to rouse Ember gives me a moment to check my phone. A text message has pinged through.

Ethan: Heard you're home. Welcome back, bud.

God, there are days when I miss our old teammate. He kept us all sane with his level head. Warner is a great leader, but Ethan brought a balance that we've been missing since he left.

Hyland: Thanks. How's Briar Valley?

Three dots appear before his reply arrives.

Ethan: Quieter than London. Come visit sometime? Willow would love to see you.

Hyland: I need to see this case through, but I'll come soon. Give her a hug from me.

Ethan: Will do. Be safe.

Hyland: You too.

Tucking it into my pocket, I study Ember as she moves around the vehicle to join me. She looks like shit. Pale, shaky and visibly antsy. I thought the same when she opened the bathroom door earlier.

I don't care what bullshit she's fed her brother. She's refusing to get checked out for a reason, and I intend to find out what that reason is. Whether she wants to tell me or not.

"Everyone is waiting upstairs." I watch her fiddle with her damp braid. "This is a standard, initial interview. Nothing to panic about."

"Nothing, huh?" She lowers her gaze to study the concrete.

"We're gonna go at your pace. If it takes a few days or even longer, that's okay."

"I can handle it."

"I'm saying you don't have to. We'll take things slow."

"Let's just head up," she insists. "I want to get this over and done with as fast as possible."

Waving off the arm that Tom offers her, Ember sets her jaw in a terse line. That fucking sass. It isn't my job to notice these details—I'm here to protect her—but hell, if her fiery spirit doesn't make my pulse thrum.

After scanning my security pass and checking in with the two hard-faced guards posted at the staff entrance, we head inside. Sabre's reception is a sprawling, brightly lit display of pure authority and influence.

"I forgot how insane this place is," Ember mutters.

With impossibly tall ceilings, endless metres of polished glass and huge, crystal droplets casting light on every clean white surface, insane is an adequate description for the high-security paradise.

"Nothing much has changed since you were last here. Just a few new faces."

"And a few old ones." She flashes me a tight smile.

"Is that your subtle way of calling me old?" I cock an eyebrow at her. "Because for the record, I'm a whole twelve months younger than Warner."

"Damn. Don't forget those precious twelve months, old man."

"Don't you forget either."

Escorting them to the elevator, I return the respectful nods shot my way by other staff members. We've risen through the ranks and gained a high level of authority in the company throughout all the changes it's undergone.

Our team works closely with senior leadership, leaving the investigative teams to trickle down in descending order of authority. Now our offices sit alongside the Knight brothers and other executives.

Stepping inside the elevator, Ember's tense shoulder brushes my torso. The slight touch causes my muscles to spasm, locking up tight. She casts me a long, searching glance.

"How come you drew the short straw?"

"Huh?" I blink at her.

"You've clearly been assigned to me for security. Why you?"

I punch the button for the top floor. "I'm the team enforcer,

Ember. It's my job to protect our clients. I leave the talking to Warner and the torturing to Axel."

"Right," she deadpans. "You're just the muscle."

"Again with the compliments? I'm blushing."

Ember breaks out in laughter. "Don't flatter yourself."

"Before we get up there… We're training the Falcon Team at the moment, so their team leader wants to sit in on the interview. Are you comfortable with that?"

Ember shrugs. "Whatever."

"I can tell Archer to clear off. He won't mind."

"I've got nothing to hide," she says in an unconvincing tone. "Unless you're planning to throw me in some fucked up holding cell in the basement."

"What?" Tom gasps, reminding me that he's behind us. "Why would you even think that?"

Her eyes watch the flashing floor numbers escalating higher. "What I did isn't exactly legal. I've hurt a lot of people."

"You weren't given a choice," I point out.

"Does that really matter?"

"Yes," Tom cuts in. "It matters."

Falling silent, Ember smashes her mouth shut. Fuck, I want to tilt a finger beneath her chin and make her look at me. Tell her that I've bloodied my fists for Sabre more times than I can count and still feel guilty for it.

Shoving my hands in my cargo pockets instead, I bounce on the balls of my feet. Nope. Not my job. They told me to collect Ember, and guard her with my life—that's all I'm here to do. Be her damn bodyguard.

But hey, it isn't illegal to look.

Since the shit went down with Jayce a few years ago, I haven't dared to even think about a woman, let alone show interest in one. Not when I managed to fuck up my marriage so badly.

This line of work isn't compatible with a healthy relationship. Working for Sabre puts me in the line of fire every day, and by extension, my loved ones too. And I'll never make that mistake again.

We're admitted onto the top floor, high above the bustling

levels of offices, training facilities, interrogation rooms and more. This isn't just Sabre's HQ. It's a self-contained city of agents and shadow operatives.

"In there." I gesture towards the conference room. "The team's waiting."

Down the thickly carpeted corridor, lined with floor-to-ceiling, frosted glass walls that conceal the office's occupants, our destination is the final door on the right.

While Tom lets himself into the room, I snag Ember's wrist at the last second. She halts to peer back at me through bruise-ringed eyes. The swelling has gone down enough for me to see her muddied gaze clearly now.

Blue flecks blend with her swirling, slate-grey irises, creating an intense thunderstorm that seems intent on decimating me. Yet beyond her defensiveness, something else hides.

"What?"

I wait for the door to swing shut. "Your brother's worried about you. I don't know what the deal is, but I want to help. Sabre has in-house medics who are *very* discreet."

"Like I told Tom, I don't want to see a doctor."

"You were held captive for six years and faced more fights than I can even begin to fathom. At least let someone here check you over. It won't hurt."

"Why do you care?" she demands icily. "We hardly know each other."

"And I'm sure it'll look great if the client I'm supposed to be protecting keels over on my watch," I hurl back at her. "You've been shaking ever since I picked you up."

Sure enough, her still-trembling hands quickly jam into the back pockets of her jeans. Those curve-hugging, tight fucking jeans... Yep, I've counted every last muscle she's packing.

"Leave me alone, Hyland."

"No can do. You're my assignment. Get used to having me on your ass when I think something's going on that may jeopardise your safety."

"If I'm your assignment, shouldn't you respect my wishes?" She cocks an auburn brow. "I'm telling you to back off."

"Cute. Nice try."

"Listen up," Ember growls. "I'm here to tell you what I know, and that's it. I don't need you sticking your nose in where it doesn't belong."

During our brief flash of privacy, her caustic tone dissolves any misgivings I have about stepping into her personal space. She backs up into the door as I advance, trapping her between my chest and the light wood.

Her chin tips up, those fierce eyes pinning me without ducking once. *Huh.* It's been a while since someone's looked at me like that rather than scuttling when I tower over them.

Before I can help myself, I've captured her pointed chin between my thumb and forefinger. Her pink lips part, drawing in air.

"You may have everyone fooled with this hard ass act," I whisper knowingly. "But I'm not buying it."

"So this how you help people? By intimidating them?"

My thumb skates across her skin in a light stroke. I swear, I see a shiver roll over her. I'd be fired faster than I can spit out an excuse if anyone saw this, but pure instinct has taken over.

"If that's what it takes."

"Then by all means." She waves her hand. "Continue."

"I'm not here to intimidate you. Believe it or not, I do want to help."

"Sure," she scoffs.

"Why don't you believe me?"

"Because you have me pinned against a fucking door?"

Forcibly shackling the beast raging inside me, I silence its possessive demands, whispering ideas like throwing her over my shoulder, marching her to the medical centre and tying her to the damn examination table.

After I take a step back to put space between us, Ember deflates against the door. She's still trembling, but there isn't an ounce of fear in her gaze. Instead, it burns with challenge.

"You can keep putting on this brave face, but I know what it feels like to have your entire life ripped away from you."

"What the hell do you know about it?" she snarls.

"I know the devastation that it leaves behind. I know how it feels to look in the mirror and not recognise yourself or your life. I know what it's like to yearn for something that's lost forever."

An aching sadness infiltrates the glimmering blue flecks in her storm cloud eyes, telling me all I need to know. I don't know why I want to help her so badly, but fuck me... I do.

"When you're ready to talk, you know where to find me," I finish. "You don't have to pretend around me."

With that, I gently push her aside then walk past her into the conference room, holding the door open for her to follow. Ember doesn't meet my gaze as she scuttles in, her head ducked.

She looks oddly vulnerable. Afraid. Like she can't even contemplate the vast reach of her own demons, and acknowledging them will open floodgates that will never close again.

We might have rescued her.

But I don't know if we can save her.

CONFIDENTIAL
Suspect
DO NOT CROSS
POLI
Suspect?
NOT CROSS
POLICE L

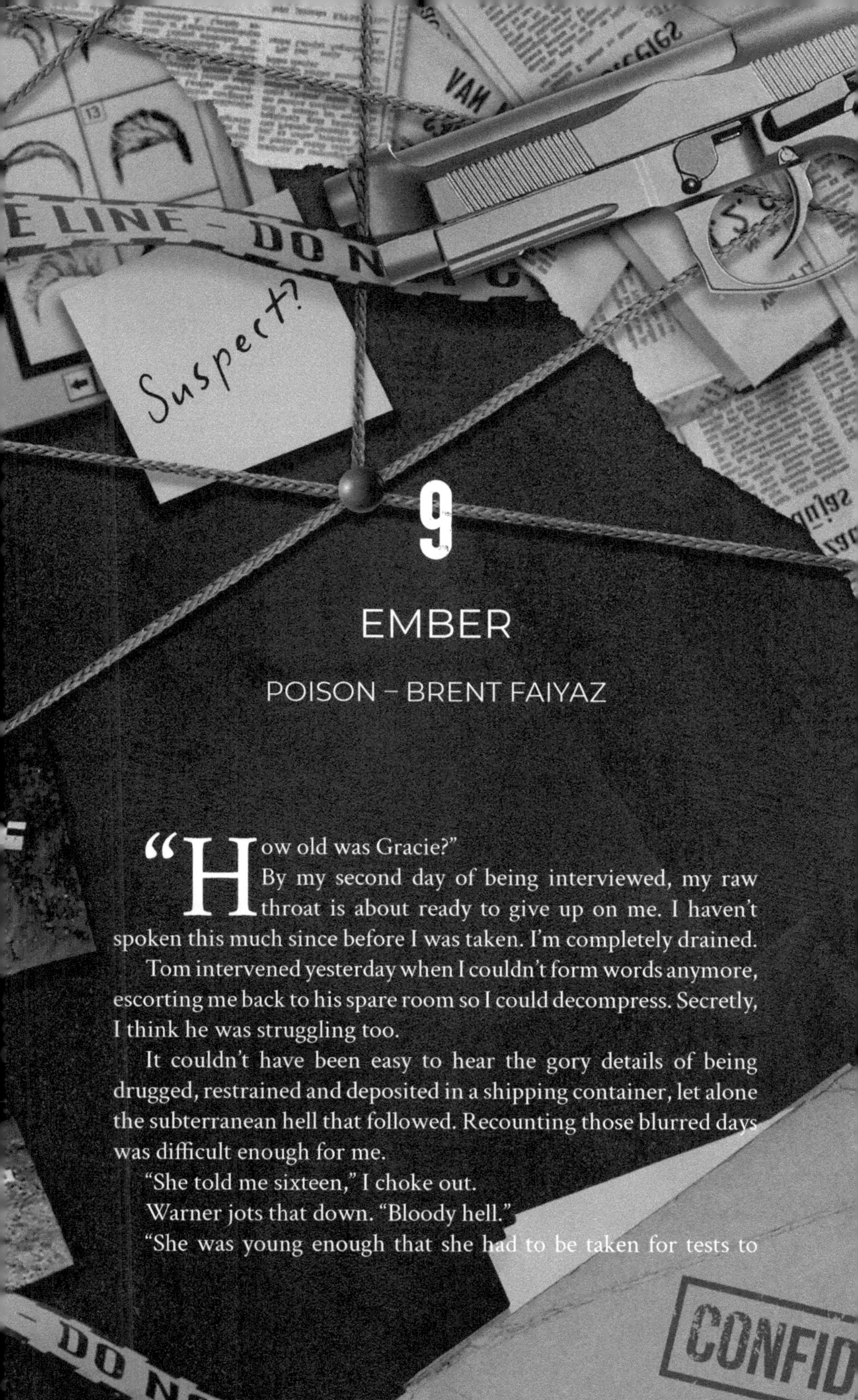

9

EMBER

POISON – BRENT FAIYAZ

"How old was Gracie?"

By my second day of being interviewed, my raw throat is about ready to give up on me. I haven't spoken this much since before I was taken. I'm completely drained.

Tom intervened yesterday when I couldn't form words anymore, escorting me back to his spare room so I could decompress. Secretly, I think he was struggling too.

It couldn't have been easy to hear the gory details of being drugged, restrained and deposited in a shipping container, let alone the subterranean hell that followed. Recounting those blurred days was difficult enough for me.

"She told me sixteen," I choke out.

Warner jots that down. "Bloody hell."

"She was young enough that she had to be taken for tests to

determine if she was a virgin."

Features crumpling in a disgusted look, he continues to take fast notes. "What kind of tests?"

"There was a doctor. He worked for the cartel."

My eyes remain fixed to the conference table. Beads of water condensate on my glass, rolling down the clear surface to pool on the table. Each rivulet sparkles like an individual teardrop.

Warner audibly clears his throat. "Were you tested?"

"Not for… that."

The entire room seems to draw in a collective breath.

"But all of us had examinations, measurements taken, questions asked. They wanted to know anything they could use to market us to their buyers."

"They did that to you?" Warner clarifies.

All I can do is nod, my voice failing.

"Em…"

"Don't say anything." I look up to cut him off. "I don't want to talk about this anymore."

"That's fine, Em. Take a breath for me."

Fingers anxiously twisting together, I fight back flashes of the doctor's thin lips, beady eyes and hooked nose. He looked like a rat. A revolting, invasive rat. The kind that bites to kill.

Giving me a few moments to steady myself, Warner ceases notetaking so he can watch me breathe. I struggle to lift the water glass in my trembling hand to sip, but thankfully, no one mentions it.

"Okay," I grit out. "Let's continue."

"We will track down Gracie's identity and get in touch with her family." Warner quickly moves on. "It won't be hard to correlate missing persons reports with your intel."

"I don't know if she's still alive."

"I'm sure they will want an update regardless."

All I have to offer is another nod. If I speak, I'm scared every last shameful taunt my mind is whispering at me will come flooding out. How I failed Gracie. Left her to be ripped apart by animals. And never returned.

It doesn't matter that I spent all that time fighting my own war.

She needed someone to keep her safe, and I promised to do that. I promised I wouldn't leave her alone. Now I have to live with the knowledge that I abandoned her.

"Em?" Tom murmurs to me. "Do you need to stop?"

"No. Keep going."

Reaching for the water again, I take several more gulps. The distant thuds of where Axel's feet knock into the ground as his legs jiggle fills the silence. He can never seem to sit still.

"Tell us about Blaine Madden," Warner redirects to safer ground.

"You already know what happened."

Warner gestures towards the voice recorder between us. "For the record."

Placing my glass down, I lace my fingers together then drop my chin on top to hold my head up. "Fine."

Tom continues jotting notes in a legal notepad between worried glances in my direction. He's on his third black coffee already. Hyland has remained silent from his perch in the corner, staring at his scuffed boots.

Sabre's newest recruit—bald-headed Archer with his intense silence and cutting gaze—joined us yesterday. I'm relieved he isn't here today to study my every move. He's an odd guy.

"Blaine intercepted me in the changing room after my last fight." I lick my dry lips. "His team had taken out my trainer, Carlos. They paid off security to allow us to slip away from the club."

"Carlos?" Warner tilts his head.

"Morello. He's high-ranking in the cartel."

Nodding, I watch Warner write his name down then circle it several times. He's been scribbling thoughts at random on top of recording the interviews as he pieces my tale together.

Axel squeezes a bright-yellow stress ball between his hands. "How many in Madden's team?"

"Um... Three. Two male, one female. She was called Raye. Short blue hair, lots of piercings, real shitty attitude. I can't really remember what the men looked like."

"Tom?" Warner looks up at my brother.

"Yeah, got it," he replies while writing fast. "I'll check it out, but from memory, I don't recall a Raye from our criminal case."

"Check anyway. He found allies from somewhere, and the Madden empire was reduced to rubble. I want to know how he's paying for their loyalty."

"Who is this guy?" I look between them.

Pinching the bridge of his strong nose, Warner sighs. "Someone with a grudge against Sabre and our team. We put him away for his family's crimes. I don't know what his angle is now."

"I helped build an airtight legal case against his family before Madden was arrested." Tom places his fountain pen down. "He was convicted and serving a hefty sentence when he escaped custody."

"Who escapes prison that easily? And isn't found?"

"Someone with inside help," he answers.

"You think he's that well connected?"

Tom nods solemnly. "I know he is."

"How?"

"The Madden family has ties to London's criminal underworld dating back a whole century. In their heyday, they ran this city and every illegal import inside it. They're bad news."

"The point is…" Warner easily controls the conversation. "Madden helped you to ingratiate himself to us despite hating our guts. We need to know why."

"I already told you everything I know. He didn't hurt me. Hell, he even cut the tracker out of my arm before he gave me the phone then chucked me out."

A short, surprised silence follows until it's broken.

"A tracker?" Axel strangles his stress ball.

Warner has stilled, his attention fixed on me. "You didn't mention that before."

"You saw my bandage."

"They put a tracker in you?" Tom demands.

Wincing, I look down at the table. "It was surgically implanted by Gael's physician."

"Fuck!" Axel spits a curse.

"Raye sliced it out of my arm. They took it with them to throw Gael's men off the scent."

"What the hell?" Warner rakes a hand through his hair. "That is just so screwed up."

Rolling up the sleeve of my loose, blue dress shirt, I try not to focus on the thin scars that encircle my wrist. The adhesive bandage I stole from Tom's medicine cabinet is stark against my forearm.

Peeling back the edges, I tilt my arm to show them the raised, stitched wound. It's healing well. Madden's stitches are neat and regimented in perfect, symmetrical lines.

"Gael couldn't have his property wandering off, right?" I say bitterly. "Had to keep it chipped and tagged like a mutt."

"What's that?" Axel grinds out.

Feeling the weight of his agitation fixed on me, I realise he's referring to the ugly burn mark near the wound. It's been concealed so far, but now the lumpy scar is on full display.

768.

It's odd how three little numbers can define your entire existence. Chip away at your identity and damn near rewrite your entire life story. To remain Ember, I had to preserve my mind. I had to block it all out. I had to compartmentalise. Bury the pain. Then fight.

"My name."

"Looks like numbers," he replies pointedly.

"Well, it's my asset number. That's the only name I was allowed."

"An asset number?" Warner parrots.

"We all had them. Every last woman he bought or sold."

A sudden, loud smash causes my head to snap up. Across the room, a framed piece of abstract art has been flung onto the floor. The frame scatters all around Hyland's vibrating frame.

"Breather," Warner barks at him. "Now."

"I'm going to destroy that motherfu—"

"Now! Out!"

Slamming a hand against the wall, Hyland doesn't look at any of us while storming from the room. The door crashes shut behind him, creating a loud reverberation.

"I'm sorry." Warner fixes a forced smile in place. "He's protective. Even with people he doesn't know well."

I want to laugh. *Protective.* More like a prying, confusing, hot and cold asshole.

"Let's refocus." He clears his throat. "We need descriptions of all the clubs you fought in. We've already moved Mexican authorities in to close the locations we were scouting out."

"A lot of it is super blurry. I wasn't given much information."

"Whatever you have is better than nothing. We also need a description of Gael's estate so we can begin looking. I'm not waiting for him to track you down first."

The implication sends chills down my spine. We all know that Gael is already searching for me. I was told about the online chatter that followed my grand escape.

He'll be out there right now, turning over every last grain of sand to find me. Gael has connections that extend beyond his homeland. His poisonous roots reach South America and even across the globe.

I'm not safe here.

I'm not fucking safe anywhere.

"Hyland will remain assigned as your personal security," Warner continues crisply. "You're to remain under our protection as a cooperating witness."

"Great. More imprisonment."

"We're trying to help, Em."

"I know." I wrestle with the rising frustration inside me. "How did you even end up in Mexico? You never explained what led you there."

Pausing, Warner looks at my brother. "A suspect in your kidnapping was identified early on. He left the country not long after you. We arrested him about eight months ago when he returned to the UK."

Frigid cold flushes over me. "Charles?"

From his seat, Axel snickers. "That's such a shitty fake name."

"Seconded," Tom agrees.

"How did you find him?" I ask curiously.

"CCTV footage from the docks," Warner answers. "He's a trained professional—fast, efficient and damn near invisible. It's pure luck that we later caught images of his team leaving."

"But you couldn't track us down?"

"That dock exports half a million shipping containers every

year." He massages his creased forehead. "We searched for months but couldn't narrow it down."

Head buzzing, I try to recall my date that night. We went to a cheap pub in Liverpool, far from the student-orientated clubs and bars.

It was nondescript, perhaps a little rough. But I didn't care about niceties. When Charles offered a nightcap at his place, it didn't occur to me that I was walking into a dangerous situation.

Opening up a manilla folder, Warner rifles through thick stacks of paperwork. He flourishes a glossy photograph then slides it across the table towards me.

"Does he look familiar?"

"Oh my God. Yes."

Nausea crawls up my throat at the ghost staring back at me. It's boring Charles but not. The tightly-buttoned, strait-laced bore I dated looks vastly different in jeans and a slouchy t-shirt.

I don't recognise the three thugs with him. There were others that night, transporting us to the docks to be offloaded. Between the terror, drugs, and six traumatic years since then, their faces are a blur to me.

"Tanner Stillwell," Warner reveals. "Thirty-five years old. Spent the last six years bouncing around South America, judging by his passport."

"It's him."

"We partnered with international law enforcement to track him down, but the man vanished for years. This was clearly not his first rodeo. You were just the final delivery before he split."

My hand shakes as I lift the photograph. "I knew it. He's some kind of honeypot, isn't he? That's his role in this whole charade."

"Appears so. Lucky for us, he's a loose-lipped honeypot. It didn't take long to get enough information to trace you to Mexico. But his intel was limited beyond the basics."

"Loose-lipped?" I reiterate.

"They loosened with some encouragement." Axel playfully winks at me. "That was a fun two weeks. I didn't know that a man could shit himself in fear so many..."

"Ax," Warner scolds.

Pouting, he resumes massaging his stress ball. "Spoilsport."

Slapping the photograph down, I smash my clenched fist above the bastard's face. "Gracie was taken from her family because of him. I hope you tore him apart, limb from limb."

"I can give you the details." Axel smirks.

"I'd appreciate a play-by-play reenactment."

"Mmm, sadistic. My kinda woman."

Scrolling on his phone, Tom halts our exchange with a sharp inhale. All eyes turn to him.

"I found an old news report." He taps the screen several times. "Gracie Livingstone. Disappeared shortly before Ember, from Bolton. Presumed dead."

When he passes me his phone, a hot burst of sickness rises in my oesophagus. The report features a school portrait with a smiling, uninjured version of the young girl I tried to protect.

If Stillwell were here, I wouldn't need Axel's description of his agony. I'd fucking inflict it myself. That evil piece of shit fed Gracie into a system of exploitation and abuse. One she's still lost in.

"Where is he?"

"Prison," Tom replies. "Where we put him."

"He should be dead and buried!"

"Stillwell is one cog in a large, sophisticated machine." Warner steeples his fingers. "Gael's cartel could have any number of honeytraps operating across the globe. His operation is beyond vast."

Each bleak word breezes over me unacknowledged. All I can do is stare at Gracie's young face. The same face that I last saw warped and misshapen to the point that she was unrecognisable as this sweet, carefree girl.

I tried so hard to escape Gael and his men before I was carried away. Even when I was re-cuffed and stabbed with a hypodermic needle while Luis negotiated my price.

It still wasn't enough to escape their bondage. The last thing I saw before the room faded into nothingness was Gracie's terrified face, mouth frozen in an 'O' as she screamed my name.

"We need everything you have on those involved in your captivity." Warner doesn't realise I've checked out. "Don't leave a single person out, Ember."

"Stillwell is still in HMP Wakefield," Tom chips in. "The place is a shit hole. We could run Ember's intel past him, try a little bribery. See who he'll verify as key players."

"Send the interview request."

"He's just a foot soldier." Axel stands up to begin pacing the room. "Stillwell won't know shit."

"We have to start somewhere," Warner reasons.

"No, we need to identify who's organising the shipments from the UK to Mexico. Someone official who knows what's in those containers."

"We tried that angle years ago," Warner dismisses his suggestion. "Spent months interrogating freight workers, dockyard bosses and even executives from the shipping firms. We didn't find a scrap of evidence."

"Then who is being paid to keep quiet?" He throws up his hands.

Between their back and forth, no one has stopped to realise that I've inched my chair backwards from the conference table. The longer I sit there, the louder Gracie's photo screams at me.

When I abruptly stand up, Tom turns to me. "Em? You okay?"

My tongue feels thick and heavy in my mouth. "I... N-Need to get out of here."

"Okay, trouble. We can be finished for today. I'll take you home."

"No... Not there. Not... Fuck!"

Words mixing and jumbling, I can't vocalise the riotous confusion running through my mind. My thoughts have scattered in the rising winds of fury, sending me into a free fall.

The moment I lay down in his spare bed, I see women being brutalised all around me again. I can still hear their sobs when I remain awake at night. The begging and pleading. Agonised wails. Fists pummelling flesh.

Even at Gael's estate, the onslaught was relentless. Evil lurked around every corner. If it wasn't in the fights I was forced to endure, it was the sight of others being controlled and degraded while I remained untouchable.

"One date!" I lash out. "One fucking date, and I lost my entire life. Everything! And Gracie... She... She never even got to..."

Grabbing the back of my chair, I angrily fling it across the room. The metal legs crash into the wall, leaving a large dent. It still isn't enough to quell the fury corroding my insides.

"Em…"

When I feel Tom's hands landing on my arms, I recoil so fast, he stumbles backwards. My first instinct is to slam my fist into his face in case he's trying to attack me.

"No!"

"Okay." He backs off, hands calmly raised. "Just take a breath for me."

"I don't need to breathe… I need those animals burned alive! I need to know if Gracie is still out there so I can go find her and save her!"

"Ember." Warner circles the table to approach us. "I know you're angry—"

"Angry? Fucking angry?"

Grabbing my half-full water glass, I send it sailing into the wall next. The wet explosion satisfies me for half a second, then the red-tinged rage comes rushing back at full speed.

"I'm beyond angry! I need to do something!"

"You have to let us do our jobs," Warner attempts to explain. "It's what we're trained for. Give us all the information you can. We'll take it from there."

"Like you've been doing for the last six years?" I growl at him. "You didn't even find me first! Blaine fucking Madden did!"

Heartbreaking pain and regret flashes over his face. Regardless of Warner's role in keeping my case alive when the odds seemed insurmountable, I want to rage at him now.

Focused on him and my brother, I don't notice Axel's quiet approach behind me. He moves like a stealthy predator before resting a hand on top of my shoulder.

"Easy, Ember."

"Fuck off!" I hiss at him.

"Why don't you come with me?"

Shrugging off his inked hand, I glower at him.

"Or you can stay here and scream at people who don't deserve it." He cocks his head in question. "Your choice. But I have something that may help."

"Like what?"

"You've spent all this time fighting, right?" His usual grin is nowhere to be found. "That's what your body is craving right now."

The thought of kicking the living daylights out of something, anything, is enough to pique my interest.

"So I thought." Apparently, he read something on my face. "Come on."

Axel stretches out an inked hand, giving me a glimpse of his thick, layered tattoos up close. Two ornate timepieces are etched onto the backs of his hands, packed full of intricate details.

He wriggles his fingers in invitation. "You trusted me before, right?"

Reluctantly, I nod.

"Then trust me again. If there's one thing I know about, it's what you're feeling right now."

Not even the other two worriedly whispering to each other can break the strange emotion pulsing between us. It feels like a kind of kinship. An understanding. He recognises that I'm blinded by wrath.

My hand slips into his, my movements controlled by sheer desperation. I don't want to hurt Tom or anyone else, but I need to fucking hurt *someone*.

"We're just going to step outside while you two chat," Axel advises them. "Back soon."

"You aren't taking my sister anywhere!" Tom bellows.

"Last I checked, she's a grown woman. We'll be back."

"Not a chance!"

"Tom." Warner drops a hand on his shoulder. "Sit down. Let Ember take a breather while we review what we've got so far, yeah?"

"That man is a psychopath, and if you think I'm going to—"

"Bye, then!" Axel chirps loudly.

Turning his back on Warner attempting to hold a still-ranting Tom at bay, Axel steers me from the conference room. I can't even look at Warner. Not after what I said to him.

Exiting the room, the corridor is a haze all around me. I'm

thankful that at least Hyland hasn't stuck around and can't interfere. I don't know if I can lie to him again right now.

Axel keeps a tight hold on my hand, pulling me alongside him. We pass several offices and wind around the corner before coming to a stop outside a door labelled *Axel Slaughter — Anaconda Team.*

"My office." He scans the security pass attached to his belt loop. "Follow me."

Tailing him into the room, I do a double take. Rather than standard office furniture—laptop, desk, perhaps a chair or sofa—the room is dominated by a full-size boxing bag hanging from the ceiling.

"What the fuck?"

Axel shuts the door behind me. "My work doesn't really require a desk."

"Is your work beating up a punching bag?"

"Nah. Usually it's some wanker's face. Occasionally breaking a leg or two. Maybe an arm or skull. Sometimes dislocating a few joints or a shoulder or perhaps cutting off…"

"Axel!"

With a smirk, he heads towards the red-leather bag, hanging from metal chains. "Too much information again? My bad."

I walk over to join him by the bag. It's far enough from the tinted, high-rise window to offer a decent safety zone, though a messily organised bookshelf is in the near vicinity.

"You're up, dimples. The space is yours."

"Dimples?" I grunt, touching the supple leather.

"You've got a couple that pop out when you smile. I like them."

Staring into his honey orbs, I try to decide if he's pulling my leg. "You're so weird."

"As advertised."

The man who just freely admitted that his job role consists of punching people when he isn't breaking or dislocating their limbs… likes my dimples?

"Show us what you've got," he encourages, clasping the bag in place. "Get all that rage out before it eats you up inside."

"Why are you helping me?" My heartbeat hammers in my ears.

Axel shrugs, still wearing that curious smirk.

"That's not an answer."

"I have my reasons." He hikes up a shoulder.

"Which are?"

"Truthfully, I'm intrigued by you. I want to see what you can do. Or you can go back to smashing chairs and water glasses, if you'd prefer."

Looking down at my clenched fists, memories of how I gained each mottled scar across my knuckles fill my mind. Every last vicious, potentially life-ending fight. All the times I limped back to my room, barely able to walk.

I would do it all again if I could save her.

Hell, I'd take every blow twice over to set Gracie free.

"You need hand wraps?"

Shaking my head, I let my fist fly into the solid mass. The impact enrages my still-tender skin, bearing the marks of my last fight. The final bout of violence that did little to satiate my thirst for more.

Axel absorbs the momentum, stopping the bag from swinging too far. I smash my other fist into it. Then again. Again. Again. Each hit delivering another burst of relief to my soaring adrenaline.

Bringing both fists to my chest, I take a measured step forward then shift my weight onto my left leg. My right flies forward in a powerful kick, slamming the ball of my foot into the bag.

"That's it." Axel nods, watching my tight form. "Nice."

After landing several hard kicks, I lunge forward to punch the bag again, landing a rapid combo. Every time the leather kisses my aching skin, the relief increases exponentially.

His head peeking around the bag, Axel appraises me. "Feel good?"

"More."

"Fuck yeah. I love watching you move like that."

Stopping for a breath, a dark-purple blur streaks across the room before it crashes into me. The momentum propels me backwards until I land sprawled across the office carpet.

"Axel!"

"What, dimples?" He rolls us so he's braced above me. "Can't take a real person?"

"You're fucking insane!"

"Meh. Old news."

Bucking my hips, he lurches sideways before I punch him in the gut. Axel grunts in pain, bracing a hand on my right side to stop himself from sliding off my body.

"Get off me!"

"Make me," he taunts.

"What the hell are you on?"

"I said make me! Fight back!"

Hitting him again, I aim higher to punch him in the patterned sun rays that cover his throat. Axel chokes on a laugh, the sound cut off by his hissing breaths.

His hand flashes out, seizing a handful of my braid. Pain races across my scalp from the harsh tug. The crazy asshole is pulling my hair. Oh, I'm going to fucking kill him.

"Come on!" he goads.

We trade fast blows—my fist connecting with his ridged abdominals, his fingers twisting my hair until tears prick at my eyes, our bodies thrashing and smacking together.

We're evenly matched as he meets my ferocity blow for blow. I suspect he's holding back because each time I think I'm getting the edge on him, he deftly cuts off my next move.

When his forehead smacks into mine, causing my teeth to clang together, I see stars for a few seconds. Then I hit back, managing to punch his round jaw hard enough for him to curse.

Rolling us over, I've stolen the advantage when Axel comes to his senses and quickly flips us back to our original position. He has more muscle mass than me, though not by much.

"You're decent," Axel tries to antagonise me. "But I expected better."

"You wouldn't survive my best, dickhead."

"Oh, ho. Fighting talk."

"You bet."

If I had a weapon, I'd be driving it into his throat right about now. I'll have to settle for fighting dirty instead.

Writhing beneath him again, I force his body to rise up long enough to expose his denim-covered crotch. My knee lifts rapidly, slamming between his legs.

"Bitch." Axel's eyes bug out comically.

"Been called worse."

Hands braced over his crotch, he slumps to the side, allowing me to throw him off. While the crazy bastard half-laughs and half-moans, I sit up to rub my sore head, feeling where he's rumpled my braid.

"My hair? Seriously?"

"That was a cheap shot," Axel admits, his legs curled inwards. "So was kneeing me in the dick."

"Well, it takes one to know one."

"Fair. It's a draw."

Slumping on the carpet once more, we lay side by side, both gasping for air. My limbs are humming with energy, but at least the screaming voice has quietened. For now.

"You want to go again?" He rolls over to face me.

"Nah. I feel better."

"Like you can think straight and pretend to be a regular human again, right?" He chuckles under his breath. "You know where to find me when it wears off."

Twisting, I look at him. "How do you know it will?"

"You're not the only one who was conditioned by violence. I know how that addiction works. This right here is the only rehab people like us will ever get."

Curiosity loosens my lips.

"What happened to you?"

His Adam's apple lurching betrays a hidden tale. "I wasn't always an orphan. And I wasn't always angry."

Waiting for him to reveal more, I watch the conflicting emotions filter over his cute features. For once, the jokes and banter have stopped.

"Life had other plans for me, I guess."

"When did you lose your parents?" I dare to ask.

"I was thirteen."

"That's young."

His long, inked fingers smooth out his purple faux hawk. "And I didn't lose them. My mother just decided to drive a knife through

Dad's gut while he slept and land herself a life sentence. Hence orphan."

"Oh my God."

"Yeah, that's most people's reaction."

In the quiet solitude of his office, I can finally see past the humour and jesting. Past his incessant playfulness and constant need for stimulation. Past every last defence mechanism he protects himself with.

And I see a kid.

A lost, angry, lonely kid.

"I walked in on her sobbing next to his dead body, knife still in hand." Axel's eyes cloud over. "Had to call the police myself. She was taken away in cuffs, and I ended up in foster care."

"You found them?" I breathe unsteadily.

"Her screaming was hard to ignore. Turns out, he was having an affair for the best part of a decade. That's why she had a breakdown and killed him in cold blood."

I've seen some harrowing shit, but this is next-level traumatising. No wonder his brain is wired differently.

"Whatever you're about to say, don't bother. I've heard it all from foster parents, bullshit therapists and the know-it-all shrink Warner made me see when I joined the team."

"I've never really gotten on with therapists either," I empathise. "My mum had multiple sclerosis. I was grown up when she passed away, but Tom convinced me to see a grief counsellor."

"How'd that go?" Axel snickers.

"Didn't quite work out."

"Can't talk your way out of some things."

"But I can punch my way out of them?" I counter.

"Is that so crazy? I didn't have to fight like you did, but after what happened, I sure wanted to."

Studying his bee-stung lips and youthfully rounded face, it isn't hard to imagine a younger version of Axel. The child embroiled in a tragedy and left to fend for himself,

"I know that feeling."

He touches the tip of his index finger to my cheek, a crease between his brows. I can feel his pain-hardened callouses on my skin, the roughness causing tingles to spread.

"Maybe you can find a way to use all that anger," he suggests.

"Like you have?"

His lips curl in a grin. "Exactly."

"What are you suggesting?"

"Got an idea. May take some convincing."

His fingertip circles the dips in my cheeks until he's stroking along my jawline to my parted lips. Axel traces the outline of my mouth, pausing on my split lip, his pupils expanding wide.

Each reverent touch makes my pulse thrum with a feeling I haven't experienced in a very long time. Something akin to want. Urgent need. Desire. Something I couldn't allow myself before.

"Convincing who?" My whisper is barely audible.

Axel shifts, his head nearing mine. "Everyone."

He's close enough for his breath to swipe across my over-sensitised skin. The rich, earthy smell of coffee blends with his own unique scent—a perfect balance of tantalising musk and enticing spice.

Axel embodies danger. Threat. Calculating strength. Yet the playful curiosity pouring off him creates space for a different side. A partially concealed, vulnerable soul behind his jokes and brutality.

Our noses nudge, bodies lightly brushing on the carpet. The danger flickering in his eyes feels like it's calling my name. Offering unconditional acceptance and recognition of what the anger that's taken root inside me desires.

It desires acknowledgement. Release.

And he can see that clear as day.

"If you need to punch something again, I'll happily volunteer my face. Free of charge."

A shudder rolls over me. "How thoughtful."

"What can I say? I'm a giver."

"Can't relate," I reply quietly. "I'm a taker."

And that's exactly what I'm going to do.

The gap between us feels like leaping across a deep cavern without hope of reaching the other side. But for the life of me, I don't care to examine the recklessness of doing exactly that.

Axel's lips are firm, all-encompassing, the swell covering my mouth and leaving no room to second guess the risk I've taken. His kiss betrays no hint of hesitation nor concern for what we're doing.

The initial kiss dissolves into another, then another, until his mouth is moving confidently against mine. I kiss him back with the same enthusiasm, desperate to relieve the ache inside me.

His fingers thread into my hair, pushing loose tendrils back where they've escaped my braid. Fingers press against my skull, holding my head in place as his tongue darts out to swipe across the seam of my mouth.

With a gasp, I relent and grant access. His hot tongue thrusts into my mouth, dancing against mine as he catalogues my taste. Explosions have begun to detonate in my belly, creating intense waves of need.

I bunch my hands in his baggy shirt, the over-washed cotton soft and worn. He has zero regard for Sabre's smart dress policy. Just like he has no regard for what anyone else thinks about him.

The kiss softens, our lips entangled and breath trading places. Somewhere along the way, my leg has hooked up on his hip, bringing us flush together. The hard press of his muscles send heat flooding straight down south.

"Axel," I moan languidly.

"Yeah." He rests his forehead against mine. "I know. We should get back before they come looking for us."

His raspy voice is barely audible through the roaring in my ears. Distantly, I realise this was probably incredibly stupid. Not to mention crazy after all I've seen since a man last touched me like this.

But I don't care.

Not when I've lost so much.

For the first time in so long, I've taken something for myself. Something I wanted. And it felt fucking amazing. I want to take more and fill this aching chasm inside my chest.

"I guess so." I release his t-shirt. "Um, what exactly do you need to convince everyone of?"

Excitement widens his smile.

"You joining Sabre Security."

CONFIDENTIAL
Why?
Suspect?
Gael?
DO NOT CROSS
POLICE LI

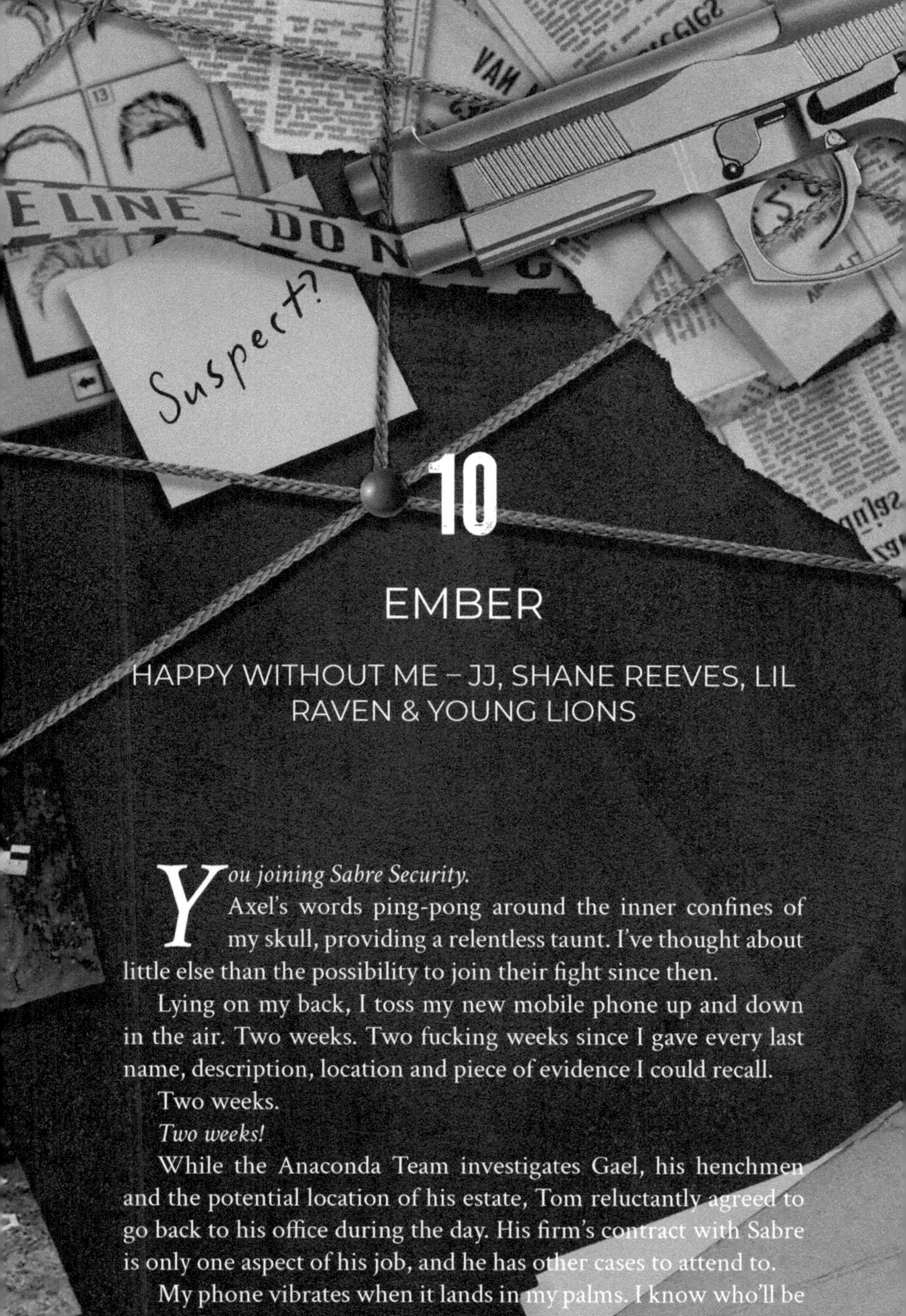

10

EMBER

HAPPY WITHOUT ME – JJ, SHANE REEVES, LIL RAVEN & YOUNG LIONS

You joining Sabre Security.

Axel's words ping-pong around the inner confines of my skull, providing a relentless taunt. I've thought about little else than the possibility to join their fight since then.

Lying on my back, I toss my new mobile phone up and down in the air. Two weeks. Two fucking weeks since I gave every last name, description, location and piece of evidence I could recall.

Two weeks.

Two weeks!

While the Anaconda Team investigates Gael, his henchmen and the potential location of his estate, Tom reluctantly agreed to go back to his office during the day. His firm's contract with Sabre is only one aspect of his job, and he has other cases to attend to.

My phone vibrates when it lands in my palms. I know who'll be texting me without having to check. The day that Warner delivered the phone after I went to buy clothes, Axel started spamming me.

Sighing, I check our conversation.

Axel: 🍔🌮🥟🍕

Ember: What the fuck?

Axel: That was me telling you I'm hungry.

That damn-fine kisser has a brain full of monkeys. His messages vary from out of context thoughts to random selfies and even the odd request for a photo back.

Ember: Then go eat, duh.

Axel: Warner's making me comb through maps of rural estates that fit your description. I've been staring at the screen for eleven hours.

Jolting upright, my thumbs race across the screen.

Ember: You found anything?

Axel: Nah. I'm gonna hand this over to the intelligence department.

Ember: Why didn't you do that in the first place?

Axel: I stuck a printout of Hyland's face on my target in the shooting range. Warner got pissed, and he knows I hate desk work.

Trying to drum up a response, I'm struggling to find adequate words. I've heard little from Hyland or Warner since we wrapped up my exhausting interviews.

While Warner investigates and Axel flirts, the complicated grump remains on security detail. I haven't ventured out much, but he's always there if I do, providing a constant shadow at a respectful distance.

Another message arrives.

Axel: Talk to meeeee.

Axel: I can still taste you on my lips.

Ignoring him, I drop the phone onto my stomach. His suggestion that I join their ranks and put my skills to good use is intriguing, but given their radio silence, I gather it didn't go down well with the others.

I'm not sure how much longer I can sit around, watching bruises fade from purple to yellow, itching to do something but stew. Literally anything.

When my phone buzzes again, I pick it back up with an annoyed sigh. Axel's a classic double-texter. AKA, he's a needy little fuck. Though I'd never admit to him that I quite like it.

Unknown number: How are the stitches healing, sweetheart?

A cold flush of recognition sweeps over me. Surely not. This is a brand-new number with encrypted text messages, courtesy of Sabre's programming. No one can find it. Especially not him.

Another message comes through.

Unknown number: Come to Unit 17b, Albatross Industries.

"Shit!" I jolt upright.

That ridiculous, aristocratic accent swims through my mind, calling me *sweetheart* before the psycho flung me out the back of the van. It's Blaine Madden.

There's a chance that someone else is trying to lure me in. I don't know who would know about his ridiculously British pet name, but I can't be too careful right now.

> Ember: How do I know this is you?

It's a few tense minutes before two back-to-back texts arrive.

> Unknown number: I told you I'd be more of a gentleman next time.

> Unknown number: Find me.

Indecision is a warring force, but the possibility of information seals my choice. I've been tearing myself to bloody shreds while battling night terrors and trying to be patient for two weeks.

No more.

Quickly dressing in the sports bra and workout leggings I found in a box of old work clothes, I throw my hair into a high ponytail before shoving my spare cash into my bra.

I'm twitching all over, full of anticipation and nerves. I have no idea what Blaine's intentions are, but if he wanted to harm me, he had ample opportunity. Instead, he saved my life.

I need to know why.

And I'm done being patient.

As I'm throwing on my running shoes in the hallway, the door clicks open with a loud buzz from the security system. Tom stumbles in, wearing his usual tailored suit and carrying a box of files.

"Oh, Em. Little help here?"

Rushing towards him, I wrestle the heavy box from his grip. "Did you lug this all the way home?"

"I had my assistant deliver it downstairs," he grunts, dropping his leather laptop bag. "So technically, only up four flights of stairs."

"You really need to start working out again."

"Probably," he admits through pants. "Between work, Jamie, life... I dunno, it never seems like a priority."

"Well, you're not getting any younger. Gotta keep up that

cardiovascular health."

"Oh, thanks," Tom says sarcastically. "You've hit the big thirty yourself now. So watch it."

"Ugh. Don't remind me."

Placing the box down on the floor, I roll my shoulders to relieve the slight twinge the weight created in my spine. While my injuries are healing up, I still get stiff.

"Are you going out?" Tom looks me over.

"I'm gonna take a run." I try for a placating smile. "Get some air."

His furrowed brows communicate his disapproval.

"I have security. I'll be fine."

"Well… Hyland is still parked outside glowering at everyone who walks past." He sighs through his nose. "Fine, but make sure you take him with you."

"Like I have a choice."

Reaching to tug my ponytail, Tom studies my face. "Everything okay?"

"Yeah," I lie. "Just need to get out of here."

Shucking off his suit jacket, he hangs it with the other coats and jackets next to the front door. While June has arrived with infrequent bursts of heat, the weather remains unpredictable.

"What did you do today?"

"Just hung out." I shrug listlessly. "Did some stretches. Watched some stupid dating show."

"Since when do you watch reality TV? You hate that shit."

"Since I've been declared a prisoner of your apartment building?" I joke flatly. "My life and business are gone, Tom. I have nothing else to do and nowhere to go."

"I'm sorry. That was insensitive."

"Don't worry about it."

Sympathy invades his expression, and it turns my stomach. It's no secret that I'm mourning the destruction of my entire existence while I was gone. But I don't want nor need his pity.

"I know you're bored out of your mind, Em."

Shrugging, I finish lacing up my running shoes. "What was your first clue?"

"You have the same look on your face as when Mum used to ground you for getting into scraps at school." He smiles at the memory.

"Those bullies deserved to be punched."

"I'm not sure she agreed, Em. You know her policy was *always be the bigger person.*"

An unexpected surge of grief infiltrates my mind. It isn't often that I allow myself to think of our mother. She struggled as a single parent, but even in the depths of her illness, she did the best she could.

I credit a lot of my determination to be independent and build my own life to her. Seeing her illness slowly steal everything from her—including her life—terrified me as a young adult.

"I don't have to go into the office, you know." Tom watches my facial expression. "It feels crappy, leaving you here alone with all this going on. I'd rather be keeping you company."

The thought of Tom hovering like a mother hen all day long and just waiting for me to break is infinitely worse than watching Destiny, the blonde Barbie from Beverly Hills, try to find love.

"You have a life and a career. I don't need you to babysit me."

"I know. I'm just worried about you."

With my laces secure, I reach up to press a kiss on his clean-shaven cheek. "Don't be."

"Isn't it kinda my job?" Tom teases, loosening his striped, blue tie. "If I didn't worry, I'd be a shitty big brother."

"Like you could ever be that even if you tried. I want you to go to work and continue living your life. Who knows how long the investigation is going to drag on for?"

Tom kicks off his shoes. It's his routine. He gets home after six o'clock most nights, yanks off his formal persona then snuggles up with me to binge watch TV.

While I love the normality of his routine—waiting for him to come home, bickering over dinner, gossiping about his boyfriend—it isn't enough. Pretending this is all normal is slowly killing me.

"You need to rebuild, Em. Find a new purpose."

"Like it's that easy. I can't even leave the apartment without a guard. We don't know who we can trust or who works for Gael.

I'm barely fucking alive!"

"Hey." He stretches out a hand to squeeze my arm. "I know this is hard, but we need to know you're safe while Gael is still at large. I won't allow him to hurt you again."

"The investigation could take years! I can't hide behind a bodyguard forever."

"You won't have to. With your intel, Warner and the Anaconda Team will hunt these bastards down. Once they've been apprehended, you'll be safe."

A million different versions of the bright future he's dangling in front of me dance through my mind, yet all I feel is hopelessness. I'll never live a normal life. Or return to the person I was. Or forget all that I've seen. Or sleep soundly without nightmares ever again.

Gael is too powerful to be caught. My life will always be under threat as long as he's out there, determined to reclaim his prized champion. That means I'm indefinitely stuck in this awful limbo.

Tom can't handle that truth, and I understand why. Just like I refused to entertain the specialists who told us that our mother's life was coming to an end. Sometimes, the truth is too much to bear.

"I only just got you back, trouble." Tom's voice cracks as his shining eyes duck to the floor. "Let me take care of you now."

Sealing my lips shut to trap my next complaint inside, I nod jerkily. He isn't trying to hurt or control me. I can see that. His protectiveness is how he shows that he cares.

As much as I appreciate his concern, I need control. I can't go another night tossing and turning, imagining the parade of battered women being shipped in and out of Gael's estate.

"I'm gonna get some air." I grab the light jacket and baseball cap hanging next to the door. "Eat without me. I want to do at least ten miles."

"You bloody health freak." He deflates with a strained smile. "Any requests?"

"Nope. Surprise me."

"Alright, Em. Be careful."

Taking my phone and my copy of his apartment key, I blow him a kiss. "Always am."

FRACTURED FUTURE

The moment the door clicks shut behind me, a tense breath heaves from my lungs. I love my big brother. But honestly, I'm about ready to remind him that I'm a grown, thirty-one-year-old woman.

With the cap pulled into place, I shove my phone and key into my pocket then take off. I'll have to play this smart. Hyland is monitoring the entrance to the building, and he can't know where I'm going.

At six thirty, he always swaps over with another Sabre agent. They rotate every twelve hours, allowing him to return home overnight. If I time it right, I can slip out during the distraction of the changeover.

With ten minutes to go until his shift ends, I hang out in the stairwell just out of sight. His blacked-out company SUV is visible outside, allowing me to watch him.

When another of Sabre's cars pulls up, parking a few metres ahead of Hyland, I zip up my jacket and tilt the baseball cap farther down to cover my face. I'll have only one shot at this.

Archer climbs out of his SUV, easily recognisable by his gleaming bald head and steely expression. I watch him approach Hyland's window so the pair can exchange words.

All it would take is one look for Hyland to spot me. Shit, I'm never going to slip past unseen. But when Archer points towards his car, my inner-meltdown halts.

Climbing out, Hyland gestures for Archer to show him something. The pair walk over to examine the rear tyre. It looks a little low from here.

Bingo!

While they study the tyre, I break out of the apartment and quickly dart away. They won't even know I've left if I'm careful, but I have to make this quick. Tom won't buy my story if I'm gone for hours on end.

Once I'm a safe distance away, I yank out my phone to check the location that Blaine sent me. I'll have to flag down a taxi to get across London to the industrial estate marked by the map.

This is probably a stupid idea.

But so was underestimating me.

After the taxi drops me off two streets from the industrial estate, I walk the rest of the way while taking in my surroundings. We're deep into northeast London, far from the chic residences of Marylebone.

The early summer sun hangs low on the horizon, casting streaks of red and pink across the tightly packed, metal warehouses. Evening shifts must be in full swing. The estate hums with noise and activity.

No one has tried to call or text me yet, so I can only assume my ruse hasn't been uncovered. Steeling my shoulders, I resolve to hunt down the address, confront Blaine, then book it home.

Easy, right?

Each manufacturing warehouse is labelled with printed signs. All manner of companies, small and large, hold factories here. The numbers pass in a blur as I walk between corrugated metal structures, counting into the teens.

14. 15. 16.

The next row of units roars with thumping bass music, blending into the constant soundtrack of urban life all around us. London is permanently loud and over-stimulating.

Unit 17a looks like a basic office for warehouse employees. Something to do with a delivery company, by the looks of it, though the blinds are drawn. I carry on to unit 17b.

More thudding bass music echoes from the structure, beckoning me inside. Searching for an entrance, I snake around the side, spotting a reinforced door set far back from the path. But it's guarded.

"Wasn't sure you'd show up," a voice calls.

Smoking a roll-up, a beefy man lingers outside. I immediately recognise his light hair and seemingly permanent glower from our introduction in Mexico. He helped Blaine to free me.

"You."

"Me," he deadpans.

Walking up to him, I keep my head on a swivel. "What is this?"

"Besides a stupid risk, fuck if I know. You alone?"

"Obviously."

"It's my job to protect the boss, lady. Don't bite my head off for asking the obvious."

"Your boss invited me here," I point out.

"Don't fuckin' remind me."

With a low curse, he wrenches open the rusted steel door. The sound of music grows even louder, accompanied by enthusiastic shouts and cheers. It's a familiar symphony.

"What is this place?"

"Nowhere special." He flicks his wrist dismissively. "But it's ours for the night."

Casting the thug a wary glance, I step inside the warehouse. It's dimly lit inside, the din intensifying when he slams the door shut behind us to block out the remaining daylight.

We're in some kind of backroom staff area. Not exactly what I was expecting. From the Post-it note laden bulletin boards to overflowing paper baskets and the lifeless coffee machine, it's an ordinary space.

"Not exactly a typical criminal haunt."

"You talk too much, woman."

"So I hear." I look around in a circle. "Have you got a name?"

"Spyder."

A snort rips free. "I'm sorry, do you think this is a TV show or something?"

"Keep your opinions to yourself around here." He glares ominously. "You'll get stabbed for less."

Grumbling under his breath about what a bad idea this is, Spyder leads me deeper into the unit. It's chilly, despite the summer warmth outside, with frigid shadows enveloping the space.

The farther we wind through metal shelving stacked with unlabelled boxes, the louder the shouts grow. After delving deep into the warehouse, a break in the labyrinth finally arrives.

Flickering lights and grunge music overwhelm my senses all at once. Surrounded by packed boxes and shelves, a large space has been cleared in the centre.

"Fucking hell," I mutter in shock.

"You should be used to this kinda thing."

Similar to the Mexican fight clubs I've become familiar with, the set-up is rudimentary but functional. Bloodstained concrete. A circle of onlookers. Two smoking thugs overseeing the fight taking place.

There are no barriers. Not a single wall nor rope to hold back the grappling pair in the centre. A full-on dogfight is taking place, spurring on the cries of all who watch their battle.

"She's savage," Spyder observes from beside me. "I wouldn't take that bet."

Blinking hard, it takes a moment to realise I'm staring at familiar blue hair. It's cut short and dyed the colour of a midnight sky, showing off ears laden with rows of multicoloured piercings.

"Yield!" Raye screams like a banshee.

"Piss off!"

The younger guy she's attempting to strangle from behind spits the insult back at her. They're well suited, both gangly and muscled, seemingly unafraid of close-contact confrontation.

"Come on, Lee," she cackles. "You can't beat me."

Despite his packed abdominals, visible without a shirt on, Lee seems to know he's screwed. The poor bastard is thrashing and flailing, trying to wrestle his way out of the headlock.

Every time he attempts to pull Raye off balance, she tightens her grip around his neck. For a relatively thin woman, she's unbelievably strong. I can't help but feel impressed.

"I'm bored now." Raye pretends to yawn.

"Fuuuuuck!" he screeches.

"That's it. Scream!"

One arm still locked around his neck, she smashes her fist into his face. Blood squirts from Lee's shattered nose, covering the concrete below. Still, she doesn't relent or show any mercy.

Another blow knocks him for six. He wavers against her body, clearly running out of steam. His fatal mistake was allowing himself to be cornered in the first place. Now he's done for.

"Do you yield, bitch?" Raye's spittle flies from her mouth onto his inflamed cheek.

Nothing.

Another direct hit to the face opens up a weeping cut above his eyebrow. My admiration increases when I notice she's dislodged a piercing, causing the hoop to tear free and fall to the floor.

"Argh!" Lee's wails mimic a terrified animal.

The sound only seems to fuel Raye's savagery as she lands punch after punch, trapping him in place with her arm while her fist goes to town.

"Yield! Now!"

Her racerback tank top reveals colourful floral tattoos up her arms and shoulders, both sweaty and tensed. She squeezes his throat to what must be excruciating proportions, her muscles rippling.

"P-P-Please," Lee wheezes faintly. "I yield."

His hand flaps in the air, finally begging for relief. One of the smoking men, clearly acting as a referee by presiding over the match, drops his cigarette to intervene.

"Time!" he calls out. "We have a winner."

Raye releases her arm, yelling for applause. The gaggle of onlookers go wild, screaming their praise and waving cans of beer in the air. I can't help but smile a little.

His knees giving out, Lee collapses on the concrete in a limp puddle. Two figures from the crowd come forward to drag his ass away while Raye saunters off to lavish in her victory.

She has to know where Blaine is lurking. Last I saw her, Raye was acting as his closest support. I'm about to follow her when the referee calls everyone to attention.

"Alright, alright! You know who's up next, but we don't have an opponent yet."

An odd hush falls over the warehouse. It's thick with palpable tension, silencing the applause and excited yells in an instant.

"Now you're in for a show," Spyder mumbles.

"How so?"

"Just wait and see."

Sweeping his gaze around the circle, the referee smiles broadly. "Who dares to challenge the Phantom himself?"

The... Phantom?

Circle parting to allow space, someone approaches the makeshift fighting ring. My whole body goes rigid, swarming with electric recognition.

I absently notice his half-shaved, tousled raven hair, visible facial scar and determined onyx eyes first. But honestly, it's his bare chest that grabs my attention and refuses to surrender it.

My throat dries.

Lungs seize.

Brain sputters in shock.

For someone who looks to be covered in more scars than skin, Blaine Madden sure doesn't seem to have a problem parading around in little more than denim and visible tattoos.

His defined chest is a harrowing sight to behold, littered with silvery marks. Long. Short. Mottled burns. Faded stripes. His pectorals, smattered with dark hair, boast small, circular marks.

Cigarette burns?

Despite this, Blaine doesn't show an ounce of hesitation. Suave confidence practically drips from his gait. Even his posture is self-assured—ripped shoulders back, head held high, black gaze fierce.

"Anyone?" His formal accent calls out. "Don't be shy now."

For an intimidating man who talks like a member of some upper-class, royal offshoot, he certainly doesn't look the part. Especially not bearing the marks of untold violence.

"Well?" Blaine grins at the room.

Not a single person volunteers or steps forward. I assume at least some of these people are part of his... well, organisation. Perhaps gang isn't the right word, if I want to avoid getting stabbed as Spyder warned.

Turning his back to face the other side of the circle, strong arms spread wide in challenge, I get a clear view of his spine. Ink swirls from the base of his neck to his tailbone, spelling out a phrase across each nodule.

My brain works fast. It's been years since I helped Tom study for his Latin finals as part of his law degree, but I remember enough to puzzle out the words.

Vincit qui se vincit.

"He conquers who conquers himself," I whisper to myself.

Spyder shifts on his feet. "He's always been a poetic son of a bitch."

"Won't anyone fight him?"

"Nah," he chuffs. "No one is brave enough."

Blaine rotates around again, his attention casting over the whole warehouse. When those coal-black irises land on me, swimming with awareness, a hot flush electrifies my skin.

We stare at each other across the warehouse, locked in an open appraisal. The scar that warps the entire right side of his face is stretched thin to accommodate the smirk that he unveils.

Realisation dawns at the sight of his little spectacle. The invitation. His grand, half-clothed parade. Looking to pick a fight.

Is he... showing off for me?

"If no one volunteers, it's luck of the draw," Blaine calls out. "Choose wisely."

The cocky psychopath is actually going to force one of these people to fight him. Even though they're all clearly terrified of whatever authority he holds over them.

Fuck that.

He isn't my boss.

I pull off my jacket to chuck at Spyder, already rolling my shoulders back. "Steal my shit and I'll be the one doing the stabbing."

"What do you think you're doing?"

"He wants an opponent. I'm willing."

Barking a laugh, he drapes my jacket over his shoulder. "Now this I want to see. You ain't gonna need your shit after the boss snaps your spine."

"Thanks for the vote of confidence."

Abandoning him in the crowd, I push through onlookers to approach the inner circle. Blaine's eyes widen with each step I take towards him. For the first time, he looks surprised.

"I'll challenge the Phantom," I call loudly.

All attention turns to me, accompanied by varying sounds of shock, awe and trepidation. If I wasn't preoccupied by Blaine's smirk transforming into a glare, I'd be amused.

"Not a chance." He shakes his head, hands on his tapered hips.

Circling him, I stretch my arms and joints. "Scared, Phantom?"

There's no way in hell he'll back down in front of the countless criminals gathered all around us. His reputation would be toast.

"What game are you playing?"

My eyes narrow in response to his glare. "You asked me to come."

"I did, but that invitation wasn't to fight." Blaine lazily trails his obsidians over me, shoulders rising with each breath. "You look good, sweetheart."

"I'm not here to flirt."

"Too bad." He cracks his knuckles. "Thought I owed you a drink."

"You do. Perhaps not here, though." I motion to our surroundings. "Is this what you do now?"

Blaine erupts in laughter that licks my alert senses. "Among other things."

"Things like rescuing the family members of the people who put you behind bars?"

Sobering, he openly appraises me. "I told you before, sweetheart. Spoilers."

"Right. Is that a second date kind of topic?"

"Depends on how the first date goes." Blaine rolls his neck.

Clearly, he isn't going to spill his grand master plan or provide any information about Gael so easily. I'll have to bargain with him.

"You have two choices here," I spell out. "Fight me or back down in front of your entire crew. But if I win, you're going to answer all of my questions. Including how you found me."

"That's a tall order."

"It's a reasonable bargain. Take it or leave it."

The referee looks to Blaine, then when he eventually receives a nod, he begins to call for bets. Suddenly, the murmurs around us erupt into blaring noise as everyone rushes to get a piece of the action.

"I suppose it would be un-gentlemanly of me to refuse your bargain," Blaine acquiesces with a wink. "Though I doubt laying you out would win me any brownie points either."

Stretching my legs, I can't hold back a laugh. "What makes you think I'd let you?"

Blaine shrugs, rolling his lip piercing with his tongue. "I've never lost."

"Well, there's a first time for everything. I'm going to enjoy ripping that inflated ego out of you by your throat."

Lips parting on a chuckle, he halts in front of me. He's close enough for the scent of peppercorns and bergamot to waft from his exposed skin and tickle my awareness.

Unlike Axel, Blaine isn't completely covered in tattoos. There are a few odd pieces dotted here and there—a feathery pair of angel wings dipping into his jeans, a geometric design above his left pec, scrawling text along his ribcage.

The urge to trace each intricate piece with my fingertips overwhelms me. It's quickly followed by a burst of irritation. This man threw me out of a van and abandoned me.

I'm not interested in him.

I just want his intel.

"This suits you."

"Fighting in a dirty warehouse?" I spread my feet in preparation. "Gee. Thanks."

"Standing by my side," Blaine corrects. "Surrounded by my people. In *my* territory."

"Cute."

Mouth now curled in a grin, he shamelessly looks me up and down. "You want to arrange that second date now?"

"Depends on the outcome of the first," I throw his words back at him. "And since this is a street fight… rules don't apply, right?"

Ignoring the bets being placed around us, I lunge at him to strike the first blow before the match has begun. Fuck the rules. I've had enough of cocky, self-entitled men… Even when they have a body like his.

CONFIDENTIAL
Why?
Suspect?
Gael?
POLICE LINE
DO NOT CROSS

POLICE LINE - DO NOT CROSS
Gael?
TIAL
DO NOT CROSS
POLICE L
8:20 AM
Incoming Call
Victim
Unknown

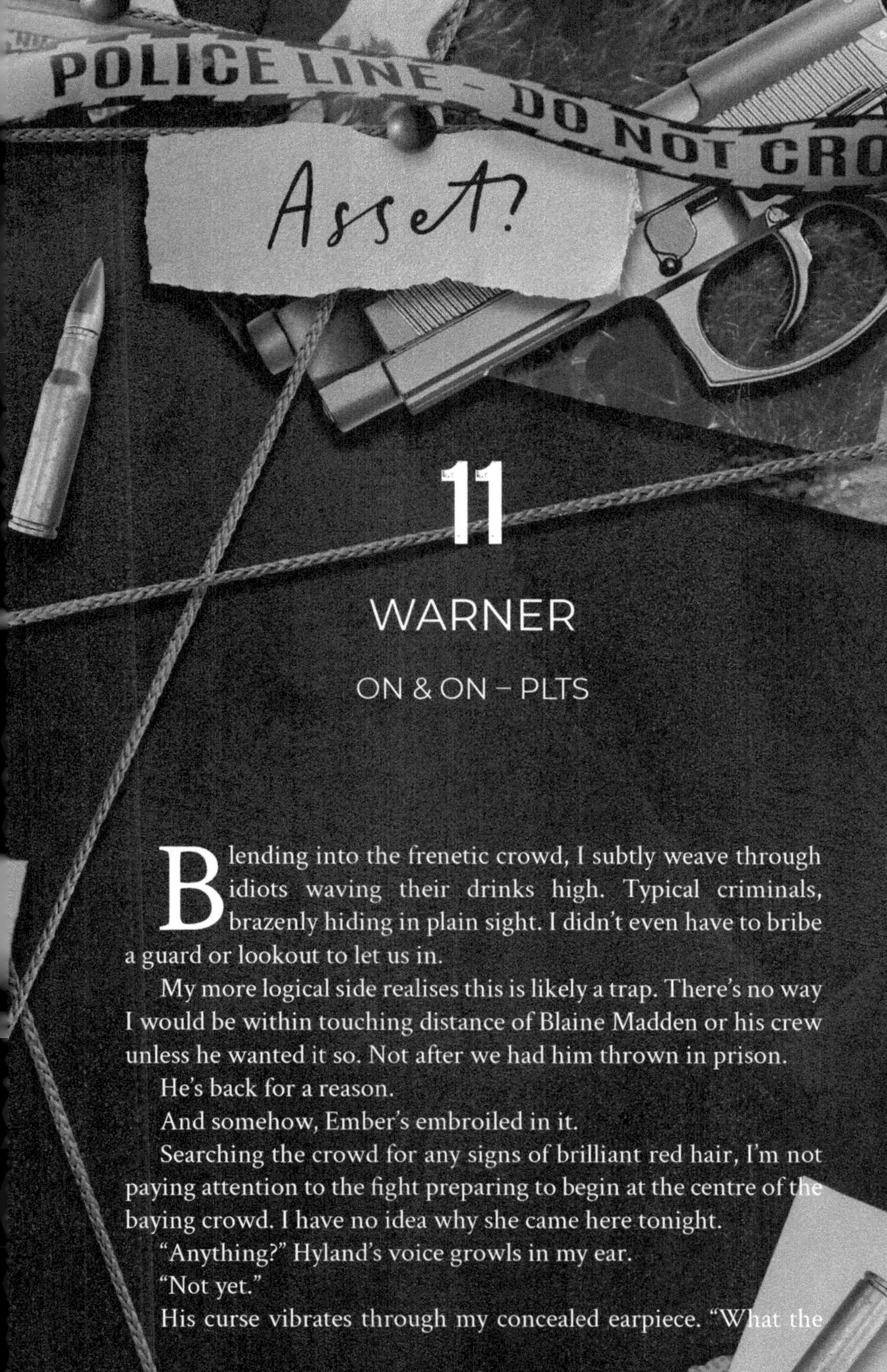

11

WARNER

ON & ON – PLTS

Blending into the frenetic crowd, I subtly weave through idiots waving their drinks high. Typical criminals, brazenly hiding in plain sight. I didn't even have to bribe a guard or lookout to let us in.

My more logical side realises this is likely a trap. There's no way I would be within touching distance of Blaine Madden or his crew unless he wanted it so. Not after we had him thrown in prison.

He's back for a reason.

And somehow, Ember's embroiled in it.

Searching the crowd for any signs of brilliant red hair, I'm not paying attention to the fight preparing to begin at the centre of the baying crowd. I have no idea why she came here tonight.

"Anything?" Hyland's voice growls in my ear.

"Not yet."

His curse vibrates through my concealed earpiece. "What the

hell is she thinking?"

"She isn't."

"If I hadn't checked her fucking tracker..."

Anger bleeding from his tone, he doesn't finish the sentence. Admittedly, using the standard-issue tracking software that we had added to Ember's phone is bending several of my morals.

However, our disregard for her privacy came in handy tonight. Without it, Hyland never would've realised that she'd slipped away, a fact he shared with us when he walked into our penthouse and promptly exploded.

"You check that thing often?" I prod.

"It's my job to keep her safe."

"Uh-huh."

"What does that mean?" Hyland snaps.

"Nothing."

Speaking of a lack of boundaries, he epitomises that exact red flag. I told him to head up Ember's security knowing full well that he'd protect her with his life.

The ways in which he achieves that can be eyebrow-raising at times. Of course, Hyland doesn't see it that way. But this isn't the first time he's gone above and beyond when protecting a client.

After all the shit he's been through, he developed an obsession for safety. Those harrowing memories have intensified his protective instincts to a new level of crazy.

"Oh, shit!" Someone next to me jerks. "She just went for him!"

"Is that allowed?"

"Hell if I know."

Brushing off my shoulder where the idiot shoved into me in his excitement, I peer through the crowd to make out the fight. I've investigated far too many of these seedy places to feel at ease.

A swinging, auburn ponytail causes alarm to slice into me. I hurriedly push through two more people, uncaring about subtlety. I'm too busy praying my eyes are playing tricks on me.

"Oh, fucking hell."

"What?" Hyland yells in my ear. "What is it?"

No wonder I couldn't find Ember in this turbulent crowd. She's in the middle of the circle, bouncing around like a live wire against some gnarly-looking guy with no bloody shirt on.

"She's fighting."

"Tell me you're kidding," he huffs out.

"Wish I was."

"What the actual fuck?"

My concern increases tenfold when the circling pair swap sides, both narrowly dodging the other. I get a glimpse of her opponent's face. Blinking several times doesn't reveal a different scene.

Blaine motherfucking Madden.

I must be tripping. Not only is that scheming snake in the country, and in my fucking city no less, but he's eyeing my best friend's little sister up like a meal he wants to devour.

"Madden is here."

"Blaine Madden?" Hyland repeats. "How?"

"He's up against Ember."

Several seconds of astonished silence follow.

"You copy?" I check under my breath.

"Yeah. Copy."

"There must be sixty odd people in here. Presumably some work for him." I cough into my hand to cover my words. "Even if you joined me, we'd still be severely outnumbered."

"Shit! Has she lost her mind?"

Unfortunately for us, Ember looks perfectly sane bouncing into Madden's personal space to jab at his midsection. The asshole lets her take a shot, a grin slicked across his face.

With Ember's strike levied, he shoves her left shoulder hard. She skates backwards, her running shoes scratching against blood-splattered concrete. It throws her off-balance.

"Come on, Em," I plead.

"Tell me what's happening."

"He's pushing her around."

"I'll kill him with my bare hands," Hyland snarls in a menacing tone. "Fuck prison. He'll be six feet under this time. Bones ripped apart and buried in pieces."

"As much as I agree with you, we need to play this smart. Get her out of here then deal with Madden once and for all."

"Yeah," he agrees, though his tone drips with reluctance. "I suppose so."

With Madden stalking towards her like a hungry lion set on devouring its prey, Ember seems to be outgunned. She's fast, but he has brute strength on his side.

Yet as he nears with his fists raised and a warehouse full of supporters cheering him on, something visibly changes in Ember's stance. Her back lengthens, red head thrown back and chin jerked upright in breathtaking defiance.

Hidden among the very criminals I've built a career hunting down, I watch Ember transform. Up until now, I've seen the cheeky little kid I grew up with when I looked at her. The sassy astronaut who always demanded my attention.

Hanging out at Tom's place was far better than returning home to divorcing parents tearing each other to shreds on a daily basis. Their home became my safe haven.

That brazen young girl quickly grew up, developing supple curves, shapely legs and lips so full they enticed me with each sassy barb she landed. It became a full-time job not to pay attention to every way her gorgeous body beckoned.

Watching her advance, ducking his wide swing to land a direct hit to his abdomen, I get my first glimpse of the new Ember. The one who survived six years working for the goddamn cartel and lived to tell the tale.

"Shit."

"Talk to me," Hyland pleads urgently. "Is Ember okay?"

"She's going for him."

"Fuck! Stop her!"

"I can't do anything."

Ember's enraged eyes narrow into slits, her lips mashing together and limbs tensing. She dodges two of Madden's strikes while landing her own shallow blows.

Seeing that man attempting to hit her boils my blood. I dismantled his entire operation once before. This time, I'll shred it down to the last fucking atom and bury him alive beneath the rubble.

But Ember isn't giving him the chance to take her down. She holds her own with practiced ease, dodging each strike and pivoting around him like they're waltzing rather than fighting.

This person isn't the girl I know anymore. She isn't even the battle-hardened survivor I've become familiar with in recent weeks. I'm seeing 768—the asset who survived unthinkable violence she can barely speak about.

"She's good, but she'll never beat the Phantom," a tattooed woman whispers on my left. "Who would dare?"

"I don't recognise her." The man standing next to her snickers. "Maybe she doesn't care about showing him up."

"Come on! Everyone knows who he is."

Unfortunately, we do.

The Phantom is exactly that—a ghost.

When Madden manages to sweep her feet and send her plummeting to the ground, I almost break cover. Even if it'll rain down the wrath of his organisation on my head.

How dare he touch her?

Ember lands heavily, but she braces her bent arms behind herself and flips up onto her feet before Madden can revel in the applause. Several gasps sound out all around me.

No one has time to take in the rapidly shifting power play. She's on him in an instant, landing two firm punches to his gut before following them up with a perfect roundhouse kick.

Madden stumbles backwards, absorbing the kick with that smirk still plastered over his face. The son of a bitch isn't just performing for the crowd, he's actually enjoying this.

Hell, it looks like Ember is too.

They're two flames dancing in each other's orbit.

"As much as I agree with you, we need to play this smart. Get her out of here then deal with Madden once and for all."

His loud exhale whooshes through my ear, his annoyance undeniable. "Be careful."

Darting forward, Ember wipes the smirk from his face with another powerful punch, this time to the jaw. Madden's head snaps sideways, a globule of saliva tearing from his lips.

"Go on!" I urge under my breath. "That's my girl."

"Are you… enjoying this?" Hyland mutters disbelievingly.

"You should see her. She's talented."

"I don't want to see her getting beaten up! Fuck!"

Another skilful kick lands Madden flat on his ass. The crowd can't seem to decide whether they should be applauding or booing while watching the fight unfold.

I've seen the Phantom fight before on numerous occasions. Back when we were investigating his family for single handedly propping up London's drugs trade, I infiltrated several of their shady clubs.

Their business model was clever. Hiding an illegal empire behind legitimate business ventures like bars, casinos and strip clubs, they concealed their misdeeds while drawing in a captive audience to purchase their wares.

Blaine Madden fought regularly at the street fights his father used to organise. I've seen him prance around bare-chested and bloodied more times than I can count while doing surveillance.

This isn't his best.

Sure, Ember's very good. Her skill and the ease with which she manipulates the fight is undeniable. But Madden is obviously thrown off by something.

The way he looks at her...

Beyond my relief at finding her safe and sound, I've maintained a professional distance. She's my client first and foremost. But perhaps more importantly, she's my best friend's baby sister.

Now this motherfucker is looking at her like she's his new favourite toy, and fuck if I don't want to tear out his eyeballs with my bare hands, grind them into a paste and feed them back to him before I slit his throat.

Looming over Madden, Ember appears to whisper something to him. Despite blood dripping from his pierced lip, he's lounging on the ground like he doesn't have a care in the world.

Ember straightens like she's about to walk away. At the last second, she twists her body around to deliver a final, bone-crunching strike that leaves Madden star-fished across the ground.

There's no applause. It's as though no one knows how to react as Ember wipes sweat from her forehead with her bare arm. The warehouse pulses with energy when Madden drags himself up.

He peers up at Ember, a trail of blood now dripping from his chin onto his heaving pecs. Concern intensifies in my chest at the long, loaded look silently shared between them.

Then he claps.

The Phantom fucking *claps*.

Cheers and applause form an ear-ringing cacophony all around me. Drinks sail through the air as toasts are exchanged at his apparent yielding. The yelling reaches an enthralled fever-pitch.

When Ember stretches out a hand to yank Madden up, I'm astonished to see that he takes it. Not only did he lose the fight, but now he's publicly accepting her help.

"Warner?" Hyland rumbles in my ear.

"I'm here. She won."

"Ember… won?"

"Damn near knocked him out too."

"Ah, hell." He sighs. "Get her out of there before that cheering turns to something else."

"Copy. Be ready for a quick departure."

While Ember steps out of the circle and farther into the warehouse, Madden lingers behind to speak to the referee. I move fast, dodging through the still-celebrating crowd to catch Ember before he follows.

She's taking her jacket off a broad-shouldered thug when I get close enough to seize her elbow.

"We're leaving."

Startled, Ember turns her head towards me. "What the fu… Warner?"

"Right now. Move."

"What are you doing here?"

I manage to pull her slightly away from the man eyeing me like a piece of meat he'd like to pummel.

"Bringing you home, obviously. We need to go."

"No." She yanks her elbow from my grip, visibly seething. "I'm here to speak to Blaine. I want to know why he saved me in Mexico and what he wants from us."

"And you thought walking head-first into his territory, surrounded by his people, was a good idea?"

"Better than sitting at home like a prisoner and doing nothing!"

"You could've been killed tonight! Or even taken again!"

Ember scoffs, lips twisting in a sneer. "I can handle myself."

"Against bought and paid for operatives looking to drag you back to Mexico? Trained professional killers? Or Madden's insane crew?"

Throwing on her jacket, Ember's neck and throat have flushed a deep shade of pink. I have a feeling I'm going to be on the receiving end of her wrath shortly.

"You won't let me help. You won't let me fight. I can't even leave the house without an escort. What the fuck am I supposed to do?"

"Be safe!" I hiss back, checking to ensure no one is listening to us. "If you got taken again or worse... What do you think that would do to Tom? Or us? Or me?"

"Then give me the chance to fight back! Train me! Anything!"

Ember shoves my chest, stalking off towards the warehouse's entrance. Relief blurs with my shock at her words. Axel suggested something similar a couple of weeks ago, but I didn't pay much attention.

Is that what she wants?

I glance over my shoulder, a cold stab shooting through me when my eyes lock with Madden's midnight spheres. That stare always unsettled me, full of calculation and criminal greed.

He's still in the centre of the circle, surrounded by revellers. Madden pays them no attention. He clearly isn't here for their praise.

Indignant determination fills his face. The kind of determination that tells me he isn't going to surrender his new toy without a struggle. Lucky for him, I don't mind a fight.

Though I'll never admit it to anyone...

Ember's always been mine to protect.

CONFIDENTIAL
Why?
Suspect?
Gael?
DO NOT CROSS   POLICE LI

CONFIDENTIAL

Suspect?

DO NOT CROSS

POLICE

Suspect?

NOT CROSS

POLICE L

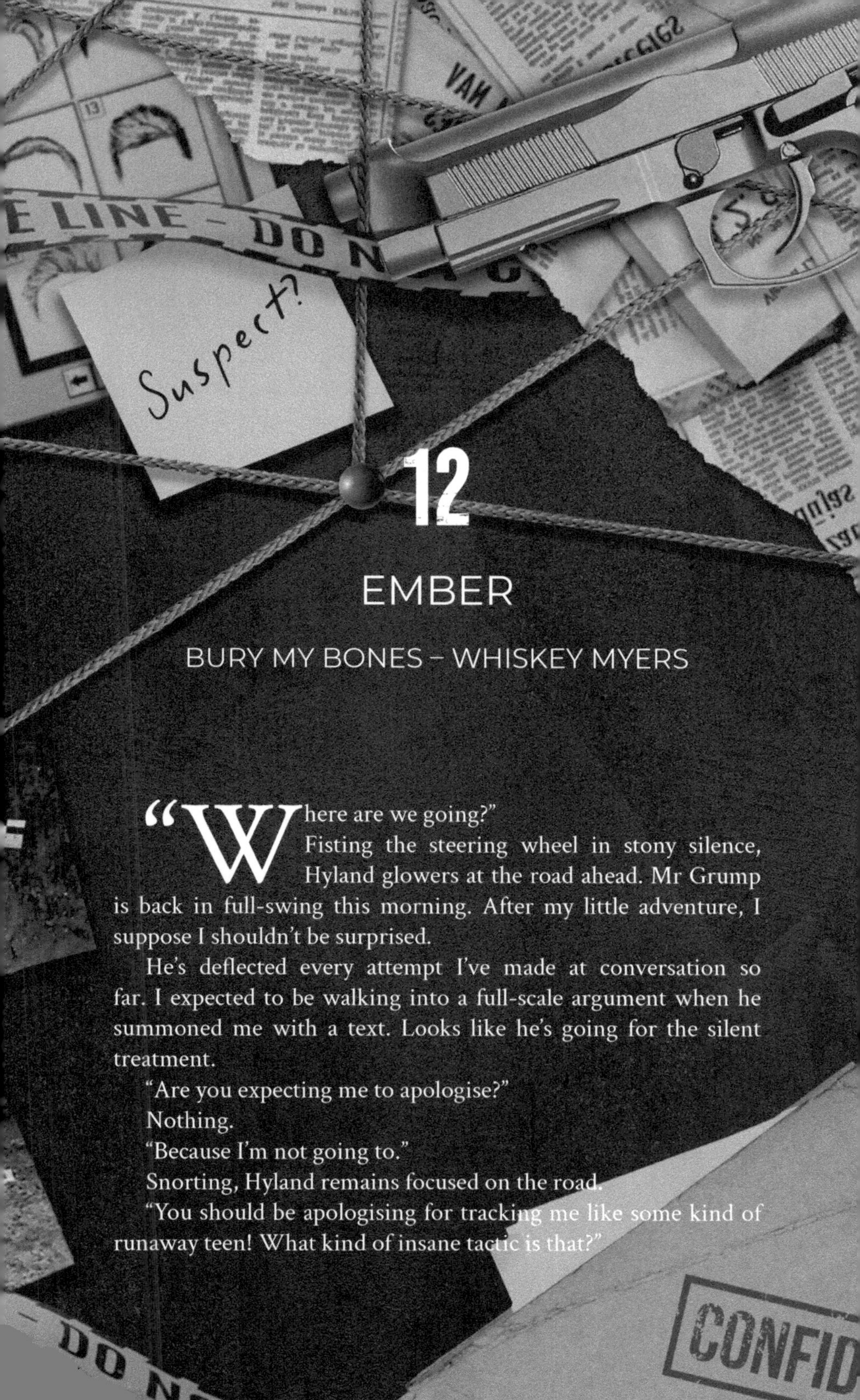

12

EMBER

BURY MY BONES – WHISKEY MYERS

"Where are we going?"

Fisting the steering wheel in stony silence, Hyland glowers at the road ahead. Mr Grump is back in full-swing this morning. After my little adventure, I suppose I shouldn't be surprised.

He's deflected every attempt I've made at conversation so far. I expected to be walking into a full-scale argument when he summoned me with a text. Looks like he's going for the silent treatment.

"Are you expecting me to apologise?"

Nothing.

"Because I'm not going to."

Snorting, Hyland remains focused on the road.

"You should be apologising for tracking me like some kind of runaway teen! What kind of insane tactic is that?"

Still not a peep. He just stares ahead, strangles the steering wheel and acts like he can't hear me.

"Fine. Don't talk to me, then."

Nothing.

"I won that fight," I say acerbically. "So if you're mad at me for sneaking out, perhaps you should pull your head out of your ass and realise that fact."

His stubbled jaw tics, betraying his annoyance. The grump is mightily mad. He can join the long line of people I've pissed off in the last twenty-four hours.

"If Warner hadn't intervened, I could've gotten answers. I know he has information about Gael! He found me! Blaine can help."

"Don't call him that," Hyland finally speaks.

"What?"

"That criminal piece of shit doesn't get to be on a first name basis with you."

My laughter bounces around the car. "Oh, grow up."

"I went back to that fucking warehouse last night to burn it down with him inside." His head shakes in disappointment. "Too bad the bastard had already cleared out."

"So you're mad because he outsmarted you?"

"I'm mad because he's dangerous, and you can't see that! You can't trust Madden!"

Studying his side profile, I try to fathom what goes on in his thick skull. Hyland is complicated. His hot and cold attitude gives me whiplash on a good day, but this feels like something far more complicated.

Neither of them had much to say to me on the drive back to Tom's apartment last night. I felt like the problem child being sent home from school. After Tom finished yelling at me, I curled up in bed with the sound of fists hitting flesh ringing in my ears.

But it was the first night since I came home that I didn't dream of Mexico. Gael's victims. The sound of my skull cracking against concrete. Endless nights spent battling to survive. Debilitating black outs and constant anxiety, never knowing when the next will hit.

My dreams were filled with bottomless onyx eyes and confident smirks instead. While I went looking for answers, I got something else from Blaine. Now I want more.

"I shouldn't have snuck out," I try to appease him. "But I don't regret going to look for Blaine. I'm a part of this case."

"You're the heart of it! And we're trying to protect you."

"I have the skills and the right to help."

Hyland harrumphs, scratching his light blonde scruff. "Be careful what you wish for."

Slumping in the passenger seat, I kick my legs up to rest on the dashboard. "I'm wishing you'd admit that you're salty about missing my fight."

"Hah. Dream on."

"You're totally jealous because I kicked Blaine's ass while Warner had you relegated to the role of getaway driver. I know I'm right."

"Delusional, more like."

His mouth twitches as he fights a smile. Hyland likes to pretend that he's all terrifying and aggressive with his insane height and stacked muscles, but I can see beyond that.

I worried him.

Because... what? He cares now?

Fuck if I know.

Looking out the window, I watch the dizzying heights of Canary Wharf rise above us. Beyond being the beating heart of London's business district, this canal-side suburb boasts multimillion-pound apartment buildings, endless cocktail bars and high-end restaurants.

At the feel of my phone vibrating, I quickly check my messages. I was half-tempted to leave it behind, knowing that the guys are tracking me. Seeing as I'm with Hyland anyway, it felt pointless.

> Unknown number: I want a rematch, sweetheart.

> Unknown number: If you still want those answers.

Lungs sputtering, I quickly shove my phone back into my

pocket. Blaine bloody Madden is the whole reason I'm in this mess. As much as I want to, I can't think about him or his fascinatingly scarred body right now.

When Hyland indicates right to pull into one of the huge apartment buildings' parking garages, tapping a code into the keypad so the barrier will rise, realisation hits.

"Wait. You live here?"

"Don't sound so surprised."

"I guess I am."

"Warner, Axel and I share a penthouse apartment here. We moved in a few years ago."

I know Sabre pays my brother's firm a small fortune for his legal jiu-jitsu, but I hadn't stopped to consider how the Anaconda Team has risen through the ranks too. They're top dogs now.

"How come I'm getting a magical mystery tour?" I joke dryly.

Hyland swings his SUV into a parking spot. "Team meeting."

"And I get an invite?"

Casting me a look, he doesn't answer.

Huh.

I climb out of the SUV, adjusting my blue jeans and tee. Tom turned his nose up at the big rip in the right knee this morning. While he's mad at me, he still found time to insult my style in typical brotherly fashion.

After fiddling with his sandy-coloured man bun, Hyland shoves a few loose tendrils behind his ears as we head inside. The doorman stands to attention when he sees us coming, the pair exchanging nods.

"One of yours?" I mutter.

"Yeah. James is on our pay roll."

He steers us over towards the elevators, glistening beneath modern glass chandeliers that illuminate the marble floors. Hell, this place is grand. It feels like some luxurious five-star retreat.

"We have 24/7 security, Ember. This line of work paints a target on your back."

"Speaking from personal experience?"

Hyland jabs the button for the penthouse. "Something like that."

The doors click shut, sealing us in the tight space. I'm drumming up another line of conversation to get him talking to me when Hyland abruptly spins around, barging into my space.

"Woah!"

I'm backed up by his intimidating frame until my spine presses against the mirrored wall. His hands land on either side of my head, bracing him in a dominant position while his scowling face leans in close.

The rapid shift makes my head spin. I'm caged by his oversized frame, locked in a steely prison of muscles and golden skin.

"What the fuck were you thinking?"

"Now you want to talk?" I crane my neck to see into his mossy pools. "We had a whole car ride to hash this out."

"I'm in charge of your security! You made me look like a complete fool."

"Oh, shucks. Did I embarrass you?"

"This isn't a joke," he hisses back.

"No, it's not! And I'm not your prisoner. This isn't protection. It's a fucking insult. I'm more than capable of looking after myself."

"That really helped last time someone took you!" Hyland throws the accusation like it's a weapon he can use against me.

And his aim is true, causing indignation to flutter in my gut. When I hammer a curled fist against his chest, Hyland doesn't even flinch. God, I'd love to punch his stupid, handsome face next.

"How dare you," I snarl at him.

"It's not a fair observation? You were trafficked."

"And spent six years being made into a weapon!"

His strong, rugged features are pulled tight in annoyance. I'm going to settle this now before I cave in his skull.

"I was held captive. Starved. Sold."

"Em—"

"Whipped. Humiliated. Threatened. Beaten almost to the point of death for good measure. I was forced to fucking fight for the right to exist!"

We're almost nose to nose, his nostrils flaring with each sharp inhale. Warring emotions tangle in his olive eyes—regret, concern, anger, frustration.

Well, fucking same.

"While other women were being distributed to be gang raped, I was trying not to get my spine cracked by a revolving door of thugs looking to make a quick buck."

"Okay, Em. I get it."

"No! You don't!"

Now that the frustrated tsunami is pouring out of me, I can't stop it. I want him to know exactly why I went to that warehouse in search of answers.

"I almost died once."

His visible flinch offers a taste of satisfaction.

"I lost plenty of fights," I continue. "But one nearly took my life from me. My opponent was vicious. He cracked my goddamn skull against the ground, putting me out of action for months."

The colour drains from Hyland's face, making his blonde-stubble gleam like shining gold threads against his translucent skin. It only spurs me on further.

"That didn't stop Gael from putting me back in the ring as soon as I could move again." I laugh coldly, a phantom pain slicing through my head. "All I could think was that I wished I had died."

Still deathly silent, Hyland doesn't respond.

"But something in me just wouldn't stop fighting to get home. I had to pick myself up and continue fighting every day, earning them even more money."

"Fuck, Ember…"

"The men who did that to me are still out there. In fact, they're looking for me at this very second, planning to drag me back to that life. And you want me to sit still?"

"Okay." His voice is a sorrow-filled plea. "I get it now."

"No. You don't get to barge in here, throw your weight around and accuse me of being weak. Not when I've fought tooth and nail to be the exact opposite of that ever since I was taken."

"That's not what I was doing," Hyland rushes to assure, shaking his head. "I don't think you're weak."

"But it's my fault I was taken?"

"No! No. That's not what I meant."

"It's what you said," I argue hotly.

"It's not what I meant. I just want to keep you safe."

"You can't protect me! Not from this!"

Still braced above me, his eyes are swirling with panic. It stokes the rage that fuels me even more. I'll never let anyone talk shit without facing the consequences of their careless words.

"This is a case for you, but for me... this is my life. It's the life that I couldn't see a way out of for a very long time. It's the life I survived."

"I know." Throat undulating, his deep tenor swells with emotion. "You deserve credit for that."

"Then what's your problem? I went to that warehouse for answers!"

He drops his eyes, breathing raggedly. "I don't... I'm not..."

"Not what? Capable of admitting I can handle myself?"

"No..."

"Then what?" I press urgently. "Spit it out!"

"Em. Enough."

"Just tell me! What is your problem?"

"I'm pissed because you put yourself at risk last night!" His hand slaps against the elevator wall beside me. "And I need you to be safe."

"Because I'm your client? Your burden?"

"Because, you infuriatingly insane woman, I care about you!"

His words bounce around the inside of the elevator as I silently gape at him.

"I care what happens to you, Ember!"

Nope. Still not a word.

"Is that really so hard to believe?" He releases a strangled huff. "I care about protecting you from those traffickers. Clearly, I care too bloody much. As usual."

The elevator dings when it reaches the top floor, but neither of us move to exit into the corridor. We're suspended in an impenetrable bubble, the invisible boundary pulsating with anger and tension.

Hyland's entire body seems to be vibrating. I'm shaking just as badly. Anger and shock collide hard enough in my chest to split the organ into individual atoms, but still, I can't leave him.

"You want the truth?" He finally breaks the silence.

Throat constricted, I can only nod.

"I think you're strong." His baritone softens to a low rumble. "Strong enough to survive horrors I can't even dream of. You're powerful. Formidable. So goddamn beautiful, I want to destroy anyone… fucking anyone… who dares to mean you harm."

My tongue glues to the roof of my mouth.

"You're a ball buster, and I've never been happier to let someone walk all over me." His mouth crooks in a smile. "The way you storm through life like it's a mountain to be conquered is so hot, I can't even begin to tell you."

When his huge hand lowers to cup my face, I forget how to suck in air. His massive palm is rough and warm, sparking an electric storm inside my veins that threatens to decimate my entire being.

What was my plan here?

Whatever I hoped to achieve, it's obliterated by pure instinct as I lean into his palm. Anger has distilled into a concentrated shot of longing. For his touch, his harsh words, his gentle declaration. Any and all of it.

I want to take.

I want to feel.

I want *everything*.

"So why do you treat me like I'm made of glass?"

"Because you survived a living nightmare," he replies simply. "I don't want anyone to try to break you ever again."

"But why? I'm not your responsibility."

"You're my client. My assignment."

"So what?"

"That makes you my responsibility." He shrugs. "If I have one job in this miserable life, then it's to protect you from experiencing pain ever again."

Peering into his expanded pupils, the black point drinking in all light and colour around it, I wait for Hyland to take the next step. Lord knows, I want him to break this stifling tension.

Regardless of our location. Regardless of the kiss I shared with Axel. Regardless of the fact that we're client and bodyguard. Something is screaming inside me, begging to be released.

And I want him to silence it.

I want him to *devour it.*

"I didn't protect someone once before." His admission comes in a rough rasp. "I failed, and she paid the price."

"Who?" I ask in a whisper.

He shakes his head, actively dislodging the painful memories. "I was so stupid, Em. My family got hurt because of me. That's why I'll never fail anyone again."

My insides twist at the sight of anguish leaking from his expression. "I'm sorry, but you can't protect the entire world."

"Watch me," Hyland challenges. "I can, and I will."

Just as a delicious heat begins to pulse between my thighs, he straightens then steps away from me. The space that opens up between us makes me want to pathetically sob and plead.

I must be losing my mind if I'm expecting him to do... What, exactly? I'm his client. His assignment. That's it. For all his grandiose words, our relationship will always boil down to that dichotomy.

"We're late." He clears his thick-sounding throat. "Shouldn't keep them waiting."

Unable to speak, I can only summon another uncertain nod. I'm still distracted by thoughts of him pinning me against the wall and destroying my mouth with his tempting lips.

I bet his muscles would fit snugly against mine. I'm hardly short, but compared to him, I have to wonder how I'd take the brunt of his raw desire. Damn me to hell, I want to find out.

"Ember?"

Shaking off the thought, I push away from the wall to follow him out. "Coming."

Walking out into the plush corridor feels akin to a fever dream after that intense moment. My legs are wobbly and unstable. I mentally berate myself to get a grip as we approach the apartment door on their private floor.

"Are you sure you want to do this?" Hyland hesitates, hand wavering over their security system.

"What is *this*, exactly?"

"You getting what you want."

My gaze darts between him and the door. Surely not.

"You mean...?"

"It's not too late to change your mind," he replies in confirmation. "Once you do this, there's no turning back."

Holy shit. It's happening.

"I can't believe I'm saying this," Hyland mutters in disbelief. "But you'll be part of our team. Our… family."

Surprise sends my stuttering brain into overdrive. After Axel's suggestion and the total silence that followed, I never thought they'd consider recruiting me. And especially not after last night.

Do I even want this?

Watching Hyland scan his thumbprint to unlock their front door then hold it open for me to step inside, my feet won't respond. The weight of this decision feels crushing.

All I wanted was to go home.

The woman who built that life died in the ring. She died time and time again until all I was left with is the person I am now. The broken shards of my former existence are scattered across the Mexican desert.

"You can still walk away." Hyland watches as I internally debate. "Let us investigate. When it's safe, you can start over."

"I thought I wanted that." I lick my suddenly dry lips. "But I don't care about that life anymore."

"What do you care about?"

My answer is immediate.

"Justice."

Feet carrying me forwards without having to think further, I feel my anticipation build. I want the chance to take back my power and fight the monsters who did this to me. I want vengeance.

"Why are you doing this?" I ask over my shoulder.

"Warner thinks you proved yourself last night." Hyland follows behind me. "And at least this way, I can keep an eye on you. We can train you. Keep you safe."

"You're seriously on board with this?"

"On board?" There's no mirth in his olive-green eyes when he chuckles. "Hell no. Reluctantly agreeing to stop you from taking unbelievably stupid risks, more like."

"Fuck you."

Hyland rolls his eyes, stepping over the threshold. "I said you're strong, red. I meant it. Our team needs a bit of fire right now."

The nickname rolls over me like a welcome embrace. I find myself smiling at the asshole.

"I can bring that."

"Of that, I have no doubt." He looks over me in a slow, sensual perusal. "Why do I feel like I'm going to regret this?"

"Because I'm going to make your life hell, tough guy."

"Great." He sighs loudly.

Inside the penthouse, endless lines of polished glass, exposed metal beams and clean lines of grey and muted blue greet me. Bright light spills through 360-degree windows in dazzling beams.

The entryway is huge in itself, divided by a glossy, black bookcase several metres long. My gaze catches on rows of framed photographs, nestled in the shelf's cubbyholes with other valuables and trinkets.

"Who's this?" I study a gold-gilded frame.

Hyland stops at my side, the door clicking shut behind him. "That's my son, Luke. He's six years old."

"I had no idea. Why haven't you mentioned him?"

Hyland deliberates for a moment, his suddenly sad gaze locked on the image of the blonde-haired kid showing off a toothy grin. The heaviness that settles over him is palpable.

"I don't see him much with my work schedule. My divorce from his mother wasn't amicable, and she got full custody. They live down south near her parents now."

"You're divorced?"

"For a few years." He shifts uncomfortably on his feet. "Like I said… my family got hurt because of me."

Cutting off the conversation, Hyland walks farther into the apartment. I follow in his looming shadow, looking back over my shoulder at the sweet little boy one last time.

He looks a lot like his dad, though his wide eyes are a beautiful shade of turquoise-blue, and his features are rounded with youthful innocence. I wonder if he's the reason Hyland needs to protect the whole world.

Maybe that's his monster.

He's forever bound to protect others because he failed those he loved most in the past.

"Hyland? Ember?"

At the sound of Warner calling our names, Hyland halts, gesturing for me to walk ahead. The ceiling rises sharply at the end of the entrance hall to a dramatic, ten-foot expanse supported with huge steel beams.

The penthouse is open plan and boasts a living space that could probably fit my entire old apartment. Sunken floors lead into the impressive lounge, marked by two cream, L-shaped sofas, a stone fireplace and massive flatscreen TV.

In the nearby kitchen, spotlights and concealed beams of muted light illuminate the space, dominated by speckled-black marble counters, multiple barstools and several high-end burners.

I've never seen such a grand fridge. It's one of many top-end appliances, the array of gadgets failing to fill even half of the available counter space. Their ten-seat dining table next to the window is equally large.

"Damn."

Behind me, Hyland snorts sardonically. "It's a bit excessive for me too."

"Are you kidding? This is awesome."

"Glad you like it."

The view out of the floor-to-ceiling windows captivates me. London's vast wealth and urban landscape stretch on for miles like a breathtaking, panoramic painting.

"Over here," Warner's voice calls.

At his words, I turn to face him. "Oh, hi."

The sight of him in navy-blue workout gear stuns me. It isn't his exposed metal prosthetic peeking out of his shorts that steals my tongue. I've seen it enough times since his car accident.

His built shoulders, hair-smattered forearms and strong, bulging biceps are on full-display in the vest he wears. Warner prefers to be comfortable, but I've never seen this much of him before. He's... *muscular.*

"Hey." He eyes me warily. "Coffee?"

"Um," I falter, feeling flustered. "Sure."

"Coming up."

Stepping into the kitchen, I drag my fingers over the silky-smooth countertops, trying hard not to gawp. He moves to work an intimidating coffee machine that I'm longing to drool over next.

"You still take sugar?" Warner asks, keeping his tone neutral.

"Uh, no. Black is fine."

"Sweet enough as you are?"

"You know it," I reply sarcastically.

Wincing at the awkward silence while he fixes my coffee, I search for the right words. I feel far guiltier for scaring Warner than anyone else. He risked himself to come after me, diving straight into enemy territory.

After all this time, he's still loyal to a fault. That sweet boy who played secret agents and astronauts with me grew into a devoted man who would do anything for those he cares about. Then I went ahead and scared the shit out of him.

"Look," I eventually break the silence. "While I'm not sorry for attempting to communicate with Blaine, I am sorry that I worried you. It was unfair and careless."

Palm braced on the counter, he slides my coffee over to me. "Worried me?"

"Erm… terrified you? Made you prematurely age? Dragged you into the middle of nowhere to rescue me? Shall I list more?"

"Sure. Keep going."

I fight a smile. "Nah, I think you get the picture."

Pinching the bridge of his nose, Warner drags in a breath. "I don't know whether to yell at you for taking such a risk or thank you for trying to corner Blaine."

"I'll be here when you figure it out." I gratefully accept the steaming mug then sip. "Take your time."

"You're a pain in my ass."

"But you still love me, right?"

Warner shakes his head in mock-outrage. "Damn you, Em."

Rounding the corner, he yanks me into a hard, fast hug. Luckily, I've placed the coffee back down so I don't end up spilling the steaming liquid all over him.

Since we reach the same height, I can tuck my face into his collarbone. A fragrant forest welcomes me, the invisible arms of an ever-present woodland pulling me into its safety.

"Don't scare me like that again."

"Sorry?" I hedge.

"You're not. So don't lie."

While Warner's familiar heat steadies me, it also soothes the constant undercurrent of fear and anxiety that I've been keeping buried. Luckily for me, he doesn't need to know how scared I am to show me compassion.

"I have enough grey hairs without you making things worse," he mumbles against my hair. "That's why you're going to train with us."

My head lifts so I can peer into his bottomless baby blues. "Are you serious?"

"I want to destroy the business model that allows people like you to get hurt. What do you want?"

"The same."

His frame vibrates with a long exhale. "Then help me do it."

When he tucks an auburn strand behind my ear, I feel my entire body clench in a way it never has around him before. Not with Warner. The unexpected sizzle of tension is immediate and intense.

His fingers brush the outer edge of my earlobe then move to trace my cheek. With each subtle stroke, fiery pinpricks explode in their wake.

"If keeping you safe means teaching you to use all that fighting power... then so be it." He seems to catch himself, quickly lowering his hand. "That's what we'll do."

"You mean it?"

Certainty brightens his crystalline eyes. "Come work for me. No one will ever dare touch you again."

"It's not me I'm worried about," I rush to explain. "I want to prevent more women and girls from getting hurt. And... Well, I want to do something to fix this feeling inside me."

"What feeling, Em?"

My chest spasms, tightening into a vice.

"This feeling like I want to hurt the whole world."

Despite sensing Hyland's presence in the kitchen behind us,

I'm entrapped by Warner's accepting stare. The glimmering, aquamarine ocean appraising me with nothing but concern and care.

A vulnerable part of me wants to dive deep into those calming waves and never resurface. I want to sink into his gaze and surrender my breath for the chance to rest there. Even if only for a second.

"I can't undo what's been done, Em." His forehead creases with deep grooves. "But I can give you the chance to seek justice."

"Please. That's all I want."

"Then join our team. Train. Learn. Let us protect you. In return, we can hunt down the motherfuckers who hurt you... together."

Footsteps approach then a familiar scarred hand touches my shoulder. With Warner still holding my waist and Hyland's heat at my back, I'm overwhelmed by them. Their scents. Their promises. The unexpected salvation they're offering.

"I want to fight these fuckers," I whisper after gulping. "I want to find Gracie. Gael has to pay for what he's done."

"He will." Warner summons a small smile, his head shaking slowly. "I can't believe I'm agreeing to this."

"Agreeing to what?"

If Axel's high-pitched, singsong voice didn't announce his arrival, then his loud footsteps would. Warner hastily steps away from me, though Hyland's paw remains locked on my shoulder.

Axel bounces into the kitchen, an open laptop in hand. "I am never pulling an all-nighter with the intelligence team again. Bunch of boring nerds with zero sense of humour."

"Then I suggest you stop breaking the team rules," Warner quips in response. "Thought you would've learned after the target practice incident."

"Didn't realise working for Sabre fucking Security would come with so many rules." He deposits the laptop on the counter then moves to the coffee maker. "I hate you guys."

With an eye roll, Warner rounds the marble slab to take a barstool. His hand automatically drops to his right thigh, massaging where his leg ends and the metal prosthetic begins.

"Well? What did I miss?" Axel looks over his shoulder.

FRACTURED FUTURE

The feeling that gathers in the pit of my belly is equal parts certainty and determination. It steadies my bones and offers me the first pulse of relief since I made that fateful phone call.

"I guess… I'm joining the Anaconda Team."

CONFIDENTIAL
Why?
Suspect?
Gael?
DO NOT CROSS   POLICE LI

CONFIDENTIAL
Suspect?
DO NOT CROSS
Suspect?
NOT CROSS
POLICE

13

EMBER

EXHALE – RARITY

My breath burns in my airways, forcing the constricted flesh to expand. Each time my feet hit the ground, a flare of pain ignites inside my pounding skull.

How long will 768 take to recover?

I pump my sore legs to run faster, farther. Wishing I could physically escape the sick whispers in my mind.

Get the asset back up and fighting.

London's dense, urban streets are a grey blur all around me, moving too fast for my attention to capture.

Don't let me down, 768. Your life depends on it.

The rumble of Hyland's SUV following me while I run has long since been drowned out by the haunting voices. Flashes of those agony-filled days after my injury when all I could do was hope to die.

The severe head injury didn't kill me. No matter how hard I

wished it would. Weeks turned to months, and gradually, my strength returned. The wounds healed. And the terrifying lasting effects set in.

My skull pounds harder as the distance I can push my struggling body to cover becomes my sole focus. I woke up groggy and disorientated, but rather than wallowing, I'm determined to outrun my symptoms.

After surviving another gruelling four miles, Tom's apartment building comes into view. I'm drenched in sweat, limbs shaking hard and head buzzing with exhaustion. But at least the voices have stopped.

At the sight of Warner sitting on the wide steps outside the building, a stack of folded cardboard boxes at his feet, I pull up short of collapsing in a lifeless heap.

"Woah. Easy, Em."

Wavering on my feet, I scrunch my eyes shut to battle a wave of lightheadedness. "I'm… okay."

"What the hell are you doing to yourself?"

"Keeping b-busy."

Peeling my watering eyes open, the world is still blurry, but a little less so. Warner squints in the afternoon sun, shielding his eyes as he studies me.

It takes a few minutes of panting for me to catch my short breath. He patiently waits for me to cool down, appearing ready to intervene and catch me if my legs decide to give out.

"Okay," I concede. "I'm good."

"You look sweaty." He laughs lightly.

Bracing my hands on my knees, I blink through my still-hazy vision. "Shut. Up."

"I've been sitting here for half an hour. You've never run for that long before."

"How would you know?"

Warner looks down at his black sports watch. "It's my job to know things. Especially about our clients."

"That's creepy."

"Maybe. What's up with the marathon running?"

"Needed to work through some stuff."

"You're going to have to open up and deal with some of that stuff eventually." He pins me with a stern gaze. "Sitting down for our interviews doesn't count as healthy processing."

"Thanks for the advice." Ignoring my headache, I roll my eyes. "Why didn't you wait inside?"

"Your brother called me a dickhead and slammed the door in my face. I figured waiting outside was safer."

"Your best friend," I correct in a saccharine voice.

"Yeah, yeah." He stiffly rises to his feet. "He's accused me of endorsing your, and I quote, childish and self-destructive bullshit."

"Ah. That line. He tried it on me too."

At the sound of Hyland slamming his car door shut, I awkwardly straighten. A stitch is gnawing a hole in my midsection. It's taking all my willpower not to collapse on the steps now fatigue is setting in.

"That was a particularly gruelling form of self-torture," Hyland rasps as he approaches us. "Seventeen miles, red."

"That's not even a marathon."

"It's damn well close to one." Warner narrows his eyes on me. "What's going on in that head of yours?"

When I don't entertain his prying, Hyland adds to the interrogation.

"Bloody lunatic didn't even stop for a water break. She was zoned right out."

"Em!" Warner gasps.

"Thanks," I snap at Hyland.

"It's the truth." He shrugs.

"I can look after myself!"

"But this isn't healthy," Warner reasons like I'm a pouting child. "If you're working through stuff... then you need to talk to someone."

"How many ways can I tell you to fuck off?" I look between the two men. "I already have a very pissed off brother upstairs, waiting to scream at me some more."

Before either of them can respond, I silence them with a caustic glare. I'm not here to be lectured about my mental health. They can stick their concern up their asses.

"Your security clearance came through." Warner lifts the stack of folded boxes. "The directors have approved your appointment to our team as a new recruit."

Whistling, Hyland braces his hands on his hips. "Well, fuck. This is actually happening."

"Yep," Warner confirms, still focused on me. "I'm here so we can pack your stuff."

"Pack… my stuff?" I squint at him.

"All teams live together. You're moving into the penthouse to commence your training."

When I glance between them and see no hint of a joke, I realise they're deadly serious.

"You want me to live with you three?"

"Want is a strong word," Hyland grumbles. "Give me the damn boxes."

Snatching the stack that Warner hands over, he stomps inside Tom's apartment building. I'm left staring at his wide, taut back and loose bun disappearing inside.

"He's clearly thrilled by the idea."

"Ignore him," he advises.

"That's a little challenging when he follows me everywhere like a lost fucking puppy."

Warner shifts down a step to move closer to me. "Hyland would have us all wrapped in bubble wrap and placed in storage if it kept us safe."

"Fantastic," I drone.

"He's harmless, really. His bark's worse than his bite."

"And I'm supposed to want to live with that?"

"No. You're not." Warner shrugs. "But it's the rules, Em. We train together, work together, live together. That's what makes our teams so strong."

"What other rules have I signed up for without knowing?"

"Beyond a full physical eval and mandatory therapy with the company shrink?"

I stumble like I've been slapped right across the face. "W-What?"

"Don't take it personally. We all have to do it." Warner winks at me. "Even me."

"You've got to be kidding."

"Wish I was, Em. You wanted this, remember?"

I'm suddenly starting to regret agreeing to this job.

"I'm not seeing a doctor, Warner. You know what they did to me in Mexico. If you expect me to trust some idiot in a white coat after that, you're mistaken."

When I brush past him to walk up the steps, he quickly follows, fingers latching around my sweaty bicep before I can escape inside.

"Wait," he urges.

"Forget it!"

"I understand what you've been through, but I can't get around this. We'll assign a female doctor—one of our best. Hell, I'll even go with you."

"No! That's not the point!"

"I'm sorry, Em," he attempts to placate. "You have to be medically cleared for training."

Chin lowering, I squeeze the bridge of my crooked nose. The horrendous violations we all endured is reason enough to give me trust issues. Add to that my debilitating episodes, and I have a lot to hide.

"Is this really non-negotiable?"

"Yes," he replies with finality.

"Shit. Fine, but I want a female. And you are *so* not coming."

Hands lifting, Warner spreads them in surrender. "I didn't mean anything by it. Just want you to feel safe and supported."

"Thanks, but no thanks."

"Alright, I'll make the arrangements. It's non-invasive, totally standard procedure. You'll breeze through it."

Nodding in defeat, I steer to safer topics. "So... us? Living together?"

His lips roll inwards as he fights a smile. "I practically lived at your house growing up. I think I can handle sharing an apartment with you. Just... don't bring any dates home, alright?"

"Um, why?"

Giving up the fight, Warner flashes me a full grin. "I'd hate to have to bludgeon any inadequate shitbag who thinks he has a chance with you."

"You… This… Jesus." I splutter in dismay while scrubbing my sweat-streaked face. "This is insane."

"I'm joking, Em."

"Are you?" I groan, my fierce headache seeming to kick up a notch.

"Mostly," Warner guffaws.

"I'm being serious! Fuck!"

"Hey, it's going to be fine. We've had women on the team before, and the guys will behave themselves. Nothing to worry about."

"Nothing to worry about, apart from living with three men?"

His shoulders quirk in another shrug. "Yep."

"Christ. Tom is really going to kill you."

Warner's chin dips, a sigh spilling from his mouth. "You can break that news to him."

"Screw that. You're my boss, right?"

"I suppose so."

"Then you get to break the bad news about our new living arrangement."

With a curse so vile I'm surprised it came from someone like Warner, he heads inside the building. Hyland lingers in the entrance hall, glowering at his phone with the boxes tucked under his arm.

"Let's make this quick. Axel has an update for us at HQ."

"He found something?" Warner questions.

"Not sure. He didn't go into detail."

"Alright." He punches the elevator button. "Let's get this over and done with."

As it turns out, Tom doesn't kill his one and only best friend the second Warner breaks the news to him. Only threatens to have him arrested on trumped-up charges of kidnapping his sister. Apparently, a grown woman can't make her own decisions.

We end up spaced out in his black-and-white tiled kitchen, multiple roaring voices lancing deep into my pounding skull. Even Hyland has intervened to try to win Tom around without luck.

The bickering rumbles on without an end in sight, causing my headache to reach bone-splitting levels of agony. I'm still in sweaty workout gear, and now I'm choking on testosterone too.

Shakily downing a glass of tepid water, I try to focus on breathing evenly to hold myself together. This is not the time to break down or black out.

"She isn't joining anything! Forget it!"

"Listen, Tom…"

"No! She's my sister. My responsibility. The answer is no."

"She's an adult!"

"Whose side are you on?"

When their yells reach a fever pitch, a hot wave of anger and indignation causes me to erupt as I slam the glass down on the kitchen counter. It loudly cracks, gaining everyone's attention.

"Enough!" I abruptly yell.

Hands raised in the air, Tom rounds on me. "Don't even get me started on you."

"What is that supposed to mean?"

"You're acting like a child. What the hell kind of idea is this, Em? You're not a spy!"

"I'm not anything!"

"You're safe and free! You've got your life back!"

Anguish is a sharp dagger, sliding deeply into my gut. "My life is fucking gone!"

When he tries to argue, a sob unexpectedly bursts out of me. The sound is guttural, animalistic. So out of my control, it makes me feel like I'm about to lose it.

"It's gone!" I scream at him.

"You're home. That's enough."

"It's not!" Something breaks inside me, the words I've been holding back forcing themselves from my lips. "I've lost everything I ever cared about!"

"You've got me!" Tom shouts back.

"That isn't enough! I lost myself!"

"Oh, fuck," Warner quietly utters.

The suffocating wave of grief hits hard and fast, taking me completely off guard. Now that I've said the words out loud, the reality of all I've lost is undeniable. And it bloody well hurts.

Tom tries to step in my direction, but I hold up a trembling hand to halt him. I don't want to be comforted. I don't even want his kindness. I just want my fury and grief to be validated.

"Enough. We're done."

"Please, Em…" He trails off, seeming to doubt himself for the first time.

"No! That's enough. Don't bother trying to talk me out of this. I'm going to use all those years of fighting to hurt the right people this time."

"Why do you have to hurt anyone?" Tom hurls back. "Why can't you just stay safe?"

"Because Gracie is still out there!" Tears pool in my eyes then leak free to scald my skin. "Just like countless other women and girls. No one else is going to save them."

"That doesn't make it your responsibility. You were a victim too."

"I'm choosing to be more than that! Why won't you support me?"

"Because I lost my sister!" Tom booms, his face flushing red. "I lost her, and I don't want to lose you too."

Silence reigns.

Thick. Heavy. Ugly.

The entire room stills as his awful words linger in the air. My whole body recoils from the devastation of each syllable. I can easily read between the lines.

I lost her.

Not me. Her. The person I'll never be again.

Glass daggers bury themselves in my heart, shredding apart fragile tissue and leaving me deathly cold. I'm not his sister. Not the one he remembers, at least.

Now I'm just a broken excuse of a person who came home six years later. A person incapable of moving on in a way that he approves of. A person he can hardly stand to look at every day.

Hearing him repeat what my mind has been cruelly whispering to me is confirmation of what I already know. That confirmation cuts so fucking deep, I don't know if I can hold the slashed ribbons of my heart together for much longer.

"That may be so," I croak around the heartbreak lodged in my windpipe. "But I'm still your sister."

"I know, Em. Shit, I'm sorry... I just want to protect you from this whole mess."

But it's too late.

The damage is done.

Glancing up at the ceiling, Tom drags in air. It's taking everything in me not to look at Hyland or Warner, silently watching our battle play out.

"You didn't escape evil just to put yourself back in the line of fire." Tom tries to steady his wavering voice. "This is your chance to rebuild your life."

"That's exactly what I'm doing. Rebuilding my life."

"You're signing up for a commitment you don't even understand!" He rubs his temples. "Do you have any idea how dangerous working for Sabre really is?"

"I think she understands perfectly," Warner speaks up. "We've explained the risks."

"So you've told my sister how you lost your leg?" Tom combats.

"I know about the car accident," I quickly intervene.

Throwing his hands in the air, Tom looks between all three of us like he can't quite believe his ears.

"An accident that wouldn't have happened if he wasn't protecting four clients being chased by armed assailants. He was left pinned in the crushed vehicle for hours!"

"Don't you dare." Warner's voice has chilled considerably. "That's enough."

"Is it?"

My eyes flick to Warner, glaring at his best friend with unfathomable anger. The story of how he lost his limb was always a confidential secret. We all got the same line—a car accident.

It was while he was working on his biggest case. The infamous Harrowdean Manor—one of six private psychiatric institutes scattered across the country—was closed down following the exposure of widespread corruption and abuse.

For years after, he fought to find a new normal. It took months of rehab and physiotherapy for him to even become mobile again, let alone able to have any semblance of independence.

"What about how Becket was killed in a bombing during the

Michael Abaddon case?" Tom continues hotly. "Or how Tara was compromised by a trafficker and shot dead by her client?"

"Don't bring her into this." Hyland flushes a dark shade of red.

"Why not? You were there! Ethan too!" Tom shakes his head. "He bailed to live on a damn mountainside rather than risk his life again. Why is that?"

Stepping closer to Tom, Warner folds his arms, a grimace twisting his lips. "Our job is dangerous."

"Haven't you lost enough friends? You want to risk Ember too?"

Even Hyland flinches at the brutality of Tom's attack. Sometimes, I forget just how savage he can be after years of courtroom confrontations.

Warner's face contorts with aggravation. He looks about ready to dent my brother's skull. They've rarely fought or fallen out in over twenty-five years of friendship, but that seems set to change.

"Collateral damage is inevitable," Warner grits out. "That doesn't give you the right to parade our losses as reasons to denounce the work we do."

"No, it gives me the right to ensure my sister doesn't become collateral damage like the rest of the Anaconda Team."

"She is a grown adult!"

"Who is clearly traumatised and not thinking straight!" Tom yells back.

"We're giving her a purpose! A chance to heal!"

"So fighting criminals is supposed to be therapeutic? Seriously?"

Fuck this.

Done with listening to them, I swipe my hands over my wet cheeks then leave the kitchen. If I stay, I may end up actually harming my brother. Even if he's being a stupid prick right now, I'm not going to risk that.

I slam the door of my temporary bedroom behind me, hard enough to rattle the picture frames hanging on the otherwise plain white walls. The freestanding lamp in the corner sails across the room before I realise what I'm doing.

"Argh!"

Not even the sight of the twisted, damaged metal abates the intense pressure growing in my head and chest. White-hot pain pulsates behind my eyes. I feel like I'm going to explode into a million pieces.

Fear isn't unfamiliar to me. I know what it does to your mind. How it warps every last fundamental part of who you are and how you think. It can turn even the sanest person into an unstable whirlwind, given enough time.

My brother is afraid.

Perhaps rightly so.

That isn't going to stop me from taking this chance, though. His fear is exactly that—*his*. Not mine. And he will have to learn to control it before he permanently hurts the people he loves.

Fisting my hair, I press my fingers into my head, hoping to relieve the deep ache. I easily find the gnarly lump across the back of my skull where Gael's physician stitched my gory head wound.

After releasing my head, I begin to randomly throw belongings into the boxes that Warner assembled. I unpacked a couple of weeks ago, having nowhere else to go. Now my entire life is back in cardboard boxes once again.

A gentle knock on the door draws my attention.

"Red?"

"Go away."

"Not likely. Can I come in?"

"I'm packing," I call back.

"Need help? Tom left. Warner's gone after him."

Great. They can verbally kill each other in public instead.

"Fine, come in."

The thud of Hyland's usual rubber-soled army boots is unmistakable. I'm focused on haphazardly folding a wool sweater when he lightly taps my shoulder.

"You doing okay?"

"Just peachy." My voice comes out strained. "What the hell is Tom's problem?"

Moving to sit at the foot of the bed, Hyland watches me pack with visible concern. "He's protective. I get it."

"There's protective, and then there's fucking insane. You of all people should get that."

"Ouch. Thanks for that."

"Welcome," I snark back.

"Talk to me, Ember. Tell me what you're thinking."

"This isn't some stupid, rash decision!" I erupt in frustration. "I'm trying to find purpose. I have skills to offer."

"We know that." He shifts, crossing his ankles. "And he will come to that realisation too. Right now, he's just worried sick."

"And lashing out like a total dick?"

"Well, yes. That too."

Giving up, I lob the sweater into a box. "That stuff he spewed about Sabre and your job was fucked up."

Hyland hesitates before replying, his hand massaging the back of his neck. "He's not wrong. We've lost a lot of people in the line of fire."

"That isn't your fault."

"I'm not sure Warner sees it that way."

"Why?" I exclaim. "He isn't to blame."

"He's been a part of this team the longest. Every loss has been personal for him, and it's been that way since he began working for Sabre."

The extent of Warner's loss isn't something I've ever considered before. When his parents finally divorced and his father left the country, I think he was relieved it was all over. But he still lost his family.

Then as an adult, not only has he lost a limb and his independence for a long period of time afterwards, but Warner's also lost multiple co-workers and friends. Especially in the army. Grief just seems to follow him.

Yet it hasn't closed him off or turned his big heart to stone. Quite the opposite. I've never known someone more devoted to his work or willing to put his life on the line to help a fellow human.

"You'll quickly learn that everyone who works for Sabre has a colourful past." Hyland releases his neck. "Our histories are what make us committed to this line of work."

"Perhaps go and tell my brother that."

"He knows it already. Tom will come around."

"I don't care if he doesn't." Grabbing a stack of t-shirts, I toss them into the box next. "This is my life. I'm entitled to do with it what I please."

When another wave of vision-blurring pain sweeps through my skull, I have to pause for a moment to lean against the built-in wardrobe. My legs are ready to give out.

"Ember?"

"I'm good," I force the words out.

"Let me help. Your folding is giving me fucking anxiety anyway."

With some deep breaths, I keep hold of consciousness and manage to respond. "Like you ever get anxious."

The bedsprings squeal as Hyland stands up. "You'd be surprised."

Nudging me aside, he begins to pull clothes from the rail inside my wardrobe to neatly fold and pack. The longer I watch him, the tighter my throat becomes, constricting with an odd emotion.

For someone who has always craved independence, having him recognise that I'm struggling and insist on helping feels weird. But also good. Soothing. Like I'm not alone in this endless fight to survive.

"Everything is going to be okay." Hyland folds the lid shut once the box is full. "You'll see."

"Are you coming around to the idea of me joining the team?"

"Hah. Don't get ahead of yourself."

If I didn't have a headache before, his constant mood swings would give me one.

"I really don't understand you sometimes." I rub my aching forehead. "One minute you want to train me so you can keep me safe, the next you're moaning and stomping off."

"I wouldn't expect you to understand, red."

"Try me."

Shoving the full box towards the door, Hyland silently starts emptying the wardrobe drawers to fill another. I'm left waiting for an explanation that never comes.

When it's clear that he isn't going to indulge me, I take another breath then move to empty my underwear drawer into a third box. No way am I letting him touch my bras and panties.

"Why do women have so many clothes?" he grumbles quietly.

"I have less than most. Don't be an ass."

Stacking his box on top of the first one, Hyland averts his eyes when he spots me sorting through cotton and lace. I think the oaf is actually fighting off a blush.

If all it takes is the sight of my underwear to freak him out, he's going to have a whale of a time living with me. I'm really not sure if Warner has thought this plan through.

Between the two of us, we get Tom's spare room packed up relatively quickly. I'm shoving my toiletries and toothbrush into a washbag when the apartment door slams loudly.

"Time to face the music," Hyland murmurs. "Ready to go?"

"I guess so. But I'm not arguing with him again."

Shaking his head, he gestures for me to go ahead. "I won't let that happen."

When I pass Hyland, who has already hefted a box to rest on his shoulder, warmth spreads through my lower back at the feel of his palm resting there. My stomach flip-flops.

Shit.

Perhaps this is a bad idea.

I've already kissed Axel in a moment of madness. Even if he hasn't brought it up since, it still happened. Now I'll be living in close quarters with him. And my heart hasn't quite realised that Hyland isn't up for grabs either.

Double shit.

CONFIDENTIAL
Why?
Suspect?
Gael?
DO NOT CROSS   POLICE LI

CONFIDENTIAL
Suspect?
DO NOT CROSS
POLICE
POLICE LINE DO NOT CROSS
NOT CROSS
Suspect?

14

EMBER

UNTITLED – KNUCKLE PUCK

Hands braced over my ears, I try to block out the sounds of abuse all around me. My plain, nearly empty room is in the guards' quarters. Their job is to ensure I remain secure at all times, but nothing more.

While I'm grateful not to be locked in a cage or worse, the nights when Gael's men take advantage of the captives on this estate are full of torment. I can't escape the noise.

"P-P-Please! No!"

Tears roll down my cheeks at the sound of begging nearby. It's no use. They enjoy any form of protest. I've watched the defiance drain from countless women since being here.

Shifting over to hide my face in an almost flat pillow, I forget about my shredded back too late. Excruciating heat cracks through me, emanating from each laceration the whip left.

I tried to intervene when Gael was assigning girls to be distributed to

his business associates today. The selection process was taking place near where I was sparring with Carlos.

"You dare to question me?"

The memory of his acid-sharp voice cuts into my already destroyed skin. I can still feel the whip that he laid into me with in front of every single sobbing, petrified woman up for grabs.

"These sluts have a purpose! As do you, 768!"

I'm not sure which of his guards carried my limp, semi-conscious body back to my room afterwards. Perhaps it was one of the men now violating another innocent nearby.

For all its grandiose architecture—stuccoed, terracotta walls, arched verandas, colourful Talavera tiles in the open-air courtyard—Gael's estate is a slice of hell on earth. No one who enters leaves alive.

Sometimes, I'm allowed to step outside to drink in the humid air. I look at tropical plants and colourful blooms, reminiscent of some picturesque honeymoon destination. And I wonder how anyone will ever find us here.

If Gael's inordinate wealth and political influence don't protect him, the remoteness of our self-contained purgatory will. No one comes here. Only his trusted men and business associates.

Gael's operation isn't just unfathomably vast, it's funded by an empire of dirty money funnelled through clubs and warehouses across the nation. His power is embedded in every level of society.

At first, I waited for help to come. I convinced myself that the authorities would come crashing in at any moment to rescue me. Take me home to my brother. To my home. To anything but this.

When they never came, the first tendrils of despair crept in. Those tendrils grew into vines that took root and strangled my hope soon after. Since then, I haven't dared to hope for a saviour.

"Noooo!" The voice screeches.

If I had the strength, I'd burst in there to attack the sick fuck. Even if it resulted in another round of brutal punishment. Someone has to fight for the forgotten souls trapped here.

Even if no one fights for me.

And I have to save myself.

Battling so ferociously to escape the dream, I twist and tangle in the bed sheets until the mattress vanishes from beneath me. My body smacks into the bedroom floor with a loud bang.

"Shit," I croak through sobs.

The feel of the cold floorboards is actually a welcome relief. Each wooden grain pulls me further from the night terror, the chill making my sweaty body break out in gooseflesh.

I've gotten good at grinding my teeth together to swallow the screams that beg to be set free at night. Perhaps all those years of silencing my fear through sheer necessity had some benefit.

Speak out of turn one more time, and I'll have your tongue!

Banging my forehead against the floor, I attempt to shove Gael's threats from my consciousness. He isn't here, but just the memory of him is often enough to pull me into the past's awfulness.

Sometimes, I dream it's Gracie screeching for mercy. Her little voice leaking through brick and mortar to torment me. Her soul being repeatedly shattered for someone else's twisted pleasure.

"Ember!"

Heavy footsteps sound out before the bedroom door is tossed open. Light from the penthouse hallway forms a glowing halo around a half-dressed Warner... holding a gun.

"Em?"

"Jesus Christ." I gape up at him. "You can put the gun down."

"What was that noise?"

His hands clenched around the silver weapon, he surveys my new bedroom. The soft grey walls with statement wood panels and a simple double bed are a functional blank canvas.

"Just me. No need to call the cavalry."

"Are you okay?" He slowly lowers the weapon to his side, clicking the safety into place. "Why are you down there?"

After swiping the hem of my oversized tee beneath my eyes, I shuffle into an upright position and lean against the leather bed frame. I'm not sure my legs are strong enough to hold me yet.

"I'm fine. Go back to bed."

"I wasn't asleep." He tentatively inches into the room. "Bad dream?"

"Something like that."

Seeming to realise that he's half-naked in little more than navy sweatpants, Warner shifts on his feet. The hem of his sweats is bunched up around his prosthetic, like it was urgently shoved into place.

"You want to talk about it?"

Fixing my gaze on the piles of unpacked boxes stacked against the built-in, mirrored wardrobe, I wave him off. His fixation on getting me to open up is exhausting.

"Em," Warner pleads. "Don't make me watch this without being able to help."

"Watch what?"

"You torturing yourself for shit you couldn't control."

Damn his stupid fucking perceptiveness. I don't want him in my messed-up head, and I certainly don't want to hear however he intends to rationalise what my brain is doing to me.

"Just leave me alone."

"You're about to get your first lesson on what it means to be a part of this team." Moving closer, he stretches out a hand. "Come on."

"We're not doing this."

"Get your ass off that floor, Ember Lawson," he says sternly. "That's an order."

Muttering under my breath, I take his hand then find my feet. The oversized t-shirt I was sleeping in gathers around my striped sleep shorts, but he keeps his gaze firmly locked on my face.

"I'm up!" I grumble. "Satisfied?"

"Fucking thrilled. Come with me."

Rather than releasing my hand, Warner entwines his fingers with mine. It feels strange, like we're breaking some invisible rule that was set long ago. Yet his tight grip doesn't relent.

I follow him from the bedroom, shielding my eyes from the light filling the long hallway. While soft and understated, it still temporarily blinds me this late at night.

"I'm sorry for waking you up," I offer.

"Don't be. I was already awake."

"Why?"

Warner steers me into the kitchen, pausing to slip the gun he carries into a console unit before flipping on the under-counter lights.

"Axel's following up a lead from Stillwell. I wanted to be awake if he called in for backup."

A quiver makes my muscles twitch. "What kind of lead?"

"We don't need to talk about this now."

When he eventually releases me, I lean against the marble counter. "Tell me."

Warner walks over to the fridge, pulling out a bottle of milk and what looks like several bars of dark chocolate. He moves to locate a saucepan from the drawer next to the stove.

"Stillwell couldn't confirm any of the identified players you've named. I figure he's too low in the chain of command for that kind of knowledge."

"We knew that was a possibility." I try not to sound disappointed.

"Granted, but he did offer us a juicy tidbit at the offer of a new prison cell that isn't infested with rats and mould."

"You're seriously bribing him?"

"Gently encouraging," he corrects while lighting a burner. "It did the trick. He's desperate to give us something after a few months in that shit-hole prison."

Realising what he's doing, I move to his side so I can begin breaking up the chocolate. It's been a long time since we made his fancy version of hot chocolate together, but Warner knows I can't resist anything sweet.

"What did he give you?"

"There used to be a biweekly meeting that takes place outside the city with other operatives." He pours milk into the saucepan to heat. "Axel is checking it out."

"Other operatives?"

"There are more honeypots working for Gael. These people operate as a network. They coordinate their hits. Plot, scheme and target women on mass."

Nearly dropping several chunks of chocolate, I make myself take a deep breath. These are the sickos providing victims to the market—the same market that Gael uses to feed his exploitative trafficking machine.

Just thinking about them all huddled together, listing off their hits and relishing in the earnings they will provide makes me want to break into the prison and cut Stillwell's face off.

"Axel's gone to track these other honeypots down?" I grit out. "They may be long gone."

"Perhaps."

Locating a wooden spoon, Warner begins to gently stir the milk. He appears calm as ever while I'm internally spiralling at this revelation.

"Stillwell's directions weren't exactly clear. Axel is scouting out a few potential places to find the location of the meet if it's still taking place."

"Why is he alone? Those people are dangerous!"

"Have you met Axel?" He snorts to himself. "I love the guy, but I wouldn't want to meet him on a dark night. He'll be fine."

With all the chocolate broken up, I scoop up the piles between my two hands to deposit them in the saucepan. Warner's bare arm brushes mine, emanating heat and patchouli-scented musk.

The faint touch seems to startle him. He stares into the depths of the saucepan, his hand tightening around the spoon. Unsure if I've made him uncomfortable, I move back.

"Once we've narrowed down the location, we'll wait for the next meeting to see who turns up."

"Those operatives must be funded by Gael and others like him," I point out.

"Most likely. Yes."

"What if they could lead us back to Gael?"

"They're just foot soldiers kidnapping women to sell onwards. Hardly a direct route to the head of the cartel. But it is a start."

Huffing, I hop up onto the counter while he locates two mugs. I know the wheels of justice move slowly, but a part of me wants to march down to that warehouse and slit the throats of every last person in it.

Something tells me Axel would agree.

Perhaps he'd even help.

Setting two large mugs next to the stove, Warner dips into a drawer to search for something. He straightens with a pack of pink marshmallows clasped in his hand.

"I haven't made this in ages."

"Why do you even have the supplies?" I snicker at him.

"You're not the only one with a sweet tooth."

"I forgot you're almost as bad as me."

"Yeah." He laughs under his breath. "Axel too."

"You and Axel make hot chocolate together? Aw. How romantic."

"Zip it, Em."

Catching the bag that sails through the air towards me, I tear into it to shove marshmallows into my mouth. His gaze is locked on the bag. Eyes rolling, I toss him a fluffy marshmallow.

Warner ducks to capture it between his lips. "Thanks."

"You're such a big kid."

Mumbling around his mouthful, he returns to stirring the hot chocolate. I cross my bare legs at the ankles, looking around their shadow-filled apartment.

The idea that I'm now living here and will soon be training as a member of their team is crazy. I know Tom doesn't approve, but somehow, this feels right. Like I was meant to be here.

"When can we start training?" I look back at him.

Turning off the stove, Warner pours our two drinks. "You've got medical and psychological assessments in a few days. Once you're clear, we'll begin."

"I'm not sitting in some dumb therapy office and pouring my soul out. Forget it."

"Talking will help." He slides a mug over to me. "Keeping all that pain locked up isn't going to do you any favours, Em. Trauma has a way of surfacing."

"I am not traumatised."

"Do you repeat that to yourself in the mirror every morning?" Warner blows his steaming hot chocolate. "You're having night terrors and run daily marathons."

"Stalk much?"

"Beyond being your new team leader, I'm your friend. I have a right to be concerned. And frankly, struggling to process what you endured is nothing to be ashamed of."

Hands wrapped around the warm ceramic, I let the rich, chocolatey nectar slip down my throat. The sense of comfort is immediate and heady.

"I'm not ashamed," I admit in a hushed voice.

"Then what's going on? Help me to understand."

Staring into the cup, a rush of nerves makes my scalp prickle. "I just… I don't want to let that pain in. I can't. If I do, I don't know how I'll come out the other side."

Placing his drink on the counter, Warner moves closer to me. His bare torso presses against my crossed legs, and when his hand clasps my knee, immediate warmth spreads through me.

"Letting the hurt in is how we move on from the past," he whispers without an ounce of judgement. "You need to feel it to heal it."

"I don't want to feel it."

"And that's understandable. But you *will* feel it. One way or another, those demons will claw their way out and wreak havoc on your life."

His soft fingers circle my skin, tattooing a reassuring pattern that sinks deep into my muscles and nerves. Even when I was a kid, scared of the sight of my mother wasting away, he could always comfort me.

"You want me to go through that willingly?" I squeeze my eyes closed.

"Better to do it on your terms, Em."

When I reopen my eyes, Warner's carved chest and patient eyes fill my vision. I can't look away from him or dodge his gentle words. The weight of his hand on my knee provides a feverish pressure.

"I've already agreed to do the medical evaluations. What more do you want from me?"

"I want you to know that it's okay to open up," he replies. "That you can lean on me. On the others. On the family we're inviting you to be a part of."

A bottomless ocean, still beneath vast swathes of cerulean sky, burns into me. His undivided attention ensures I feel every last promise tangled in his words.

"I'm not good at talking," I reveal.

"That's okay. To be honest, we can all be shit at it. The point is that we hold each other accountable. We look out for one another and offer support."

"So this is a two-way thing?"

"Sure." Warner nods. "You're not a burden. Come to us, and we will come to you. We'll figure out anything that comes our way together."

"I'm not weighing in on your girl trouble or shit like that." I wink at him to lighten the mood. "You're coming to the wrong person if you want relationship advice."

His chuckle pierces the intensity. "Noted."

"Glad we cleared that up."

"For the record, none of us are seeing anyone. So no relationship drama."

"Thank God. I'm not that kinda girl."

His handsome smile growing, Warner lifts his hand from my knee to lightly touch my sleep-rumpled hair.

"You never have been."

That budding feeling flourishes in the small gap between us again. The same feeling that took me by surprise before. It's an illicit spark, tinged with longing for what can never be.

"I need to check in with Axel." Trapping his bottom lip between his teeth, Warner steps back from me. "Try to get some more sleep."

"Okay." My voice comes out raspy.

"If you need me, just shout. I'll be awake."

"Sure. Thanks."

"Goodnight, Em."

With a final meaningful look, Warner picks up his hot chocolate and leaves the kitchen. I know they have a shared office on the far side of the penthouse for when he has to work from home.

The moment he disappears, the tension drains out of my body. I almost slump over on the countertop. A volatile concoction of unspoken need and confusion is sending me into a tailspin.

I must be losing my mind. There's no way that Warner feels

anything but duty towards me. Our friendship has always revolved around his love for Tom.

Taking my hot chocolate, I find my way back to the room he showed me into when we arrived. I know that Hyland is next door—I can hear his deep snoring from here.

With the door shut between me and what just unfolded, I slump against it. My bare-bones room feels lifeless without Warner in the doorway like an avenging angel, body taut and gun in hand.

He flew in here to save me from something unknown. Without a single beat of hesitation, Warner was willing to endanger himself if it meant getting to me when I needed him.

That knowledge sinks deep into my heart.

The heart that now holds a forbidden yearning.

A yearning for what it can't have.

CONFIDENTIAL
Why?
Suspect?
Gael?
DO NOT CROSS POLICE LI

Sec
Reasoning?
Suspect?

15

AXEL

TWO YEARS – HAVE MERCY

Crouched in the window of a barren, ten-floor building left derelict since the nineties, I peer into my sniper's scope. Any minute now, the meeting should adjourn.

I've been scouting out the local haunt on the outskirts of London ever since I located it by sifting through thousands of hours of CCTV footage.

It took days of searching to identify a few of the players described to us. While our singing jailbird is terrible at giving directions, his intel is sound. The meeting between operatives is still taking place.

We've finally caught a break.

At fucking last.

"Well?" Warner prompts in my ear.

"No sign of them yet."

"It's been two hours. What could they possibly be discussing for that long?"

"You saw that listing on the dark web," I murmur back. "Gael's offering a hefty price for any information on Ember. He has to know that she's back in the UK."

The extortionate offer popped up while I was doing a routine search in a heavily-used forum last night, advertising all manner of illegal products. Drugs. Hitmen. Abuse material. Even people.

If there's a demand, you'll find it on the dark web. While it isn't illegal to access that side of the internet using a Tor browser, it is challenging. The anonymity makes it a breeding ground for all things illicit.

"Did you tell Ember?"

"Yeah…" He sighs in clear fatigue. "It was rough, Ax. She's trying so hard not to be scared, but I can see it written all over her face."

"Gael will never get past us. She's safe."

"We've gotten comfortable before. That's what gets people killed." An unspoken guilt fuels his words. "I won't make that mistake again."

"You know we will all protect her."

"I know. Listen, I have to make a call. Check in when they're out."

"Copy that."

With his voice falling silent, I feel a sense of relief. I never worked in a team during my counterintelligence job. Instead, I surveilled espionage suspects, stalked foreign diplomats and collected evidence in peace.

Joining Sabre was a shock to the system. All of a sudden, I had to learn how to be a team player rather than a solo agent tailing suspects on government watchlists or relaying intelligence to military commanders.

"Bingo." I watch the warehouse doors fling open. "At last."

I'm already dreaming of a salt beef bagel from Mary's and an ice-cold beer. Sitting in the same position for two hours and obsessing about what Ember's doing right now is not my idea of a fun time.

Three people shuffle outside, all dressed in dark clothing and making a hasty exit. The human skin trade is indiscriminate, so I'm not surprised to see a female face among them.

But at the sight of the bobbing black head leaving the abandoned building with his two bodyguards, my blood runs cold. Icy spikes tear into my flesh, filling me with violent desire.

"You're kidding me," I mutter.

Blaine Madden may have been before my time, but I've been briefed on the prolific mobster and all his immoral deeds. Assassinations. Underground drug factories. Gang wars. His family rained hell on the capital.

So when I see the cocky son of a bitch swaggering outside like he belongs with the other bought and paid for assholes, my shock is startling. The two-faced piece of shit must work for Gael.

Lifting the camera from my backpack, I bring the shot into focus then snap a few pictures of Blaine leaving with his thugs. They disappear behind the warehouse, leaving me to capture the others leaving behind him.

As much as I'm twitching with the urge to chase after Madden and plant a bullet between his eyes, I know we need his intel. He succeeded where we failed and rescued Ember from the cartel.

Is this how?

Tapping my earpiece, I patiently wait for Warner to return. "Come in, boss."

"What?" His voice is muffled.

"Meeting's over. Got something for you."

"Anyone we recognise?"

My laugh is short and caustic. "You could say that."

"Meet us at HQ. Ember's still in for her evals."

"Affirmative."

It takes a matter of minutes to dismantle and pack my sniper. I slide the compact case into my backpack then sling it over my shoulder, ensuring the camera is safely secured in the front pocket.

The walk back to my motorcycle takes twenty minutes. I had to park far enough away to avoid arousing suspicion. With my backpack secured tight, I nestle my head inside the helmet then take off.

Fuck, I missed this thrill.

Leaving my beloved 1978 Harley Davidson behind when we were sent to Mexico broke my heart. I did the whole rebuild myself, including the fresh red paint job. It's a slice of history, restored to its former glory.

The roads are bustling with evening traffic, but with my thighs wrapped around the purring beast, I can easily weave past dawdling motorists. Nothing compares to the feeling of total freedom that riding provides.

When work drives me insane, I like to pack a bag and run for the hills on my Harley. Nothing but me and the open road. The roaring engine. Wind freezing my skin. Heart soaring and mind at ease.

Pure bliss.

Second only to fists on flesh.

Tapping two fingers against my visor, I salute the guards lingering near the entrance to Sabre's underground parking garage. I have an assigned spot next to Warner and Hyland's spaces.

"Hey!" I shout at a smartly dressed figure slamming his car door shut. "You have something on your head, dude."

A brown leather satchel in hand, Kade Knight meets me halfway to the entrance door. The co-director of Sabre Security is formidable in his own right but widely known as the lesser of two evils.

His brother, Hudson, is the real asshole. The two brothers took control of Sabre when the previous owners emigrated to Australia after a particularly harrowing case involving a serial killer.

"Oh, shit." Kade drags the plastic tiara from his pearly-blonde hair. "Thanks, Ax."

"Fun Tuesday night?"

"Don't even ask. Raising kids is a damn sight harder than running this place. Logan's going through a dressing up phase."

The thought of their cute little boy making Kade and the rest of his crazy-ass family dress up like princesses is enough to break me. I almost double over from laughing so hard.

"Yeah, laugh it up," Kade groans.

"A fucking tiara?"

"I tried to get him to play with a football or something else, but the boy loves this Disney princess shit. Brooklyn thinks it's hilarious."

"She has a point. It's kinda funny."

"You're as bad as Phoenix. He's the instigator."

Now that isn't surprising. The blue-haired member of their complicated polycule may work a serious job at a London-based rehab clinic, but he's known for his uncontrolled chaos.

Kade and Hudson's family has always been interesting to me. Sure, the word polyamory is common now. It's becoming more mainstream and less taboo to have multiple partners. Seeing how their family unit functions up close is fascinating.

"You finish up that stakeout?" Kade follows me inside.

"Just heading up to debrief now. Ember's having her eval."

"I should come introduce myself soon." He stiffly nods at several passing agents. "Assure her that we're not all lunatics and assassins."

"Hope you're a good liar."

"Shit. Me too."

Smiling to himself, Kade summons the elevator by scanning his black security pass. He's older than me—closer to Warner's age, in his late thirties—but we get on well enough. Kade is a good director and a solid agent.

When his phone rings, Kade curses and fishes it from his jacket. "Yeah?"

The sound of yelling emanates through the speaker.

"Jesus, Eli. Take a breath. If he doesn't want to take the pink dress off, then don't make him. The little tyke will fall asleep soon enough."

Smothering my chuckling takes great effort. The shouting continues, sounding a lot like terror.

"You've got this, man. Leave Brooke and Jude alone. You know it's their date night tonight."

After several more seconds of loud yelling, Kade wraps up the call. He stuffs his phone away then exaggeratedly rolls his eyes at me.

"Not sure Eli's figured out solo parenting yet."

"Clearly," I snicker.

"He's an incredible dad, but he gets anxious about messing up. I told Phoenix to leave him to it. He's got to get over this fear sometime."

The elevator deposits us on the top floor, and Kade smacks my shoulder before heading for his office. Letting him stomp off to track down his less-friendly brother, I head for Warner's office.

Barging in without knocking, my heavy pack slides off my shoulder to hit the blue office carpet. Warner sits behind his monitor, a work phone pressed to his ear. He gestures for me to sit down while still listening to whoever is on the line.

"Yes. Understood."

Taking a seat in the comfortable leather chair opposite his desk, I drop my motorcycle helmet onto the seat next to me then work on pulling off my leather jacket.

"Send an information request to the Mexican feds. If they have permits or land records, I want them. Thank you."

Ending his phone call, Warner slumps back in his chair. I ease my leather jacket off my shoulders while watching him deflate.

"Good news?"

"That was Fox down in intelligence. He and Rayna have narrowed down approximately seven estates in the vicinity where Ember thought she was held by Gael."

My spine stiffens ramrod straight. "What do we know?"

"Right now? Nothing. Not until that information request comes back. Could be a while until we hear."

My jacket's well-worn leather twists in my hands. The idea that we could track down Gael's base of operations and commence surveillance has felt impossible. This is much-needed progress.

If we can locate his headquarters, we'll be one step closer to apprehending him. Gael is the head of the snake. With him gone, his ring of fellow monsters will soon collapse.

"What did you find?" Warner prompts.

"Right." I shake myself back into the present. "The meeting unfolded exactly as Stillwell said it would. You need to get him a new cell."

He impatiently waves his hand for me to continue.

"Nobody I recognised from our past investigations, but it won't be hard to get IDs. I took photographs of the attendees. Including one very familiar face."

Warner patiently waits while I bring up the shots on my surveillance camera. Handing it over so he can look at the built-in screen, I watch his expression flit between surprise and fury.

"What the fuck?" he exclaims.

"My thought precisely."

"Blaine Madden. Again!"

"Yep. Who saves someone from trafficking if they're part of the goddamn ring?"

"This makes no sense." Warner clicks through the different shots. "Madden was always adamant that he wanted nothing to do with the skin trade."

"What about his father?'"

Jaw clenching, he places the camera down. "They had different points of view on it. But we haven't had eyes on Nolan Madden since we convicted his son, and he vanished into thin air."

Deep in thought, I look up at the wall-sized board behind Warner's desk. We've collated years' worth of investigating across the huge panel, pinning countless news articles, surveillance reports and possible players with red tacks.

Until Ember's call came in, the pieces were all fragmented. Cartels. Shipments. Missing persons reports. Those pieces still lay scattered, but at the heart of the puzzle, Ember unwittingly resides.

"There's a connection here."

"I agree." Warner nods thoughtfully.

"Madden knew where Ember was. He saved her from Gael and delivered her straight into our laps. Why would he help us if he works for Gael?"

"Beats me. If he's embroiled in the trafficking ring, he doesn't stand to gain from double-crossing them."

"Exactly," I hum in confusion.

"We didn't know Madden was sniffing around when this mess began. It will feel shitty, but we have to wait. We need more time to figure out what his play is."

"Do we?"

Warner's intense blue gaze fixes on me. "What are you suggesting?"

Stringing my thoughts together, I'm thankful Hyland isn't here. He'd have my spine ripped out and tossed from the window in a heartbeat if he knew what I'm thinking.

"Madden contacted Ember to offer information. He gave her a location and invited her right in. We'd be foolish not to use his interest in her to our advantage."

"Absolutely not," Warner instantly disagrees, his forehead creasing. "I'm not letting that snake anywhere near Ember ever again."

"This is our way in."

"I said no! End of discussion. We're here to keep Ember safe, not expose her to wanted criminals."

"Right..."

"That's final, Ax."

"Sure. I hear ya."

Hyland gets a bad rap for being stubborn, distracting from the fact that Warner's just as hard-headed at times. His insistence on defending Ember is laughably transparent.

Even letting her on the team is a guise to have her close. No one searches for a missing person for half a decade out of brotherly obligation. I doubt he even realises what's fuelling his desire to have her safe and sound at his side.

But I do.

Oh, I've noticed it alright.

His refusal to let her near Blaine Madden isn't coming as a team leader. It's not even coming from his sense of duty as Tom's best friend. He's simply longing for the one thing he can't have, the one thing off-limits to him.

Ember.

"Now that we've identified the meeting location, we can stage an offensive at their next gathering." Warner nods to himself. "I want those sickos arrested and interrogated."

"There were twenty assailants, at least."

"Then we have two weeks to plan a safe take-down." He tears off a fresh sheet of paper from his memo pad then grabs a pen. "Enrolling the Falcon Team will bulk up our numbers. We take them hard and fast."

Watching the invisible cogs turn in his mind, my thoughts stray back to the red-haired goddess with a tongue softer than velvet. Fuck, I can't remember that hot kiss without getting hard.

I've been searching for the opportunity to pin her delicious curves to the floor and bruise her mouth with mine again. Now that the little minx is living with us... perhaps it'll come sooner than I think.

"And Ember? You know she won't sit this raid out."

Warner swallows, his neck muscles working. "Then she has two weeks to train and be ready for her first active operation."

Two weeks.

She's in for a fucking baptism of fire.

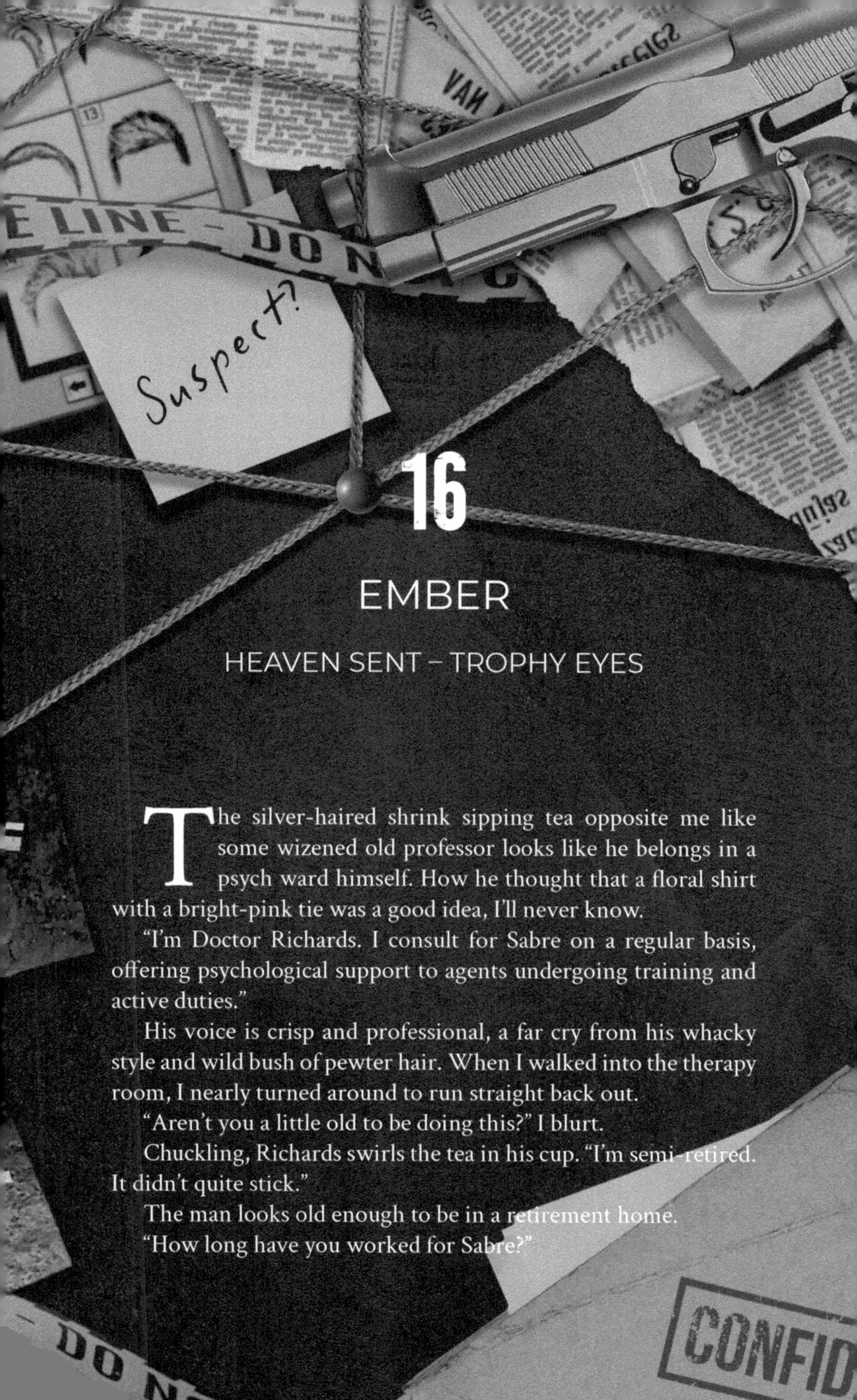

16

EMBER

HEAVEN SENT – TROPHY EYES

The silver-haired shrink sipping tea opposite me like some wizened old professor looks like he belongs in a psych ward himself. How he thought that a floral shirt with a bright-pink tie was a good idea, I'll never know.

"I'm Doctor Richards. I consult for Sabre on a regular basis, offering psychological support to agents undergoing training and active duties."

His voice is crisp and professional, a far cry from his whacky style and wild bush of pewter hair. When I walked into the therapy room, I nearly turned around to run straight back out.

"Aren't you a little old to be doing this?" I blurt.

Chuckling, Richards swirls the tea in his cup. "I'm semi-retired. It didn't quite stick."

The man looks old enough to be in a retirement home.

"How long have you worked for Sabre?"

"Long enough to know what I'm doing. I consulted for the last owners for over a decade and have personally supported hundreds of clients and staff alike."

Unconvinced, I remain on the edge of the chair, ready to get the fuck out of the spotlight. I don't care what Warner says. I don't need some pointless psych eval to join their team.

"Your physical examination was all clear." Setting down his tea, he flicks through the stack of printed reports balancing on his knee. "That's a relief, given your circumstances."

Gulping down the noxious bubble in my throat, the safest response is to mutely nod. While the female doctor did question the scarring across my back, I was deemed a healthy weight and in good shape.

The examination was thorough and went better than expected. I only felt the urge to break her neck once or twice. And I was able to avoid revealing anything too telling.

I'm not sure how long I can keep my black outs a secret—I am living with the Anaconda Team, after all. Perhaps it's foolish to keep this a secret, but I can't risk losing this fragile chance now that I have it. They don't need to know how damaged I truly am.

"I've also read your interview transcripts, so we don't have to rehash the last six years." Richards peers at me over his wire-rimmed glasses. "Unless you want to."

"I'll pass, thanks."

"Given your history, it has been determined that you'll have weekly debriefs with me throughout your time here. We're well-equipped to support survivors of trauma."

This time, I can't help but shudder. At least he didn't use the V-word. If I'm referred to as a victim one more time, I won't be held responsible for my actions.

"This is such bullshit!"

Richards steeples his fingers over his belly. "Talk to me about why you're frustrated."

"Nice try. I refuse."

"You can refuse. I can also decline to clear you to commence training."

Holding eye contact, he merely waits. Watches. Scrutinises me with his beady, little eyes. The pressure to speak and get him off my case builds to an unbearable level.

"I don't need anyone digging around in my brain." I unclench my fists, my palms stinging from where my nails have been cutting into them. "And I have zero desire to rehash what happened to me. I just want to train and get to work."

"You'll have that opportunity, Ember. However, we cannot have agents working for Sabre who are not stable enough to endure the stressors of this career."

"I'm perfectly stable!"

"No one is saying you're not," he replies calmly. "My job is to keep it that way. I have no ulterior motive here."

Overwhelmed by frustration, I stand and begin to pace the small interview room. It's been painted a muted shade of blue, filled with dark-wood furniture and forest themed photos on natural canvases.

Everything about this space pisses me off. The false sense of comfort. Richards and his scheming smiles. Warner's encouragement to open up and be honest. It's all designed to entrap me.

I don't want to remember. Feel. Talk. Anything that will break down the internal brick wall I've haphazardly rebuilt. If it falls again, I don't think I'll be strong enough to build it up once more.

"Tell me why you've decided to join Sabre Security."

"Why?" I groan.

"Humour me, Ember."

Running a hand over my face, I move to study one of the images up close. "I want to do something useful."

"Useful, how?"

Nosy fucking prick.

"You've read my file." I flap a hand in his vague direction. "You know about the street fights. I have a skillset that will prove useful here."

"That's a very well-rehearsed answer," Richards remarks.

"Excuse me?"

"Tell me what actually motivates you."

Rounding on him, I have a million unkind words to offer in

retaliation. His presumption to understand what I'm thinking and feeling is downright infuriating.

"Isn't that good enough?"

"It's a start." He arches a brow. "But after years spent taking orders, being controlled and confined… it's curious that you would opt to undergo a process which will assign you a new master."

"I'm not here for a master."

"Then why are you here?" Richards challenges.

Contemplating hurling the canvas at his head, I flex my stiff neck. The fierce pain in my head is back. It hasn't really abated since the blistering argument with Tom. Nor in his silence since I left without another word.

While I haven't had another full black out yet, I can feel my body failing me. The chronic pain is constant and blinding. Pretending that everything is fine while fending off the symptoms is becoming challenging.

"I want to capture the men who hurt me. Who hurt all of us."

"For revenge?"

"No." I jerkily shake my head. "For justice."

"One would be forgiven for thinking they're one and the same thing."

Reluctantly retaking my seat, I avoid the old doctor's penetrating stare. Something tells me he can see through my motives without me having to expose them.

"Anger is a dangerous emotion in this line of work." Richards closes the file resting on his leg. "If you wish to be effective here, you need to find a way to see past it."

"What are you saying? I'm not cleared?"

"I'm saying you need to sit in that chair every week and work with me to understand what you've been through. If you don't do that, your time at Sabre will be short-lived."

His honesty is strangely refreshing. It's different from the grief counsellor that Tom insisted I speak to after Mum's death. She tiptoed around me until it became insulting. I hated her mind games.

"What happens to what I share with you?"

"These sessions are confidential," Richards assures me, that damn smile reappearing. "Unless I have cause for concern, our conversations will remain private."

"You don't report back to Warner? Or senior management?"

"All I provide is a stamp of approval that clears you for duty. Why I give that approval, or perhaps rescind it, remains my business alone."

Mistrust curdles inside me, but I can feel it morphing into defeat. I won't get past him. Not without giving him something to dissect. If I can give just enough to placate him, perhaps I'll pass his tests.

"So..." Richards picks his tea back up to continue sipping. "We have forty-five minutes. Use them as you see fit."

Resolving to play along with his charade, I talk a little about my old life. The studio. My regular clients. How close Tom and I were, growing up with a chronically ill parent.

Richards listens intently, opting not to take notes. By the time his cup is empty and my throat aches from talking, we've ran over the allotted forty-five minutes.

"Friday morning." He unfolds his legs then stands. "Nine o'clock every week, Ember. I need prior notice and a damn good reason if you're going to miss a session."

"I'm not sure forced therapy is particularly ethical."

"Who said anything about therapy?" Richards flashes me another cooky smile. "I'm just a listening ear, giving you an outlet for all those pesky feelings. That's all."

"Does that mean you'll clear me to join the team?"

He tucks his stack of files under his arm. "You may commence training."

"Thank you, doc."

"Remember the deal, Ember. Weekly meetings. I'll be keeping a close eye on you." Richards fishes a business card from his jacket to hand over. "You're to contact me if anything comes up."

Taking the embossed card with no intention to save the number, I fold it in my hand. "Sure."

"Then you're free to leave."

Richards's stare follows me out of the interview room. I slam the door closed to escape him, slumping against it and sucking in several gulps of air.

The old man has a way of getting under my skin. I went in anticipating a fight, so his careful words and quiet observation were unexpected. I need to watch myself around him.

"Dimples!"

"Axel?"

Straightening from his perch against the wall, Axel bounces over to me. With his usual ripped jeans in place, he wears a typically colourful t-shirt displaying another crazy slogan.

"*Disguised as a responsible adult?*" I read aloud.

"Do you like it?"

"Well, it's better than the pizza shirt at least."

Yanking me away from the closed door, I'm dragged into a bone-creaking hug. Tattooed muscles smash into me from the force of the collision.

"You've been gone for hours!" he whines dramatically.

"You know, evaluations and stuff."

Axel slowly releases me. "How'd it go?"

"I've been cleared to commence training. Clean bill of health."

Fist pumping the air, he beams brightly. "Then that's cause for celebration. Wanna get food?"

"Um… sure? What time is it?"

"Past eight. Hyland and Warner are dealing with some mission planning. We're all going to talk when they get home."

"Planning? What happened?"

"I located the meeting and identified some players."

"Who?" I quickly demand.

"Nuh-uh," he tuts. "Food first, team meeting later. They want to be there for the big debrief. And trust me, you do not want to see me hangry."

I roll my eyes at him. "Like hangry Axel is any different."

"That's rude." He slings an inked arm around my neck. "Come on, the local cafe does a mean burger. It's just down the road."

Smothered by him, I happily let Axel strong-arm me from the building. Anything to put distance between Doctor Richards and the whispered secrets swirling inside me that I do not want him to unearth.

"Don't we need security?" I ask as we step outside.

Axel pats a bulge in his supple leather jacket. "I am your security, babe. You're safe with me."

Honestly, I feel far from it with his body heat wrapped around me. Axel's inability to maintain boundaries is far more dangerous than anyone who would dare attack me.

When he snags hold of my hand and tangles our fingers together like it's the most natural thing in the world, I bite down on my bottom lip. He has to know what he's doing.

Even at this hour, the crush of traffic and pedestrians fail to relent. Night and day don't really exist in London. It's always in a perpetual state of motion.

We walk in comfortable silence to a scary-looking cafe down the street. Seriously, the place is complete with a striped, red-and-white overhang and neon lighting outside.

"What is this place?"

"London's finest greasy spoon!" Axel excitedly rubs his hands together. "Home to the juiciest cheeseburgers in town. I know you're a fan."

"I'm just easily pleased," I joke.

"That ain't a bad thing, dimples."

Disentangling myself from his body, I step inside the cafe and grimace at the sound of blaring rock music. With its cheap Formica tables, cracked vinyl seats and plastic menus, the entire place screams tacky and cheerful.

A skinny chef flipping burgers behind the serving counter gleefully sings along to an old *Nirvana* tune while plating dishes. His counterpart—the scowling waitress scribbling on a small notepad—startles me when she yells out an order.

"It's not exactly Michelin star dining," Axel admits somewhat nervously. "But I didn't think you'd care."

"You're right." I laugh under my breath. "I really don't."

He releases his held breath. "Thank God."

"But I want three burgers with extra bacon and a portion of cheesy fries as an apology for calling me a cheap date. You also don't want to see me hangry."

Tugging the end of my loose braid, he cracks a wide grin.

"Whatever the lady desires."

I find an empty table while Axel places our order, handing over a few crumpled notes to the harried-looking cashier. After receiving a laminated table number, Axel joins me with a selection of drinks.

"Take your pick, babe."

Considering the options, I steal an apple lemonade. "Thank you."

"You're a bit weird, you know." He wrinkles his nose. "That was my wild card."

"What? I like fruity stuff. More than the shit you're drinking."

Cracking open a Diet Coke, he shrugs before taking a long sip. "I'll eat or drink anything put in front of me. I'm not fussy."

"So I can see."

Dropping his chin onto his palm, Axel trains his focus on me. The full force of his curious, autumnal eyes causes uneasy goosebumps to break out on my skin.

"What did Richards say?"

"How did I know that dinner was a guise to pick my brain?"

"Because I'm laughably transparent?" He wiggles his eyebrows.

"You really are."

"Come on then. Spill the beans."

"Aren't my sessions supposed to be private?" I glare back at him.

Axel shrugs dismissively. "I'm trustworthy."

"That's not the point."

Lifting his head, he slumps back in the creaking plastic chair. I should've known one of them would attempt to dig into today's evaluations. But he was my last guess.

"We're going to be training you first thing in the morning, Ember. We're working together. Living together. That means we have to trust each other."

When I don't reply, Axel cocks his head to the side.

"Don't you trust me?"

"It's not you I don't trust, Ax."

"Then who?"

Myself.

Lapsing into silence so I don't have to find an answer to throw him off, Axel seems content to quietly wait. When the waitress eventually smacks a plastic bag filled with food containers in front of us, she huffs as she stalks off.

"Let's go eat outside." Axel doesn't wait for my response, scooping up the bag. "That woman's pissing me right off."

"No arguments here."

Following him out of the café, we wind back into the evening crowd. We're not far from the riverbank, dotted with streetlamps that illuminate the winding route of the Thames.

"Over here." Axel hops up onto the brick barrier. "Follow me."

"Wait, seriously?"

"Don't be scared, dimples. I'm not going to drown you in the dark."

"How thoughtful!"

"Well, not until you've eaten, at least."

Axel disappears from sight when he drops down the other side. I clamber onto the barrier, cursing when I see there's a decent jump down onto the stony riverbank below where he's waiting at the bottom.

With a cursory glance around, I follow him down. Lights from surrounding bars, pubs and fancy eateries illuminate the darkness, though London glows fluorescent even in the dead of night.

"Here." He sits on a large chunk of fallen wall, already fishing in the food bag. "This is much better."

"I didn't take you for someone who needs peace and quiet to eat."

"Everyone needs a bit of peace sometimes." He hands me a grease-stained container. "Even me."

Joining him on the hard rock, I dig into my first burger. Despite the café's scary décor and their staff's shitty attitude, it's a bloody good burger. Thick, juicy and dripping with melted cheese.

Diving into the loaded fries next, I silently hand Axel the container so he can help himself.

"Oh, sweet," he yips. "S'good."

"Just save me some."

"No promises."

It feels oddly natural to sit and share a meal like this. Eating with our bare hands, sharing food, enjoying the comfortable silence. There's no pressure or expectations.

By the end of my second burger, I'm starting to think I overestimated my own stomach size. Axel's already hoovered up his chicken sandwich and bacon cheeseburger in record time.

"I'm going to need a self-imposed time out after this," I groan.

"Need a hand there?"

Wordlessly handing him my leftovers, I let him scarf down the remnants while rubbing my bulging food baby. I've never been short of an appetite, but Axel's craziness encourages it even more.

"Now I can think straight again." He passes me a wrapped wet wipe from the bag. "That was fucking good."

"Thanks for the invite. I needed to get out of there."

"I'll eat your extras anytime." Axel winks at me.

"So chivalrous."

"That's me." His easy smile falters, hardening into a rare serious look. "I'm glad you're on the team, Ember."

Despite the sound of the river lapping nearby, the distant cheers and thudding music as the night unfolds, I feel like the last human alive, caught in Axel's stare. He sure looks at me like nothing else exists around us.

When the jokes stop, his vulnerability is arresting. All that sorrow and heartache trapped behind a cheesy grin and penchant for violence. The contrast is what consumes my fascination.

Even as thoughts of Warner and Hyland bubble in the back of my mind, I leap up to climb into his lap. Axel's arms wrap around my back, allowing me to straddle his trim waist.

Sliding a hand into his tousled faux hawk, I toy with the coarse amethyst strands. His lids have fallen to a half-mast, the long length of his eyelashes hiding his blown pupils from sight.

"Why?" I challenge throatily.

"Just because."

"Because you want me to do this?"

"Partly," he admits in a rasp.

Tugging on his hair, I savour the groan that emanates from his inked throat. It's a submissive sound that pours fuel on the sense of power that being around him sparks within me.

"What about that?"

"Yes." His eyes squeeze shut.

Tugging again, I trail my parted lips along his jaw and up to his ear. Axel practically whines when my teeth sink into the plush lobe.

"We're co-workers now," I purr into his ear. "That means we have to be professional."

"Hmm. Professional."

His hips flex beneath me, lifting to show me just how much his body disagrees with that statement. The hard press of his rising erection tells a different story.

"We can't touch," I chastise him. "Or kiss. Or do anything inappropriate. It isn't allowed."

"Of course not."

"And we definitely, definitely cannot sleep together."

"Why would you even think about it?" Axel grunts deeply.

Letting my breath warm his skin, I slide a hand up to his throat. The tattoos there are beautifully intricate, each individual sunbeam filled with ornate, abstract patterns that disappear beneath his t-shirt.

My hand cinches around his neck, giving a light, teasing squeeze. I'm grinding on his lap without realising it, pushing down on the throbbing heat that strains against his denim.

Each move is furtive. I'm toying with a piece of forbidden fruit, not quite plucking it free. Toeing this thin line with my new teammate is clearly a bad fucking idea.

But I do not care one ounce.

Right now, I want to take. I want everything he's offering and more. I want the safety of knowing that Axel will let me pillage his soul to refill my own with everything that's been stolen from me.

Still holding his throat, I seal my lips on his. Axel lets me take control of the kiss, his mouth softening against mine. Salt still clings to his lips from our meal.

It isn't slow or passionate. Not when the gaping chasm inside me is demanding something fill it. I kiss him hard, our teeth clanging from the rough collision, his mouth opening to accept my tongue.

Axel's pulse hammers beneath my palm, stretching the ink that covers his throat. His cock is rock-hard beneath me, pressing into my core with tantalising promise.

Part of me loves how foolish this is. How awkward it'll be now when one of us gets hurt and we're still living together. The sick thrill of knowing this is stupid and reckless only makes me want it more.

"Ember," he moans into my mouth. "You need to stop before I get arrested for bending your sweet ass over and plunging my cock inside you in public."

His words hit right between my thighs where heat has pooled. "How would you take me?"

"Hard and rough, babe. I want to feel you clenching tight around me while I fuck the sass straight out of you."

My inner walls clench and pulse, frantic to be filled. I'm viscerally aching. Every inch of me feels like it's screaming out for a release that I can't give it.

"Please," I whine desperately.

"Fuck, Ember. Why did you start this here?"

Writhing against his thick erection, I think I'd happily let him take me right here. Damn the public. Need so acute has taken over, it's to the point that I hardly recognise my own behaviour.

"Please. I need... I..."

"Shh. I've got you, dimples." Axel presses his lips on mine again. "I'll make it better."

Shucking off his leather jacket, he pulls it around my shoulders to offer some coverage. It's too big for me, giving a small amount of protection along with the high wall at our backs.

Hot, rapid kisses are pressed against my neck and throat, sucking the skin between his teeth to leave a mark. I let Axel lay his claim, pushing my chest forward to urge him on.

The scoop-necked t-shirt I threw on for today's evaluations easily lifts to reveal my nude lace bra. From the moan in the back of Axel's throat, he likes what he sees.

"If we were home right now, I'd be spreading you wide open to eat your pretty cunt." He sighs in disappointment. "But I guess that'll have to wait."

Tugging my left bra cup aside, Axel plucks my nipple free to roll it between his fingers. I quietly mewl, staring at the city lights while sizzles radiate from my chest to my throbbing pussy.

"I bet it's soaked for me." Axel toys with my bud. "Are you wet right now?"

"Yes," I gasp.

"But I thought this was all a bad idea, huh?"

"It is. Fuck, Ax."

"Such a terrible idea," he exaggerates.

When he ducks his head to suck my nipple into his mouth, the stars that burst behind my eyes erase any concerns about the complications this will cause.

All I care about is his wet mouth on my skin. His frenetic touch. The slick swipe of his tongue teasing my tingling flesh. Each lick and tease serving to increase my need for more.

My fingers weave back into his vibrant hair while I faintly remember to keep an eye out. We're tucked out of sight enough to give us a little privacy, but still, anyone could interrupt.

Every time his tongue swirls around my bud, I feel the bite of his teeth. Flashes of pain and sweet bliss create a symphony inside me, reawakening every last pleasure cell.

"You're so fucking gorgeous." Axel releases my nipple with a *pop.* "And perfect."

Rubbing myself against him again, I long for more. The clothing between us feels like a personal insult.

"Needy, aren't you?" he teases.

"Fuck off."

His chest vibrates with a chuckle. "It's a compliment. I think it's hot."

Reaching between us, he finds the waistband of my leggings. I opted for comfort instead of formality for today's crap. I'm thanking myself for the stretchy fabric now.

"Tell me to stop at any time, Em."

When I don't respond, Axel grabs my chin with his other hand.

"You hear me? I need you to tell me if this is too much. There's no rush."

"Yes. Please." I frantically writhe against him. "God, yes. I need you. Just touch me."

Easing his hand past the flexible Lycra, his fingertips skate over my lower belly and down to the edge of my panties. I wait for him to plunge inside, biting back another moan.

When Axel pushes into my panties, forcing me to lift from his lap to adjust my position, I internally celebrate. His hand moves to cup my pussy, giving a playful squeeze.

"I can feel the heat pouring off your cunt." His hooded eyes lock on mine. "You're loving this. Aren't you?"

All I can do is mewl in confirmation when he pushes a finger through my slick folds. I can feel how much I'm dripping. It's been a long, long time since I felt this way.

Sliding his digit inside my entrance, Axel slowly works it in and out of me. Each deep thrust delivers a brief snippet of relief, but it fails to satiate me. All I want is more.

"You're going to ride my fingers, babe."

"Right now?" I moan.

"Yes, Ember. Fuck my hand until you come all over it. Understood?"

Nodding frantically, I gasp when he pushes another finger inside my pussy.

"Say it out loud."

The way his ministrations stretch my internal walls is a welcome sensation. With a foot planted on either side of his seated body, I have leverage to lift my hips up and down.

"Yes! God, yes. I understand."

"Perfect. Keep moving."

Each time I move to work myself on his scissoring fingers, Axel pushes them back inside me to deepen the impact. His thumb moves inside my panties, lifting to locate my clit before pushing down on it.

"More," I plead.

"Fucking stunning. You ride my hand so well."

Working myself on him, I find a fast, driving pace that he matches. I had no idea that getting finger fucked on a riverbank could be so hot, but here we are.

When Axel pushes a third finger into my slit, my head falls back on my shoulders. Everything feels tense and overheated. My muscles have tensed to breaking point.

"Ax…"

"That's it, babe. Are you going to give it up for me?"

"Yes… Please…"

"Come on. Soak my hand. That's it."

The intensity of his fingers pressing inside my core drives me to the edge. He's dragging against my walls and pressing the sweet spot buried far inside me, but it's his praise that finishes me off.

Staring up at the glowing night sky, I have to mash my lips together to hold a loud cry of ecstasy inside. The moan reverberates from my throat and chest instead, echoing with my orgasm.

"Oh, God," I mewl.

"Dammit. That's a sight, Em."

Undulating on Axel's hand, the last vestiges of my release engulf me, spreading heat into every last molecule of my being. The way he watches me in awe makes it even more satisfying.

"That was so incredibly hot, I think I actually came myself," he announces proudly. "Bloody hell."

Cheeks flushing, I feel him ease his hand from my panties and leggings. I'm not prepared for him to raise his fingers to his mouth and lick each glistening digit clean.

"You even taste sweet. Fuck."

"You're insane, Ax. And that was insane too."

"Does insane mean good, amazing or mind-blowingly fantastic in your language?"

With his fingers sucked dry, Axel gives me a lascivious smirk. I crash my forehead into his chest, unable to provide a single, level-headed retort back.

Yep. I am well and truly screwed now.

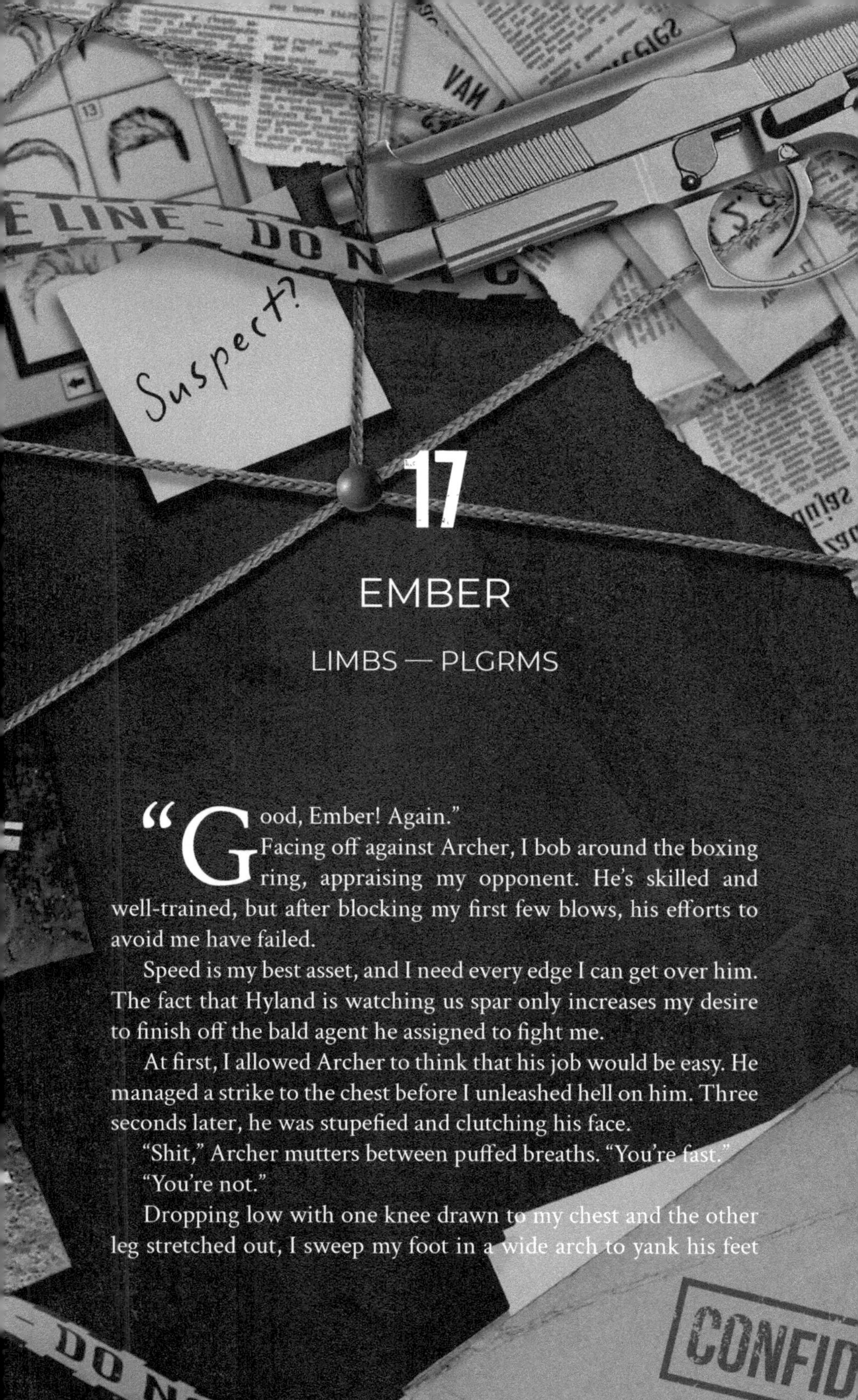

17

EMBER

LIMBS — PLGRMS

"**G**ood, Ember! Again."

Facing off against Archer, I bob around the boxing ring, appraising my opponent. He's skilled and well-trained, but after blocking my first few blows, his efforts to avoid me have failed.

Speed is my best asset, and I need every edge I can get over him. The fact that Hyland is watching us spar only increases my desire to finish off the bald agent he assigned to fight me.

At first, I allowed Archer to think that his job would be easy. He managed a strike to the chest before I unleashed hell on him. Three seconds later, he was stupefied and clutching his face.

"Shit," Archer mutters between puffed breaths. "You're fast."

"You're not."

Dropping low with one knee drawn to my chest and the other leg stretched out, I sweep my foot in a wide arch to yank his feet from underneath him. Archer goes down faster than a collapsing building.

While less bulky than Hyland, his considerable weight causes a seismic thump when he makes impact with the mat. I rise to my feet, fists raised to my chest and ready to respond if he tries to get back up.

Beating him was fun at first. It got the blood pumping and reminded me why I earned such a formidable reputation overseas. Now I'm bored and want a bigger challenge.

"You asked for that!" Hyland calls out.

Grunting, Archer blinks rapidly while staring up at the training room's ceiling. "Touché."

"You're strong but slow." I shrug at the sight of him flopping around. "We can keep doing this all day."

"Rain check?"

Wrestling himself upright, Archer rubs his spine. He's already sporting a big, black bruise across his cheekbone where I first clocked him. I bet he's regretting accepting Hyland's request now.

Looking over at the blonde brute, I gesture for him to join me with a crooked finger. His sandy locks are pulled into a low ponytail today, leaving several silky flyaways to frame his face.

I've never seen Hyland out of the all-black cargos, tight t-shirts and signature army boots he's always wearing. Not even in the mornings when I emerge from my room to find him gulping coffee.

"Nope." He shakes his head.

"Scared?"

"I'm not in the business of beating up my teammates. We have Axel for that."

Smart man.

After the debrief and discovering that Blaine Madden was at the underground trafficking meet, I was beyond ready to step into the ring. Hyland attempted to put it off, protesting against the idea of me aiding their upcoming offensive.

I'm not going to tolerate his macho, overprotective shit. If that means handing him his ass in the training ring to prove my abilities, that's exactly what I'll do.

"You can have a go, dude." Archer grunts in pain as he finds his feet. "I've got a surveillance job tonight. I don't need any more bruises."

Hyland rolls his eyes at the grumbling agent, limping off with little more than an unenthusiastic wave in my direction. While his team is still learning the ropes at Sabre, something tells me Archer didn't expect to be humiliated so easily.

Stretching my arms above my head, I roll my warmed-up muscles. It feels amazing to do what I'm good at again. The fight against Blaine was a taste of power, and now I want more.

Ducking between the ring's ropes, Hyland hefts a hardshell case onto the mat. It lands with a heavy thud. He kneels beside it and unclips the hinges.

"Forget it, Em. I'm not gonna lay a finger on you. We're moving on to weapons."

"We've only been in the ring for two hours." I pout at him.

"Clearly, there's nothing more about physical combat that I can teach you. You're already better than the head of our newest team."

"Well, shucks. You're giving me a compliment?"

"Uh huh," he mumbles.

Sauntering over to him, I'm gifted a view inside the equipment case. A variety of weapons are nestled in black foam, including two shiny handguns and a wide selection of knives.

"Sabre needs agents," Hyland continues. "Being one means learning how to be invisible, to stalk a target and identify their pressure points. How to manipulate, subjugate, and ultimately, capture. Not just punch your way through life."

"You're spoiling all my fun."

Scoffing at me, he sits back on his haunches. "You ever handled a gun?"

"Sure," I state sarcastically. "Gael let me walk around with a loaded AK-47 for the hell of it. I just never thought to kill everyone and escape before."

The look he shoots me is full of ire. "Be serious. I know you shot someone at that auction."

"Yes," I admit gruffly. "I told you what happened. But I stole that gun, and my aim was pretty shit."

"It's lucky you didn't blow your arm off, firing a weapon without training.”

“I had to do something.”

Hyland gestures for me to join him on the mat. “After today, you’ll never be in that position again.”

Squatting down to join him, I study the array of weapons he has on display. “What are we learning?”

“I’m going to talk you through the basics on a standard issue, semi-automatic pistol. You need to take this seriously, Em. Respect the weapon. This is life and death right here.”

“Got it.”

He lifts the sleek, silver and black pistol. Hyland is thorough, explaining each component and pointing out the muzzle, barrel, trigger and grip.

He racks the slide to load the gun then talks me through reloading the magazine with more ammunition. To my surprise, he doesn’t grumpily bark at my questions but carefully explains each step until it’s clear.

“Sabre agents are authorised to use force when needed.” He checks the safety before placing the gun back into the foam. “That isn’t a license to run around doing whatever the fuck you want.”

“Noted. Don’t I get to hold it?”

“We’ll go to the shooting range downstairs for that.” He lifts a wickedly sharp switchblade with deep grooves in the grip. “How are you with knives?”

“Um… I’ve cut vegetables with them before?”

Hyland exhales dramatically. “Why did we waste two hours in here?”

“Hey, I told you I could fight with my fists. You’re the one who insisted on a demonstration.”

“Well, enough dicking around. You clearly can handle yourself in a physical altercation, but we’ve still got a lot of other ground to cover.”

Uncertainty makes me chew on my bottom lip. Glancing up at me, Hyland’s golden brows pull together in a concerned line.

“What is it?”

“How am I supposed to learn all of this in less than two weeks?”

“You don’t have to,” he replies easily. “Skip the raid. We’ll handle it."

"No chance. I want to be there!"

He passes the blade between his hands. "I'm willing to give this a shot, but that doesn't mean I'll let you walk into enemy fire unprepared."

"Then help me get prepared," I implore.

"We train new recruits for at least three months before assigning them to active duty. And even then, it's nothing too risky or intense."

Placing a hand on his vein-studded arm, I gain his attention. "I'm not the average new recruit. Teach me what I don't already know. Help me be ready."

His nostrils flare. "You're asking for too much, red."

"I'm asking for your help. Your guidance. I'm asking for your trust."

Gazes locked, I can see his reluctance. It twists and tangles in the earthy threads that sculpt his irises. Hyland can't decide where his priorities lie—protecting me or letting me retake my life.

Sucked into the magnificence of his olive-toned orbs, I find myself wondering when I last pleaded with someone. It's not something that comes naturally to me. Pleading equals vulnerability in my books.

But I feel safe enough to occupy that fragile space with him. I've let Hyland see glimpses of the real Ember, beyond the caricature I play so well. And he hasn't hurt that broken woman. Not yet.

"I do." His reply offers some assurance. "We wouldn't be doing this if I didn't trust you."

"Then let's get to work. I need to be ready for the raid."

Gaze softening, his reluctance drains away to leave a familiar look of concern. "Why put yourself through it? There will be other chances."

The scent of a fresh, salt-laced breeze pours from him, a perfect match to the raw strength of his voice. He talks like the ocean is spilling from his lips, full of deafening waves and almighty force.

In another life, Hyland could've passed for a surfer. Perhaps even a modern-day Viking. He certainly has the cut muscles and unruly hair to fit the stereotype.

FRACTURED FUTURE

Most would find his intimidating stature exactly that: downright terrifying. Yet he selflessly wields his extreme strength by helping those who wash up on Sabre's doorstep.

"I need to prove to myself that I can do it," I whisper back. "That I can take all the evil they poured inside me and use it for good. I won't know until I try."

"You aren't evil." His gentle smile causes warmth to seep through my veins. "What they made you do was evil, but you… are not."

"Tell that to the trail of people left behind me. Shit, I did far worse than leaving them unconscious after a fight. I don't know if they all survived."

"That's irrelevant." Hyland flicks his wrist dismissively. "What you did was under threat of death or worse. You had no choice."

"But I chose to enjoy it."

"Ember…"

"It's true. I chose to become the violence I was forced to inflict. I chose to let it make its home inside me."

The stubbled lines around his mouth tensing, Hyland lifts a big paw to smooth hair from my face. Several chunks have fallen out of the braid after sparring all morning.

"Fine… You're evil. You win."

"That's not funny." I glare at him.

"My point is that what you do now is your choice. For the record, I think choosing to work for Sabre is brave. Regardless of the shit I give you for it."

"I think that's the nicest thing you've said for a while." I laugh under my breath.

"I give everyone a hard time, Em. It's only the people I care about who get to see why I'm like this. And why I care so bloody much."

"The more you care, the more of an ass you become?"

A smile unfurls on his mouth. "Something like that."

"Then you must really care about me."

"Perhaps I do."

The sound of the air-conditioning system whirring is the only distraction to our moment. Crouched in the ring, the limited air between us feels charged, laden with the possibility of something unknown.

It's the same feeling that crawls under my skin when Axel cracks a joke that makes me laugh so hard, I can barely breathe. Or when Warner sends me hurtling back to a safe, uncomplicated time in my life with a caring smile alone.

Inching my head closer to his, I relish in the torment of Hyland's breath whispering over my skin. Weeks' worth of loaded looks and gruff, reluctant smiles have built a tension inside me that I wasn't prepared to acknowledge before.

Then Axel happened.

That tension fucking exploded.

The smooth-talking jokester showed me that I can have what I want again. That I have the freedom to take it. The ability to choose for myself. Whether it's right or wrong, my body is begging for something from Hyland too.

"If training to meet this stupid deadline is what you want, then I'll help you." He closes the weapons case. "I'll give you whatever you need to face these demons."

"You will?"

"For you." He nods. "I want you to have your proof. I want… Goddammit, Em. I want you to see yourself like I do."

The screaming organ trapped behind my breastbone skips straight over its next beat and launches into a full-blown gallop. His hushed, borderline-secretive words ignite a flame inside my core.

My hand inches across the firm sponge mat, snaking ever closer to his. When our fingertips brush, heat erupts at the faintest graze of his skin on mine.

One stroke is enough to send me into the deep end of my greedy desires. My lungs have seized and feel heavier than a lead balloon. I'm running through the infinite forest that lies within his gaze and wilfully losing myself.

"What do you see?" My breathing grows short.

"Didn't we have this conversation not so long ago?"

"I want to know if your answer has changed."

Hyland scrutinises my face. "It hasn't changed."

Irrational longing envelopes me, urging me to take what I want with no regard for the consequences. Never mind the complication that my stolen time with Axel may cause.

Starved of all free will and affection, a gaping cavern developed inside me. That excruciatingly empty space is now aching to be filled with all I've missed out on.

Hyland's index finger lifts to skate over the back of my palm, slowly caressing me. It's perhaps the most innocent touch I've ever received, but it still feels like being hit with a lightning bolt.

"Red," he grates out.

My teeth sink into my lip, holding back every last traitorous syllable I want to throw out.

"We should head downstairs."

No, I'm desperate to scream.

"When I let people get close…" Hyland audibly swallows. "It only ends in hurt."

"Then it's a good thing I'm already hurt."

"So what? You want me to add to the shit you've already suffered?"

My hand clenches over his, squeezing his rough skin. "You don't hurt people, Hyland. Quite the opposite, in fact."

"You don't know what you're talking about."

"I know enough to say that you're one of the kindest, most protective people I've ever met… Even if that manifests as a miserable, old grouch at times."

He offers a thin smile at my assessment.

"That's the opposite of hurting people," I add.

The tip of his tongue peeks out, moistening his lower lip. That generous pillow, surrounded by blonde scruff and golden skin. God, I want to bite it. I want to feel it against my mouth.

"All love is hurt, Em." His finger drags over my prickling skin. "If you stick around long enough for it to become painful."

When his hand pulls from beneath mine, I'm swamped with disappointment. Just like the near-miss in the elevator. I get achingly close to breaking his defences only for him to withdraw.

No.

He can't choose for both of us.

Grabbing his wrist, I yank hard to make him look back at me.

The ardent intensity of the craving in his eyes steals the limited breath I have left.

"I survived this long by hurting other people and letting them hurt me," I spell out. "Pain is all I've known for the longest time."

He seems to grit his teeth, like he's holding something back.

"What does it tell you that I'm willing to join this team, to let people get close to me, knowing I could get hurt all over again?"

"I... don't know," Hyland admits.

"Then let me illuminate you. It means I'm choosing this. I'm choosing to trust you. To get close to you. To join this family and this team."

Still, his firm jaw remains locked tight, keeping himself closed off. He won't even allow himself to consider his own wants and needs, so I land the killer blow.

"I'm *choosing* to get hurt if that's what's required. You don't get the right to tell me whether that's allowed or not."

Releasing his wrist, I press a chaste kiss to his cheek before standing up. The sudden departure seems to penetrate his overwhelming doubt.

"Ember!" he thunders from behind me.

Walking to the edge of the boxing ring, I look back over my shoulder. He's still crouched on the mat, frozen and fiercely staring at me.

"There are marks on your neck. Marks that weren't there before you had dinner with Axel."

Heat floods my cheeks, but I don't look away. "And?"

"And... If you tear my family apart, I will truly have nothing left. Do you understand that?"

"I understand perfectly."

"Then why are you playing this game?"

Every shitty answer I could placate him with flashes through my mind, but I won't lie to him. I'm not that person. I've created this mess, and I will own it just as easily.

With a jittering hand, I gesture between us. "Does this feel like a game?"

"This being... us?"

I nod sharply.

"No," he answers.

Struggling not to squirm under his intense attention, I watch him square his shoulders as if charging into battle.

"This isn't a game for me, and I don't think it is for you either." He studies me intently. "Which begs the question… Why are you doing this?"

"Axel showed me that it's okay to laugh and smile again. He gives me the space to feel light. Carefree. To feel alive."

Hyland's eyes shutter, anticipating a rejection. "I see."

"And despite how unbearably overprotective and downright infuriating you can be… You make me feel safe. I feel like nothing and nobody can touch me when I'm in your presence."

"Nobody would dare." His tenor deepens into a hair-raising growl. "Not while I'm here."

"Exactly."

Tiny butterflies of fear take flight behind my ribcage, but I pay them no attention. I want him to understand. No, I *need* him to understand.

"Do you have any idea how many times I wished I had someone there to protect me? Someone who could save me? Someone capable of making the pain stop?"

His face wrinkling in a look of immense pain, Hyland drops my eyes. "I can imagine."

"Then perhaps you can begin to understand why it means so much to me now, no matter how much of a hard time I give you. The truth is, I want to feel safe. I want to feel protected."

When he climbs to his feet, disregarding the weapons box, I press against the ropes at my back. Hyland huffs a short breath then stomps over to me, stopping mere inches away.

My neck protests at the sharp angle it takes to look up at him. Gruff, grumpy, asshole Hyland. The handsome face hiding a hurting heart with so much left to give.

"You're playing with fire, red. Someone will get hurt."

Stepping into his space, my sports bra brushes against his torso. "I guess I'm greedy because I don't care."

"I don't have that luxury."

"Because you won't allow yourself to have it," I correct him.

"What would it feel like to take exactly what you want for once? Can you imagine it?"

His loaded pause almost convinces me that he's going to stalk off. Until his hand finds the back of my neck while the other moves to clasp my Lycra-covered waistline.

The forest-green of his eyes has been nearly swallowed whole by impenetrable blackness. If I could throw myself into the depths of his pupils, I doubt I'd be able to crawl out again.

"I don't have to imagine, Em."

Euphoria smacks me in the face and nearly knocks me off my feet when his mouth brushes over mine. The featherlight touch screams through my extremities and sets each limb alight with need.

"Just once won't hurt," Hyland adds hoarsely.

His lips press on mine again in a more commanding kiss. The kind of kiss that stakes an irreversible claim on a person's soul. A kiss so hard and demanding that I gasp into his mouth.

Trapping me against his barrel chest with the hand that cups my neck, Hyland's lips are possessive and firm. He kisses like he's trying to communicate something through his touch alone.

I pour my confusing emotions into it—my appreciation and desire for him, my need for belonging and the turbulence of being pulled in different directions by the way they all make me feel.

Hands sneaking up the solid lines that carve his chest, I curl my arms around his neck and reach onto my tiptoes to deepen the kiss. Hyland responds in kind, a rumble echoing from his throat.

My tongue glides over the seam of his mouth, offering another vulnerable plea. He relents immediately, allowing me to sweep inside and taste every ounce of desire that fuels his movements.

The thought that I've broken this strong, usually unaffected man enough for him to give me this one moment of relief is staggering. He's relented for me.

Lord fucking forgive me, I want to break his resolve again. Over and over. Smash it apart, collect the pieces, then admire them while he fucks the life out of me.

At the sound of a very loud, very deliberate throat clear, Hyland's mouth tears from mine like I've scalded him. Sheer panic infiltrates his face as he looks over my shoulder at something I can't see.

"Training is going well, I see."

Fuck, fuck, triple fucking fuck!

"We're just heading to the shooting range," Hyland rushes to explain.

"Sure looks like it." Warner's voice is unmistakable, albeit unimpressed. "You're wanted upstairs. Go."

Abruptly releasing me, Hyland avoids meeting my eyes as he collects the weapons box and exits the ring. I work on catching my breath before I turn to duck through the ropes after him.

Dread invades my body and makes itself at home when Warner doesn't move from where he's leaning in the doorway. He lets Hyland pass without sparing him a glance.

I've never quite understood the expression *caught red handed* until now. Not even when Tom caught me making out with my first boyfriend and promptly threw him out of the house.

As I scurry across the room, hoping Warner will let me escape without confrontation, my cheeks feel like they're aflame. I didn't mind toying with Axel or Hyland. But Warner? That's a whole other ball game.

"Not you." His arm shoots out to block the exit.

Internally wincing, I halt in front of him. "Um…"

"Enjoying yourself?"

"It isn't what it looks like."

"What does it look like, Em?" He inclines his head.

"We… uh, we're training. Going over weapons. Hand to hand combat."

"What sort of combat requires sticking your tongue down my agent's throat?"

When the ground doesn't open to swallow me up like I'm praying it will, Warner steps closer to me. I've never been afraid of my brother's best friend before. Now I'm fucking petrified.

"We don't fuck around in this family." His low, threatening tone makes my stomach lurch. "So be careful where you put those lips, or you may get more than you bargained for."

My shocked brain nearly implodes, unable to fathom his words. This feels like a loaded threat. Perhaps far beyond merely kicking me off the team.

"Do you understand?"

"Yes," I squeak.

"Good. Now get out of here."

Nodding with my gaze still lowered, I dart past him to flee the room without looking back. If I do, I'm not sure what I'll find written on his face—resentment or rejection.

I can't handle either.

Not from him.

POLICE LINE DO NOT CROSS
POLICE LINE - DO NOT CROSS
LE LINE - DO NOT CROSS
Weapon!
CONFIDENTIAL
2
3

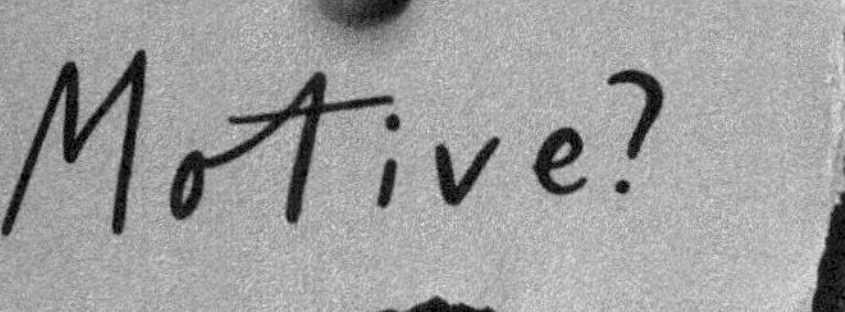

18

HYLAND

STONE — WHISKEY MYERS

Standing beneath the glassy height of the apartment building, I watch rain clouds bubble in the afternoon sky. Dammit. There go my plans for a trip down to Hyde Park today.

The kid always loves the outdoors. Raising him in a quiet cul-de-sac off the beaten path was my priority before I worked for Sabre. I wanted to give Luke a calm, solid upbringing.

When the offer to take this job came in, my ex and I fought for hours about what to do. Choosing to uproot our newborn son, our marriage, our family home… It wasn't easy. But the money was good.

How was I to know what would happen?

We don't know we're making fateful decisions that will hold ramifications for our entire lives when we make them. Does an innocent bystander go out for a walk knowing they're going to be hit by a car? No.

Yet the car hits them regardless.

And a fully loaded semi hit us.

When a mud-splattered Jeep pulls up at the curb, the rapidly expanding anxiety in my gut blooms into suffocating poison ivy that strangles my lungs. Jayce yanks the handbrake to park up, twisting to look into the back seat.

I shouldn't hate that she looks good—what appears to be freshly dyed brunette hair, a face full of well-applied makeup and glowing skin. But fuck it. I hate that she's thriving after leaving me.

She climbs out of the car with barely a glance at me. "Hi."

"Hey," I grumble.

"You made it home safe, then."

Nodding, I look up at the greyscale clouds for an ounce of grace. "Yep."

"The case all wrapped up?"

"Not exactly."

Halting with her hand on Luke's door, she casts me a searching look. When our eyes meet, I'm thrown back to the sheer bliss of our wedding day. The love and happiness that felt like it would go on for an eternity.

Reality kidnaps that happiness, holds it hostage for a short amount of time while we share a moment, then beats it into the ground with a fucking sledgehammer when she speaks.

"You will not put our son in danger again, Hyland. Do you hear me?"

"I hear you."

"This case must be pretty damn serious if it took you halfway around the world for five months. Now you expect me to believe it's safe?"

"Please, Jay. I need to see him. I can't be his dad through odd text messages and phone calls."

Her laugh is bitter and full of grief, far more painful than a stray bullet to the heart.

"You haven't been a dad for a very long time. Not since you chose this career over our family."

"That isn't true."

"Isn't it?" She flaps a hand towards the building behind me. "This was never us."

"You told me to take this job," I hit back, unable to hold it in. "You told me to get out there and earn for our family. You wanted this!"

"I wanted a husband who could provide!" Her eyes shine with a layer of unshed tears. "Not to be nearly killed by criminals in the dead of night looking to blackmail you."

Recoiling at the whip-like impact of her barb, I stare down at the pavement. Shame and too much regret to ever reconcile pulsate through me in a toxic plume.

The memories of that night are too awful to bear. Seeing my wife, clothing ripped and bloodstained while holding our screaming son, killed something fundamental inside me.

It never should've happened. The case was cut and dry—a corrupt CEO funnelling illegal revenue through his hedge fund. Who knew the crafty son of a bitch would go to such lengths to manipulate me?

By the time we apprehended him, it was too late. The men he paid to intimidate me hit where it hurt most. My family. They later felt the full weight of the law, but I'm the one who was punished.

Jayce left soon after.

And she never came back.

"Please." I force the word through my thick throat. "All I want is to be his dad."

"You lost the right to be any kind of father when you brought that mess into our home." She brushes away her tears. "Be thankful I'm allowing you visits at all."

Jayce visibly takes a breath then opens the Jeep's back door. I work on schooling my expression before Luke can see that we were fighting again.

"Come on, baby. Dad's here to see you."

"Yay!"

Two legs quickly hop out of the car. For his age, Luke's a big kid. He inherited that much from me, at least. He got his angelic features and pouting smile from his mother.

Squatting down to get closer to him, I look at my little boy. His shining, golden hair is similar to my own dirty-blonde colour. He's grown so much. Every time we reunite, he looks different.

"Hi, buddy."

"Dad." He breaks out into a big, cheesy grin. "You're back!"

As he launches himself into my hurriedly thrown open arms, it's like no time has passed at all. I sweep Luke off his feet and hug him tight enough for him to squeal in protest.

"You were gone for so long," he complains.

"I know. I'm sorry."

"Where were you?"

"Working, bud. You know how it is."

"I know." Unhappy, he juts out his bottom lip.

Cupping the back of his head, I steal a deep pull of his scent before I release him. Leaning against the Jeep, Jayce watches us cuddle and chat with tears still brimming in her eyes.

"Thank you," I mouth sincerely.

Lips pursed, she swipes underneath her eyes. "Don't make me regret this."

Luke wriggles out of my arms to wish his mum goodbye, squirming when she covers his face in kisses. Then he grabs his bright-red Spiderman backpack and returns to my side.

"Come on, bud." I ruffle the top of his head. "Let's get going."

His hand feels tiny wrapped in mine. Like I could break his little bones with a single squeeze. No one warns you how terrifying it is to become a parent, knowing full well you have the power to make or break your kid.

Inside the elevator, Luke punches several buttons so we end up stopping on multiple floors. By the time we reach the top, I'm laughing my ass off.

"You're as bad as Uncle Axel."

"Is he here?" Luke spins towards me excitedly.

"Yeah, he's in."

"Oh, cool! I want to learn more karate."

Shit. I should find the kid a few less insane uncles.

Unlocking the front door, I frown at the sound of yelling emanating from somewhere in the apartment. Luke peeks around my leg to follow the noise, but when I pick out Ember's voice, I relax.

"It's alright. We have someone new on our team who I need to introduce you to."

"Really?" Luke brightens up.

"She's nice. You'll like her."

"She's a girl?" He looks up at me with a wrinkled nose. "I don't want any of her germs."

A laugh spills from my chest. "Girls don't give you germs, Luke."

"They so do. Emily at school said she was my girlfriend, but by break time, she said Morgan Reeves was her boyfriend!"

Pinching his cheek, I fight to hold in a laugh. "I'm sorry, kid. That's mean."

"Yes!" He stomps his foot. "And that's why girls have germs."

"Well, this girl doesn't have any germs. I promise."

As we walk into the living area, the sound of yelling intensifies. Though it sounds like only Ember is shouting while Axel's voice is punctuated by guffaws of laughter.

"I said neutral colours, Ax! What is neutral about orange paint?"

"You could've gone to the DIY shop yourself."

"And you know I had to go see that idiot, Richards! You are such a fucking dick."

"I thought a bit of orange would brighten up the place. I even started painting for you."

"And that's why you're a fucking dick!"

"Language," I call into the hallway. "Little ears present."

Both of them falling into a hush, footsteps precede their heads poking around Ember's bedroom door. Axel straightens with a massive smile when he spots Luke yanking off his shoes.

"Hey, man! You're back."

"Uncle Ax! Uncle Ax!"

The pair run at each other to exchange a hug. The moment Axel joined our team and our lives, my son took a fast liking to his pranks and endless energy for playdates. They adore each other.

"Why are you covered in paint?" Luke asks the big oaf.

"I was helping out our new friend." Axel shrugs, placing him back on his feet. "She's redecorating her new bedroom."

The *friend* in question has emerged from her room to join us at the edge of the sunken living area. Ember shoots me a terse smile, visibly uncertain of how to proceed.

It's been awkward between us since the boxing ring. We've worked our way through several more training sessions before I handed her over to Axel for his help, but we haven't touched again.

"Ember, this is Luke." I gesture towards him.

"Your son?"

"The one and only. He's here tonight. Sorry, I should've said."

When her face lights up in that effortless smile that I'm slowly becoming obsessed with, I let my tense muscles ease. She wanders over to Luke and offers him a high five.

"Hey. I'm Em."

"Luke." He eyes her suspiciously. "Do you have girl germs? My dad said you don't, but I'm not sure."

A hand propped on her hip, Ember quirks an eyebrow at me. I shrug wordlessly.

"That depends." She lowers her raised hand. "Do you like pizza? Because Uncle Ax owes me an apology pizza. But we don't have to share if you think I have germs."

"I like pizza! I'll share!"

"Alright, then. I guess I don't have girl germs. Go get your credit card, Uncle Ax."

Mumbling a curse under his breath, Axel rolls his eyes then vanishes to locate his wallet. I watch Ember lead Luke into her bedroom then follow them in a state of shock.

True to his word, Axel certainly did start painting. The entire back wall behind Ember's pushed aside bed has been badly painted a lurid, disgusting shade of orange.

"Oh." Luke covers his mouth with his hand to laugh. "That's so gross."

"Right?" Ember titters.

"I hate orange!"

"Me too. What colour should I paint it?"

"I like blue. But dark-blue, like the sky at night."

Nodding, Ember stares at her bedroom wall. "That's a great idea. What colour's your room?"

"Red!" he exclaims. "It's my favourite colour."

"I like red too."

Eyeing her critically, Luke sucks in his lips. "Your hair is kinda red."

"It sure is. That's why red is so cool."

"I guess your hair is cool. You look a bit like Black Widow."

"Want to hear a secret?" Ember asks him in a conspiratorial hush.

Nodding enthusiastically, Luke awaits the big reveal.

"I'm far cooler than Black Widow," she explains. "And I bet I could kick her ass."

"Language," I drone again.

His reticence forgotten, Luke makes big heart eyes up at Ember. "I bet you could!"

While Luke's always been friendly enough, Ember clearly has a knack for winning kids over. Which is odd considering how standoffish she can be with the adult population.

Propping my shoulder against the doorframe, I watch Ember crouch down to Luke's level. Honestly, seeing her laughing and smiling with my kid is making my heart sputter uncontrollably.

I've been kept awake most nights since I pinned her tight, hard body to my chest as I plundered her hot mouth. The thoughts of what is possible but can never be between us are constant and cruel.

To top it off, Warner hasn't spared me a glance. I know what I did was stupid, but I'd like to see any man refuse the minx and her sexy taunts. He wouldn't be immune either.

"Are you drooling over Ember right now?" Axel whispers over my shoulder.

I glance backwards to glower at him. "Shut it, pup."

"That's not a denial."

"She's really good with him."

"She is. But you can't impregnate our new teammate."

"Ax! Jesus Christ."

"Just saying." He winks at me. "Not yet at least."

Spinning around, I shove him into the hallway. "I do not want to do that. Perhaps have a word with yourself about respecting boundaries with our new co-worker."

"Respect." His nose scrunches with a confused look. "Boundaries.

Huh. Nope, *no comprendo.*"

"I'm serious, Ax! She's our colleague!"

"Then why is Warner giving you the stink eye every single day and not me?"

Stumped, I mash my lips together.

"Ah," Axel coos knowingly. "Someone isn't taking his own advice. I see."

"I have no idea what you're talking about."

"It's cool, bro. I'm not territorial. Whatever the lady wants, she can have. I won't complain."

Irritation sears behind my eyeballs. "She doesn't want me!"

"Doesn't look that way to me."

When I smack him across his purple-dyed head, Axel ducks beneath me to escape into the bedroom. He's such a little shit stirrer.

I'm not dumb. I know he's playing games just like Ember is. Axel will happily tear apart someone else's life if it keeps him entertained for five minutes. What I don't know is what he hopes to achieve.

We can't both be with her.

Right?

Leaving the trio, I return to the kitchen to pull out soft drinks and plates. I can hear them discussing pizza toppings, moving on from the mess Axel has made of Ember's new bedroom.

By the time they emerge with the pizzas ordered, I've set everything up on the breakfast bar. Axel has Luke attached to his back like a spider monkey while running around, screaming and laughing.

"He's a good kid." Ember takes a seat on a bar stool. "Real sweet."

"Yeah, he is."

When she stares directly at me for several emotionally loaded seconds, I lift a hand in challenge.

"Got something to say?"

"Don't go all mega-grump, Hulk mode on me... But you said that it's hard to see him."

"Yeah." I wrestle to keep an even tone. "It's tough."

"Well, he clearly adores you regardless."

Cautiously nodding, I try to puzzle out her weirdly thoughtful expression. The two boys have collapsed on one of the L-shaped sofas, giving us a second of privacy while they browse the TV listings.

"I didn't know my dad." Her expression stoic, Ember feigns nonchalance. "Mum did the best she could, but it was tough. I saw my friends with their happy families, and I wanted a piece of that."

"Having two parents doesn't always equate to happiness."

She nods jerkily. "No, it doesn't."

"So what's your point, Em?"

Trailing a finger over the speckled blackness of the countertop, she seems to choose her next words carefully.

"Luke is lucky to have you in any shape or form. You don't have to be the perfect dad to be his whole world. You should give yourself some credit for showing up."

Thorny vines wrap around my throat and squeeze tight. It doesn't take long for thoughts and memories of that night to poison my bloodstream.

"I put him in danger. Me."

"He'll be in danger every day of his life as long as he's living in this world," she counters. "Maybe he'll be thankful to have a devoted dad there to look out for him despite his mistakes."

"You're saying he'll forgive me when he learns about what happened?" My voice comes out as a warble.

"I'm saying… I don't think there's anything to forgive. Not from him. Perhaps the issue is you need to forgive yourself."

After everything happened, I had several months of sessions with Richards. We dissected the entire timeline until I thought I'd processed my destroyed life. Perhaps things aren't as tidily put away as I thought.

With a wash of surprise, the urge to take her into my arms and crush those perfect, plump lips again takes over me. Fuck the consequences. Fuck whether or not it's allowed. Fuck it all.

Ember sees the world in a unique way. She strips all the bullshit away to get to the core of what matters. Right now, Luke matters. Raising him. Making him feel loved. I can't do that as half a man.

"You have a big heart, Em."

"I'm just telling it how it is." She speaks without looking at me. "You're punishing yourself for stuff you couldn't control back then."

Sidling around the counter, I dare to reach for her hand. When her fingers slide against mine, an intense longing seizes me, obliterating every last misgiving I hold about whatever this is.

Two blue-grey celestites full of unresolved pain flit up to me. She's still holding it all in. Denying herself the possibility of leaning on anyone but herself.

"I know how much that shit hurts."

"How would you know?" I ask softly.

"Don't push it, Hy."

"It's a simple enough question."

"I've only done two therapy sessions guised as some debrief crap." Her lips form a thin smile. "I'm not going further than that."

Battling my own smile, I'm desperate to lean into her beckoning personal space and tuck a fiery-red strand behind her ear. Even if she'd stab me for it.

"Answer my question, and I'll make sure Axel repaints your bedroom whatever shade you want. And he has to apologise for being an asshole."

"What if he won't?" Ember challenges.

"He'll have to live with no fucking limbs."

"Hm. I like that idea."

Licking her bottom lip, she peers at me through devilishly thick lashes. Fuck me, the way I'd happily fall into those curiously mixed eyes and let myself be crushed by her internal gravity.

"How do you know it hurts, Em?" I push her.

Teeth repeatedly sinking into her lip, the war that unfolds on her oval face makes my fingers twitch. I won't cross a line with her again. That's what I have to tell myself. That's the law I must live by.

"I didn't hurt Gracie." Ember blinks rapidly. "But I hate myself for it anyway. Just like you hate yourself for how your family got hurt."

"It wasn't your job to protect her."

"I don't care. I still failed at it."

Needing to do something to stop the chasm in my chest from opening further and sucking in all the reasons why I shouldn't touch her again, I dare to inch a little closer.

"I failed them too," I whisper back, my gaze straying over to Luke, watching a movie. "People I was supposed to protect. It eats you up inside."

Ember silently nods.

"Every time I help a client or solve a case, it heals a bit of that pain. Not all of it—I don't think those scars will ever heal. But it helps enough for me to continue living."

When her gaze lifts to meet mine, I feel like my heart is going to spill from my throat. The lost look on her face is tempered by an almost imperceptible flicker of hope.

"You're gonna get there too, red. I know you will."

"I think you have a lot of faith for someone who's barely looked at me in days." She tears her eyes from mine to stare out the window.

Overcome by conflicting emotions, I can't stop myself from brushing loose, velvety hair over her shoulder.

"You know why I can't look, Em. Why I can't do this with you."

"No." Her hand clenches around mine when she looks back at me. "I really don't."

The feel of her warmth sinking into my palm is a hateful taunt. It screams of endless possibilities that will never be within my reach, no matter the passion we so recklessly shared. It can't happen again.

"Napkins." I change the subject, pulling my hand away from her grasp. "We still need napkins."

"Napkins. Sure."

Turning my back on her pains me, but it's easier to breathe when I don't have to look at her. Busying myself, I focus on ripping sheets of kitchen towels.

By the time I turn back around, Ember has returned to the living area. They're all watching some superhero crap with the volume turned up high. Already I can tell that Luke is enthralled.

Content to watch them rather than the movie, I answer the door when the security system shrieks for attention. Warner waits on the other side, a stack of steaming pizza boxes in hand.

"The delivery guy was downstairs." Frowning, he casts me a reluctant look. "Luke here already?"

"Yeah." I take the boxes from him. "Why?"

"We need to talk. Privately."

Warner walks into the apartment behind me, shrugging off the light jacket he wears over his plain t-shirt and jeans. He ditches his work ID and lanyard on the kitchen counter.

"What is it?"

With a quick look at the others to ensure they're distracted, Warner scrapes a hand over his stubble-marked jaw.

"I received a call from an MoD official today."

"Why is the Ministry of Defence calling us?" Confusion burrows beneath my skin.

"I have an old army friend who works there now. We keep in touch. He knows about our current case."

"Right. Get to the point?"

"This news hasn't broken yet." His throat moves with a heavy gulp. "A shipping container washed up in British waters today. The bodies of twelve women were inside."

Twelve... women.

I feel my mouth fall wide open as a riot of thoughts batter the inner confines of my skull. Right or wrong, the first person that comes to mind is Ember.

"I don't know if it's connected to our case yet." Warner massages his temples. "But this may give us a break in figuring out who's arranging these shipments."

Trying to wrap my head around the contents of that shipping container, Warner gives me a second to process before he adds the sweetener.

"If it's an official taking bribes from multiple mobs and trafficking gangs to approve these shipments without being checked or caught... we can nail them."

"It's a start." I numbly bob my head in agreement. "Fuck. Twelve women? All dead?"

"I know," Warner replies solemnly.

"This is so messed up."

"We don't have IDs yet, but they've been in there for a while. We have to tell Ember."

Too choked up to find a response, I stare at our team leader.

Homing in on his visible eye bags, weighed down by fatigue. Every last exhausted line that marks his face.

He may disapprove of our recent behaviour, but that hasn't stopped Warner from working night and day to ensure Ember's safety. He's relentlessly determined to give her back her life. Almost too determined.

We're up against a powerful system.

He knows it isn't a fair fight.

My gaze strays over to Ember, snuggled up next to my son and loudly debating the merits of the superhero prancing around in spandex tights on the screen. Her laughter lights up the whole penthouse.

She could've been swallowed by that system.

And I don't know if we can protect her from it now.

CONFIDENTIAL
Suspect!
DO NOT CROSS
POLICE
Suspect?
NOT CROSS
POLICE

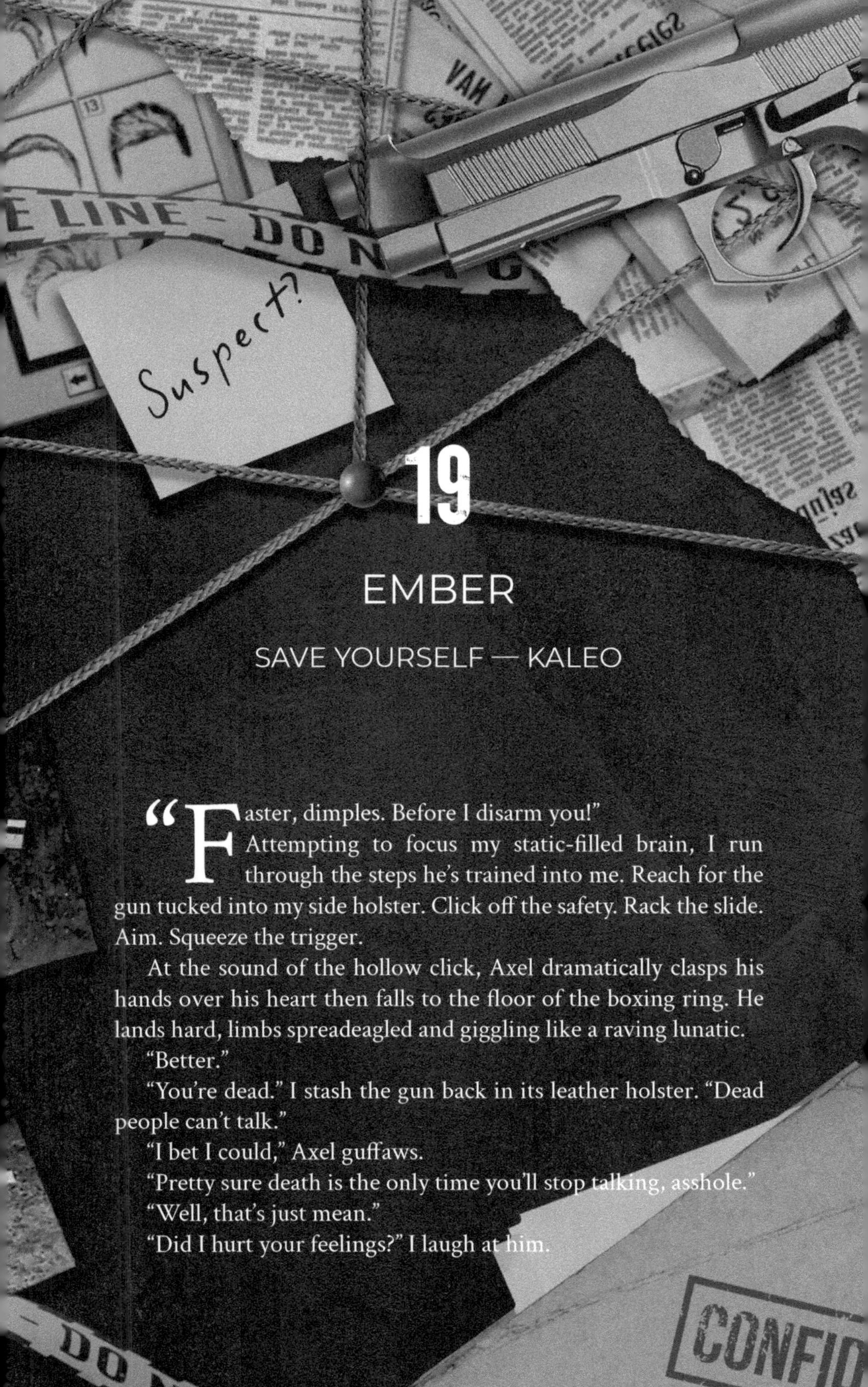

19

EMBER

SAVE YOURSELF — KALEO

"Faster, dimples. Before I disarm you!"

Attempting to focus my static-filled brain, I run through the steps he's trained into me. Reach for the gun tucked into my side holster. Click off the safety. Rack the slide. Aim. Squeeze the trigger.

At the sound of the hollow click, Axel dramatically clasps his hands over his heart then falls to the floor of the boxing ring. He lands hard, limbs spreadeagled and giggling like a raving lunatic.

"Better."

"You're dead." I stash the gun back in its leather holster. "Dead people can't talk."

"I bet I could," Axel guffaws.

"Pretty sure death is the only time you'll stop talking, asshole."

"Well, that's just mean."

"Did I hurt your feelings?" I laugh at him.

"Nah. I'll live."

Flipping back up onto his feet, he lifts the hem of his oversized tee to dab his forehead, revealing a flash of mouthwatering abdominals. His shirt is an obnoxious shade of red displaying the words '*I dressed myself today*' in childlike scrawl.

Dropping from the ring to take a swig of my iced americano, I watch him fiddle with his amethyst hair. It's all ruffled and messy from sweat after our latest sparring session.

We've been working on weapons for several days now in preparation for Thursday's raid. As the hours tick down, my excitement grows, along with my trepidation.

"I don't think red is your colour, Ax."

"Get lost," he snarks back. "I love this shirt."

"It's clashing with the hair."

"What? No, it's not!"

"I preferred yesterday's selection."

"You did?" His eyes widen into round spheres. "Well then. I'll burn everything I own and only wear that t-shirt from now on."

"And when it needs washing?"

He saucily winks at me. "I'll be naked, obviously."

Shaking my head at him, I work on stretching out my muscles. We've been working harder than ever since Warner's news. Though my motivation to train non-stop now stems from more than my desire to attend the raid.

When I'm not in the ring, all I can think about are those twelve women. Twelve bodies currently being autopsied, after they were left to float and rot until the container washed ashore. Twelve lives… gone.

The number repeatedly throbs inside my tender head.

Twelve.

Twelve.

Twelve.

The thought of what they endured is horrific. Every night, I dream of the container we were trapped in—dark, freezing cold, filled with sobbing and raw bodily waste. The constant swaying and tipping.

Twelve.

Twelve.
Twelve.

Eyes scrunching shut, I brace a hand against the raised platform that holds the boxing ring to ride the wave of vertigo that engulfs me. My current headache has been tormenting me for days now.

Holding back memories and every last emotion entangled in them is becoming a full-time occupation. I can hardly get through a waking moment without hearing rain on the roof of that container again.

"Ember? You good?"

"Fine," I grit out.

"You don't exactly look it."

There's a thud as Axel hops down next to me, then his hand lands on my lower back.

"We've been at it non-stop. You should take a break."

"No! I need to—"

"Rest." He grips my shoulders to hold me steady. "Jeez. You're trembling."

"Just tired."

"You sure? Are you getting sick?"

"No, no. I said I'm fine." I pull from his grasp, rolling my neck to relieve the stress. "Let's go again."

"Again? Hell no!" Axel watches me with tightly knitted brows. "You're pale too."

"Ax, stop. I want to keep training."

"Nope. We're done."

"I have to be ready for Thursday!"

"Yes, by resting and recuperating. You won't be worth shit if you're sick or dead on your feet."

Steeling my spine, I'm about to lay into him when I realise a quiet figure is typing on his phone near the entrance to the room. He must've slipped in while we were busy training.

Although he's wearing his usual tailored suit and tie, Tom looks rumpled. His auburn locks are hastily arranged, not neat and sleek. Even his shirt collar is unbuttoned, navy tie askew.

"Aw, shit." Axel looks over at our intruder. "Shall I get rid of him? You should go home and nap."

"It's alright. I can handle my brother."

"Or I could beat his ass?"

"Ax!" I exclaim.

"What? He's not my brother or best friend. I'll happily do it."

"Well, he is mine."

"Sooo… You're gonna beat his ass then? I have a new knife you can borrow. It's in my coat. Custom blade and grip too."

"No ass beating! No knives!" I flap my hands around with increasing dismay. "For fuck's sake."

Axel's honeyed eyes roll in outrage. "You're so dull."

"Better to be dull than fucking insane."

"See, that's where we disagree."

Shoving his shoulder, I decide to face the music rather than put it off. Tom and I haven't spoken since I left his apartment, and the silence has been excruciating. But hell if I was going to be the one to break it.

Ditching my cold coffee, I limp over to Tom's slumped-over state. He quickly slips his phone away to train his tired focus on me.

"Hi," he offers warily.

"Hey."

Looking over me, Tom summons a minuscule attempt at a smile. "It's good to see you."

"Can I help you with something?"

He shuffles his feet, appearing awkward. "I was hoping we could talk."

"I wanted to talk the last time we saw each other. All you did was yell."

"No more yelling." Tom surrenders by showing me his palms. "I promise."

"Why should I believe that?"

Face folding in visible pain, his eyes are pleading. "I heard the news. I'm here for you, Em. Nothing else."

Taking a moment to debate his motives, I decide to steer him out into the corridor for some privacy. Tom follows close behind me as I head for Sabre's empty changing room a few doors down.

"So talk." I wave towards him.

Resting against a bank of shiny silver lockers, he averts his eyes while I change into fresh leggings. It hurts my head to bend and yank them up, but I suck it up.

"I want to apologise for the things I said. And I intend to apologise to the others too."

"You were a complete dick, Tom."

"I'm aware of that," he agrees wholeheartedly. "Throwing the past in their faces was unfair."

"You know Warner has been through hell."

"I know. I'll make it right."

Throwing a plain white t-shirt over my sports bra, I sit down to brace my palms on my knees. I need a moment to rest. My vision is hazy at the corners.

Moving to crouch in front of me, Tom clasps my forearms. His fingers graze my brand, causing discomfort to slither up my spine. It takes great effort to look up and meet his eyes.

"Let's talk about this, Em."

"You literally called me mentally unstable for choosing to do this. I don't know what else I can say."

"That's not… Shit." He sighs heavily. "I didn't mean to be such an idiot. I really am sorry. It's just… I wanted to protect you."

"By screaming your head off?"

"By convincing you to be something you're not."

Tom averts his eyes, but not before I see how much shame fills them. My brother isn't one to apologise. His career and world are far too cut-throat for that. But we've never fought like this either.

"I can see how foolish that was now. You're braver than me. Strong. Determined. I should've trusted you."

Softening, I lift one hand to place it over his, drawing his sad eyes back to me. "Thank you."

"When Mum died…" His throat works up and down. "You held it together for the both of us. You looked after me and struggled alone. Just like you did when I left for university."

"You're being too hard on yourself."

"No, Em. It's always you keeping us together."

My vocal cords spasm, filling with sharp pain. Someone had to take care of the funeral arrangements and our mother's estate.

Although Tom was older, he was a grieving wreck. I had no choice but to step up.

"For once, I just wanted to be the one to look after you. That's all."

"I love you for it," I rasp throatily. "But I have to do this."

"I know that. I'm proud of you."

"You've no idea how much I needed to hear that."

We wrap each other in a tight hug. Tom's face tucks into the crook of my neck while I suck in his minty, ink-stained scent, letting it soothe me.

Losing our only parent fucked us both up, but I don't think either of us quite realised how much until now.

"I'm not going to lie... I really hate that you're living in an apartment full of men." He laughs into my neck. "Who do I need to have thrown in prison first?"

"No one," I rush out.

Pushing me backwards, Tom cocks a brow. "That was a fast answer."

"I can handle the Anaconda Team. They're harmless."

"I trust Warner, but the moment the others try to cross any professional boundaries... You tell me, alright? I'll handle it."

My stomach twists and flips traitorously. He really doesn't need to know about Axel publicly fucking me with his hand or Hyland kissing me so hard, I swear I saw stars.

"You got it."

Smiling, Tom tugs the end of my ponytail. "Good."

"Did you come all the way here just to win me over in person?"

"Partly." His smile soon fades away. "The authorities are investigating the shipping container that washed up. I wanted to make sure you're okay. But first, I have something for you."

Sitting back on his haunches, Tom reaches into his suit jacket. He pulls out a folded yellow Post-It note to hand over to me.

"What's this?"

Unfolding the paper, I see a scrawled phone number.

"We contacted Gracie Livingstone's parents. They want to speak to you when you're ready."

A miasma of shock, terror and alarm nearly bowls me over.

I quickly refold the note so I don't have to see the ink smears screeching their accusations at me.

"Why? I don't know where she is."

"Em, breathe." He lightly squeezes my knee. "They just want to hear about her. That's all. They miss their daughter."

"I c-can't… I can't do that!"

"Hey, hey. It's okay. There's no rush."

Gracie's swollen, purple face flashes across my vision, an endless scream trapped on her tongue. She could barely walk when she returned from her examination, her legs were so shaky and weak.

Do they really want to hear about that? Or how she was repeatedly battered with fists and humiliation? How sick men drooled over her, imprisoned and prone, negotiating their best offer?

Soon they'll think about their precious little girl the same way Tom now looks at me. Like she's a broken doll. A shattered memory. Eternally lost to a trauma too extreme to ever recover from.

"Do they hate me?"

Tom passionately shakes his head. "Of course not. Why would they?"

"Because I left her there!"

"You escaped, Em. It's different."

"But I didn't just escape, did I?"

I was freed.

Eyes straying over to the backpack I stole from Hyland to use on training days, the urge to reach for my phone is stifling. I blocked Blaine the moment it was revealed he attended that meeting.

It's hard to comprehend that he was playing me all along. Though he owes me nothing, part of me still believed there was more to him and his actions. That on some level, perhaps he even cared.

Knowing that I was just a pawn in some unknown game stings. I don't have to understand his scheming to feel used. Despite all his flirting and weirdly gentle touches, he never really gave a shit.

"You don't have to speak to them," Tom adds, his emerald eyes full of understanding. "Not if it's going to be too hard. But I promised I'd pass the message along."

"I'll think about it." I nod robotically.

"No matter what you decide to do… What's happened to Gracie will never, ever be your fault. No one else thinks that, so you don't need to either."

When his phone begins to ring, Tom reluctantly releases my knee to answer it. When the voice on the other line rattles on about some urgent client matter, he mouths an apology to me.

"Take it. I need to freshen up."

Nodding, Tom rises to his feet. "I'll be back."

Once he's left the changing room, I pull my knees up to my chest and rest my hot, pounding forehead there. It took all of my strength to hold my mask together in front of Tom. Like I do every other day for the whole world.

With him gone, the building blocks that fortify my mental wall come tumbling down. No matter how many times I rebuild that fortress, it never lasts long. I just don't let anyone see the inevitable destruction.

Shivers overtake me, the first tremors of an apocalyptic earthquake that will level everything in its path. I shook so hard in that container. Not even Gracie's hypothermic body clinging to me stopped the quakes.

I don't know that my bones have thawed since those endlessly cold days. An eternal frost crystallised around my nerves and organs in the time I spent waiting for us to die or be rescued.

I'm s-so c-cold, Em.

I want to g-go home.

It took all of my strength and remaining energy to whisper reassurances to the sobbing sixteen-year-old. Everything I had to give, I gave to her. I wanted her to feel safe with me.

The tears come thick and fast, coating my skin in an unbearable reminder of how badly I've failed. It doesn't matter that what happened wasn't my fault. Honestly, I don't care whose fault it was.

I still made a promise that I couldn't keep. I failed to protect that terrified girl who just wanted to go home. Now I'm safe and free while she's still lost.

Slumping onto my side, I curl up in a ball on the changing room floor. My chest heaves as relentless sobs tear through me, each thunderous clap causing my ribs to shudder.

My cries pour out in a never-ending geyser, ripping free from the broken remnants of my soul. The anger and hatred leave no space for air. I don't deserve any. Not after breaking my promise.

At the sound of the door reopening, I can't even attempt to pick myself up. The last thing I want is for Tom to see me like this, but the floodgates have splintered, and I've got no chance of rebuilding them.

"Em? You in here?"

More footsteps. Then a sharp inhale.

"Oh, love."

Metallic thumping betrays Warner's unmistakable steps. His hollow prosthetic would give him away to anyone. Knowing it's him only intensifies my embarrassment.

He grunts while struggling to lower himself to the floor a short distance away. I peer through enflamed, tear-logged eyes to look at him. The sweet, broken boy who once harboured so much pain. I know he will understand.

"Tom gave you the number," he guesses.

"How can I face them?" I weep uselessly. "How can I tell them that I left their daughter behind?"

"You had no choice, Em. You were sold."

"She needed me!"

"You needed saving yourself," Warner murmurs.

His soothing words slice into the tissue rupturing inside me until it feels like I'm going to bleed out. I want him to blame me. To scream at me. To tell me he hates me. Anything to validate my guilt.

Instead, he reaches out a single hand towards me. Just one. No expectations, no gruff demands. Just five fingers and a hope that I'll let him share this burden with me. Hell, with *anyone*.

"You don't have to do this alone. Not this time."

"I'm so tired of hurting," I whimper.

"Then let me help you. We talked about this, Em. We're a family. You can lean on us."

"I don't know how... I'm alone. Always alone."

"No. You're not."

Warner doesn't wave his hand in invitation or wriggle his fingers. He doesn't even inch closer. It's all on me… He's giving me the choice to accept his support or not.

The unconditional love in his motiveless care breaks me. Limbs locked tight, I shuffle across the floor to near him. Our fingers bounce off each other before his hand cinches around mine.

I drag in a startled breath.

"That's it, love." His firm grip on my hand tightens. "I've got you now."

Warner pulls me close until I can crawl into his lap. I clamber on top of him, a leg on either side of his waist as I flatten my chest against his. Comfort thaws my frozen bones as two strong arms curl around me in a vice.

Every part of us ends up touching, not a single inch of air or space separating us. We're locked tighter than two lost puzzle pieces, desperate to reveal the final image.

As the cyclone inside me continues to spin, I let myself be held by him. Comforted. Offered support and assurance. I've never given myself this luxury before.

Warner is what he's always been to me—*safe*. The steady, constant presence of the tide lapping at the shore, regardless of the storm raging above. It doesn't stop him from providing his love and care.

"I can't face them," I hiccup into his t-shirt. "How can I?"

"You don't have to. Not yet. Not ever if you don't want to. You owe them nothing."

"But… They must hate me. I left her behind!"

"You did no such thing." He gently kisses my hair again. "Did you plan to abandon her?"

"No!"

"Did you want to?"

"God, no. No!"

"Did you laugh as they dragged you away?"

"Fuck… No!"

"Or celebrate in the knowledge that she was left alone?"

Tears continue to pour down my cheeks, resembling an

overflowing waterfall.

"N-No. I didn't do any of that."

"Then stop punishing yourself for something you didn't choose. You were both captives. One of you just got lucky and found their way home."

"B-But it didn't deserve to be me." My tiny, broken voice sounds so fucking childlike, it makes me sick.

"But it is."

His arms tighten further, forming a snake-like coil that refuses to surrender me to the demons trying to drag me into their lair. Warner won't let me drown. I know he won't.

As long as he's holding me, I'll always come up for air. The same way I did when he held my hand at my mother's funeral. And the same way I did when he found me in that coffee field, battered and broken.

He's seen me at my worst. The lowest, most harrowing points of my whole life. No matter what heartbreak I've allowed him to see, Warner never judged. He never left. He never stopped caring.

"You were given the chance to escape and begin again," he says into my hair. "Now look what you're doing with that chance, Ember. You're fighting back."

"H-How?"

"By continuing to live. You're taking all that pain and evil and doing something with it. You're fighting for the right people now. I am so fucking in awe of you."

Those words land the killer blow against my fragile state. My sobs intensify into backbreaking bawls that old, independent me would've been utterly disgusted by.

My keening must be audible out in the hallway; I have no idea how no one else has come in, seeking the source. The sound of my animalistic wailing feels deafening in my own head.

"Let it out." Warner's lips repeatedly press into my head. "You're safe with me."

With the feel of his hand stroking my hair, his quiet murmuring and each breath he draws in expanding against my chest, I find a lifeline. A tiny glimmer at the end of a suffocating tunnel.

And I take it.

Over and over again, I take that lifeline.

I take the strength he's giving me.

Because if Warner can forgive me—the man who has seen me change into this broken version of myself, leaving my old self behind like a ruined chrysalis—then I can forgive myself too.

Or I can at least try to.

For him. For us.

For our team.

CONFIDENTIAL
Why?
Suspect?
Gael?
DO NOT CROSS
POLICE LI

CONFIDENTIAL
Suspect?
DO NOT CROSS
PO
Suspect?
NOT CROSS
POLICE L

20

EMBER

BURN THE MONEY — YOUNG LIONS

Clustered on the ground floor of an empty office building, I linger at the back of the group of black-clad operatives. It's controlled chaos as weapons, bulletproof vests and instructions are handed out.

At the heart of the wild scene, Warner barks orders at each Sabre agent gathered around him. With the Anaconda Team and the Falcon Team—including Archer and his teammates, Josh, Kyle and Oscar—we're a decent-sized group.

"We have ten minutes until we estimate the meeting will end," he calls over the murmured conversations. "Let's go over this one more time."

When platinum-blonde haired Oscar fails to fall silent, Warner shoots him a cold look. This Warner's a far cry from the man who held me tight not so long ago.

It's odd to see him in his element. He's worked for Sabre long enough for me to know he's good at what he does, but reconciling this strict disciplinarian with the gentle man I know is tough.

"Sorry," Oscar mutters.

"This is your first real raid, Falcon Team. Pay attention, and don't fuck this up. You don't want to piss off the bosses."

There's a chorus of nervous laughter.

"Believe me," Warner continues in good humour. "It isn't pretty when you do."

While I have yet to meet the infamous Knight brothers or the family I've heard gossiped about so many times, their reputation precedes them. Sabre's directors are equally respected and feared.

After looking at each of his team members to ensure they feel the gravity of Warner's words, Archer defers to him with a nod. Since I beat his ass, he's taken to taunting me about a rematch. Though never in front of his team.

"You will be around the back, covering the rear exits." Warner's gaze lands on each man. "I want all escape points blocked."

The younger-looking Falcon member, Josh, awkwardly sticks his hand up. "Are we apprehending or... uh, shooting to kill?"

"Jesus." Archer runs a hand over his exasperated face. "Did you idiots forget all of your training?"

"We only shoot to kill if there is no other choice." Warner frowns at Josh. "You know that. Use of force is permitted when your life is at risk."

With a nod, Josh lowers his hand.

"Hyland, Axel, Ember and I will make up the advance party," he explains, hands clasped behind his back. "We will be covering the front entrance to catch attendees off guard when they leave."

"How many are we anticipating?" Kyle asks in a gruff timbre.

"I counted approximately fifteen assailants entering the meeting," Axel answers him. "Fewer numbers than before. Some are missing."

"Why?" I speak up.

Looking back at me, Axel shrugs. "Unclear."

The thought that we won't catch all of Gael's honeypots tonight, and some may be left to disappear, sets my teeth on edge. Word will soon spread. The cartel will know we're gunning for them after we do this.

Tonight could be our one and only shot to gain an advantage over Gael and the intricate web that feeds his business model. We can't reach him, but we can reach those who prop up his enterprise.

"Our priority is Blaine Madden and his three associates—two male, one female." Hyland folds his bulging arms. "We need them taken alive."

Distracting myself by checking my dark cargo trousers, bulletproof vest and attached gun holster, I try to ignore the weight of his gaze on me.

They all seem hyper-aware of the fact that Blaine is here. Sure, I'm hyper-fucking-aware of that fact too. He's half the reason I'm here.

I want to look that snake in the eye and demand to know what his game plan is and how he knows Gael. What I don't appreciate is being treated like Blaine is some kind of sore spot for me.

He showed his true colours. Communication was cut. End of story. I don't care about him or his crew. I'll be professional tonight and ensure he's in cuffs.

"We have a few agents on standby at the rendezvous point three blocks over," Warner continues explaining. "Should you need to, you can call for backup. No injuries tonight, please."

"Only theirs." Axel cracks his knuckles, flexing dark swirls of ink. "The fatal force rule doesn't apply to me, right?"

Everyone gapes at him like he's joking. Only the punchline never comes. It rarely does with Axel.

"What?" He glowers back.

"Yes." Warner wearily rubs his jaw. "It does apply to you. Perhaps even more so."

"Hang on, I didn't sign up to dance with these motherfuckers. You can take some alive, but I reserve the right to break a few skulls tonight."

"He has a point," Kyle mumbles.

Shooting a thumb's up at his co-conspirator, Axel smirks at me. I wink in return. We need some of them alive, but if he wants to crack a few skulls, I can think of no one more deserving than these operatives.

"Enough!" Warner snaps. "Everyone in position, prepared to advance."

All making agreeing sounds, we fan out into two separate groups. Archer exchanges a few words with Hyland before leading his team from the building to find their place outside.

Tailbone still propped against the white wall, I watch my three teammates confer. I didn't sleep a wink last night in anticipation of the raid. Coupled with my recent symptoms, this feels like a shitty idea.

But after spending all these weeks working tirelessly to be ready for this exact moment, I'm not going to admit defeat that easily. I've fought under worse conditions. I just need to focus and hunt down Blaine.

A spasm in my hand causes me to look down at my contorted fingers, twitching and jerking tellingly. I quickly curl them into a fist before anyone can notice.

Not now. Not now.

Wandering over to me, Warner summons a smile. "Ember? You ready?"

"Sure. Lead the way."

"You've got this. Just keep calm."

"Yes, boss."

I feel far too vulnerable to meet his eyes. Not after the state he saw me in a couple of days ago. He's checked in regularly since my breakdown, ensuring I'm up for my first mission.

As sweet as it is, his fussing only reminds me of the utterly broken state he found me in that day. I never want anyone to see me like that. Even if I allowed him to in a moment of weakness.

"Remember to follow our lead, stay alert and watch your back." His hand is warm on my lower back as we walk towards Axel and Hyland. "We're going to get to Madden while the others take care of the spineless fucks who'll inevitably flee."

"He won't go down without a fight."

"I'm counting on it." Warner's hand leaves my back to rest over the pistol tucked into his hip holster. "I'd like to have a word with that cunt."

"Wait your turn," Axel throws at him.

"Like you'll even get a chance, pup," Hyland scoffs. "He's mine."

"Enough dick measuring," Warner snarls at them. "We've got enough of that going on with these other fools as our backup."

"Learned behaviour," I point out.

When both Hyland and Axel look at me in mock-outrage, I smile broadly back. Being the only female in this all-male, testosterone-filled environment doesn't bother me. If anything, I enjoy being the one to tear them down.

"Can girls dick measure?" Axel pouts pathetically. "Because it sure feels like you are."

"I wouldn't need to, Ax. I'm obviously far more well-endowed than you are."

"Don't encourage them, Em," Warner pleads.

"Sorry. Couldn't help myself."

Walking past Axel to prepare to leave, I smack my hand against his when he offers me a high-five. Only the lovable psycho himself would take my insult as reason to applaud me.

With Warner and Hyland taking the lead and Axel moving to the rear so I'm sandwiched between them, we exit the office block to head for the warehouses located in the distance.

This is a quiet, industrial suburb with little to no pedestrians. The location of the meet isn't far, so within a few minutes of walking, the derelict structure comes into sight.

"We want them out in the open," Warner murmurs, his attention fixed on the front entrance. "I'm not having any of us set foot in that booby trap."

"Booby trap?" Axel repeats. "This isn't Scooby Doo."

"You wanna go in there? These dickheads don't mess around, Ax. You'll be walking into a death trap."

"I could take them," he declares confidently.

"Be still, and shut up, pup." Hyland tightens the strap on the extra-large vest that covers his long-sleeved tee. "You're giving me a migraine."

"I haven't succeeded yet? Damn. I need to up my game."

"Don't you fucking dare."

All crouching behind a brick half-wall that sections off the warehouse's deserted car park, we bide our time. Warner checks in with Archer via his earpiece while we ensure ours are all connected.

"Come in." Axel puts on a posh announcer's voice. "Testing, testing. Ow!"

Lowering the paw that's smacked into Axel's head, Hyland spits a choice curse at him. Honestly, if I didn't already have a headache threatening to take me out, their antics would give me one.

"I can see movement inside on my scope." Kyle's voice whispers into my ear. "Seems like an impending exit."

"Copy that," Warner acknowledges.

A shoulder nudges into mine as Hyland sends me a stern nod. "This is it."

"Okay. I'm ready."

"You can still sit this out."

"Not a chance, Hy. I've trained for this."

He flourishes a proud half-grin. "Just testing you. I'm gonna be right behind you watching you take their asses down."

"Just here for the show, huh?" I tease him.

Reaching for his gun, Hyland checks the magazine one last time then replaces it. "Damn straight."

"And here I was thinking you'd be my partner in crime tonight."

Ignoring the others nestled close by and inevitably listening to us, Hyland stares deep into my eyes. His olive-toned spheres brim with pride, making my heart patter even harder.

"I'll be the fuel to your fire, red. Just tell me who you want to burn first."

My mouth twists into a smile just for him.

"Blaine Madden and his crew."

"Deal. We'll give them hell."

Treacle-like pleasure slicks down my spine at the dangerous spark in his eyes. "Yes, sir."

"I see doors opening," Warner announces. "Let's roll."

Creeping along the half-wall, we circle towards the side of the dilapidated warehouse so we can catch their backs while exiting the meeting. Sure enough, two conversing men have walked outside.

"No one exiting at the rear yet." Archer's update comes through our comms. "We're in place for any runners."

Raising his balled-up fist, Warner gestures for us to hold

position. His entire focus is locked on those swinging, dented doors. We need to wait for everyone to clear before we move in on them.

Through my wavering vision, I squint hard to keep the doors in focus. Waiting for Blaine Madden to show his stupidly handsome, scarred face. I'm going to cave it in for making me feel foolish.

What I'm not prepared for is the slow gait of a tall, well-dressed man who emerges, deep in conversation with three others in rapid, exotic Spanish. The familiar mug of the guard at his back makes my innards contract.

"Oh my God," I blurt.

Immediately, Warner spins towards me. "What is it?"

Words fail to surface as the four men light up cigarettes, completely brazen in the open air despite being in *our* territory. Thinking their power still protects them. Just as much as their money does.

Not for much longer.

I couldn't hurt them last time. No more than I did before they drugged, sold and shipped me off to the highest bidder. Now I have the chance to inflict an ounce of that pain on them.

Disregarding the plan, I ready myself to launch at none other than Luis—the man who sold me to Gael—and his disgusting lackey, Diego. He survived that shot to the leg after all.

"Forget Madden," I rush out. "Get them! Now!"

"Ember, wait!"

"No time!"

Warner's shouting registers, but all I can focus on is the roaring of fast-moving blood in my ears, demanding that I lay hands on the man who set me up to endure such depravity before my body fails me.

I'm going to destroy every last joint, bone, ligament and fucking tendon in his body. One by one. Alphabetically. Numerically. I don't give a shit—as long as he tells me who he sold Gracie to.

Giving the rest of my team no choice but to follow, I execute the approach we planned, moving fast alongside the warehouse's exterior. Smoking, the four men are now sharing laughter with the other two who first emerged.

At the sound of our rapid approach, one of them startles. Miguel, I think. I recognise his sneering, rat-like features from our time in the cages. His eyes widen when he spots me barrelling towards them.

"Mierda!"

I drop to the ground and propel myself towards his exposed legs before he can draw his weapon on me. My outstretched foot connects with his ankle, causing him to catapult towards the ground.

Miguel lands hard on his side, head smacking against cracked concrete. I have long enough to look up into Luis's surprised eyes as he watches me take out one of his men.

Before he can react, Luis is side-tackled by a growling Hyland running full-speed into him. In his element, he resembles an angry boulder rolling over a trapped animal.

"Fucking bitch!"

Scrabbling to reach me, Miguel gets hold of my leg and yanks. I'm dragged towards him close enough to receive the punch he haphazardly throws. It brushes my jaw, barely making contact.

"Is that the best you've got?" I cackle desperately.

Spitting an insult, Miguel wails another foreign curse when I whip out my other leg to kick him in the face. He's thrown off balance, blood spurting from his mouth.

Without hesitating, I tackle his slumped form to continue landing blows. *Smack. Smack. Smack.* I need to take this motherfucker out so I can get to those who really matter.

Luis and Diego.

They're *mine*.

My knuckles burn and crack with each blow I levy against Miguel, caught flat on his back and too disorientated to put up much of a fight. When the back of his head whacks the ground again, I watch the light in his eyes wink out.

"Stay down," I spit at him.

The sense of euphoria from knocking him out is fleeting. Looking around, I find that a few others have emerged from the warehouse to join the fight. Hyland and Luis are locked in a violent battle of fists while Axel and Warner pick off incoming thugs, one by one.

Panic takes root at the realisation that Diego has vanished. I haven't laid eyes on Madden or his crew yet either. I resolve to deal with the consequences of their bullshit *no force* rule and start taking people out.

"768! You made it!"

A lilting voice hollers from behind me.

"Over here, 768! Yoo-hoo!"

Lifting onto my feet, I boot Miguel's unconscious body in the stomach for good measure before looking over my shoulder. My bloodstream freezes into an arctic dagger that buries in my gut.

"You still alive?" I shout back.

Hand resting on the weapon tucked into the front of his jeans, Diego sneers at me. "Last I checked."

"Too bad. I was hoping I'd caught an artery."

"Hope you're a better shot now than you were six years ago, *puta!*"

With a sick grin, Diego turns and darts around the side of the warehouse. He's gone faster than I can draw my weapon to take him out. I know it's a trap, but I don't care all that much.

This time, he's mine.

Without glancing at the others, still knee-deep in the rush of assailants, I chase after Diego. Like hell am I going to let him escape. I want his boss, but I also want him.

As he vanishes out of sight, memories of the last time we faced each other fill my mind, piercing the woozy fog that's gradually worsening.

With Gracie's sobs still ringing in my ears, dim light guides me into the overgrowth that creeps up the exterior of the abandoned husk. All manner of litter, detritus and smashed glass pepper the long grass.

"Come get me, 768!" Diego's voice echoes.

That same voice haunted so many of the bleak days we spent trapped behind rusted bars, stomachs screaming for sustenance and bodies blue from hypothermia.

For Gracie. For myself. For every single woman left to rot in that hell. I don't care if I die trying—I'm going to make this motherfucker bleed for what he's done.

"I know where your bitch friend is!" he adds with a hyena-like laugh. "Do you want to know?"

Steps growing wobblier and more unstable, a loud ringing fills my ears. Shit, I can feel myself fading. Still giving chase, I push past the exhaustion sapping my strength.

Not now. Not now!

My limbs are now jerking, growing heavy under the strain of crashing adrenaline. I have to reach him before my body pulls the plug. This may be my only chance.

Pushing past every last warning sign telling me to stop, turn back and find a safe spot to collapse in, I refuse to let Diego get away. I can't see him or take aim, but he can't be far ahead.

"Though she's probably dead and gone by now!"

"I'm going to kill you!" I screech back.

"Come and try, whore!"

Towering weeds and shrubbery cut me as I tear through the wilderness, keeping the warehouse on my left. The thick overgrowth thins out a little ahead, revealing what looks like an outdoor smoking area.

Hunched over as he pants for air, Diego watches me emerge into the evening din. The sounds of the fight unfolding behind us have lessened, enveloping our showdown in anticipatory silence.

The entire world is wavering now as alarm bells howl through every sense. Head-splitting pain has grown into a raging firestorm that feels strong enough to break bone.

Not now. Not now.

Diego is mere steps away from me. The man who helped to ensure my suffering is within touching distance, and I refuse to let him walk away free.

"You know, I heard rumours about what Gael turned you into." He straightens, still smiling like a lunatic. "But I didn't quite believe it."

"You sold me!"

"We saved you." He snorts.

"This isn't what being saved looks like."

"You think anyone else would've given you the chance to fight?

To avoid your tight little cunt being passed around like an ashtray? You should be glad we let Gael take you."

"Is that what happened to Gracie?" I roar back.

His laughter causes my rage to expand until I think I might burst into icy, hate-filled chunks. All I can hear, see or conceive of is his disgusting chuckling.

"You know, I don't even remember who bought the screaming virgin." He winks at me like this is all a big joke. "I have no idea where she is now."

The sight of his smarmy grin is broken by flashes of light streaking across my vision. Rapidly spreading spots erupt like neon fireworks painted onto my eyeballs.

Wobbling on my feet, I quickly draw my gun while I can still use it. "I don't believe you!"

"It's the truth, 768. She could be anywhere. Dead. Alive. I don't know or care."

Terror seeps into my bones and joints, weakening my stance further. My knees are sagging, promising to take me down. Clicking off the safety, I shakily aim my pistol at him.

"Last chance. Tell me the truth."

He doesn't even flinch.

"She's gone. You'll never find her."

"You're lying!"

"I'm not." He chuckles darkly. "But that doesn't matter. We're here for you. I'm going to enjoy the reward Gael will pay for the return of his precious champion."

With a feral scream, I fire off a shot. The bullet soars straight past Diego without making an impact, thrown off course by the continued jerking of my failing limbs.

"I'm here, 768!" He waves his arms, taunting me.

"Goddamn you!"

Another two quick shots fail to take the son of a bitch down. I want to attempt a fourth, but somewhere internally, a plug is yanked out. All of my waning energy instantly drains away. The gun falls from my unresponsive hands.

My spasming legs quickly give out. Knees cracking against the old pavement, an anguished shriek lodges in my throat, cut short by my clenching muscles. Everything pulls taut and stiff.

The bright strobes have intensified, blurring darkness into breathtakingly white nothingness. My vision cuts in and out, offering snapshots of Diego casually strolling towards me.

"What's this?" He leers down at me. "I haven't even touched you yet."

As much as I want to yell, shout and rave back at him, not a single word can escape. Only guttural whimpering that seems to satisfy my opponent as I collapse in a locked-up heap, chin wet from leaking spittle.

Moving into a crouch, Diego watches me shudder and involuntarily convulse, imprisoned by my own malfunctioning body. His confusion fails to rival his delight at watching me suffer.

"Gael really fucked you up, didn't he?" Diego's lips curl downwards. "This is a sorry sight."

When the flashing white strobes give way to encroaching blackness, I know I'm in deep shit. All I can hope is that someone heard the gunshots. I'm not going to be conscious for much longer.

"You're so weak, 768. Pathetic."

Convulsions sweep through my extremities, straining muscles and tendons. Pain becomes an acute force, holding me in the cruelty of consciousness as a black out races closer. All I can do is gag on my own saliva.

I can't feel Diego's hands on my body when he straddles himself above me in a position of supreme power. Trapped in my own skin, I silently choke on my terror, infused in the moisture that fills my mouth.

"Does he know that his product is damaged?" Diego wonders aloud. "Perhaps he won't mind if I deliver you in pieces instead. Maybe I'll ruin that cunt of yours first."

My vision dims and sputters. The darkness overwhelms me, receding in a hateful taunt for split-seconds until it rises once more. Every time the world comes back into focus, I see him.

Laughing. Relishing in my paralysis.

His twisted face inching ever closer.

When the next wave washes over me, I let the shadows swallow me whole. In the darkness comes relief in the form of defeat. I don't have to see Diego here. I don't have to think about what he's doing.

Open your eyes, Ember!

Fight back!

The tear-stained face yelling at me is young. Bruised. Familiar. She's shouting so loud, but I can't figure out why. Who is she? How does she know my name?

Get up! Now!

Wait. It's… Gracie. I know her voice. The sound of her pleading. I want to reach out and swipe her tears aside, but there's nothing around me but an empty, black void.

Fight for me, Ember!

Fight!

Her wails hit like a direct defibrillation to the heart. The darkness shudders and splits wide open, filling with flashes of blinding light. Agony infects every nerve ending and skin cell.

When the light fades enough for me to blink through great, murky tides, I see dark sky. Emerging stars bursting forth through beautifully stormy clouds. A nearby building's roof.

The haze parts enough to reveal someone looming over me. Face blurred. Hair swimming with each woozy wave that hits. Two soulful black pits emerge through the confusing obscurity.

My tongue feels like an oversized lump of dead skin in my mouth, refusing to move or carve out a single syllable. I can't find my limbs through the steadily increasing pain that scurries through me with each sharp breath.

Then the black pits vanish. Eaten by blinking lids and fascinatingly curled lashes. Oh, they're eyes. I'm staring into onyx orbs, sparkling with a midnight sheen.

"Easy. Don't try to move."

That voice.

"You're okay. Just breathe now."

The aristocratic drawl slicks over my still-shuddering body, burrows inside my cavities and finds a new home in the hollowed-out carcass of my skeleton.

Looking past the black eyes that seem to drink me in, dark stubble, carved cheekbones and a twisted scar are all obscured. Each identifying feature is covered in brilliant-red splats.

Blood.

He's covered in blood.

It's *everywhere.*

"Miss me, sweetheart?" my captor croons. "You didn't have to pull this dramatic crap just to get my attention."

The smell of crushed peppercorns and citrus-sharp bergamot offers undeniable proof that I'm awake. From what exactly, I'm not quite sure. I don't know why I'm sprawled out or how long I've been out for.

I'm cradled in a pair of wiry arms while blood-speckled fingertips stroke over my face, easing the ache that emanates from my clenched teeth.

I'm being soothed. Comforted. Protected.

By Blaine motherfucking Madden.

CONFIDENTIAL
Why?
Suspect?
Gael?
DO NOT CROSS
POLICE LI

Sec
LINE – DO NOT CROSS
Reasoning?
CONFIDENTIAL
?
Suspect?
DO NOT CROSS
POLICE
ret

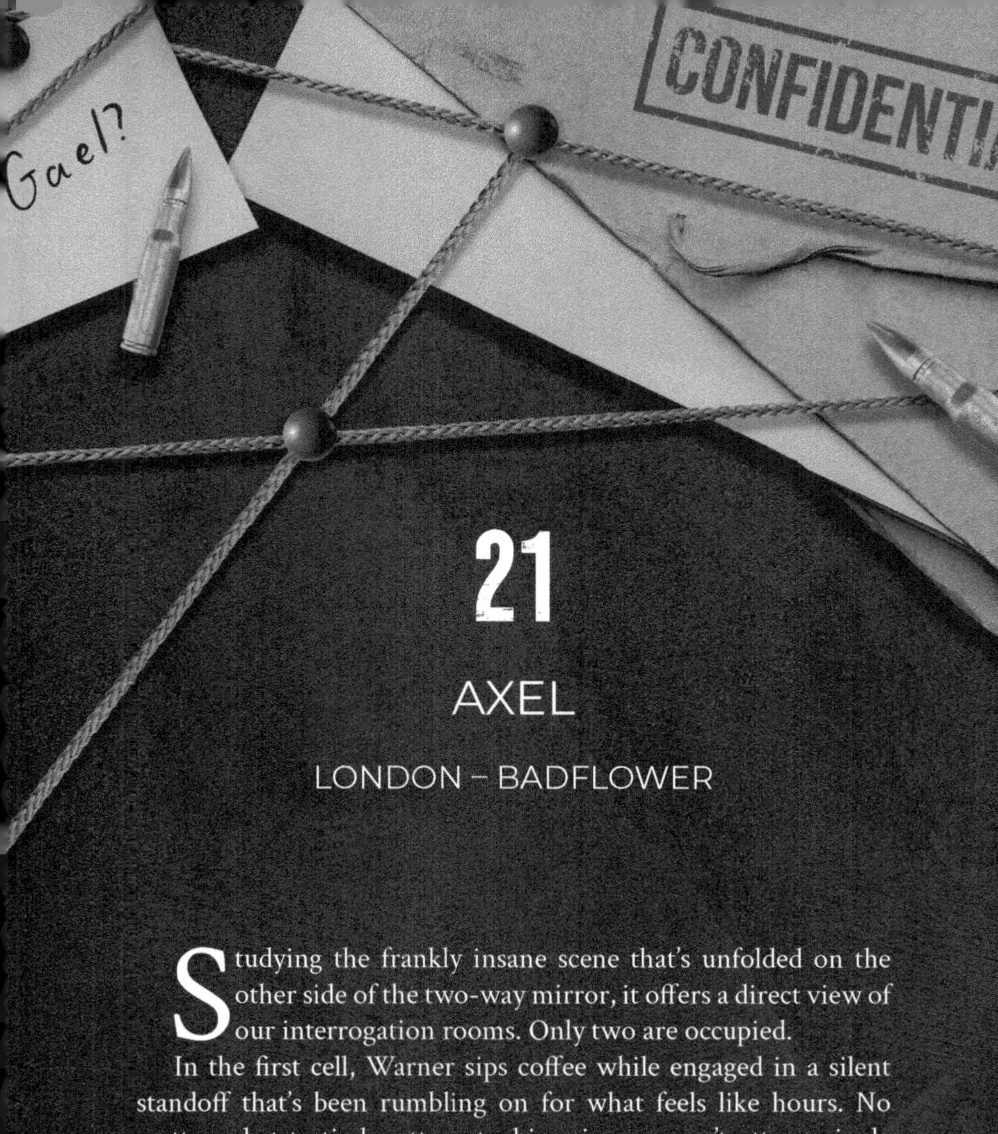

21

AXEL

LONDON – BADFLOWER

Studying the frankly insane scene that's unfolded on the other side of the two-way mirror, it offers a direct view of our interrogation rooms. Only two are occupied.

In the first cell, Warner sips coffee while engaged in a silent standoff that's been rumbling on for what feels like hours. No matter what tactic he attempts, his prisoner won't utter a single damn word.

Opposite him, Blaine Madden lounges in the steel chair he's handcuffed to by his ankles and wrists. I'm not quite sure how he manages to make being incapacitated look so comfortable.

"Why did you come back to England, Blaine? You were free overseas. Why risk it?"

Still, Madden refuses to open his mouth. He simply stares. Smiles. Silently waits. For what, I'm not quite sure. Warner has no intention of letting the criminal bastard see the light of day ever again.

"Did you come back for Ember?" Warner directly asks.

Nothing. Not a fucking peep.

"Why did you help her last night? Why not let her be taken again?"

Still dressed in dark clothing saturated with blood, Madden looks every inch the unhinged powerhouse that his reputation suggests. His face, hair and body are all crusted with dark-red splotches.

"You've been meeting with Gael's associates. Why is that?"

With a quiet chuff, Madden flicks his gaze over to the mirror. I know he can't see me, but it feels like he's challenging me with his stare regardless. I want to go in there and rip his fucking face off.

It doesn't matter that he saved Ember. Sure, without him there, she'd be lost all over again. Perhaps even dead. None of us care, though. We'd rather understand why he was there in the first place.

Looking away from the tight-lipped crime lord, I peer into the second room. Hyland should be interrogating this sick fuck, but he's with Ember in the hospital right now.

With a half-smoked cigarette clasped between his fingers, legs outstretched and feet propped up on the table, Hudson Knight stares down a beaten Miguel. The lucky bastard survived his run-in with Ember.

"It won't be a challenge to tie you to decades worth of international crimes, Miguel. The Mexican authorities are in full cooperation with us. We will bury you."

Hudson's terrifying voice is enough to put me on edge, let alone anyone who doesn't know the heavily-inked brute. To everyone but those he cares about, he's a stone-cold, merciless bastard. I love the guy.

Taking another drag from his cigarette, Hudson eyes Miguel without a single care in the world. He's completely calm.

"How much did Gael offer for Ember's safe capture?"

"*Chinga tu madre!*" Miguel spits saliva at him.

Unfazed, Hudson wipes his face then lifts his legs to stand up. "I'm going to assume that was something unpleasant. And I dislike uncooperative people."

When he smashes his still-lit cigarette down on Miguel's exposed collarbone, the asshole wails like a baby. His cries are so shrill, they even soak through the double-glass mirror to bite into my ears.

Hudson lifts the now-extinguished cigarette butt then flicks it aside. A red welt, already weeping with blood and puss, is left behind on Miguel's skin.

"Care to answer my question now?"

"Hombre loco!"

"I know you speak English, dickhead. Start talking, or I'll go fetch another pack of cigarettes."

Turning away, I peer into the empty third room. By the time we located the source of the gunshots after losing Luis then subduing the maniacs throwing themselves at us, Diego was dead.

Perhaps decimated is a better word. Madden did a hell of a job when he covered himself in all that spilled blood. He sure exceeded expectations. I hate that.

Disregarding the interrogations when my phone vibrates in my ripped jeans, I almost hang up by accident in my rush to accept the call.

"How is she?"

"No idea. She won't let me in the room." Hyland's voice drips with weariness. "Still having tests done, I think. They called in a neurologist from St Thomas's hospital."

"Wait, a neurologist?"

"She had a seizure, Ax. A really fucking bad one."

Several elongated seconds stretch on, filled with my disbelief. Surely not. If Ember was having seizures, we'd know about it. She would've told us. That's too big a thing to hide.

"That can't be right," I eventually reply.

"It's their medical opinion. I lifted some of her paperwork because the doctor won't tell me shit. She's having an EEG, CT scan and blood tests done."

"Well… Maybe this was the first one?"

Hyland's sigh rattles down the receiver. "I tried to listen in. She told them she can handle it. This is clearly not the first episode she's had."

"I don't believe this. She would've told us."

"Would she?" he retorts.

Uncertain how to respond, I stare at the wall. A bulletin board filled with scraps of paper, sign-up sheets, health and safety posters grabs my attention like it holds the secrets of the universe.

"If Madden hadn't found her and killed that son of a bitch, there's no telling what he would've done while she was incapacitated."

"He didn't just kill Diego," I reply hotly. "He damn near took his head off. Forensics had to collect the shattered pieces of his skull to toss in the body bag."

"So what? You're jealous he got there first?"

"Yes! That shithead laid his hands on our girl!"

"*Our*." Hyland's laugh is dark and bleak. "She isn't our anything, Ax."

"Don't you dare. Ember's our teammate. Our friend. Our fucking family!"

"Families don't lie to each other."

The line clicks as he disconnects the call. Clenching my phone tight, I fight the urge to hurl it at the goddamn bulletin board until both objects break.

Hyland can say whatever the fuck he likes—he's still glued to his seat in the waiting area, ensuring Ember isn't left alone in the emergency ward. That doesn't scream of giving up to me.

Emerging from the interview room, Warner sags against the door that slams shut behind him. He's barely able to walk. One of the bastards we took down landed several strategic blows when they spotted his prosthetic.

"You should go home." I watch him wince in discomfort. "Take your leg off. I can handle this."

"Fuck off, Ax."

"That's professional, team leader."

Shaking his head, he downs the last of his coffee as he looks towards the room he just left. "That slick shit isn't saying a goddamn word."

"Why would he?"

"To save himself?" Warner supplies. "To negotiate a plea deal? To avoid being tossed in a maximum-security prison? One he won't escape this time?"

"Madden clearly isn't afraid of you or being punished."

"He should be!"

Head falling, Warner's shoulders shake with each ragged breath he pulls in. None of us have had a spare moment to clean up or change. He's still blood-streaked and wearing ripped clothing.

I'm not faring much better. Though I took down seven men singlehandedly, only succeeding in killing two of the fast fuckers, I still caught a decent beating. My lip is split and sore while my face stings from bruises.

"We ambushed the meet, seized Madden and Miguel. Diego is dead. Sure, we lost Luis and Madden's crew in the chaos, but I'm still considering last night a win."

"A win?" Warner scoffs to the floor. "You said it yourself. We lost Luis. Fuck, we almost lost her too."

Walking over to him, I place a hand on his shoulder. "We didn't lose Ember though, did we?"

"Not this time. She's so reckless!"

"Come on, man. Are you telling me that if you saw those responsible for hurting you or your friends, you wouldn't see red? Or take the first chance you got to batter them?"

"I..."

Trailing off, Warner lifts his head to the ceiling like he's searching for patience or understanding. None of us seem to have the answers today.

"She reacted on instinct. I'm sure she regrets it."

"Well, that instinct almost got her killed," he growls. "I don't know why Madden stuck around alone to save her, but I'm damn well going to find out."

Before he can head back into the interrogation room, I clamp my hand down to halt him.

"You need to go to the hospital. Hyland's losing his shit because he's being kept in the dark, and Ember's in for a slew of tests with a neurologist."

"What? Why?" He visibly startles.

"They reckon she was passed out because of a seizure. He's been snooping in her medical notes."

"A… Seizure?" Warner repeats thickly. "Like, epilepsy or something?"

"I don't know, man."

"Surely we'd know about that?" He frowns to himself. "She never had seizures before."

"That's all I know. You need to go be with her."

"Why me?"

"Besides the fact that I'm sure Tom is freaking the fuck out, Ember's being an uncooperative bitch, and Hyland's talking like she's off the team? You're her friend!"

His lips sealing shut, Warner nods. "You're right."

"Leave Madden to me. Hudson's still in with Miguel."

"We need him capable of forming words, Ax. Don't cut his fucking lips off."

"Dude, that was one time!" I protest.

His tired eyes rolling, Warner pats my hand on top of his shoulder then shrugs himself free to limp away. Once he's gone, I refocus on his abandoned task.

Madden will talk.

I'm not going to ask nicely.

Picking up the rolled, black fabric case I retrieved from my office safe, I saunter into his interrogation room. Madden's gaze locks on me the moment I shut the thick metal door then engage the lock.

"Warner sending his latest pet project in to take a crack?"

"Something like that." I smile widely at him. "I'm his favourite pet project."

"So I hear." Madden shifts against his shackles, still appearing relaxed. "Axel Slaughter. Thirty-one years old. Orphaned at thirteen. Eight years in MI-5 and now… Sabre's bitch."

"Congratulations. You can profile."

Setting my fabric case down on the table, I work on untying the silky knots to release the flaps. It rolls open easily, revealing an array of neatly secured scalpels, blades and instruments of torture.

"Someone else profiles for me," Madden corrects, sparing my toys a disinterested glance. "I can read words on a page."

"Aren't you a clever boy?"

"Not as clever as you. Tell me, Axel Slaughter. Does anyone

know the truth?"

His words cause my movements to still for a moment before I quickly shake the uncertainty off. He'll stop chatting shit as soon as I slide my stainless-steel needles beneath his nail beds.

"Oh, Axel," Madden drawls in that stupidly formal accent. "The truth was buried so well, wasn't it? Maybe you even convinced yourself it was real."

"I have no idea what you're talking about."

"I bet not even your team leader knows what really happened to your family, does he?"

Selecting a wickedly sharp, carbon steel scalpel—one of my favourite pieces—I turn to face Madden's knowing grin.

"I've been instructed not to cut bits off you. However, I think you can still talk without eyelids. So perhaps I'll start there."

"Go right ahead." He quirks a brow. "It won't change the fact that I know your little secret."

"I have no secrets."

"No?"

"No. My past is a matter of public record."

"Quite," he hums. "Just the way dear old mum planned it, right?"

Each word he utters threatens to undo almost twenty years of carefully placed memories. The memories I crafted, refined and planted like baby trees to grow over the reality I dare not recall.

"Enough!" I slam my fist onto the table.

"Give me what I want, and I'll stop right there." Madden casually raises a shoulder. "No one has to know about *him*. I won't spill your secrets."

Those three traitorous letters pierce my body like rapid-fire bullets. *Him.* The ghost I've long erased from my memory. For all intents and purposes, he never even existed.

"What do you want?" Both palms on the table, I lean into his space.

"I'll only speak to Ember. That's my terms."

"You're joking, right?"

"Not much of a joker, I'm afraid. Bring her to me."

My laughter is a short bark. It feels alien. Uncomfortable. This man is tearing every last thread from inside me and pulling them tight until it feels like I'm being played like a violin.

"Ember's in the hospital. She can't and won't see you."

"I have time." He reclines in his seat. "I'll be waiting."

"No one will allow it!"

"That sounds like a you problem, Axel. Go cut someone else's eyelids off, and bring me what I want. Or else I'll be taking a trip down memory lane."

The urge to throw him from that chair, press my blade into his jugular vein and bleed him dry until I'm dancing in his essence is all-consuming.

"Run along." Madden jerks his chin towards the door. "I'll wait."

Conflicted, I consider executing him even though it would end my career. Potentially my life. I'm not sure who would kill me first—Ember, Warner or Hyland.

Shoving the scalpel back into place, I quickly refold my weapons case then tuck it under my arm. The longer I'm breathing the same air as him, the more acute my need to silence his wagging tongue becomes.

Moving to the door, I stop at the last second to look over my shoulder. His beady, black eyes are watching me, full of intense calculation.

"How did you know?"

"Know what?" Madden smirks at me.

"About… *him?*"

"Ah. Now you want to acknowledge his existence, hm?"

Nausea and the need to flee war for supremacy inside me. I haven't opened this Pandora's box for years now. It became easier not to acknowledge his existence as I grew older. Like second nature. I pretended to forget.

"You may have forgotten about your brother, Axel… But I know that he hasn't forgotten about you."

Blinking several times, the scene refuses to change. A dream-like haze doesn't lift to reveal a reality in which this conversation never happened. This is real.

I don't reply before leaving the room. Madden's satisfied chuckling follows me out until the door slams shut with a metallic thud, and I slump against it.

He hasn't forgotten about you.

If the sibling I've written out of my life is tangled up in this, I'm on a collision course with a part of my pitch-black past. A course that offers no hope of there being any survivors in the wreckage.

Ember lied to us, but that's forgivable.

Because I lied to all of them first.

CONFIDENTIAL
Suspect?
DO NOT CROSS
POLICE
Suspect?
NOT CROSS
POLICE

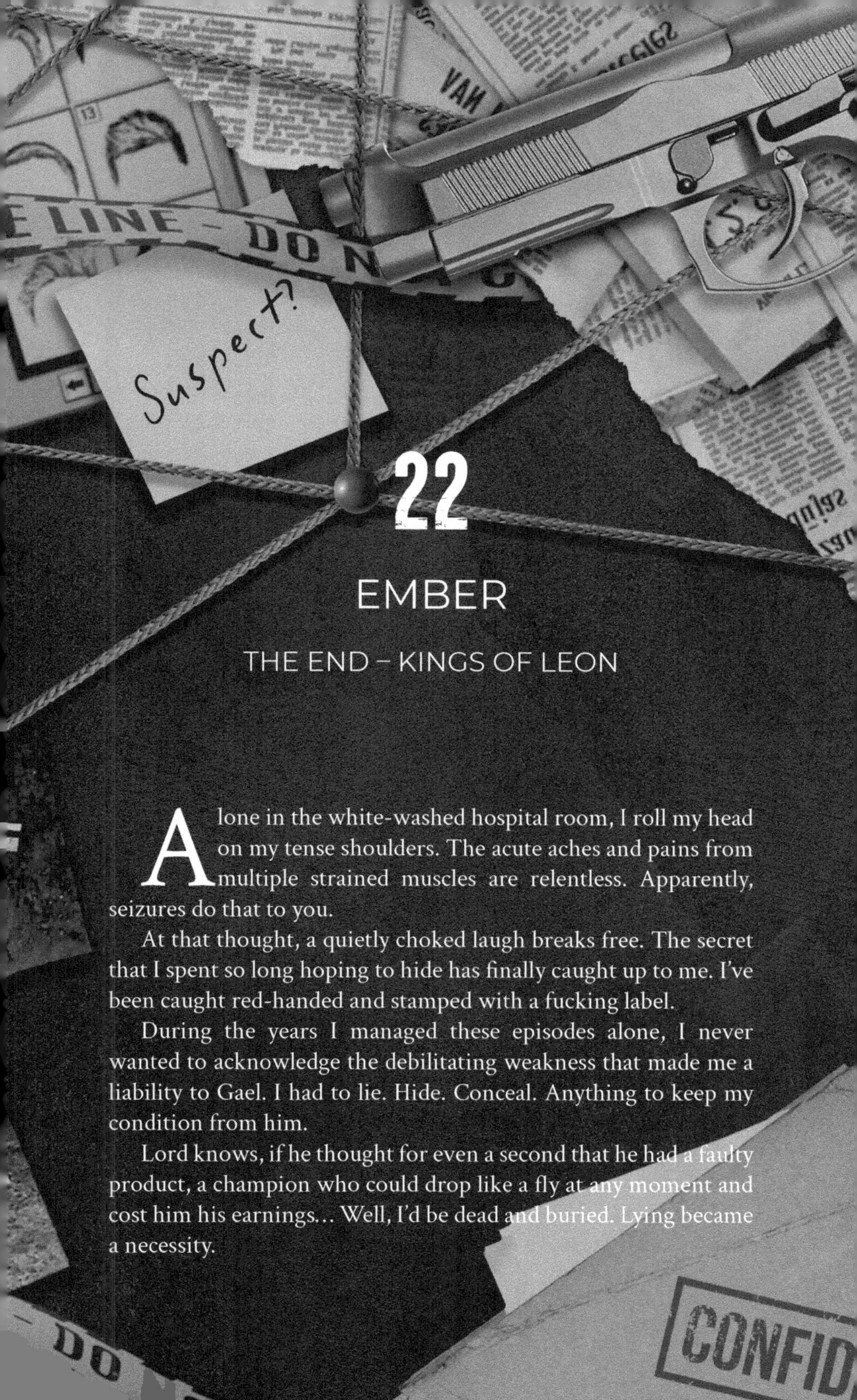

22

EMBER

THE END – KINGS OF LEON

Alone in the white-washed hospital room, I roll my head on my tense shoulders. The acute aches and pains from multiple strained muscles are relentless. Apparently, seizures do that to you.

At that thought, a quietly choked laugh breaks free. The secret that I spent so long hoping to hide has finally caught up to me. I've been caught red-handed and stamped with a fucking label.

During the years I managed these episodes alone, I never wanted to acknowledge the debilitating weakness that made me a liability to Gael. I had to lie. Hide. Conceal. Anything to keep my condition from him.

Lord knows, if he thought for even a second that he had a faulty product, a champion who could drop like a fly at any moment and cost him his earnings… Well, I'd be dead and buried. Lying became a necessity.

FRACTURED FUTURE

But that's the thing about survival instincts. They don't switch off once we're safe. Ask anyone who has survived pure evil itself. The things we did to keep ourselves safe don't vanish overnight.

They burrow. Cling on. Metastasise into silly rituals or easily told lies. A self-harmer may not cut themselves on a daily basis anymore, but they'll still sleep with a knife beneath their pillow or keep a stash of pills *just in case.*

When the specialist returns, clipboard in hand, I work to summon a speck of patience. Doctor Fawn intervened several hours ago when my case was handed over to him after arriving at the emergency department in a semi-lucid daze.

"Ember. Out of bed I see. How are you feeling?"

"Brilliant," I clap back.

"Bit stiff? Headache? Disorientated?"

Rather than create a lie that will only worsen my sore head, I simply nod. All of that and more. Beyond the physical aftereffects and exhaustion the seizure left behind, I feel raw and exposed.

"Thank you for your patience while we examined your test results. I know it's been a long day for you."

"I just want to go home. Can I leave now?"

"Not quite yet." He takes the empty seat next to mine. "You have several visitors waiting outside. Would you like someone with you while we discuss these results?"

My first reaction is to decline. I don't want anyone to hear whatever shit he has to say. I know it isn't going to be good news. But the events of the last twelve hours give me pause.

The truth is my knife under the pillow. My stash of pills in the bedside table. I've kept it close and allowed it to hold a terrifying power over me, even after escaping Gael and his abuse.

When I broke down in that changing room, Warner begged me to let someone in. Literally anyone. I didn't think I'd ever want that, but sitting here… drained, scared and in pain… I want someone.

"My brother," I croak. "Is he here?"

"Allow me to go look. Wait here."

Placing the clipboard down, Doctor Fawn leaves the room again. I'm left staring at the clipped paperwork he carried in. Those sheets hold my entire future in their individual grains.

At the sound of footsteps returning, I drag my gaze from my signed death warrant. I'm expecting Tom to rush in and engulf me. I asked the staff to hold him back with Hyland up until now.

When a warm hand encircles the back of my neck, patchouli and pine form a protective woodland around me. The soft touch vanishes, allowing Warner to stiffly take the spare seat next to me.

"You're here?" I gawp at him.

"I have been for a couple of hours." He searches my face. "The doctor's just giving us a minute."

"Where's Tom?"

"He had to take a call outside. I didn't want you to do this alone."

Too overwhelmed to find adequate words, I try and fail to hold tears back. Heat spills down my cheeks, prompting Warner to swipe the moisture aside with his calloused thumb pad.

"Is everyone safe?" I ask, afraid to hear the answer yet needing to know.

"Everyone's fine. We've taken six people into custody including Madden and the man you knocked out, Miguel."

Terror cracks through me. "What about Luis?"

"We almost had him, Em. When we heard the gunshots and realised you were gone, we split fast to find you. I'm sorry, but Luis escaped. He's in the wind."

"Shit! This is all my fault."

"He'll turn up soon enough. The good news is that Diego is dead."

At the mention of his name, I clamp down on a rush of perplexing emotions. Of all the people to intervene and halt whatever Diego had planned, I didn't expect it to be Blaine.

"Let's focus on you now. The rest can wait."

At the feel of his thumb caressing my cheek, I find a timid nod. "You don't have to stay. I'll be fine alone."

"I told you that we look out for each other," he whispers back. "Through thick and thin."

"Thank you."

"I've got you, Em."

Calling Doctor Fawn's name, Warner entwines his hand with mine as we wait for him to return. The clinician returns, standing opposite our two chairs.

He looks between us questioningly. "Ember?"

"Go ahead." I nod in consent.

"Right." Doctor Fawn clears his throat. "Well, as you know, we performed an EEG, CT scan and several different blood tests. We determined that what you experienced was an intense, post-traumatic seizure."

When I remain silent, Warner speaks up.

"Can you explain what that means?"

"While there are different types, seizures are essentially bursts of electrical activity in the brain. This can temporarily affect a person's muscle control and behaviour. It can even cause a loss of consciousness."

Staring down at my sock-covered feet, I let his words beat over me in a ceaseless wave. Hearing the doctor outline every way I'm vulnerable against my own damaged body is excruciating.

This is precisely why I didn't want anyone to know. The lack of control is scary enough. Knowing anyone can see, target and exploit those weaknesses is petrifying.

"Some people may experience convulsions or spasms. There can be visual disturbances—flashing lights, floating orbs, loss of vision altogether."

"Convulsions?" Warner repeats in alarm. "Aren't they dangerous?"

"Try not to worry too much. It's important to cushion the person's head during a seizure and ensure there is no tight clothing around their neck. Mostly they need reassurance that they're not alone."

Hell, I can already hear the gears in Warner's head turning as he takes mental notes. He loves an action plan. For some reason, that intensifies my sense of humiliation. I don't want to be just another problem.

"People who suffer from seizures may also have mood swings." Doctor Fawn addresses both of us. "Bursts of anger or crying fits. And bouts of dizziness, chronic headaches, weakness or fatigue."

"We get it," I grit out. "Move on."

"Em," Warner scolds under his breath.

"What?"

"This is important. I need to know what to look out for if you're going to have another episode."

"You don't need to look out for anything. This is my problem."

"If you think I'm going to watch—"

"Just tell me what's wrong with me," I cut him off to address the doctor. "I don't need to hear all of this medical bullshit."

Pausing to assess us both, Doctor Fawn flicks through his paperwork. "Ember, I know this is a lot. It's okay to feel afraid right now."

With a shrug, I look down at Warner's hand still gripping mine. As much as I want to run and find somewhere to hide from this, I know that I won't get far.

"I'd like to discuss the results of your CT scan next."

"Go on," I whisper defeatedly.

"You have an eight-centimetre scar beneath your hair. The CT scan shows a healed fracture in your skull. Perhaps a few years old."

Warner's palm tightens to the point of pain. "What?"

"Do you recall how you obtained that injury?" Doctor Fawn queries.

I clear my throat, ignoring the pressure of Warner's stare burning into me. "Yes."

"Perhaps you could talk me through what happened." He glances at the man by my side. "I've been made aware of your history and the ongoing investigation."

Attempting to unlock my clenched jaw, I fight through my weariness. Tensing up is making every protesting muscle I strained feel even worse.

"There was a street fight a few years back."

Doctor Fawn nods in encouragement.

"I suffered a bad head injury that put me out of action for months. My captor's physician kept me alive, but it took a long time to recover."

When Warner mutters a curse to himself, I know I'm in for a bollocking later. I kept some details to myself during my interviews, including this unveiled secret. He isn't going to let that slide easily.

"That would correlate with the results I'm seeing." The doctor nods again. "You're lucky to have made a full recovery."

"I didn't feel so lucky at the time."

"When did you experience your first seizure after the injury?"

"Maybe a few weeks. Perhaps a month."

"I see." He seems to ponder for a moment, lips puckering in thought. "And how often after that?"

I'm acutely aware of Warner's fingers digging into my hand. He's clinging onto me for dear life–whether for his benefit or mine, I'm not quite sure.

"It varies." I shrug.

"Give me an estimate."

"Um… Perhaps every few weeks. Sometimes more. If I'm overwhelmed, stressed or exhausted… They can hit more often."

"Fucking hell." Warner's curse is much louder this time. "We've been pushing you to train for weeks now!"

Wincing at his harsh tone, I refuse to look at him. I haven't seized since the episode in the shower before my first interview, but it was only a matter of time.

"Sometimes, significant trauma to the skull and brain can lead to a condition we call PTE." Doctor Fawn shifts on his feet. "Do you know what that is?"

"No."

"PTE—or Post-Traumatic Epilepsy—can take the form of trauma-induced seizures after a severe head injury. It's less common but still a possibility."

And there it is.

The label I've battled to avoid.

"Don't look so crestfallen, Ember." The doctor smiles kindly. "Epilepsy isn't the end of the world. You have a serious chronic condition, but it can be managed. Now we know what it is."

"If you're going to tell me to stop fighting or work—"

"No, no. Let me stop you right there. I'm not about to recommend you remain in bed for the rest of your life."

Surprise holds my tongue.

"However, I am going to prescribe medications that you will take daily. Anticonvulsants and perhaps an anti-epileptic. This could be a long trial and error process until we find the right fit, though."

Faint hope sparks within me. "I understand."

"What about lifestyle changes?" Warner questions, apparently pushing his anger aside for now.

"There will be some." Doctor Fawn adopts a serious tone. "You'll need to surrender your driver's license. If in the future you remain seizure free for a set period of time, you will be able to drive again."

Now I'm the one squeezing Warner's hand to a breaking point. We're both strangling the blood from each other's veins.

"Simple changes like diet, exercise and avoiding excessive stress need to be considered," he adds. "You do not have to give up your career, Ember. But you have to be careful."

"I can do that," I quickly confirm.

"That means resting when needed. Avoiding further trauma that may trigger a seizure. Learning to manage stress and recognising your triggers. You need a good support system."

Perking up, Warner leans forward in his seat. "She has that. We can look out for her."

"Then you need to learn how to help." Doctor Fawn turns his gaze to Warner. "I can recommend reading on supporting a loved one with epilepsy. What to do, warning signs, after care."

"Yes please. Write me a list. I'll share it with the whole team."

"You'll need to be on the lookout for..."

Their voices quickly fade from my awareness, swallowed by the blood pounding in my ears. The hospital room becomes greyscale as I simply stare at Warner.

I'm fascinated by his endless passion. The way his voice fills with excitement when he discovers a purpose. His steadfast commitment even when he's mad as hell.

Who cares that much?

He hasn't abandoned me to do this alone because I lied to him. To all of them, really. This secret was theirs to know too, but still, I kept it to myself. Yet Warner hasn't given up on me.

Snapping back into the dreary hospital room at the sound of my name being called, I glance at the doctor. He's pressed his clipboard to his chest in preparation to leave.

"I'm going to give you some time to process while I discuss

treatment options with our clinical pharmacist. We'll get you sorted, Ember."

My tongue unpeels from the roof of my mouth. "Thank you."

"Of course. Please try to get some rest."

When he leaves the room, I deflate like a popped balloon. The pressure to hold it together in front of Doctor Fawn has drained what little energy I had left.

I sink into the arm that Warner wraps around my shoulders. His body feels firm and steady against mine, bathing me in the intoxicating scent of the forest I hold so dear.

"Thanks for being here," I murmur.

"Always."

"Aren't you mad at me?"

"Oh, I'm fucking furious. You lied, Em. That's not okay. But it doesn't matter right now."

My eyes slip shut, offering me a brief reprieve. "I'm so sorry."

"Believe it or not, I understand why you did it."

"You do?" I bleat.

His torso vibrates with a long-suffering sigh. "You spent a long time taking care of yourself out there. That included hiding this from the world, right?"

"It still freaks me out when you read me like a book."

"Quick study," he jokes tiredly. "I am pissed off, Em. But I'm also here for you."

"You don't have to make me feel better about this."

"Again, it's kinda my job."

"Well, I could've come clean weeks ago. I could've told you what's been happening. Instead, I put everyone on that raid at risk."

"You did. We'll be having words about that later."

Bathing in his soothing scent, I crane my neck to look up at his handsome face. Those devastating baby blues hold so much unconditional care, it's hard to stare directly into them.

"May I?" He looks up at my head.

Instinctively, I know what he's asking for.

"I guess so."

Warner slips a hand into my hair, loose and flowing after I removed my ponytail to be examined. His fingers glide over my skull, searching for the scar I know he'll find.

When he locates the raised skin I keep hidden, his lips part on a fast inhale. I rarely look at it in the mirror or touch it, but I know the scar is unpleasant. They didn't exactly care about stitching me up neatly.

"Christ," he mutters. "It feels huge."

"Big enough."

"I don't know how you survived their evil all alone, love. But I'm so fucking glad you did."

"Why?" I laugh listlessly. "I've been nothing but a pain in your backside since I called you."

Amusement mellows the hard, tired lines that mar his face beneath his five o'clock shadow.

"Hardly. I'll always take care of you, Em."

"Because you love Tom, right?"

It's foolish and dangerous to ask, but I do it anyway. An indecipherable emotion fills his sparkling aquamarines. It's the same look as when he caught me locked in Hyland's arms.

"He's my best friend." Warner's answer comes slowly, deliberately. "I love him like a brother."

"Right."

His eyebrows curve in a concentrated frown. "That doesn't obligate me to be here, Em."

"It doesn't?"

"Perhaps it did before. But no, not now."

"Now... You care about me too."

"No." He shakes his head. "I always cared about you."

"Then what?" I ask breathlessly.

Cradled in his arms, mere inches of air separating us, Warner's mouth opens and closes. Neck bobbing, his facial lines pull into stressed ropes as he struggles to vocalize whatever he wants to say.

I don't know what he feels for me. What he's thinking. Or what this charged feeling bouncing between us like two misfiring power lines is. All I know is that I need something to give.

"Help me to understand this. Please."

"This is... Us." He grimaces at his own clunky words. "We're us, Em. We've always been us."

"And what is us? What are we?"

"That's it. We're us."

"We're colleagues?" I push him, hoping for something unknown. "Childhood friends? Acquaintances?"

"Why does it matter?" Warner bites his lip.

Unwilling to reveal my own confusion, I drop my eyes before I'm drawn into something we can't ever come back from. Something that would implode the bond we created through our shared childhood.

The act of pulling my soul back from the edge of a dangerous precipice unlatches something inside me. A collapsing, taped-together box of youthful lust and repressed emotion.

I'd blame it on the fatigue and stress from what we just endured, but I know it's far more. Putting words to what it really is won't help anyone, though.

"Forget it. I want to go home."

"Look at me, Em," he pleads.

Shaking my head, I ignore the way my eyes sear with more tears. "Let's just move on."

"Please, love. Look at me."

"No. I'm fine. It's fine. We're..."

"Fine?" Warner volunteers.

"Exactly."

Sliding his rough fingertips beneath my chin, Warner lifts it so I have no choice but to look at him. A confusing sheen rides the waves that undulate in his gaze.

He strokes my falling tears aside, mouth twisted and nose scrunched like the sight of me crying causes him physical pain.

"You test every last ounce of patience I have, Ember Lawson."

"I don't mean to—"

"Let me finish," he interrupts with a teasing smile.

Lips sealed, I hold myself back.

"You drive me insane. You infuriate me. You make me question my choices, my loyalties and my goddamn priorities."

Warner tenderly brushes his knuckles against my wet cheek. The slight touch creates tingles that raise the fine hairs on the back of my neck.

"You make me want to do things that I've only ever dreamed of. Forbidden things, Em. Things that would destroy the family who took me in when I needed it. You and Tom."

"He loves you." I shudder a breath.

"And I love him."

With the final nail in the coffin, I resolve to pull away from Warner. It's for the best. His arm pins me to his side when I try to shift, preventing me from fleeing.

"But I think I feel something else entirely for his little sister." His forehead lowers to rest against mine. "And I know for a fact he will not like it."

Our noses nudge, teasing each other with a light brush that skirts the edge of innocence. My shock is overridden by the sense of urgent need that having him so unbearably close provokes.

It's foolish.

Dangerous.

Totally insane.

This is Warner. My childhood friend. The man who rescued me. A constant presence in my life since I was a kid, and he was a lonely boy in need of a new family. That's all we've ever been.

Tell that to my racing heart, sending litres of hot, fizzling blood through my nervous system. I'm drunk with the heady feeling of unchartered desire.

"We can't do this," he whispers.

"Do what?"

"You know what. Don't make this harder than it needs to be, Em."

His breath tickles my lips, causing a slow shiver to roll over my limbs. The weight of countless years of friendship hang in a fragile balance between us.

"I'm not doing anything," I murmur back, forehead pressing against his.

"You know damn well what you're doing."

Warner's voice is strained, laden with conflict. The same emotion beats its fists against the imprisonment of his baby blues. I want to reach my bare hands into his eyes and rip the indecision clean out.

FRACTURED FUTURE

With the silent promise of his breath licking my skin, Warner's lips hover millimetres from mine. Every last reason why I shouldn't indulge what my body is screaming out for vanishes.

Looking up at him beneath my lashes, I skate my tongue over my bottom lip in clear invitation. A single breath and he could take exactly what he wants from me.

"Please stop," he whispers in a pained tone. "We can't do this, Em."

"Why not?"

"You're already toying with my teammates. I don't know what your game plan is, but you're going to tear us all apart in the process."

My hand trembles when I raise it to his stubble-smattered jaw, stroking the strong, defined length of bone.

"You guys make me feel whole. I want to be whole again. I want the family you're giving me. I want this and more."

"You're asking for too much, love."

"I know." I slip my hand into his trimmed salt-and-pepper locks. "But I never once apologised for being greedy before, and I'm certainly not about to start now."

My mouth hovers over his in a ruthless tease. Warner's eyelids lower, shielding the orbs that have held so much love and care for me over the years.

The boy I once knew disappears.

A powerful, protective man takes his place.

"You know what?"

Hope stretches the bounds of my skeleton. "What?"

"Fuck it," he growls.

Then his mouth crashes onto mine.

Hard. Rough. Demanding.

Drowning us in relentless passion.

The lips that have whispered so much comfort to me now attack mine with the ferocity of a full-size army invading enemy territory. His mouth captures mine and greedily accepts my surrender.

Powerful longing and crumbling restraint collide in an explosive firework display. Warner's mouth urgently moves against mine like he's drinking in every second together before this is taken away from him like everything else he's lost.

Desperation forms an unbreakable coil that entraps us in its fleeting bliss. The swipe of his tongue, hot and wet against my mouth, intensifies what feels like an admittance of defeat.

I twist his hair between my fingers, holding his head in a vice. Anything to prevent this assault from ending. The sharp tug causes a groan to swirl in Warner's throat, making my core clench.

The arm still wrapped around me responds in kind—pulling taut, locking me in a prison of muscles and skin. Lips and teeth suspend me there, and I wouldn't complain even if I could.

When the kiss eventually breaks, our lips linger in each other's orbit. Breathless. Tingling. Hearts battering ribcages like caged birds, frantic to escape their enclosures.

Daring to open my eyes, I'm met with a fatal concoction of desire and guilt spelled across Warner's flushed face. His mouth is swollen, trapped open to steal each short gasp.

"I'm in so much trouble," he mutters.

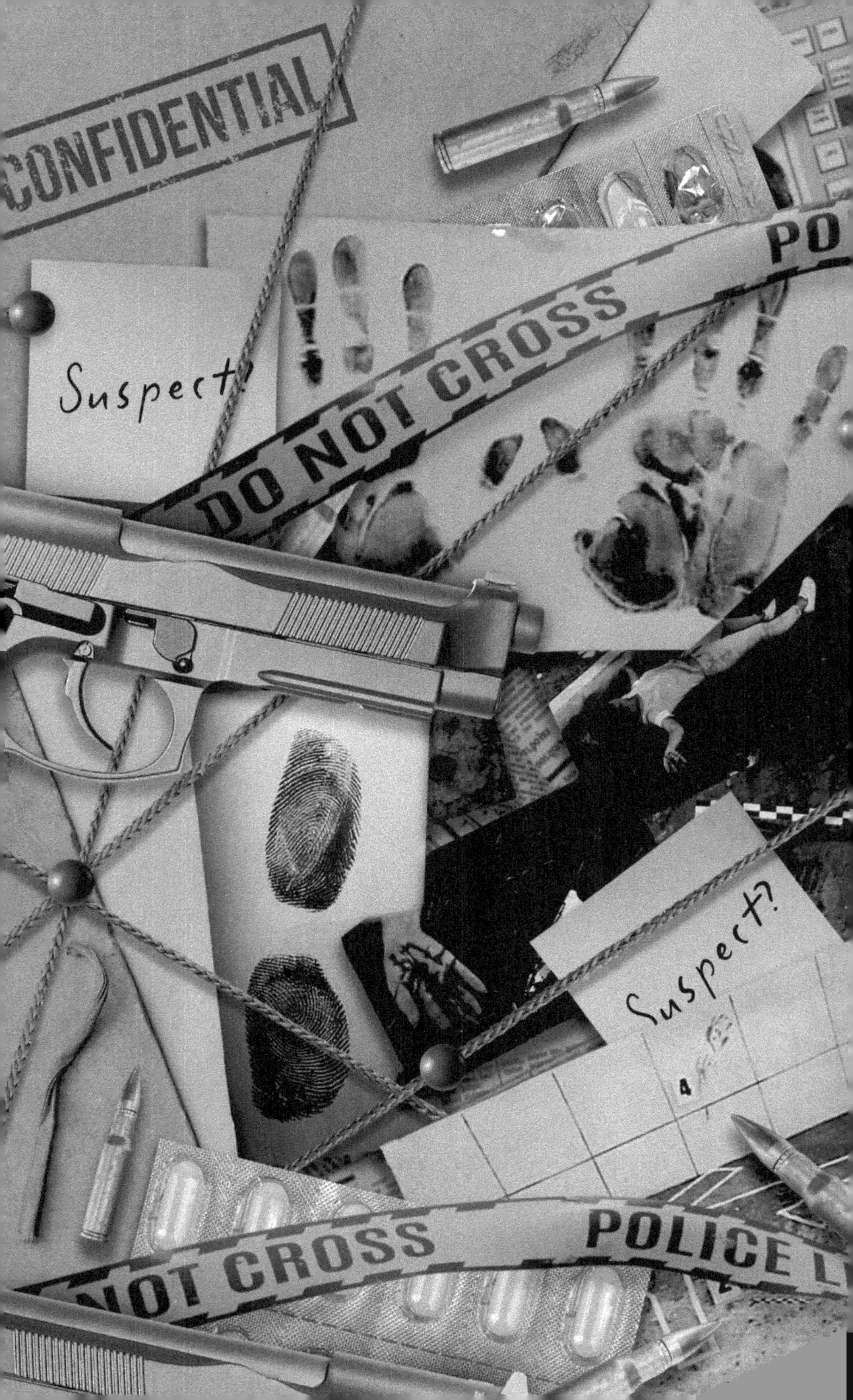

CONFIDENTIAL

Suspect?

DO NOT CROSS

PO

Suspect?

NOT CROSS

POLICE

23

EMBER

RED VELVET – JUTES & ARI ABDUL

"**A**bsolutely not!"

His fist thumping down on the dining table, Hyland's menacing expression would melt the skin from my bones if I gave a shit. Perhaps he should try it on someone who's actually intimidated by his crap.

While his hot and cold behaviour does make him a pain in the ass to be around, I'm not going to cater to his stupid, protective demands. I didn't before, and I won't start now.

"I don't recall asking for permission," I reply curtly.

"You've been home from the hospital for less than twenty-four hours."

"So?"

"Already you're planning to throw yourself in the deep end with that lunatic!"

His yelling is really not appreciated by my still-fragile brain.

While I slept well, I'm still feeling sore and worn out. The pain medication I've been prescribed is helping my chronic headaches, though.

"Blaine is refusing to speak to anyone but me," I try to reason with him. "What choice do I have?"

"She isn't throwing herself anywhere," Axel pipes up from the kitchen. "We will be there. She'll be supervised and perfectly safe."

"There's no such thing as perfectly safe around Blaine Madden!" Hyland blusters.

Rolling my eyes, I accept the steaming coffee Axel delivers to me. His bruised face morphs into a smile at the appreciative look I gift him. At least someone has forgiven me.

"That one's on the house, babe."

"You're too kind," I tease back.

"Consider it a gift in lieu of grapes."

"Grapes?"

"That's what you bring sick people, right?" His dark brows pull tight in obvious confusion. "Grapes?"

"Pretty sure that's what you take your grandma when she's in the hospital after breaking a hip, but sure. I'll accept it."

"Thanks, dimples." He flourishes a boyish grin. "You can stay a while."

"I already live here?" I sputter out a laugh.

"Well, obviously. I don't pull out my impressive coffee making skills for just anyone."

Flirtatiously winking at me, Axel disappears back into the kitchen to continue organising my morning medication. He declared it his top priority after coaxing me out of bed to eat and rehydrate.

"Um, hello?" Hyland gawks at me like I've lost my mind.

Taking a sip of coffee, I glare at him. "I'm listening."

"Clearly, you're not. This is a terrible idea!"

"Give it up, Hy. You're not changing my mind."

"I shouldn't have to!" He pulls at his sandy tresses. "You've just been diagnosed with epilepsy, Ember.

"I'm aware of that."

"You're supposed to be resting and avoiding stress!"

Again, the giant dick thumps his fist on the table like some kind of bat-shit dictator. I'm going to thump my fist directly into his face in approximately three seconds.

"I still have a job to do regardless of what happened. We need Blaine to talk. If I can make that happen, then I will."

"You're so infuriating!" He moves to press the heels of his palms into his eyes. "Like... fuck!"

His chair thrusts backwards with a screech before Hyland draws to his full, intimidating height. He's been in this foul mood since driving us home from the hospital, stopping to deposit Tom enroute.

The pair of them were united in their collective anger towards me while Warner seems to be taking on the role of peacekeeper. Though he still hasn't risen this morning, so I'm dealing with the grump solo.

"You have succeeded in making it impossible to protect you." He casts me an annoyed glower. "Congratulations."

With that blow levied, Hyland storms towards the hallway then disappears with an aggressively slammed door. Groaning to myself, I lower my forehead to the dining table.

"He is insufferable sometimes."

"Only sometimes?" Axel jokes.

"What I meant to say was more than ever lately."

Axel's palm slides over the back of my neck to deliver a squeeze. "You scared the life out of him, Em. The man's in a tailspin."

Lifting my head, I find Axel leaning over me with an outstretched hand. A cluster of white and yellow pills rest in the centre, plucked from the array of prescription bottles I was sent home with.

"It's not like I intended to hurt him." I wearily accept the handful of pills.

"None of us ever do." Axel shrugs, taking a seat beside me. "Hyland hurts his own damn feelings by making the entire world his problem. He'll get over it."

"I've really fucked things up, haven't I?"

"Hey, join the club. It's nice to have a fellow fuck up on board."

"Great. So glad to be here."

"I'll get you a membership t-shirt."

"Thanks." I knock back my morning medication with a deep gulp of coffee. "Hell. You make a good cuppa."

I'm sure Hyland would disapprove of this too, but thankfully, Axel doesn't question my choice of beverage. I still need caffeine even while recovering.

Grinning while he leans back in his chair, Axel straightens his bright-yellow, sixties-style tee. The lurid colour even features groovy flowers and butterflies with bubble writing.

"Life's too short to wear boring clothes?"

"I always speak my truth," he says solemnly.

"I'm almost positive that's a woman's shirt."

"Dude, vintage gear is gender neutral."

"It has butterflies on it."

"I like butterflies!" Axel juts out his bottom lip.

"Hey, no judgement here."

Swigging more coffee, I focus on steadying my hands. The tremors are still obvious. I can feel Axel watching me closely for any tiny signs of another seizure.

"Did the specialist say how long it'll take for the medication to work?"

"It's not a simple fix." I sigh while studying my coffee mug. "We have to try different types of medication to see what reduces the frequency of the seizures."

"Well, shit."

"Yep. I'll have to go for regular check-ups for the next few months and see what happens. I can't just take a pill and be normal again."

"Well, that would be boring."

"I wouldn't mind a bit of boring right about now."

Nudging my foot beneath the table, Axel encourages me to look at him. "Normal is far overrated, babe. You're perfect just the way you are."

"Dirty hair, pyjamas and unbrushed teeth?"

"Oh, yeah." He pretends to wipe drool from his mouth. "That's my kink."

"What the fuck is wrong with you?"

"Especially the unbrushed teeth. Oof, so hot."

Kicking his foot away from me, I burst into laughter. It lightens the pressure that's sat on my chest since I saw Hyland and Tom's matching anxious expressions in the hospital.

"I don't know about taking my medication—I think you need to take yours."

"Nah, I'm also perfect the way I am." Axel blows a kiss at me. "We're a match made in heaven."

Pretending to bat the kiss away, I decide to get showered and dressed before Hyland decides to literally restrain me in the apartment. I need to get to HQ to see what the hell Blaine wants from me.

"I have to get washed up."

"Need a hand with that?" he innocently purrs.

"Dream on."

"Spoilsport. At least think of me in the shower." His eyes trail over me, leaving a heated path. "Or think of how it felt when I played with your sweet pussy."

"Ax!"

"Care for a replay?"

Cheeks flaming, I quickly escape the room. The sound of his raucous laughter follows me across the living area and into the penthouse's hallway. He really is incorrigible in all the worst ways.

"Shit!"

A loud bang follows the cuss, coming from Warner's bedroom. A wheelchair holds the door ajar, wedged into the entrance at an awkward angle.

"Oh. Hi."

His head jerks up, embarrassment flushing over him. "Hey, Em."

"Haven't seen you use the chair in a few years. You okay?"

The sight of him sitting in the wheelchair is a surprise. He's dressed in shorts that expose the pink stump of his residual limb, the lack of prosthetic catching me off guard for a second.

For a while after his accident, Warner could only get around by using the wheelchair. Then he progressed to using two crutches before beginning to experiment with prosthetics.

"Just having a bit of trouble." He plays it off like there isn't sweat coating his forehead. "I'm good."

"Are you in pain? Can I do anything?"

Waving me off, Warner avoids looking at me. "Just sore today. Took a few hits during the raid."

"How bad is it?" I wince.

"Nah, not bad. I'm just swollen so I can't get the leg on."

Concern morphs into guilt that forces me into action. I don't care if it's going to be awkward after the charged moment we shared. He's in pain and needs my help.

Squeezing past him, I hold the door open with my hip then take control of the handles behind the wheelchair's back.

"Kitchen?"

"You don't have to help," he mutters.

"Pretty hypocritical for a man always lecturing me about accepting help. Tell me where you want to go, and shut the hell up."

His head lowering, Warner repositions his hips in the chair. "The kitchen is fine."

"Coming right up."

Rolling him down the hallway towards the kitchen, I realise how thoughtfully designed their penthouse is. The halls are wide and accessible, and the level floor is easy to navigate.

Even their stylishly sunken living area features a sloped section on the left that leads down. I didn't put two and two together before. It's been done for Warner's more immobile days.

"Hey! Nurse Slaughter!" I holler loudly.

"Yes?" Axel calls back.

"Got a new patient for you to play with."

Head perking up, he stands from where I left him pouting at the deserted dining table. "Oh, goody."

"Please no," Warner whimpers in what sounds like genuine fear. "Don't leave me here, Em."

"He's going to look after you."

"Please! I can't run away from him right now."

"That's good. Let him play nurse for a bit."

Slapping his hands together when I park Warner up at the edge of the kitchen, Axel appraises his state of casual undress.

"Food first, I think." He frowns in concentration. "You look a bit peaky, boss. How about a peanut butter sandwich?"

"You know I hate peanut butter, Ax!"

"Aw, shit. But I really fancied one."

"You don't need to cook for me."

"But I do!" Axel declares. "How about a chip sandwich instead? They don't look appetising, but they sure do taste good."

Glaring at me with panic overflowing in his eyes, Warner silently pleads for me to rescue him from Axel's lack of cooking capabilities. I stoop down to press a kiss against his freshly shaven cheek.

"Have fun."

"You're so dead, Em!"

"And you're so welcome!" I shout while walking away. "Happy cooking, boys."

Leaving them to bicker about sandwiches, I shower and dress as quickly as my tender body will allow. My knuckles sting when I lightly apply cream to the abrasions gained from pummelling Miguel.

It felt good to unleash some of my rage on him, but it wasn't enough. Knowing that someone else had the pleasure of ending Diego's life infuriates me. Thankfully, Luis is still alive to face me.

For now.

Pulling on plain black jeans and a basic t-shirt that clings to my toned arms, I work on braiding my wet hair. With Warner out of action and Axel on nursing duty, I'll have to ask the grump to drive me now that I'm barred.

After putting it off for as long as possible, I head next door to Hyland's bedroom. The door falls open when I lightly knock, revealing a dark interior.

"Hyland?"

Bathed in tonal shades of blue, his bedroom is a calm paradise of dark-stained wood and luxuriously thick, black curtains. Beyond his truly gigantic sleigh bed, he has a modest sized wardrobe, built-in desk and several floating shelves.

With his back to me, Hyland sits at the desk, bent over something. His headful of loose blonde hair shoots up at my voice, alarm scored across his bearded face.

"I need a ride," I announce.

"I'm busy."

Snapping the book clasped in his hands shut, Hyland rises to face me. He keeps the book tucked behind his back, triggering my curiosity.

"What are you doing?"

"Researching a new career," he snarls.

Strolling into his safe space, I let my fingers trail over the inky-blue linen sheets on his bed. You could easily fit three average-sized people in that monster.

"Come on," I goad him. "You'd never leave the team."

"I don't like people lying to me."

"Lying is such a strong word."

"What would you call it?" His jaw visibly tics.

Nearing him, I tilt my neck to drink in his ruggedness. Even when he's driving me up the wall with his possessive ways, it's impossible not to appreciate his marble-carved looks.

"Um, temporarily withholding the truth?"

"You're turning into Axel with that self-deluding crap."

Resting a hand on his bicep, I adopt a more serious tone. "I really am sorry. What I did was wrong. I had my reasons, but that doesn't make it right."

"You should've trusted us!"

"You're right."

Overcome with a rush of guilt, I resolve to confide in him. For all his quirks, Hyland cares deeply. I know I've hurt him, and I hate the thought that I've caused him pain.

"I didn't trust you," I admit. "Or anyone else, for that matter. I had to keep this secret to avoid being discarded like faulty goods. Only that would've entailed my execution or worse."

"We're not Gael, Ember."

"I know you're not, but after all these years... the lie was ingrained in me. And I was scared. Far too scared to even admit to the symptoms I've had."

"So you suffered in silence," he surmises.

"Can you really blame me?"

Stumped by my question, Hyland huffs in irritation. His wide shoulders slump under the weight of his defeat settling into each honed muscle.

"I suppose not."

"Then try having a bit of empathy for why I felt the need to lie," I reply calmly. "I didn't do it to be malicious or to hurt anyone."

"You're safe here, Em. You could've told us."

"I know that now."

"Do you?" he demands.

"Yes. I do."

Fingers itching with the urge to stroke the golden spun silk that smothers his jawline, I internally celebrate when he tugs me into his chest. A massive hand finds my lower back to pin me against him.

"You're such a stubborn creature." His chin drops on top of my head. "Do you have any clue how fucking terrified I was to find you passed out like that? In *his* goddamn arms?"

"I'm sorry, Hy."

"Stop apologising. Just promise me you won't take such a dumb risk again."

"I won't. It was foolish."

"I'm not stupid enough to think I can keep you locked up here. But you need to be smart in this job."

My cheek nuzzles his t-shirt. "I'll be careful from now on. I don't want to put anyone in danger."

"That means telling us if you feel a seizure coming on," he rumbles above me. "Even the slightest fucking twitch, Em. A tiny headache. A dizzy spell. Anything. You'll come to me."

"Is that an order?" I snort.

"You bet your ass it is."

"So much for making up. I thought you'd cut the overbearing crap."

"Believe me, red. I can be far more overbearing than this."

"Promises, promises."

Planting a kiss on top of my head, he withdraws before I can read too much into it. As Hyland reaches for his usual army boots to begin lacing them at the foot of his bed, I spot the book he's discarded.

"What's this?"

"Wait!" he calls out.

Picking up the glossy self-help book, I turn it over in my hands. The title makes me choke on a surprised laugh.

"Living with Epilepsy?"

Glancing at Hyland, his entire focus is back on lacing his shoes. If I didn't know better, I'd think a pink flush has taken over his tanned skin.

Oh, fuck.

I actually think he's blushing.

"Did you buy a self-help book on epilepsy?"

Boots now in place, Hyland rises to march over to me. "Give it to me."

"Well?" I prompt when he snatches the book from my hands.

"No."

"Clearly, you did. How'd you get it so fast?"

"Overnight delivery," he grumpily replies.

Tossing the book on his neatly made bed, he waves his hand, gesturing for me to get the hell out of his room. I don't know whether to create an even bigger mess for myself by kissing the fool or scurry away.

"You're researching my condition?"

"Leave it, Em."

"No. Tell me why."

Hyland palms the back of his neck. "I want to know what to do when it happens again. I need to be able to look after you."

"But... You were mad at me."

"So? You think that stopped me from caring?"

Mouth snapping shut, I merely shrug.

"You should know by now, Em. No matter how pissed off I am, I'll never stop caring for a second."

With that, he briefly grazes his fingertips along my cheek then departs the bedroom. I'm left to pick my jaw up off the floor and follow the most confusing man to have ever walked the earth.

A man who overnights self-help books even when he's giving me the silent treatment. I must have some kind of internal brain damage for thinking that's undeniably cute.

ONFIDENTIAL
Why?
Suspect?
Gael?
DO NOT CROSS
POLICE LI

POLICE LINE DO NOT CROSS
POLICE LINE
CONFIDENTIAL
Weapon?
2
3

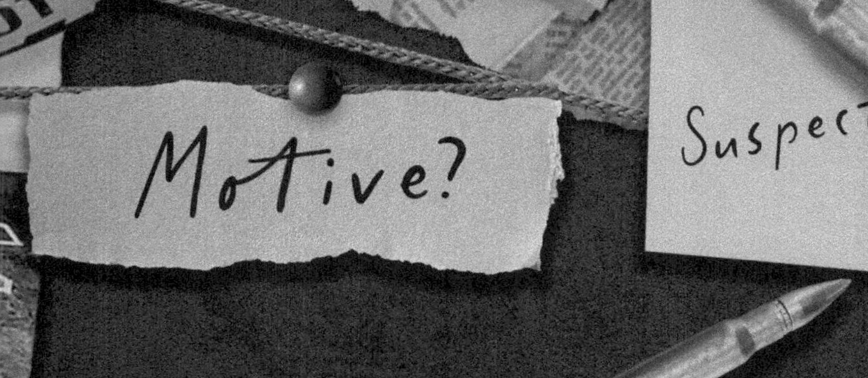

24

HYLAND

DISARM – THE SMASHING PUMPKINS

Riding Sabre's elevator down to the interrogation floor, I run through Warner's strict instructions one more time. It took a lot of trust on his part to allow this to happen while he rests up.

He was done with Axel's fussing after a matter of minutes, begging me to bring the pup along for extra muscle. Now the three of us are on our way to face the ghost that just won't stay dead.

Blaine Madden.

That name haunts me.

Deep in the bowels of Sabre's HQ, we keep an array of rooms for interrogations. Our jurisdiction covers criminals arrested in the course of an investigation, granting us the power to question them.

I'd like to think it also allows us the power to snap their legs and spines if they fuck us around. From what I've heard, our two star witnesses are being tight-lipped.

"Looks like you're learning on the job today." I glance at Ember. "This isn't a regular interrogation. You have a personal relationship with Madden."

"If by relationship, you mean he threw me out of a moving vehicle, harassed me via text message and fought me in front of a warehouse full of thugs, then sure."

Axel chuckles but remains silent.

"Trust me," I continue brusquely. "The fact that he let you walk away alive on multiple occasions means he certainly believes you have a personal relationship."

Scoffing in disgust, Ember tugs the hem of her black t-shirt down. It's slightly cropped, riding above her waistband to reveal a flash of flat, creamy-white stomach. Enough to tighten my throat.

"Be careful." I make myself focus on the task at hand. "Don't try to be clever. If the asshole wants to talk, let him. We'll document everything he wants to reveal then send him back to prison."

"Gotcha," she grinds out.

"He's restrained. You're perfectly safe."

"I'm not scared of him," Ember rebuffs.

"You should be."

She raises an eyebrow at me. "Seriously?"

"Years back, a member of Madden's family snitched," I explain. "He was cooperating with the Serious Crimes Unit to bring about racketeering charges. Then their mole disappeared into thin air."

Both Ember and Axel focus on me.

"They found him lynched and hanging from the rafters of an abandoned drugs farm in East London. Someone stapled a fucking note to his forehead. It said *DISLOYALTY.*"

"Disloyalty?" Axel tests the word.

"These families operate on strict moral codes, even while they're breaking the law. Loyalty is their lifeblood. Madden personally admitted to the killing when we arrested him."

If I'm hoping to inspire Ember's fear, I'm sorely mistaken. The crazy woman actually looks impressed by that level of commitment. Note to self: executions turn her on. That's helpful information.

"I doubt he's looking to hang me today," she comments.

"Perhaps not, but Madden's been playing an intricate game for a long time. He schemes and plots. That's his modus operandi."

"Your point being?"

"The Phantom has a plan. Try not to be a part of it."

Tense silence takes over as we exit onto the subterranean level, cloaked in low light. This is Axel's domain. As the team enforcer, I'm usually at the forefront of the fight, not interrogating those we arrest.

Skipping along with far too much pep in his step for someone heading into an interrogation, Axel is right at home. He leads the way to the suite where we've had our perps holed up.

"Hudson had Miguel in here for thirteen hours." Axel scans his security badge to release the door lock. "He's been taken back to his cell for the time being."

"Thirteen hours?" Ember gasps.

"Yeah… Hud's a little sadistic. Kept lighting and putting out cigarettes on the poor fuck."

Eyes bouncing around, she takes a moment to consider how to react. "Good. I wish we had Luis to torture too."

Honestly, her sadism probably rivals that of our company director. She just hasn't had the opportunity to explore it yet. Reckless or not, I want to give her that chance.

"Miguel did a bit more than squirm, sweetheart." Axel grins in amusement. "Not sure he has any vocal cords left to give us information with after all that screaming."

Holding open the door for us to enter the viewing portion of the mirror-lined space, Axel clicks it shut behind us. The air pressure system hisses into action, securing the suite.

Through the three-way split on the other side of the smoky mirror, only one interrogation room is occupied. The other two sit empty.

On the far left, Blaine Madden casually lounges in his chair. He's no longer covered in blood, at least. Some unlucky agent must've had the pleasure of supervising his cleanup.

Seeing his scarred face up close again only makes me want to march in there and break it. The fact that he had his mitts on Ember while she was unconscious reviles me. Even if he was helping her.

"Are you ready?" I move towards the door.

Shaking out her hands, Ember nods. "You're coming with me?"

"Axel's giving me the honour." I cast him a brief smile. "This is usually his department, but I don't think I could stand to wait out here and watch."

"You owe me one," he quips back.

"Yeah, yeah." I refocus on Ember. "I'll stand in the corner just in case. Those cuffs don't make me feel any better about sending you in there with him."

"Right."

"If he moves an inch, I intend to rip his spine out then shove it down his throat."

"Mmm. Physically impossible." Axel moves over to the mirror to observe. "Take it from me. I've tried unsuccessfully."

Pressing himself against the glass, he bobs on the balls of his feet while Ember rolls her shoulders. His playfulness seems to drain away, filling his body with visible tension instead.

"Ax? You good?"

When he doesn't respond, I call his name again.

"Huh?" His head swivels to me. "Oh, sure. Good luck."

I frown at him. *Weird.* What's weirder is that he indulged my request to take his place in that interview. I didn't expect him to actually agree to it.

There's no time to question his behaviour as I escort Ember into the farthest interrogation room. Her shoulders are now thrown back, holding her auburn head high.

The moment she enters the space, Madden perks up. A satisfied smirk curls his pierced bottom lip when he inspects his prize. The slow perusal causes my hands to curl up, begging to pummel into his body.

"You came."

"You called," Ember responds coolly.

"Is that how this works? I feel honoured."

"Don't. I'm here for answers. That's all."

Taking the empty metal chair opposite his cuffed state, Ember sits down. I move to stand in the corner of the room, giving me direct sight of them. If Madden tries anything, he's toast.

"You're looking a bit more with it," Madden observes, lazily checking her out. "Feeling any better?"

"I'm not here to talk about me."

"Ah. That's your first lie."

Body tensing, Ember stares daggers at the man across from her. "Why were you attending that meeting? How do you know Luis and Diego?"

"Straight down to business with no foreplay, hm? My kind of girl."

Breathe. Breathe. Breathe.

Crossing her arms, Ember shows no sign of rising to his teases. "Thank you for saving me. You're a fucking hero. Are we good now? Answer my questions."

"You don't do gratitude real well. Do you, sweetheart?"

"It's not my strong suit, no."

"That's okay. I'm not here for your thanks."

Ember narrows her eyes on him. "Then why are you here?"

"For you," he says simply.

Their back and forth is painfully mesmerising. I know firsthand that Ember's a certified ballbreaker, but seeing her refusing to pander to Madden is particularly satisfying.

"I asked for a rematch in exchange for answers."

"You're heading straight back to prison from this room," she denies. "No rematch. Just tell us what you know about Gael."

"You drive a hard bargain. What's in this for me?"

"Your life," I insert. "We can just as easily lose your body and falsify the records to make it look like you never stepped foot inside this building."

Head tossed back, Madden stares up at the ceiling for a moment to gather his thoughts. His raven hair is messy, long strands sticking in all directions above the closely cropped sides.

It's pleasant to see him looking unkempt, even while he talks like some aristocratic asshole. I'll feel even better when he's rotting behind bars with zero possibility of ever escaping again.

"Fine," he concedes. "I'll play."

"Then start talking," Ember orders.

"Antonio Gael is a business associate."

"So you do work for him." Her face stains red with beautiful rage. "You son of a bitch!"

"A business associate of my father's. Not mine."

Startled by his response, I look between them, trying to pull the discordant pieces of this tale together.

"Your… father?" Ember squints at him.

"Yes. I do not work for Gael."

Once upon a time, Madden spearheaded his father's criminal empire. Nolan Madden built a dynasty on blood, dirty money and extortion, with his son providing the brute force to fortify their criminal legacy.

It's no secret that Blaine Madden was resolutely against the skin trade. Years of research and investigating told us that much. He refused to dirty his hands with trafficking of any kind.

But his father?

A whole other beast altogether.

"Your new teammates at Sabre Security hauled me in to be prosecuted." Madden cuts me a sour look. "And I was punished for my father's crimes."

"You've killed countless people," I vocalise.

"Under orders. Yes, I have. But our family business operated within certain limits. Boundaries I refused to cross. I wasn't aware that my father was crossing them without my knowledge."

Elbows bracing on the table, Ember leans in. "Explain."

Darkness seeps over Madden's scar-twisted features, casting a shadow that steals the light seeing Ember had previously illuminated his face with.

"I discovered that he had money tied up in the human trafficking trade running through England and beyond. My father was loaning out our men to perform kidnapping runs and being paid handsomely."

"Honeypots," Ember murmurs.

"Excuse me?"

"Those men you were cosying up to in the warehouse. They're Gael's honeypots. The stuffed shirts he sends out to target innocent women and lure them into his trap."

"That's what you thought I was doing?" Madden grimaces in

distaste. "I am not some foot soldier."

"Could've fooled us," I grumble.

The murderous look he shoots me is full of lethal threat. "I wouldn't stoop that low."

Smiling back at him, I let the limitless, cold hatred I hold for this waste of space shine through. "Wouldn't you?"

"No! After I was arrested by you fools, my father vanished into thin air. He fled his crumbling empire and was never seen again. But he's still out there."

"No one has heard or seen from Nolan Madden in years."

"Yes." Madden nods at my statement. "Because he's protected by powerful, loyal friends. The kind of friends that years of successful business transactions earn you."

"You're saying he's working with Gael," Ember interprets, the colour draining from her face. "Shit."

The dire look Madden wears chills my skin.

"I suspect that my father has spent the last few years hiding out in some luxurious bolthole, bought and paid for by the man who held you captive."

His words rebound off the walls, landing with cataclysmic magnitude. We spent a long time searching for the head of the Madden family, unsatisfied with charging his son alone.

No matter how long we investigated, tearing apart decades of shady dealings dipped in a bloodstained trail of money, there was nothing. Not a single sighting. It's like Nolan Madden never existed.

We had to make our peace with dismantling the family legacy to the best of our ability—prosecuting hundreds of lower-ranking mobsters, taking down countless drug production sites and obliterating illegal markets.

"Were you in Mexico searching for your father?" Ember asks him.

"Partly." Madden's sparkling black orbs latch onto her. "Partly for you."

"Wait, why me?"

"Don't hurt me, sweetheart, but I needed a bargaining chip. I wanted to buy peace with these knuckleheads through your safe return because I need their help."

Pushing off from the wall, I move closer to brace my hands on the table. Madden doesn't show an ounce of discomfort at the way I loom over him in obvious threat.

"Our help with what?" I sneer at him. "You're our enemy. I'm going to take great pleasure in tearing apart the few allies you've gathered and tossing you back in a cell."

"Or you can help me track down my father and burn down the Madden dynasty for good."

"Are you serious?" A laugh bursts free.

"Deadly. I'll allow you to light the damn match, if you so please."

Reeling back, I stare deeply into his eyes. Not spotting a single hint of deception. Jesus fucking Christ, he lost his mind while on the run from the law. He actually believes we'd buy that crap.

"Track him down so you can reunite with dear old dad?" I straighten, wanting to smack the smug piece of shit. "Then you'll steamroll over my team for what we've done to that empire you once held so dear."

"Fucking fool!" Madden spits out.

His calm mask slips, offering a glimpse of the infamous Phantom. You don't earn a terrifying name for yourself with fancy accents and clever spiels. Though he was almost convincing.

"Do you really think I wish to reunite with that monster?" He strains against his wrist cuffs.

"You worked for the man your entire life."

"Not out of choice!" His hiss fills the air. "I've spent most of my life in servitude!"

Fighting the handcuffs again, Madden thrashes and lurches, unable to escape the metal restraints.

"He raised me to be this… this… machine! This violent creature! I had no choice. I've spent every waking moment doing his bidding to avoid…"

Voice failing, Madden stares intently at Ember. Something seems to pass between them. A glimpse of recognition. She knows something about him that we don't.

God, I fucking despise that.

"I did my best to steer the direction of the *family business.*"

Madden swallows to moisten his mouth. "He still found a way to subvert my efforts. Then when the time came, he fed me to the wolves and left."

When an odd sensation crawls into my heart and sinks its claws inside me, I take several big steps back. Disgust is tart and overwhelming on my tongue.

Oh, hell no. I don't think so.

Do I actually pity him?

I've worked with villains before. The worst kind. Saved a fair few of them along the way too. Some are worthy of garnering our sympathy, while others deserve their place on society's scrap heap.

Madden is evil.

He's the worst of the worst.

Right?

"You used me as a pawn." Ember loudly clears her throat. "To play some insane long game with people who despise you in hope that you could track down a missing mobster to get your revenge?"

"Something like that."

"Fuck, Blaine. I don't know what's more impressive... your scheming or your audacity."

Madden breaks out in one of his classic smirks. "I do enjoy being audacious when the situation allows."

"But why infiltrate their meeting? They must know you're not on their side."

"I like to have a Plan B." Madden shrugs. "I thought that if I could establish contact, present myself as a sympathetic party or perhaps an ally, it would lead me to my father."

Whistling under my breath, I brace my hands on my hips. "You're crazy."

"This coming from you?" Madden tosses at me.

"Takes one to know one, dick."

"Go back to scowling. You're far better at it."

The wall greets me when I turn to take a deep breath before I actually smash his head in. As usual, Madden has a game plan. I just didn't anticipate it revealing him to be an almost-ally after all.

That's the problem with this snake. You never know where his true loyalties lie. He's been playing us while keeping his cards close to his chest all along. Just to reveal his motives at the opportune moment.

We can't trust him.

Not now. Not ever.

It doesn't matter if he can gain us access to Gael. Working with Madden is suicide. He'll turn around to stab us in the back, given half a chance.

"Gael is offering eye-watering sums of money for your safe recapture," Madden reveals, drawing me back to the room. "He will never stop. Help me find my father, and we'll find Gael too."

"Why should we trust you?" Ember argues fiercely. "All you've done is lie, manipulate and plot against us. I don't see why we should believe a word of this ridiculous story."

"You've seen what that monster did to me, sweetheart. The scars don't lie. You should know—you've got plenty of your own."

Damned jealousy sears my insides as I turn back around to hit him with a death glare. If this scar comparison is another pickup tactic, he's going to be gravely unsuccessful.

"This isn't my decision to make." Ember abruptly stands, shoving her chair back.

"Then speak to your team," he suggests.

"They won't buy into this charade," I supply flatly.

Madden glowers at me. "Your investigation is at a dead end. Interview the others you arrested all you like. None of them have the information you need."

"Then we keep looking!" I burst out.

"Can you keep her safe for that long?" he challenges. "Luis and his men are the first of many who will smuggle their way into this country to take a shot at scoring the grand prize."

"Me," Ember guesses.

"Precisely."

"We will keep her safe." My declaration seems to fall on deaf ears.

"The longer this investigation stretches on, the more danger you will face." Madden ignores me to address her. "This is your only chance to defeat Gael and secure your future."

"That's enough!" I march over to Ember to haul her up. "We're done here.”

“Hy—”

“No. He's a fucking reptile, Ember! You can't trust him!”

Towing her from the room, Madden's shouts follow our retreating footsteps. The formidable Phantom has crumbled to the point of pleading for our help. He's as defeated as we are.

That doesn't mean we can team up.

Once a snake, always a snake.

CONFIDENTIAL
Suspect?
DO NOT CROSS
PO
POLICE
NOT CROSS
Suspect?
4

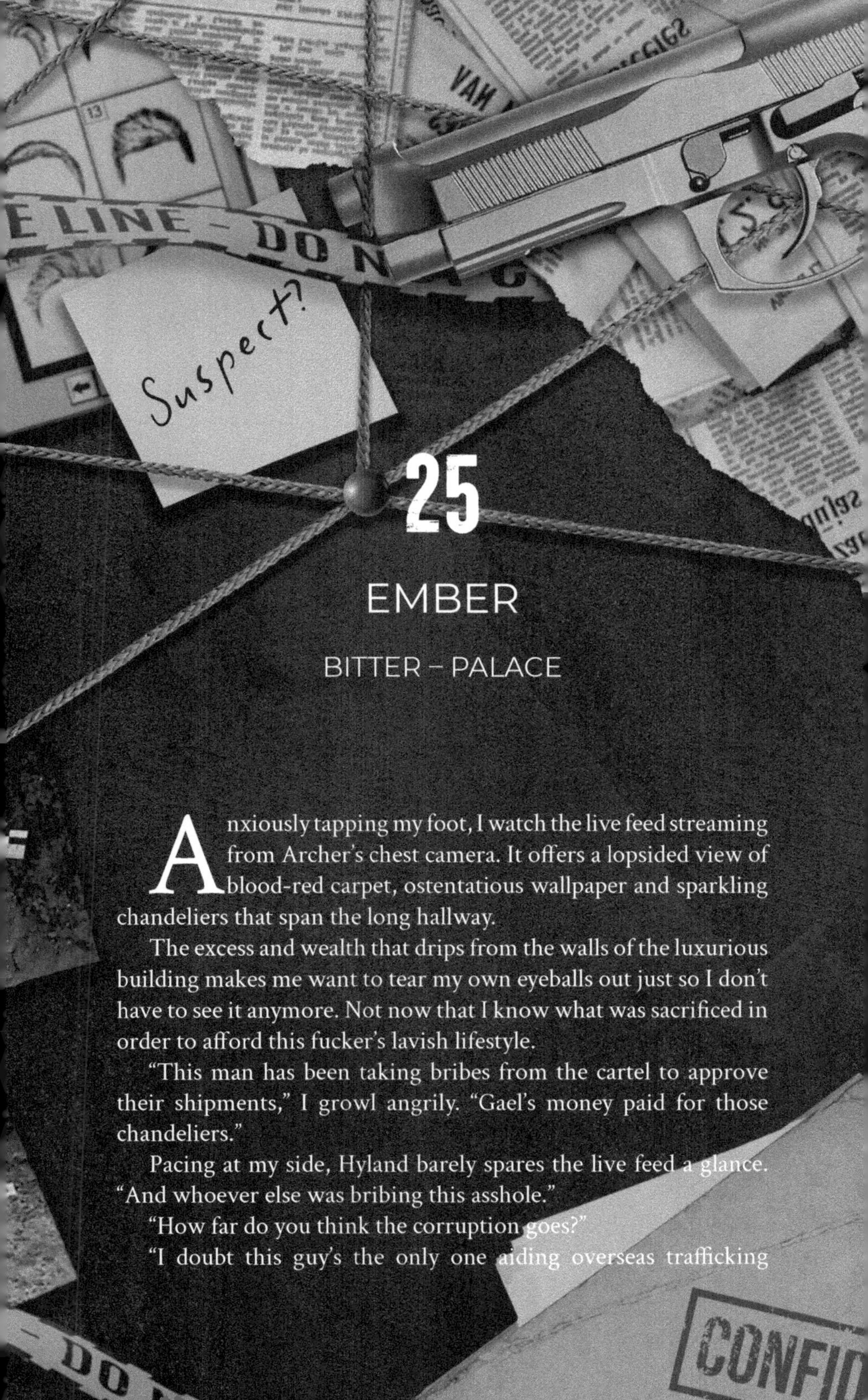

25

EMBER

BITTER – PALACE

Anxiously tapping my foot, I watch the live feed streaming from Archer's chest camera. It offers a lopsided view of blood-red carpet, ostentatious wallpaper and sparkling chandeliers that span the long hallway.

The excess and wealth that drips from the walls of the luxurious building makes me want to tear my own eyeballs out just so I don't have to see it anymore. Not now that I know what was sacrificed in order to afford this fucker's lavish lifestyle.

"This man has been taking bribes from the cartel to approve their shipments," I growl angrily. "Gael's money paid for those chandeliers."

Pacing at my side, Hyland barely spares the live feed a glance. "And whoever else was bribing this asshole."

"How far do you think the corruption goes?"

"I doubt this guy's the only one aiding overseas trafficking gangs. Money talks, red.”

“We need to identify and arrest them all.”

“We will,” Hyland vows.

No one else pays our muttering any attention. Warner sits at the head of the cluttered table, deep in conversation with his support staff, including two members of Sabre’s intelligence team—Rayna and Fox.

Today’s target was a hand-wrapped gift courtesy of Miguel. The other lowlifes we captured from that warehouse didn’t have any intel to offer, but Luis’s thug eventually sang for his life under the threat of another thirteen-hour session with Hudson.

Tyler Perez.

We’ve found a puzzle piece.

Spreadeagled in an office chair, Axel remains glued to his phone screen. I’m convinced that something is eating at him. He’s been off throughout the last few days of back-to-back interviews, searching for a lead.

“What are you studying so hard?” I move to look over his shoulder.

Slapping it against his chest, Axel plasters on a smile. “Nothing.”

“Seriously, what’s going on with you?”

“Nothing, dimples.”

Unconvinced, I resolve to pin him down later when we’re not mid-assault on a hostile target. He’ll tell me what crawled up his ass and died. I can drag it out of him.

“I have no idea why the Falcon Team were put on this,” Hyland grumbles when I retake my place. “Perez is our target.”

“Archer’s team can handle it.”

“Like they handled letting Luis escape?”

“Come on,” I coax. “That isn’t fair.”

Shaking his head from side to side, he takes a moment to calm down. Losing Luis during that raid was a blow, but it seems Hyland is taking it hardest.

“They’ve got this, Hy.”

“Perez has been ensuring shipments fly under the radar for years.” Hyland tosses his hands in aggravation. “He’s behind all those containers filled with women.”

"And you've trained the Falcon Team yourself. Trust them to do their job. They want to redeem themselves."

On Warner's laptop screen, we all watch as Archer advances with his three teammates hot on his heels. They've already infiltrated the high-rise apartment block in upmarket Knightsbridge without arousing suspicion.

"Be glad that Miguel broke," I reason, filled with an odd sense of hopefulness. "This is our first real clue."

"That's exactly why it should be us in there."

While part of me can relate to Hyland's frustration, I also understand why they're taking the lead today. After the seizure, my medical clearance hangs in the balance. Not to mention the toll from questioning every last operative we apprehended.

Warner and Hyland took the lead on interrogating the remaining suspects while avoiding the topic of Madden still rotting in a dark cell somewhere in the building. They've been working flat out as I've rested.

"I've got Perez's lease up." Rayna leans close to squint at her laptop, dislodging lilac hair tucked behind her pixie-like ears. "It's for apartment 32c."

"You catch that?" Warner reiterates into his comms. "32c. You have permission to force entry."

"Copy." Archer taps his earpiece on the live feed.

"Take him quickly and quietly," Warner instructs. "Perez can connect us to Gael. Or at least whoever receives the shipments on the other side. He's integral."

With all of my attention locked on the screen, I watch the Falcon Team inch closer to their target. Archer, Oscar and Josh hang back while Kyle lines up their handheld battering ram.

"On three." Kyle's deep voice warns his teammates. "Cover me."

I'm on the edge of my seat as Kyle prepares to make his move. We know very little about Tyler Perez beyond his role in local government handling shipping permits and freight permissions for large-scale exports.

He could be sitting behind that door with a machine gun ready to unload it into the Falcon Team, and we'd be none the wiser. The real danger of working for Sabre is at the forefront today.

Overwhelmed by nerves that feel foreign to me, I curl and release my fists repeatedly, waiting for the bang of the door collapsing in. Hyland halts his pacing to stand at my side.

"Red." His huge paw tucks around mine and offers a squeeze. "Take a breath."

"Thought I was calming you down?"

"We can't do that for each other?" He arches a brow.

"I guess I can take your anxiety if you'll take mine, big guy."

Moss-laced pools flicking over my face, he flourishes a tense smile. "Deal."

Together, we watch the scene unfold onscreen over Warner's tense shoulders. Kyle is fast and efficient, cracking through Perez's front door in two rams.

The scene dissolves into a fast-moving blur, holding us all on tenterhooks. The team rushes into the apartment in close formation, weapons raised at the ready and screaming for surrender.

"Status report," Warner booms into his earpiece, clutching the edge of the table. "Come in."

Live feed settling, a view of a sleekly furnished, high-ceilinged apartment comes into view. The classical, Victorian mouldings and brass fittings shine despite the weak daylight filtering through drawn velvet curtains.

"Clear every room!" Archer shouts his orders.

Each member of the team splits off to infiltrate a different space. It's a vast apartment, spanning multiple gold-laced marble floors and elaborately furnished sitting rooms. There's even a private bar.

Clearly, Gael pays well.

What a surprise.

"He's gone," I whisper, dread gathering to form a brick in my stomach. "We're too late."

"We'll find him." Hyland's hand cinches mine again in an attempt at comfort.

"The same way we've found Luis? Our leads keep disappearing!"

"This job is a long game, I'm afraid. You have to hold faith sometimes."

"I don't have a lot of faith left to give."

"Then I'll hold faith for you, red."

Squeezing his hand back just as tightly, I'm struggling to summon an ounce of hopefulness after everything.

On the screen, Archer is advancing closely behind Josh to inspect what looks like the master bedroom on the second floor. Their guns are raised in an attack position, prepared for any eventuality.

His camera swings around the vast space, complete with a four-poster bed draped in unmade, white sheets. A few drawers in the mahogany sideboard are yanked out, while the door to what seems to be a walk-in wardrobe is ajar.

"Signs of a disturbance," Josh whispers lowly. "I think someone tore through here."

Warner's spine curves as he leans even closer to his laptop to capture every detail on the feed. "Be careful."

"Was Perez fleeing, or was someone searching for him?" Hyland ponders in a hush.

"Why would someone break into his apartment?"

"Perhaps they've been paid to tie up a loose end. Eliminate a potential rat and search his apartment for any incriminating evidence."

After checking each corner and crevice, Archer and Josh head for the ensuite. My palm has grown so slick with sweat, it's sliding in Hyland's firm hand.

Unease is a powerful tornado firing alarm bells inside my overwhelmed mind. With Hyland's gruff words playing on repeat, I feel like that tornado is about to sweep us all into its destructive spiral.

Pausing to flick the bathroom light on, the sound of Archer spitting out a shocked curse resonates from the laptop's speakers. Josh is a couple of metres in front of him, blocking our sight.

"What is it?" Warner demands.

"Well… I'm not sure your perp is going to be up for making any phone calls to his boss."

Encouraging a still-cursing Josh to move aside, Archer steps farther into the oversized, white-tiled ensuite. His chest camera offers a perfect shot of a slumped figure sitting atop a closed toilet lid.

White tile ends where a spray of dark, congealed blood begins. Only it doesn't stop there. Crimson rivulets spatter across the walls. Floor. Nearby mirror. Bathroom sink. It's been distributed in a wide geyser.

"Fuck me gently," Hyland blurts.

"Is that… Tyler Perez?"

"Looks like it."

The source of the blood is the blown-open skull of our target. His lifeless body is lolling forwards, revealing the hole that a bullet has torn through him. I can make out a silver gun loosely clasped in his limp hand.

"No," I whisper in abject horror. "No!"

Perez is dead.

Unable to look away from the macabre nightmare, it's like something out of a slasher movie. I'm no stranger to death, but seeing it laid out in its rawest form is sobering.

He was our one lead.

Now he's gone too.

This man has benefitted from every last dollar, pound and peso funnelled through Gael's cartel and likely many others. He's taken victims from their captors, packaged them up and shipped them across the globe for a tidy profit.

The bullet was a kindness. I wouldn't have given it to him. After we'd gotten the information we need from him, I intended to ensure his grisly end myself. Now I'll never get the chance.

Axel joins us to more closely observe the death of our sole clue. "Fucking hell."

"Suicide?" Warner wonders aloud.

"More like an execution made to look like suicide." Axel studies the camera shot. "Look at the site of the bullet wound. No one can bend their arm that far."

"The gun's in his hand," I point out.

"Deliberately so. This is sloppy work. Whoever did this knew we'd be able to tell it wasn't self-inflicted."

"Okay… to what end?"

"Because it's a warning," Hyland answers my question. "Gael's leaving us a message."

This was the one person who offered us a chance of tracing Gael's exports. Reduced to little more than a warning shot. With Diego dead and Luis gone, the raid was for nothing.

Unless...

"We have no choice," I announce with grim certainty. "Madden is our best chance to reach the cartel."

Spinning in his seat, Warner hits me with an aqua stare. "Not a chance."

"He can help us."

"He's lying through his teeth to save his own skin!"

"Then why is he still in the building?"

Warner falls silent, stumped by the truth.

"Why haven't you had him shipped off to some hellhole he'll never escape from?" I push further.

Watching his shoulders sink, I wait for a reasonable explanation that he can't give. Warner could've gotten rid of Blaine the moment we told him about the proposed partnership. Yet he hasn't done so.

"Ember has a point." Axel stretches his ink-riddled arms and shoulders. "We're fresh out of options."

"Shut up, pup," Hyland snaps at him.

"What? I don't get a say in this?"

"You don't know Madden like we do!"

"I know he made a very good point!"

"What fucking point?" Hyland argues.

"That Gael is ready to expend all of his resources to recapture his champion. We need to locate him before he finds Ember."

"No one is finding Ember," Warner inserts, pulling his earpiece out. "Sabre remains the safest place for her. By our sides."

"We can only ensure her safety if we have the advantage," Axel calmly reasons. "Madden knows Gael's operations. He has a personal stake. He could be useful."

"He's a fugitive!" Hyland gestures wildly.

"Look at what we do for a living! If we didn't have these jobs to justify our actions, we'd all be criminals. I for one know I would be!"

"What is wrong with you, Ax?" Hyland squares off against him. "Why the sudden allegiance to Madden?"

Something passes between them—a mistrustful tension that turns the atmosphere to ice. I watch Axel's eyes drop as he sputters defensively.

"I don't have an allegiance to him."

"You're the one who told us what he wanted." Hyland refuses to take his eyes off him. "You pushed for Ember to speak to him. Hell, you've been off ever since you interviewed him alone."

"I have not!" Axel cries.

"I call bullshit on that."

"How dare you accuse me of having false allegiances? Who do you think you are?"

"I'm protecting my team!"

Their shouting is penetrating my skull, creating a sharp throb. I shuffle away before it builds into a full-blown headache. Hard to avoid stress when you work with a gaggle of hot-headed assholes.

As Hyland and Axel move chest-to-chest to continue their screaming match, I take the opportunity to slip out of the room. I don't care to see them call forensics to handle Perez's body.

Sabre's corridors and ceiling-height windows blur around me with each numb step I take. Stumbling in an indecipherable direction, I'm consumed by the riot of conflicting paths ahead that I have no idea how to choose between.

Think about home, Gracie.

We didn't go through hell just to die now, did we?

I told that terrified little girl to think about her home. Her sisters. The cookies she'd soon taste again. And not only did I fail to give her that fantasy, I'm still fucking failing her.

A naïve part of me was actually stupid enough to believe that Perez would provide us with information. That somehow, he would've been able to tell me where Gracie ended up. No one else has a damn clue.

Now I'll never know. The reason Gael's web is so impenetrable is that nobody knows exactly where they fit in it. Every moving part remains blissfully ignorant while he collects profits from each distinct branch.

When the familiar walls of the training room settle around me, I realise where my heart has led me to. The boxing ring that's become my home in recent weeks lies empty ahead of me.

Tearing my t-shirt over my head, I adjust my black sports bra then tighten my ponytail. In the corner behind the ring that we spar in, bags of various weights hang still.

The numbness perseveres until my unwrapped fists make contact with the blue bag. Thumbs tucked, knuckles firm, wrists tensed. Slipping into a fighting stance feels like crawling into bed after a long, exhausting day.

I batter the living daylights out of the bag until sweat coats every inch of my body. My ponytail sags, hanging over my sweat-slick shoulders and spine. The headache has receded as clarity takes centre stage.

This can't be it.

We *will* find Gael.

There's no way that Luis has left the country without the grand prize. Me. He wouldn't dare show his face in Mexico empty-handed. Especially not after losing his right-hand man and several others along the way.

When he crawls out of the woodwork, I'll be ready. He's our central line to the house of cards we need to dismantle. Find Luis, and we find a moving part. Perhaps a vital one. Maybe even Gracie.

Throat burning in protest, I reluctantly take a break to locate the water machine. When I turn around, I realise that I have an audience to my ruminations.

"How long have you been standing there?" I pant breathlessly.

Shrugging, Warner keeps his strong arms folded over his chest. "Long enough."

"That's fucking creepy."

"You left."

"Didn't care to listen to those idiots squabble like children."

"I'm sorry, Em. Emotions are high. I've sent them to cool off and deal with the crime scene now."

Brushing past him, I kick off my shoes then snag a pair of boxing gloves hanging on the edge of the ring. Hopping up onto the platform, Warner's stare follows my every step.

"Are we going to talk this out?" he calls out.

"Nope. I'm busy."

"I know you're disappointed, Em."

Ignoring him, I hope that he'll take the message and give up. I should know better by now.

"We are too," Warner emphasises. "But Perez wasn't our last shot at Gael. We're still identifying the bodies that washed up. And we have those potential locations for Gael's estate too."

I strap on the boxing gloves then bounce on my bare feet. To my delight, he accepts the silent invitation to join me in the ring.

The thought of sparring with Warner provides enough distraction from the disaster we just watched unfold. We haven't fought yet. Though I've thought about what it would be like to face him many times.

"Fighting instead of feeling isn't the answer," he proclaims in a clipped tone.

"You want to talk?" I raise an eyebrow. "Let's discuss that kiss in the hospital."

Warner smashes his lips shut.

"Yeah… I didn't think so."

Advancing into his bubble, I make the first move. My gloved hand slams into his side, landing a fast blow. Warner twists his frame to pivot, allowing him to deliver his own strike to my ribcage.

Teeth gritted, I duck his next attempt by swinging myself low then throwing a fist up to catch his jaw. Warner anticipates the move, shifting sideways to avoid my punch.

The failed strike only stokes my inner fire. Irritation spikes through the ceaseless well of rage that's kept me going this long. I can't hit Gael. I can't hit Luis. But I can hit him.

"Em," Warner pleads.

"Shut up and fight me."

"No!"

"Fine. Then I'll make you."

Focusing my mind, I launch another attack. This time, the roundhouse kick I deliver to his midsection lands perfectly, allowing me to flash forward and follow up with a powerful punch to the face.

Warner skids backwards, massaging the red blotches appearing on his cheek. Perhaps I should feel guilty. He came down here with some false hope of helping, and instead, I'm going to beat his ass.

Oh well.

He seems to snap, beginning to fight back. We parry back and forth, trading light blows. While he manages to land a few shots, I can tell he's letting me off easy.

"You're right!" he attempts to break through to me. "As much as I hate it… We need to give serious thought to cooperating with Madden."

"You hate Blaine."

"More than life itself." He ducks my next swing. "That doesn't mean we can't use him."

Rolling back my shoulders, I puzzle out his weirdly expectant expression. Hyland's reticence makes sense. No one understands Axel's brain or motivations. But I didn't expect this from Warner.

"Why the change of heart?"

He tries to inch closer to me. "Something has to give."

Foot connecting with his ribcage, I attempt to follow the kick with another strike, but he grabs my ankle. I'm pushed backwards, almost losing my balance.

"If working with our enemy will bring you the peace you need faster, then that's a price I'm willing to pay."

"And when Gael is gone?" I puff for breath. "Once Blaine's father is apprehended? What happens to him?"

"That's for me and the directors to discuss. Any cooperation would be legally binding."

Body flexing, I escape the blow he attempts to deliver. "What does that mean?"

"I don't expect Madden to help us for free; it will be a quid-pro-quo situation."

Fists dropping, I gape at him, the meaning of his words clear. He's going to strike a deal. That realisation causes a miasma of complex feelings that I'm too overwhelmed to even dissect right now.

Using my teeth, I tear off the Velcro on my boxing gloves then toss them aside. Fighting isn't helping.

"I have to find Gracie," I grind out.

"I know, Em. We will."

"Even if she's dead… I need to know. Then I can kill Gael knowing he isn't taking her location to the grave with him."

"And I promised to help you," he confirms with a nod. "You know by now, I never break my word."

The fire ants that pull at my skin haven't eased. If anything, sparring with him has worsened this intense feeling of pressure. Every inch of my skin is alight with a battlefield of burning fires.

I feel so fucking powerless.

And I need him to *fix it.*

Closing the last step between us, my hands curl in the soft material of his dark shirt, twisting the fabric tight. Not even I can fathom what I'm searching for in his cautious blue stare.

"You swore to look after me. To protect me. To help me."

His throat frantically dancing, Warner nods again. "I did."

"What if I told you that I need more than you're willing to give?"

"Please, love. Don't do this again."

"You kissed me, Warner."

"That was a mistake," he insists weakly.

"It sure didn't feel like a mistake."

Allowing myself to be sucked into the near-iridescent ocean that fills his gaze, I sink to the crushing depths of that watery expanse where he can't possibly drag me back to the surface.

"When I'm with your team, this gaping hole in my chest feels just a little smaller," I admit in a small voice.

"Em…"

"I can breathe again. It doesn't feel like it's going to suck me into a vacuum and crush my bones to ash."

My head tilts, allowing me to search his conflicted expression. He may be fighting this, but I can see where desire collides with duty in his eyes.

"This isn't a game, Warner."

"Then why are you treating it like one?"

"I'm not. This isn't me trying to tear apart your family. Truthfully, I didn't mean to feel this way for any of you. I didn't want to. But…"

"But?" He sounds like his throat is coated in gravel.

"But… I still do. I want what I can't have. I want more than I should have. And I want it with all of you."

Cursing under his breath, he grabs my wrists to prise my hands away from his chest. The incoming rejection only makes me cling onto his shirt even harder.

"I told you I can't do this, love."

"Because you can't, or because you don't want to?"

"I just… I can't do it!" He vehemently shakes his head as if he can force his own feelings out.

"Forget about Tom for a second. Forget all the years we've known each other. Forget the rest of the team and this company."

Pupils darkening the brilliant blue hue all around them, Warner's breathing accelerates into a racing staccato.

"Tell me what you want."

For several agonising seconds, I don't think he'll crack. Then he licks his lips before roughly answering.

"I want to tell you that I've battled tooth and fucking nail not to feel anything for longer than you realise."

"And now?" I breathe out.

His words form a pained growl. "Now… I'm failing."

Letting my hands release his t-shirt, I press myself into his firm chest. Every solid line of muscle provides a bittersweet taunt against my heaving breasts.

"I want to tell you that I actually don't give a fuck if my teammates want something with you too," Warner admits. "They're good men. If you make them happy, I want them to have that."

My lungs halt and seize.

"Frankly, the more protection you have around you, the happier I'll be. I would die a thousand times over before letting anyone hurt you ever again."

Hands wrapping around my waist, Warner presses the small of my back so I can feel every inch of him. The pressure is acute. He's everywhere. Invading everything. Refusing to leave any doubt.

"I'm willing to raze this entire world to the ground to grant you justice." His whisper is guttural. "Including this team and this company. All I want is to give you the peace you deserve."

Overstimulated to the point of pain, I let my weak knees collapse inwards when he starts to guide me down to the floor. The shift from denial to desire is the headiest of highs.

We sink to the mat—my spine hitting the spongy material, his body bracing above mine, our hips lined up in perfect symmetry. My entire awareness is comprised of Warner and nothing else. Every sense. Every thought. Every emotion. He consumes it all.

"You're determined to rip apart my life." His fingers clasp around my chin and squeeze. "All of our lives. Just to fill that goddamn gaping hole in your chest."

"Yes," I confess shamefully.

"You want Hyland's possessive shit? Axel's violence and insanity?"

"Yes. I do."

"You want my attention," he says ominously.

"Please. Yes."

"You want all the things I've longed to do to your tight, absolutely fucking gorgeous body for years on end, no matter the fractures it'll cause in our lives?"

"Yes!"

Deliciously forbidden heat slams into me faster than I can push the words out.

"You want me to lay my hands on these soft curves and make you cry out with my tongue?"

"Please..." I whimper. "Yes. I do."

"Or for me to strip your disobedient ass bare and bury my cock so deep inside your sweet cunt that I won't have to listen to a second more of you talking back?"

Squirming like a wild animal beneath him, I'm genuinely concerned that if he doesn't stop, something is going to tear free from my skin.

"I want all of it. I want the family you're offering."

"No, Ember. You don't. You want a hell of a lot more than what I ever offered."

Lowering his head, Warner doesn't kiss me.

"But maybe... that's okay."

His lips ghost over my throat, neck, collarbone. Down the deep canyons between my breasts until his teeth are grazing the stiff peaks of my nipples pushing against soaked Lycra.

The slightest friction causes me to moan, wantonly bleating for more. His teeth bite down on my right nipple through the sports bra, sending pulses of hunger into my clenched core.

"You want me to share you?" His hand moves to seize a firm handful of my other breast. "To share the woman I've loved since we were kids with the men I call my brothers?"

"Yes. That's what I want."

His filthy words feel so right. Like fucking kismet. That utterly insane idea somehow sounds like the only thing that will make me feel whole.

Shifting down my body, Warner seizes the waistband of my workout leggings. I automatically lift my hips when he starts to drag them down, exposing my plain, black panties.

He's moving torturously slowly. Examining every muscle, faded scar and inch of goose-pimpled skin like he's seeing me for the first time. The leggings are soon tossed over his shoulder.

"What happened to that shy little girl?" His gaze roves over me.

Back arching, I push my trembling legs open for him. "She grew up."

"And became a hell of a lot more demanding."

Just when I think he's going to relieve this endless tension sending my system into overdrive, Warner sits back on his ass. He has to lift and drag his right leg around to position it comfortably.

"What's wrong?" I prop up onto my forearms.

"You're asking for a lot from me." He shrugs, though his ablaze eyes tell a different story. "First show me how much you want it."

"I don't understand."

"I'm not going to touch you, Em. I can't do that without losing control."

Feeling the urge to punch him in the face again, I have to strangle my compounding rage. "Asshole!"

"Show me how well you take care of yourself."

"Are you fucking serious?"

"Do I look like I'm joking?"

Aghast at his newfound cocky attitude, I merely stare. Warner doesn't show a crack of hesitation. The evil son of a bitch isn't going to touch me. Not that easily.

I've never been afraid to take what I want in life. If he wants to play this game, I can play twice as hard. Soon, he'll be begging to crawl between my legs to make it up to me.

Holding intense eye contact, I trail my fingertips over my stomach and thighs, intensifying the lively tingles unfurling at my centre. Warner is completely focused on me.

Knowing he's watching but preventing himself from laying a single finger on me adds a dimension to this charade that feels entirely new. I've never performed for a man before. Or so brazenly taunted one.

My hand travels beneath my panties, stretching the bounds of the elastic. I tug the soaked cotton to one side, revealing my bareness to him. With a curse, Warner scrunches his hands into fists.

"I could be yours," I purr at the sight of his indecision. "I want to be."

"Fuck, love."

"Do you think I let many people own me, Warner?"

He quickly shakes his head.

"Yet I'd let you own this pussy. I'd let you make it yours."

"God-fucking-dammit."

Pushing my index finger inside my dripping slit, I throw my head back at the rush of relief. My digit slips in and out of my tight hole, on full display to him.

Swirling and circling, I know just how to pleasure myself. The invisible lines that I can cross to make my body sing. An audience is simply more ammunition that I'll happily accept.

Slick moisture covers my finger as I work myself over, rubbing the heel of my palm against my clit with each pump. Lavishing the sparks that creates, I quickly lower my other hand to rub my throbbing clit.

"Perfect," Warner praises. "More."

Pressing down on the bud, flashes of excruciatingly sweet warmth settle over my sensitive skin. With each thrust, I pinch and roll my clit, finding a pace that satiates my need for indulgence.

"Another finger, love." Warner greedily drinks in the sight of me fucking myself for him. "Stretch yourself wide for me."

"Come do it yourself."

"You're doing a good job all on your own."

Shoving a second finger into my entrance, I scissor the two digits inside myself to brush against my inner walls. A whiny moan pushes past my lips, filling the cavernous training room.

I'm needy enough to believe he'll give in. Lower his hard body over mine and plunder my lips. Kiss every part of me. Latch his mouth between my thighs and let me come all over his face.

But Warner just sits there—patient, observant, letting me pleasure myself for his eyes alone. It feels like a test. I don't know if I'm passing it as I quicken my hand until my fingers roughly fuck my weeping pussy.

"That's it, Em. Keep going."

Rubbing circles above my clit, I let myself fantasise about what it would feel like to be owned by him. The boy who held my sadness when no one else could. The man who rescued me from evil and gave me the safety I needed.

I think there's more to his steadily devoted self. Beneath the sweet words, assurance and comfort... I think he'd fuck like a god and leave me broken by his ferocity.

Feeling myself tighten, I maintain the constant pace, determined to show him exactly what he's missing. My walls contract and clamp down around my fingers, guiding me to a nearby cliff.

"Show me how you fall apart," Warner croons. "I want to watch your pussy drip with all those sweet juices."

"Fuck... Please. Please touch me."

"No. Make yourself come. Now."

"Goddamn you!"

Aggravation and dismay form a deadly bomb that doesn't take long to detonate. Another flick of my clit and I feel my orgasm taking hold. It barrels over me without a second's notice.

Every muscle locks up as I cry out for him, feeling moisture soak my fingers and palm. Each individual blast emanates from my centre and spreads outwards, decimating everything in its path.

The aftershocks are powerful and continuous, my legs shaking so violently, I wonder how I'll ever walk again. It takes great effort to lower my head to the mat where I stare up at the ceiling rather than collapse.

I feel Warner move more than I hear him. A hand circles around my wrist, encouraging my fingers to pull from where they're still deep inside my spasming pussy.

Hovering over me, Warner stares at my face as he brings my glistening hand to his mouth. I wonder if I'll come all over again when he sucks my fingers between his lips.

Warmth engulfs the wet digits, tingling with the feel of his tongue flicking and cleaning every drop of bliss I've deigned to offer him. He sucks them dry, releasing my hand to lick his lips.

"You did very well," he compliments, still clutching my wrist tight. "Such a perfect girl, aren't you?"

Am I into this?

Preening at his words, it's damn well evident that I am. I doubt I'd want to hear praise from anyone but him. The dynamic he's creating is making me want every domineering tactic he has to offer and more.

"Clean yourself up. We have work to do."

I sit upright when he awkwardly gets his feet beneath him to rise. "What work?"

"We're going to go see what that cocky, criminal shit's price is to help us end this."

"Wait… we are?"

"Yes. Get up, Em."

Head spinning, I struggle to catch up with his train of thought. I'm far too busy admiring the way his smart black trousers strain at the front, boasting an impressive bulge that looks in need of attention.

"Ember." Warner barks my name. "Dress."

"You make my head spin."

"Join the club, love. I haven't been able to think straight since the day you disappeared, and I realised exactly what I'd lost."

With that revelation, Warner stiffly walks away from me to exit the ring. I'm left staring after him, wondering when exactly my brother's best friend started to look at me differently.

And when I started to look back.

ONFIDENTIAL
Why?
Suspect?
Gael?
DO NOT CROSS
POLICE LI

CONFIDENTIAL
Suspect?
DO NOT CROSS
PO
POLICE
NOT CROSS
Suspect?

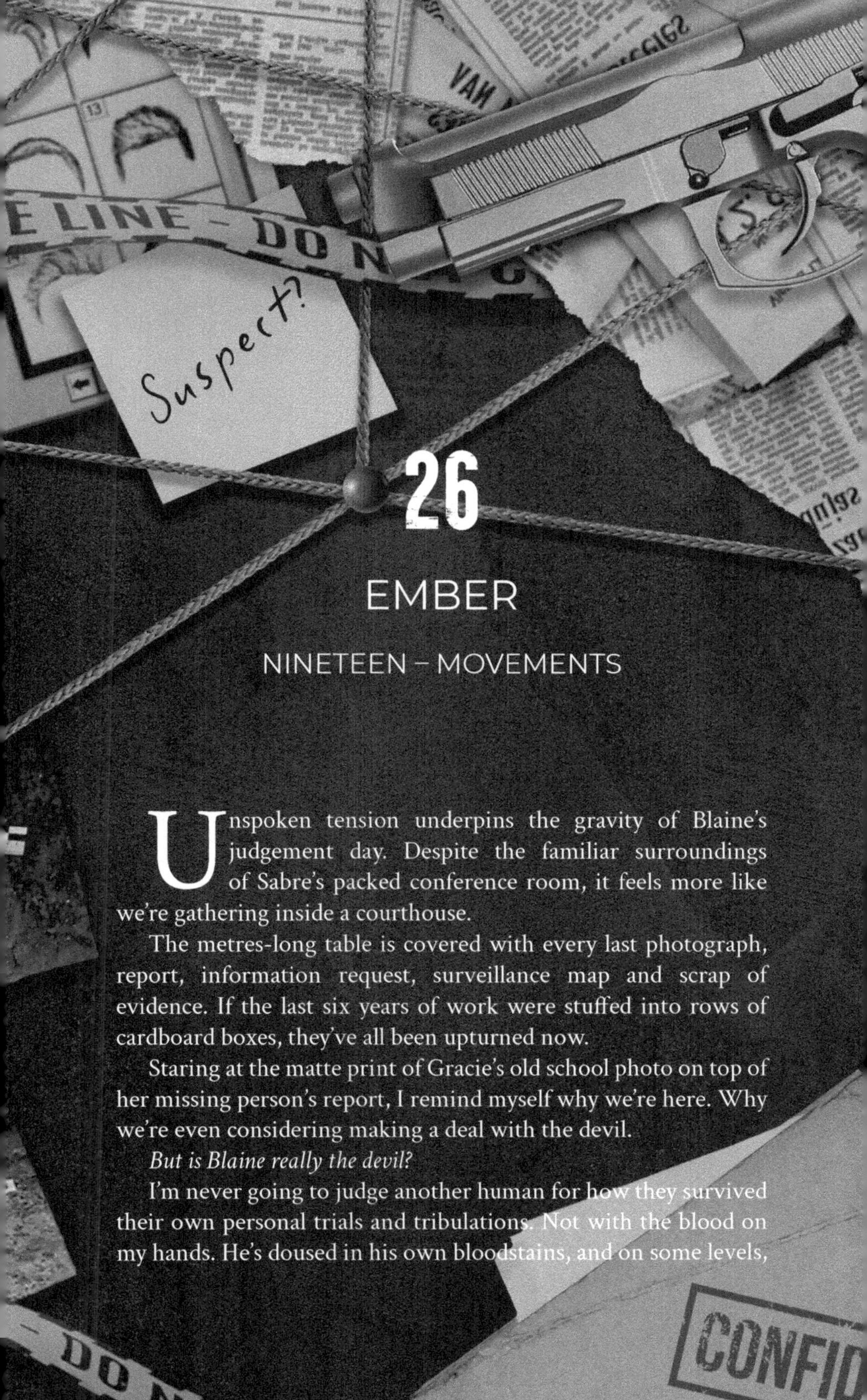

26

EMBER

NINETEEN – MOVEMENTS

Unspoken tension underpins the gravity of Blaine's judgement day. Despite the familiar surroundings of Sabre's packed conference room, it feels more like we're gathering inside a courthouse.

The metres-long table is covered with every last photograph, report, information request, surveillance map and scrap of evidence. If the last six years of work were stuffed into rows of cardboard boxes, they've all been upturned now.

Staring at the matte print of Gracie's old school photo on top of her missing person's report, I remind myself why we're here. Why we're even considering making a deal with the devil.

But is Blaine really the devil?

I'm never going to judge another human for how they survived their own personal trials and tribulations. Not with the blood on my hands. He's doused in his own bloodstains, and on some levels, that makes us kindred spirits.

"Head's up." Hyland lifts from the glass window we're leaning against. "Someone wants to meet you."

"What? Who?"

"The bosses."

Stepping into the conference room, I vaguely recognise the two pillars of authority who grace us with their presence. Everyone knows Sabre Security. And everyone knows the Knight brothers.

Striding ahead of his scarier counterpart, Kade Knight is the definition of affable golden boy. With pearly-blonde hair that he wears slicked back, intelligent hazel eyes and a penchant for expensive shirts with waistcoats, it's hard not to recognise him.

By comparison, his brother fully embodies the flip side of that coin. He's the darkness to Kade's light. Clothed in all-black, his V-neck tee shows off countless tattoos that cover his chest, neck and throat, matching his eyebrow piercing and terrifyingly hard blue eyes.

They can't be much older than Warner or Hyland, but the sense of gravitas in their assured presence commands a respect far greater than their years.

"Coffee?" Hudson's grunt breaks the silence.

Standing next to a selection of full thermoses, Axel lifts a cup towards him, emblazoned with Sabre's logo.

"Right here."

"Thank fuck." Hudson makes a beeline for Axel and the coffee station. "If any of you are considering it… don't have kids. You'll never sleep again."

"That's our son you're talking about." Kade scowls at his grumpy brother.

"And you know just how monstrous kids are."

Smoothing a hand over his hair, Kade slowly nods. "Fair."

As Hudson fills his cup, Kade looks around the room. We're only missing Warner—who has gone to retrieve our star of the hour—and my brother. He's on his way in to oversee the legal proceedings.

Upon noticing me, Kade makes his approach, straightening his silvery tie with one hand. He sticks out the other towards me, glinting with a thick wedding band.

"You must be Ember. Heard a lot about you."

"All bad?" I accept his handshake.

"I'd say fifty-fifty." He passes me a dazzling grin.

"That's disappointing. I must be slipping."

His laughter is light and friendly, revealing his smile lines and barely noticeable crow's feet. Another man who's ageing with grace. There must be something in the water in this building.

"These lot have had an easy ride since Ethan left the company. I hope you're giving them hell."

"Always." I smirk at him.

"Well in that case, welcome to Sabre Security. We're glad to have you."

Making space for his brother to join us, Hudson gives me a critical once-over while guzzling his steaming cup of coffee. I'm preparing a defensive attack when he breaks out in a weirdly friendly smile.

"Ember, right?"

"That's me."

"Is it true you handed Archer's ass to him?"

"Hey!" Archer protests from the table.

"Um... I guess." I shrug.

Switching the coffee to his other hand, Hudson offers me a fist bump. "Nice work."

Knocking our matching scarred knuckles together, I let myself relax. Formidable directors, my ass. They're a pair of teddy bears.

"We should put her in the ring with Brooke." Hudson continues to eye me over his coffee cup. "It's been a while since she's blown the cobwebs out."

"That's a terrible idea." Kade sighs.

"Why?"

"Because something tells me Ember would kick our wife's ass, and then we'll have to deal with her having a toddler tantrum of her own."

"Your wife?" I blurt before I can hold it in.

"Yes," they answer simultaneously.

I've heard plenty about the unique family setup behind the

directors of Sabre Security. I even had a couple of clients back in the day who were polyamorous. I've got a lot of questions.

"She works here too." Kade's cheeks tint slightly. "Well, she did. She's a little preoccupied at the moment."

Sauntering over to us with a mischievous grin, Axel looks between the two suddenly shifty men. "Does preoccupied mean pregnant?"

While Kade rushes to say *no*, Hudson bursts out with a suspiciously proud sounding *yes*. They glare daggers at each other soon after.

"Thought we were keeping it between us for now?"

"Fuck that." Hudson punches Kade's shoulder. "We got our girl pregnant again. I wanna shout about it."

"I want to watch when she rips you a new asshole for boasting about this."

"I can handle her." Hudson waves Kade off.

"God. You're still so fucking weird sometimes."

"Thanks, bro."

Shoving him towards the conference table, Kade takes a seat at the head while Hudson reluctantly sits down on his right. The pair are still bickering away as we watch them in bemusement.

"Do I even want to think about the mechanics of how their wife got pregnant by her multiple husbands?" I ask quietly.

Tongue darting out to skate over his bottom lip, Axel lazily winks at me. "Yes. You do."

He dances away before Hyland can smack him.

"We can even demonstrate, if you'd like!"

"Axel!" Hyland booms.

"Interested, Hy?"

The grump doesn't immediately respond, offering all the confirmation that Axel needs. Laughing unrepentantly, he moves to sit down and bother the Falcon Team.

I'm too busy attempting to get my stuttering brain in gear. The mental images in my mind are far too graphic. Particularly what it would feel like to have two men laying claim to my body... or battling over the honour.

Oh, fuck.

Peering down at me with an odd look on his face, Hyland seems to be on the verge of addressing Axel's taunts when the door to the conference room opens once more.

"Never mind," he grumbles.

Two female agents march in, closely flanked by Warner and the scarred face that still manages to haunt my dreams. With his ankles cuffed, Blaine walks slowly, a chain connecting them to the shackles still enclosed around his wrists.

"Isn't this a turnout." He gazes around the room. "Full house."

Kade clears his throat. "Take a seat, Mr Madden."

The chair at the opposite end of the table from Kade awaits. Blaine is escorted into it then secured to the legs by one of the agents adjusting his cuffs.

Both retreat to linger nearby, packing visible weapons and emanating enough threat to make me consider forming some female friendships. I like the look of those two.

Positioning himself behind Blaine, Warner remains standing as he folds his arms. A delicate shudder causes my body to spasm when his baby blues stray over to me.

Then Blaine's confidence-filled onyx orbs join Warner's, and I begin to get hot under the collar. I may as well combust on the spot when Hyland stakes a very clear and obvious claim by wrapping his arm around my back.

Then Blaine fucking smirks.

At Hyland.

"He can still sign a damn plea deal if I break all his teeth," Hyland rumbles beside me. "Then pluck them out one by one and shove them up his asshole."

"Now, now. Play nice."

Lifting my hand, I place it on top of Hyland's strong grip. While it makes Blaine draw his black brows together, Warner unveils a delicious smile that promises a repeat of the absolute filth he said in the boxing ring.

"Where is Tom?" Kade questions.

Checking the phone previously tucked into my pocket, there are no new texts or missed calls. He must be stuck in London traffic.

"He said he was coming in." I repocket my phone.

"Fine. He can catch up when he arrives." Kade focuses on our shackled guest, the friendliness now drained from his face. "Blaine Madden."

"Kade," he clips back.

"Didn't think we'd see you here again."

"Should've chosen a more secure prison," Blaine drawls. "The last one was child's play to escape."

"We have a wonderful solitary cell in Belmarsh lined up for you with the worst of the worst—serial killers, rapists, terrorists. You'll be nice and secure with them."

"Come on, Kade." Blaine shakes his head. "Don't be rash."

"Then prove your usefulness. You know we have the power to cut a deal."

"I believe you have all the proof you need. I was able to track down your missing person." He nods towards me. "Free her from bondage. Deliver her to the Anaconda Team. And infiltrate a prolific trafficking gang."

"Do you think this is a fucking job interview?" Hudson scoffs.

"Your brother is the one asking me to prove my usefulness," he responds with obvious pride. "If anything, I believe you should be begging for my help."

"Is that so?" Kade mocks.

"You're in dire need of my unique advantage. I know my father. If we combine forces, we can track them both down. I have no desire to claim Gael's head for myself."

"So that's all you want?" Warner shifts on his feet, still warily guarding his prisoner.

Glancing over his shoulder, Blaine flashes him a grin. "Perhaps the assurance that you'll leave me in peace afterwards. Punish the right man for my father's crimes."

What he isn't saying is just as obvious. Blaine doesn't just want a lifeline—he wants clemency. A clean slate. All in exchange for his help in tracking down our current nemesis.

"That's a rather large record you're asking to be erased." Kade twists in his chair to cross his legs.

"You've pardoned far worse, Mr Knight. And been pardoned for equivalent crimes."

The sight of colour draining from Kade's face is shell-shocking. In contrast, his brother seems to amp up, pushing his chair back as he slams his coffee cup down.

"There is a difference between crimes committed in the name of survival and crimes committed for power's sake!" Hudson breaks out in a yell.

"Is there?" Blaine taunts, unaffected. "I'm not aware of such a distinction."

"You have spent your entire life serving a criminal dynasty."

"And I've paid the price in blood and more," he argues back. "As I imagine everyone around this table has. We've all survived in our own ways."

His mouth slamming shut, Hudson stalks away from the table to refill his coffee cup. I'm starting to understand why he has an infamous reputation for having a temper.

"Should we discuss the misdeeds of Sabre's golden family further?" Blaine sighs in boredom. "Or can we skip the posturing and discuss the terms of your offer?"

Hands braced on the table, Kade draws to his feet. "Excuse me."

He moves to the back of the room to confer with Hudson out of earshot. Smiling to himself, Blaine returns his attention to me. Those eyes seem to speak a million words without ever opening his mouth.

The memory of the countless scars that litter his body float back into my awareness. Small, circular cigarette burns. Whip marks that match my own. A collection of shiny slashes, mirroring the path of countless knives.

So I stare back.

In acceptance.

In understanding.

When the two brothers retake their places, both wearing matching solemn expressions, I know their next words will hold groundbreaking ramifications.

"We are willing to negotiate a plea deal, Mr Madden." Kade grimaces. "In exchange, we require your full and unequivocal cooperation until Antonio Gael, Nolan Madden and their accomplices are safely apprehended."

"No!" Hyland erupts.

"That's final." Kade cuts each of us a stern look. "The decision has been made."

I have to shrug the trunk-like arm from around me before Hyland cracks my bones. He's tensed up into an iron band that holds terrifyingly extreme strength.

"By apprehended you mean…"

"Alive," Hudson supplies.

Nose wrinkling, Blaine looks physically offended. "Is that negotiable?"

"We serve justice, Mr Madden." Kade stares at him evenly. "Not executions."

"If you insist. But I doubt there is a prison in this world that could contain my father. You do not know him like I do."

"We'll cross that bridge when we come to it." Kade dismisses with a hand wave. "Do you accept?"

"Hm." Blaine flexes his shackled hands. "I should consult my legal counsel."

When his joke falls flat, he exhales through his nose.

"Yes. I accept."

Hands braced on his hips, Kade bobs his head in confirmation. "We will have our legal representative draw up the terms of this clemency agreement… When he shows up."

"Wonderful. Mind removing these cuffs now? I'd quite like my blood circulation back."

Seeing Warner grit his teeth and move to release the man he's openly called his enemy feels like a double-edged sword. Part of me wants this. Another part has no clue how it will ever work.

Releasing the ankle shackles first, Warner moves to release Blaine's wrists. The pair share a silent exchange in long, searching looks. When Warner nods tersely, Blaine sobers enough to dip his head in return.

What exactly are they agreeing?

"Forfeit this deal, and you will be prosecuted to the full extent of the law." Hudson watches the scene unfold with a grim look. "That's a damn promise."

Stretching his long legs out, Blaine massages his swollen wrists.

"Understood."

"The Anaconda Team will be your babysitters," Kade adds around his own uneasy frown. "Try not to bite the hand that feeds you."

"Oh, hell no." Hyland abruptly stalks forwards. "He isn't joining our team."

Blaine lays a hand over his heart in a dramatic fashion. "I'm wounded."

"You're a psycho murderer and scumbag!"

"Hyland," Warner scolds, his posture slumped in consternation. "We have to make this work. Finding Gael is more important than anything else."

"More important than the rule of law?" Hyland spits in disgust. "Madden is a fugitive!"

"I don't care!" Warner shouts back. "The decision has been made. He will help us to secure Ember's future. Nothing else matters."

The communicative stares shared between them cause the hair on my arms to raise. While Axel remains silent at the table, watching Blaine with intense concentration, it seems Hyland and Warner are coming to a collective realisation.

"Ember." Kade ignores the posturing at the other end of the table. "Mind calling your brother? I'd like to get this tied up."

"Oh, sure."

I'm all too glad to turn my back on my teammates... plus one. The sight of London's urban skyline, draped in beams of smog-tinted sunlight, provides a welcome break from their antics.

Dialling Tom's number, I wait for him to answer on the hands-free I know he has built into his Mercedes. When the line rings out, I frown at the screen and redial.

It's several more rings until the line connects with a click. The stressed voice I was expecting to hear as Tom navigates the traffic never arrives.

"Apologies, 768. Big brother is a bit preoccupied right now."

Horrified turmoil slashes into me and opens a gaping wound, leaving me feeling like the blood has drained from my body. With each icy wave of panic, my heart speeds up into an erratic sprint.

"Luis?"

FRACTURED FUTURE

"Sí, señorita."

Bracing a hand above me on the window, I let my head tip down, unable to withstand the dizzying numbness that tightens every limb and muscle.

"Where is my brother?" I shout into the phone.

Not even the sound of arguing behind me suddenly ceasing can break my spiralling terror. Razor-sharp spikes of dread have already sunk into my chest and taken control of my whole body.

"Thomas is just fine," Luis singsongs through his lilting accent. "For now."

"If you dare touch him—"

"You'll what? Kill or kidnap my best men? That ship's sailed, *chica.* You have no bargaining chips left."

The pressure of hands finding my shoulders and back fails to revive me. All I can see is that damned rusted cage, echoing with endless screams and sobs. Only now, I see my brother confined in it.

"I'm not particularly a fan of Señor Gael, if that wasn't obvious before," Luis reveals. "However, I am a fan of his money. He's willing to part with a significant amount in exchange for you."

"Let Tom go! He has nothing to do with this!"

"He is what you love, hm? That's relevant."

"You fucking…" My teeth grind together as I try to find a speck of sense. "I will end you."

"Such spirit. It's not hard to understand why he chose you to invest such time and resources into. I've enjoyed imagining how Gael broke you, over and over, to create such savagery."

Battling past the horror sinking its claws into me, I spin around to locate Axel. I should've known he'd be one step ahead of me. He's already placed a laptop on top of the evidence-littered table to trace the call.

My tear-blurred eyes bouncing between each person watching me unravel, I clench the phone in a death grip.

"What do you want from me?"

"I'm not stupid enough to think you'll merely surrender, 768. You already proved that once before. If only you'd set a better example for the poor virgin girl, she'd still be alive."

My vision narrows, darkening at the edges as ringing overtakes my ear canals. Reality is drowned out by the memory of the day I was sold. And the fragile life I left behind.

"You're lying," I spit into the phone.

"I'm doing you a kindness," Luis chortles. "You should be glad that she's dead. Her fate could've been far worse."

The hands on me tear free when I let my knees cave in. Rough carpet rushes up to meet me, cushioning my fall. The pounding of my failing heart has slowed to a futile patter as grief takes over.

"I'm a patient man," Luis says cheerfully. "My next instructions will follow."

"Just tell me where you are," I plead through falling tears. "I'll be there. You can have me."

"Along with the company you've aligned yourself with, no doubt." His laugh is sickeningly smug. "I want your compliance. By the time I'm finished with Thomas, you'll give it to me."

"Luis, wait—"

The call disconnects.

Letting my hand crash into my lap, I look up at the silent room through the blurry curtain that's conquered my vision. Everyone is on their feet—even Blaine and the Falcon Team. Ready to respond. Ready to fight.

"He has Tom," I croak. "Luis took my brother."

Fisting his hair, Warner spins to swiftly punch the wall. If anything matches my utterly consuming dismay, it's his shattered expression.

"What are his demands?" Kade asks gently.

"He didn't have any. Luis said he wants my compliance. He's going to use Tom to get it."

"Goddammit!" Warner roars in a voice I've never heard before.

"H-He said that Gracie Livingstone is dead." Tears make my words shrivel up into raw rasps. "I... I d-don't know if he's telling the truth or not. Now h-he has my brother too."

Looking down at the phone still clenched in my hand, every last instance I witnessed of Luis beating and torturing compliance out of his kidnapped captives forms a devastating slideshow behind my eyes.

FRACTURED FUTURE

I barely survived before.
But I know… I won't survive losing Tom.

CONFIDENTIAL
Why?
Suspect?
Gael?
DO NOT CROSS
POLICE L

FIND
ME
CONFIDENTIAL

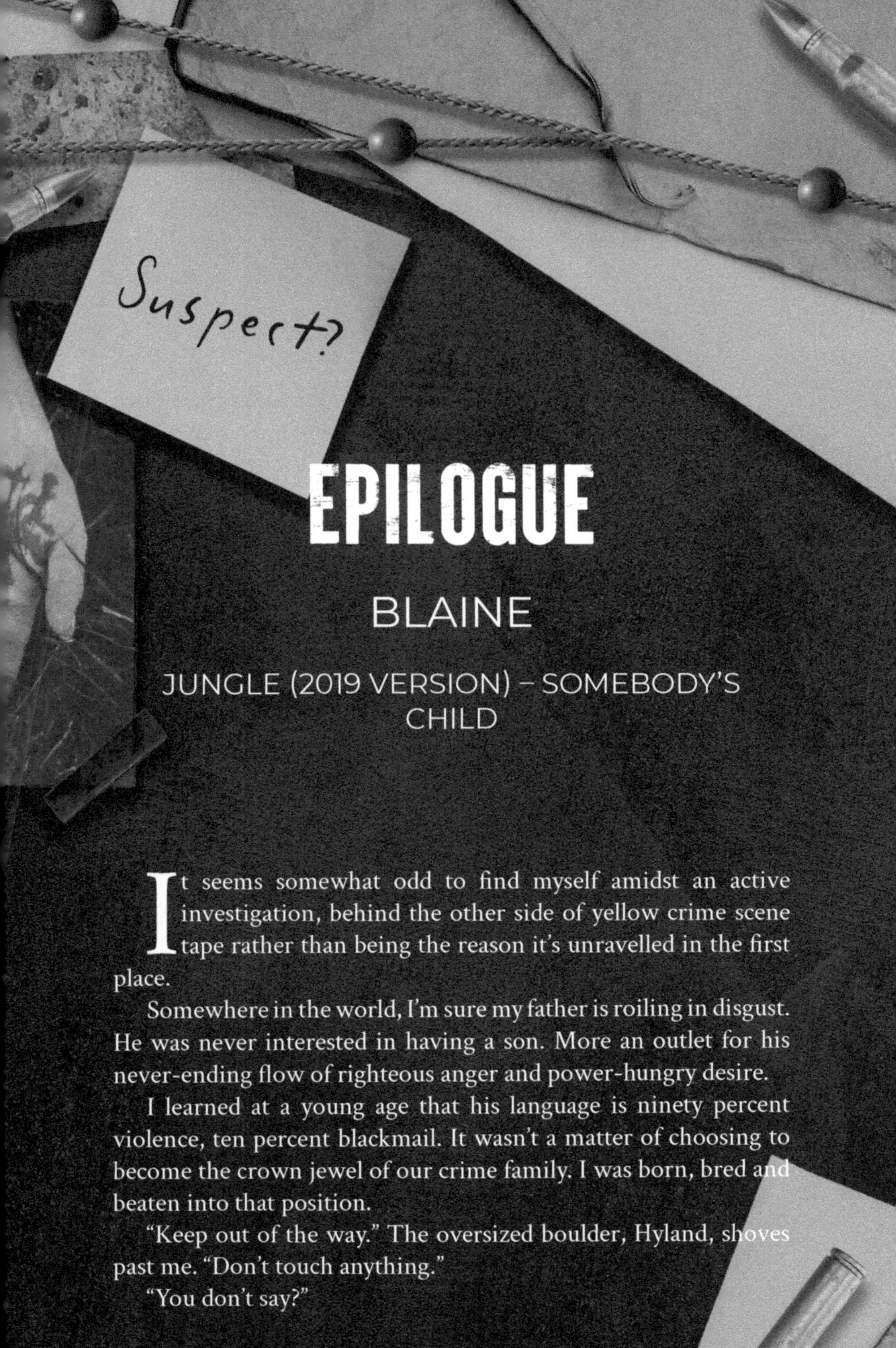

EPILOGUE

BLAINE

JUNGLE (2019 VERSION) – SOMEBODY'S CHILD

It seems somewhat odd to find myself amidst an active investigation, behind the other side of yellow crime scene tape rather than being the reason it's unravelled in the first place.

Somewhere in the world, I'm sure my father is roiling in disgust. He was never interested in having a son. More an outlet for his never-ending flow of righteous anger and power-hungry desire.

I learned at a young age that his language is ninety percent violence, ten percent blackmail. It wasn't a matter of choosing to become the crown jewel of our crime family. I was born, bred and beaten into that position.

"Keep out of the way." The oversized boulder, Hyland, shoves past me. "Don't touch anything."

"You don't say?"

"Watch it, Madden."

To say he's displeased about the tidy deal I've negotiated for myself is an understatement. I didn't quite know if the scheme I'd intricately laid would pay off. My allies—Raye in particular—doubted it would.

Yet the plan has unfurled perfectly.

Perfectly… besides one thing.

When I decided to solve a glaring issue for Sabre by locating their lost lamb, I didn't bank on that lamb being a full-blown, roaring lioness who robbed my attention and refused to give it back.

The moment I saw Ember fight, I knew I was well and truly fucked. It was her powerful poise, the subtle twists of her well-trained body, the thirst for blood in her gaze. Each revelation sucked me further into her bewitching orbit.

I've tried to enact my master plan without becoming distracted these past few months. That's hard to achieve when the lioness is constantly intoxicating me with her sheer will to survive. It's an impressive quality.

One I admire.

One I intend to cherish.

Picking past three scowling agents and two of my newest teammates—all seemingly unable to tolerate my existence—I join Axel at the living room window. Thomas Lawson's apartment is nice, albeit half-destroyed.

Luis Torres left little untouched when he swept through here. Going after the lawyer was a cheap shot. He's trying to manipulate Ember, toying with her vulnerabilities. Trying to unhinge her mind so he can capture her more easily.

"I'm in no mood for your mind games," Axel immediately states. "Fuck off, Madden."

Leaning back against the windowpane, I ignore his hard stare and watch the search unfolding all around us.

"I don't play mind games."

"That's all you do," he spits acerbically. "You got what you wanted. The deal's done. Now leave me alone."

Casting him a look, I consider his clenched jaw. "You seem

tense."

"No shit."

"Having a little trouble tracking down your lost property?"

In total disregard of our nearby audience or the dirty secret he's so determined to keep, Axel grabs a fistful of my shirt. He drags me in close until we're almost nose to nose.

"Don't mention him to me ever again."

"Oh, come on." I chuckle lightly. "I'm certain you've been searching far and wide since we chatted."

"You don't know a thing about me," he snarls.

"I know plenty, believe it or not."

"If you'd like to keep your skin intact, I'd recommend shutting up now."

"No need to make things unpleasant." I feel my smile broaden. "I was merely going to offer my help."

Releasing my t-shirt, Axel shoves me away. "I don't want or need it. His location is no concern of mine."

"After all this time, you're not interested to know what became of your long-lost brother?"

It's a risk to taunt him so brazenly, so I take a step backwards to avoid a punch. That would be a bad start for our fragile alliance.

"I don't have a brother, Madden. Get that into your thick skull and drop it."

"My apologies." I smile sweetly at him. "Would you prefer the word *twin?* The resemblance is uncanny."

Convinced I've earned myself at least a light stabbing, I'm surprised when Axel hurls a curse at me then storms off. Oh, toying with his sore spot is going to be such fun.

If my father taught me anything, it's to always have the advantage. No matter the situation or relationship—control is how we succeed in life. It's how we carve a name and a place for ourselves.

Truthfully, I do not care why Axel rewrote his own history. Nor do I care why he has an identical twin out there, running around and causing havoc. The lost Slaughter brother has proven useful to me once or twice.

I just want the upper hand.

That's exactly what I have now.

Avoiding the caustic looks that both Warner and Hyland shoot me while deep in conversation with a member of their forensics team, I slip from the apartment to enter the security-lined hallway.

The only person I've ever met who was able to gain the upper hand over me paces back and forth out here, repeatedly stabbing her phone every time she attempts to redial and gets cut off again.

"Fuck!" she screeches.

Ember hurls the phone at the floor, watching it bounce off the carpet and skate away. I quietly slink over to her, keeping my hands laced behind my back.

"Going well?"

"No one is answering me!" A muscle jumps in her jaw.

"That's kinda the point, sweetheart. Luis wants to set the time and place in which he'll deliver his first demand."

"What kind of sick game is this? Wouldn't it be quicker to just take me and skip off into the sunset?"

Drinking in the pointed curves of her face, the way her auburn brows scrunch together when she's enraged, and the endless beauty of her half-blue, half-grey eyes, I merely shrug.

"You're not a lone wolf he can simply pick off. Luis is intelligent enough to realise that where you go, an army follows. He's playing this smart."

Shoving flaming-red hair back from her face, Ember trains her storm-filled orbs on me. "You seem confident in that prognosis."

"It's what I would do." I lean against the wall.

"Oh, how comforting!"

"Come on. Look who you're talking to."

Clearly exasperated, she works on slowing her breathing for several seconds. I really don't like seeing her calm down. Her spitfire rage is what interests me the most.

"When he calls again… Don't think for a second about sacrificing yourself."

"You think I'm that stupid?" She rolls her eyes. "Come on."

"I seem to recall you begging to take your brother's place during that phone call."

Her feet spread wide like she's preparing to fight. "So I could draw Luis out into the open and bury a knife in his fucking gut!"

I'm not even remotely ashamed to admit that my cock twitches at the venom lacing her voice. I'd love to see her inner darkness unfurl as she enacts her vengeance. Perhaps I could even assist.

"If Luis harms Tom, he will hold no power over you. Therefore, Tom must remain alive in order to manipulate you. He won't be killed."

"Yet," Ember groans.

"Well... Yes. Yet."

"Then we have to find him before that *'yet'* arrives. I will not lose another member of my family."

Unable to hold myself back, I seize a strand of her curious, flame-dipped hair. The tips remain blonde from where an old dye job grew out in captivity. I had wondered if she'd cut them.

"Care for some help with that?" I hum.

Blue-tinged graphite skates over me in contemplation.

"Apparently, we are allies now." My fingertips dance over the long strand, letting it curl around my fingers. "Therefore, my services are available."

"If we find Tom... We find Luis."

"And remove pieces off him until he reveals a link to Gael's operations," I say succinctly. "I'm sure your little friend Axel has a bone saw."

"It probably needs sharpening."

"Mm. The blade will dull with overuse."

"You can be sure he's done that," she clips out.

Comically waggling my brows at her, I stoop to retrieve her discarded phone. Ember takes it from me with a small smile.

"I half expected you to take the deal then concoct some grand scheme to disappear again."

"Tempting." I sigh dramatically. "I am not built for this country anymore. Far too cold. Alas, I have decided to stick around for now."

"What about your friends?"

"They have their orders in my absence."

"All part of the plan?" Ember's head tilts.

She has me so nailed.

"You'll soon come to learn that I'm never without a plan. Though I have made some adjustments to several of my plans since we met."

She tucks the phone into her pocket. "Is that so?"

With a glance around the hallway at the steel-faced agents wearing their best blank expressions, I take hold of Ember's biceps and push her up against the wall. She grunts in protest but doesn't fight me.

Her fine body pinned against the wallpaper, I let my hand sail downwards to find the scars left by my stitches. My thumb skates over her brand next, tracing each individual number.

I lean in to let my lips meet her earlobe. "You were just a bargaining chip, sweetheart. That's all humans ever are to each other."

"What a charming thought."

"Then I got a glimpse of that savage beast you barely keep shackled, and I wanted more. I'm not in the business of denying myself the things I want."

Shivering at my touch on the marks that tell our shared story, I relish the way she turns to fucking putty. It's one thing to own a woman. Satisfying? Certainly.

But to own a dangerous menace capable of ending your entire existence? That's a thrill I've never experienced. My plans don't matter if they don't include owning Ember Lawson on the immediate horizon.

"On that note… Tell me what you want."

"I want my brother back," she demands.

"What else?"

Her beckoning body trembles against mine. "I want to hurt the people who hurt me."

"Naturally. And?" I prompt.

"And… I want to find Gracie—there's no way that she's dead. And I want to feel the warmth on my face while my enemies' carcasses burn."

Lifting my lips from her ear, I move so our heads are together—foreheads meeting, noses brushing, my lips an inch from heaven. But I don't let our mouths meet. Not yet.

"Ember."

She startles at my use of her actual name.

"Yes, Phantom?"

Pleasure seeps over me. Oh, the game is so on.

"Let's take them down together."

Ember's response is certain.

"Fucking deal."

THE END

TO BE CONTINUED IN...
RAVAGED SOUL (ANACONDA TALES #2)

WANT MORE FROM THIS UNIVERSE?

Begin this shared world in Blackwood Institute. Learn more about Brooklyn, Hudson, Kade, Eli and Phoenix by diving into the dark and twisted world of an experimental psychiatric institute.

TWISTED HEATHENS
SACRIFICIAL SINNERS
DESECRATED SAINTS
OMNIBUS

Dive into Sabre next. Set in the same shared universe, the Sabre Security series follows Harlow and the hunt for a violent, bloodthirsty serial killer. Featuring cameos from all your favourite Blackwood Institute characters.

CORPSE ROADS
SKELETAL HEARTS
HOLLOW VEINS
OMNIBUS

Follow Willow's story next as she flees an abusive marriage and takes refuge in the small mountain town of Briar Valley, assisted in her hunt for justice by Sabre Security.

WHERE BROKEN WINGS FLY
WHERE WILD THINGS GROW
OMNIBUS

Explore Warner's early days in the Harrowdean Manor duet. Follow Ripley, our morally grey antihero lead, as she wages war on a corrupt corporation with the help of her sworn enemies.

SIN LIKE THE DEVIL
BURN LIKE AN ANGEL
OMNIBUS

PLAYLIST

LISTEN HERE:
HTTPS://BIT.LY/FRACTUREDFUTURE

Destroy Me – Young Lions
Teal – Wunderhorse
Mr. Rager – Kid Cudi
Coexist – Have Mercy
Cigarettes & Saints – The Wonder Years
Please Don't Cry, You Have Swag – Hot Mulligan
Hurt – Johnny Cash
Stay With Me – Thrice
Matches – Jonah Kagen
Poison – Brent Faiyaz
Happy Without Me – JJ, Shane Reeves, Lil Raven & Young Lions
On & On – PLTS
Bury My Bones – Whiskey Myers
Exhale – Rarity
Untitled – Knuckle Puck
Two Years – Have Mercy
Heaven Sent – Trophy Eyes
Limbs – PLGRMS
Stone – Whiskey Myers
Save Yourself – KALEO
Burn The Money – Young Lions
London – Badflower
The End – Kings of Leon
Red Velvet – Jutes & Ari Abdul
Disarm – The Smashing Pumpkins
Bitter – Palace
Nineteen – Movements
Jungle (2019 Version) – Somebody's Child

ACKNOWLEDGEMENTS

We're freaking BACK! Wow. It feels so good to be writing these words. I've wanted to return to this shared world since I finished my last series and Ember's story is finally here.

I know that two of her guys—Warner and Hyland—have been waiting for a long time for their voices to be heard. Thank you for being patient and waiting with them. I hope the beginning of their angsty, slow burn love story was worth the wait.

I'd like to start by thanking someone that I haven't mentioned here before. My very own protective big brother. While writing Tom's character, I had an excellent case study to follow from my own life. Thank you, Jake, for being my wine-drinking buddy, book signing boss and the best big brother a girl could wish for.

As ever, I want to thank my loved ones. My almost-husband, Eddie, for his unconditional love. Kristen, my wife across the pond, for her constant chaos and support. My best friend, Lilith, for always giving me love and a listening ear. Lola and Nat deserve an extra special mention for celebrating this release with me in NYC — I love you both! Plus Kaya and Melinda. You all mean the world to me.

I couldn't do this without those who support me every day. Thank you to my fabulous editor, Kim, for being an absolute wordsmith as always. And to my frankly phenomenal PA, Zoe, for putting up with all my endless chaos. Not to mention my publicist, Valentine, and all the amazing staff at Valentine PR. Of course, I'm eternally grateful to everyone on my ARC and PR teams too.

Finally, I'd like to finish by acknowledging every single one of you who has gotten me here. Five years ago, I never dreamed that I'd be able to write full-time and craft imperfect love stories for a living. You made that dream a reality not too long ago.

Thank you for reading my books. For showing up. For allowing my voice to be heard. For shouting about my characters. For giving me love, acceptance, and a safe space to create.

I love you all.

Stay wild,
J Rose xx

NEWSLETTER

Want more madness? Sign up to J Rose's newsletter for monthly announcements, exclusive content, sneak peeks, giveaways and more!

Sign up here: www.jroseauthor.com/newsletter

ABOUT THE AUTHOR

J Rose is an independent dark romance author from the United Kingdom. She writes challenging, plot-driven stories packed full of angst, heartbreak and broken characters fighting for their happily ever after.

She's an introverted bookworm at heart with a caffeine addiction, penchant for cursing and an unhealthy attachment to fictional characters.

Feel free to reach out on social media. J Rose loves talking to her readers!

For exclusive insights, updates and general mayhem, join J Rose's Bleeding Thorns on Facebook.

Business enquiries: j_roseauthor@yahoo.com

Come join the chaos. Stalk J Rose here…
www.jroseauthor.com/socials

ALSO BY J ROSE

Read here: www.jroseauthor.com/books

Recommended reading order:
www.jroseauthor.com/readingorder